UNDERWORLD'S DAUGHTER

Molly Ringle

central
avenue
publishing

2014

CENTRAL AVENUE PUBLISHING EDITION

This Central Avenue Publishing edition is published by arrangement with Molly Ringle.

www.centralavenuepublishing.com

First print edition published by Central Avenue Publishing, an imprint of Central Avenue Marketing Ltd.

UNDERWORLD'S DAUGHTER

ISBN 978-1-77168-016-5

Published in Canada

Cover Design: Michelle Halket

Cover Images: Courtesy & Copyright CanStockPhoto: coka; DivaS; Artranq

UNDERWORLD'S DAUGHTER

CHAPTER ONE

𝕳 ADES LAY NAKED UPON HIS BLANKETS. WITH HIS ARMS FOLDED behind his head, he gazed up at the bed's canopy. Joy coursed through his veins.

Persephone emerged from the passageway, returning from her bath in one of the river's small underground tributaries. She wore only his damp cloak wrapped around her. "Brrr!" She hopped onto the bed and wriggled up close to him.

He drew up one of the goatskin blankets over both of them and hugged her. Her shivers ceased, and she sighed and rested her fragrant head against his shoulder. Nearly all the flowers had fallen out of her hair by now. Some still lay crushed on the pillow, tickling his ear. He had discarded his own crown and its flowers onto the floor the moment he and Persephone had arrived in the bedchamber, just before tumbling with her onto the bed.

Firelight gleamed from an oil lamp on a ledge in the wall, and two leashed spirit dogs glowed in the corner. Here and there on the surrounding cave walls, gems sparkled in the flickering light.

Hades slid his hand up beneath the mass of Persephone's hair and rested his palm upon her warm back. "A freezing cold underground river. A dark cave lit by ghosts. A man too stupid to realize you loved him. This is what you want?"

"All of it. Especially the very stupid man."

He sat up and drew her onto his lap. "Listen. Before you regain your mind from this madness, will you consent to be my wife?"

She threw her arms around his neck. "Of course, yes! Didn't you know I'd said yes?"

They toppled back onto the mattress, wrapped around each other, Hades breathing the scent of her damp skin. After a long moment lying in the embrace, he rose on his knees and helped her up in front of him. He bent and kissed her breast, over her heart. "I marry you," he said.

When he lifted his face, she leaned down and kissed his chest. "I marry you."

They broke into smiles and fell onto the bed again in each other's arms.

In most of Greece at the time, those gestures and words were all it took for two adults to count themselves officially married. They would want to carve their names somewhere together, and hold a feast so their friends and relatives could recognize and celebrate their union. But as far as Persephone and Hades were concerned, their marriage pact was now sealed.

"Barely lunchtime, and you're already married." He latched her thigh over his. "Busy day."

"Very. Speaking of lunch, I'm hungry. What food do you have down here?"

"Not much. Some nuts. A few fruits in the orchard that won't do strange things to us. We could go up and catch fish at the beach."

"Let's." She kissed him on the lips. "Then we'll come back here for a good long time."

As they dressed, a sound of clacking toenails and panting approached from the tunnel. Kerberos trotted in, tail wagging, and leaped onto the bed next to Persephone, who sat tying a rope around her tunic as a belt.

She laughed and held out her hand, which Kerberos licked. "Where did you come from?"

"Oh yes, I have a dog now." Hades pulled a dry, folded cloak from a wooden box and shook it open. "This is Kerberos."

"Kerberos? Indeed. Fearsome, I can tell." The dog flopped over on the bed and turned his belly upward in submission. Persephone scratched his ribs until his hind leg kicked.

Hades snorted. "He worships you already. Come on, boy. Get up. Fish?"

At the word "fish," Kerberos leaped to his feet and answered with a bark.

Persephone borrowed a pair of Hades' sandals and wrapped them down to her size with a few rags. It worked well enough that she could walk out of the tunnel with Hades and Kerberos, though she had to shuffle a bit.

"I meant to tell you about him." Hades waved toward Kerberos. "He was wounded from some bite and it got infected, but one of your new fruits seemed to put him right. He's been a barrel of energy ever since."

"New fruits? Exciting. I'll have to try them."

But today the excitement of being newlyweds eclipsed the appeal of all the Underworld plants. They prepared and ate their lunch with barely any notice of the food. Shaded by a boulder on the beach, they embraced on a blanket, their attention fastened to one another's words, eyes, lips, and bodies. Kerberos, after wolfing down the fire-roasted fish Hades gave him, flung himself in and out of the waves, snapped at driftwood, and chewed up sticks.

After the sun set, Hades and Persephone moved to the warm rocks above the cave's entrance and rested there. The souls poured in. Breaths of chilled subterranean air wafted up from the Underworld.

"Wouldn't you like to go tell your mother where you are?" Hades said.

Persephone shook her head and kept watching the waterfall of souls. "Let her figure it out."

The stars emerged. Though still aroused enough to be caressing Hades idly beneath his tunic, Persephone was growing sleepy, her head heavy against his shoulder. He carried her back to the chariot, called the salt-encrusted Kerberos in as well, and made the descent into the cave. Guided by the light of one of the leashed spirit dogs, Hades and Persephone walked with happy exhaustion down the tunnel to the bedchamber, disrobed, and fell asleep. Kerberos snoozed near the door, next to his ghost-dog friends.

They awoke some time later when he scrambled upright and barked. From the tunnel bloomed a glow of torchlight. A female voice shouted, "Persephone!"

Demeter burst in with the torch. Kerberos barked once more, then sat back beside the bed with a grumble and watched her distrustfully. She paid him no heed. She glared at Persephone and Hades.

They sat up. Persephone blinked against the bright torch and held the blankets around her naked body. Mother and daughter gazed at one another, Demeter's fury against Persephone's coldness.

Hades reached for his cloak and wrapped it around his waist before stepping out of bed. "Demeter, I should officially inform you—"

"She knows we're married," Persephone cut in. She kept her eyes upon Demeter. "And there's nothing she can do about it."

Demeter's chest heaved in a breath. Long blades of grass had tangled around her sandals, and bits of leaf were stuck to her cloak, suggesting she'd been tearing through meadows and forests in search of her daughter. "This is how you tell me? Not a word of warning, you just disappear? Do you realize how worried I've been, how—"

"You brought this on yourself. You meddled." Sitting tall in the bed, flower petals clinging to her rumpled hair, Persephone already had the bearing of a goddess.

"No one's seen you since morning!" Demeter said. "You left to gather flowers and simply vanished. I found your cloak and basket and sandals, all scattered across the ground—what was I to think? Girls have been raped and killed at these festivals. Finally I found Adonis and Aphrodite, and they told me *not to worry*." She said the words through clenched teeth. "They said someone had seen you in the forest with a black-haired man in a cloak. An immortal, who took you away into the spirit realm." She slid a contemptuous glance toward Hades, then returned her gaze to Persephone. "I should have guessed from the start."

"Yes, you should have. Now you know I'm married and safe. You may go."

"Safe? With him?"

"I won't get pregnant," said Persephone, at the same moment that Hades said, "I will never hurt her."

Demeter finally rounded on him. "To you I say only this. If you do hurt her in any way, or you leave her or betray her when she ages and you don't, I will have the rest of eternity to hate you and punish you for it."

Defenses rose to his mouth, but he held them in check. His gaze moved to the torch, which she must have brought with her from above. "You've never come down to the Underworld before," he said gently. "Certainly not by yourself, at night, and without knowing your way in the tunnels. That would take a lot of courage for anyone. I know what Persephone means to you, that you'd brave this place to find her."

"I still loathe it. Seeing it firsthand hasn't changed my mind."

"But she's queen here now," Hades said. "Does that change your mind?"

Demeter shuddered and turned back to Persephone. "This doesn't have to be your future. You can still leave him, find a normal life. There are men who'd have you."

"This is the only man and the only life I want. If you can't accept it, you know the way out."

Demeter lowered the torch and turned, but stopped at the doorway. "I'm sorry I lied to you. Both of you." Her voice was strained. "Persephone, I'm sure you realize I only did so to keep you safe. To keep you with me."

"You'd prefer I never grew up? Some of us don't have that luxury."

Demeter bowed her head, and departed into the tunnel.

Hades sent a concerned glance at Persephone. Her brows were lowered, her eyes troubled and stormy. She gathered dried petals off the blanket and crushed them in her fist.

Kerberos rested his chin on the bed and gazed at her.

"Don't you want to go after her?" Hades asked.

"No. This is what she deserves, tampering with our lives."

He sat beside her, and she leaned against his chest. "Look," he tried. "Long ago, when Demeter found out she was going to have you, I told her I'd always be her friend, and the friend of her child. Now I'm...well, she must think I've utterly stolen and violated her child. Not to mention her trust."

"You haven't. This is her wrongdoing, not yours." She looked up at him. "I promise you, this is where I want to be. And she must live with it. Let's go back to sleep."

"If you wish."

They lay back and he cradled her in his arms until she breathed deeply and peacefully. But he stayed awake a long while, disquieted by the echo of Demeter's words: *I will have the rest of eternity to hate you and punish you for it.*

Chapter Two

$\mathfrak{I}$т's gone." Adrian's voice sounded puzzled, almost flat.

Sophie stared at the little tree. A few days ago she had touched the one remaining orange on it, which she had come here today to eat. But…

"It's gone," she echoed.

"Why is it gone?" Adrian said. "It shouldn't be gone."

"Did an animal eat it, you think? A bat, a…I don't know, are there raccoons down here?" She would not panic. They'd figure this out. She'd still become immortal.

"Animals have never done that before. And no, then it'd be all ripped apart on the ground." He circled the tree and shone his LED flashlight around it. "It's just gone. Like someone took it."

"But who would take it? Who *could*?"

He lifted his face toward the cave's entrance. His features hardened in anger. "Who indeed." Adrian seized her hand and pulled her through the tangled orchard, back toward the fields.

"Where are we going?"

"Niko!" he roared as they broke free of the trees. He dragged her along.

They were nearly running, and Sophie did her best to keep up and not stumble on the bumpy fields. "You think Niko knows?"

"Who else? Niko!"

They crested a hill, and found Nikolaos climbing it on the other side to meet them. "Yes, what are you shouting about?"

Behind him at a distance stood Freya, with a middle-aged

Indian woman whom Sophie assumed was the wife of Sanjay—the reincarnation of Apollo, lately murdered by members of the Thanatos cult. The woman was talking to the souls of Sanjay and Rhea, and she looked sorrowful. Niko and Freya must have just returned from India, fetching her here to visit, as they'd promised Sanjay.

But Sophie only had a moment to consider all of that, for in the next second Adrian seized Niko by the front of his black denim jacket and slammed him against a tree trunk.

"What did you do with the orange?" Adrian said.

"What orange?" Niko said.

Adrian jerked him forward and slammed him back again, making him grunt. "You *know* what orange."

"Don't hurt him," Sophie said.

Adrian glared at Niko. "It won't hurt him."

Suddenly Adrian flew backward and sprawled upon the grass. Niko had shoved him with both feet in a nimble kick. Niko straightened his jacket and smirked. "Quite right. Won't hurt me. Now would you care to discuss this like a grown-up?"

Adrian growled and leaped up. He lunged at Niko and crashed down atop him on a rock outcrop, one hand around Niko's throat.

Sophie cringed at the thud Niko's skull made against the rock. "Adrian—"

"What did you do with it?"

"What on Earth?" Freya shouted. She ran to them.

"Stop choking me," Niko rasped out. His face was turning purple.

Sophie hauled on Adrian's arms, but might as well have tried to move a boulder. Freya dived between the two men and shoved them apart. While she held Adrian back, Niko scrambled to his feet.

"Are you going to admit it?" Adrian yelled, from the restraints of Sophie and Freya's hold. "Or do I ask the souls? They'll tell me who's been down here recently, visiting the little orange tree. They never lie."

Niko lifted his chin, unabashed. "It was going to be a nice surprise for you. For heaven's sake."

"Sophie was going to eat it. Today." Adrian's voice shook with fury.

"Well, I didn't know that. I texted you to ask, a few days ago, and you said she wanted to think about it a while."

"I didn't say, 'Go ahead and feed it to someone else.' I'd never say that. You knew we were saving it for her."

"It wasn't a written contract," Niko said. "And it isn't her last chance. It's still blooming. More fruit's going to grow."

"Who did you give it to?"

"Look, we need more immortals on our side, as soon as possible. It was clear even before what happened to Rhea. So I considered all the—"

Adrian tried to lunge at him again, but the women held him back. *"Who did you give it to?"*

Freya sent Nikolaos an entreating look. Niko's gaze moved to Sophie, and his face changed into what might have been subtle apology. For a moment both dreadful and thrilling, she wondered if he had made her father—Demeter's old soul—immortal.

But finally he answered, "Dionysos."

Adrian stopped struggling. His mouth twisted in disgust. "You didn't."

"Have you met her? She's awesome."

Sophie stared at the white grass. Her mind traveled back. She knew the name Dionysos—god of wine, among other things, according to her mythology book from childhood. But she remembered him from the Persephone lifetime too. He had joined the immortals later. No, he had been someone she'd known. Hadn't he? And he was definitely a "he," so why had Niko said "she"?

"What were you thinking?" Adrian said. "Without even consulting us? Did you talk to anyone about it?"

"Well. Not beforehand."

Adrian snarled, broke free of the women's hold, and threw himself at Niko again.

But Niko met him halfway, anger finally surfacing on his

face, and caught Adrian's arms. While Adrian fought him, Niko slammed his knee up into Adrian's stomach, then shoved him to the ground. Sophie cringed and covered her mouth, though she knew Adrian couldn't be injured for long by a move like that.

Niko planted his foot on Adrian's side. "Stop it, Ade. It's done. What is this temper tantrum going to accomplish?"

"Thrashing you would feel really good right now." Adrian seized Niko's leg and pushed him, but evidently not hard. Niko kept his balance and merely hopped away a few steps, allowing Adrian to roll onto his side and get up.

"It's done," Niko repeated. "We have new strength on our side. Let's be happy, eh?"

"Who is Dionysos now?" Sophie directed the question at Adrian.

Wiping dirt and grass off his shirt, he sent her a long, stormy look. "Tabitha," he said.

Her mouth fell open. Jubilant delight fought with intense jealousy. Then a sense of betrayal stabbed at her as well. Adrian knew Tabitha had been a god, and he'd never told Sophie?

"She's awesome," Niko said again. "You have wonderful taste in friends, Sophia." He glanced at Adrian. "Not so much perhaps in boyfriends."

"Out," Adrian said. "Get out."

Tabitha. Tabitha was immortal, and used to be a god, like Sophie. Why hadn't Tab called her? Did Tab know about Sophie?

Sophie whipped out her phone and tapped Tab's speed-dial number. But nothing happened. Of course; they were underground, in a cave. No cell reception. She lowered the phone and looked again at Niko and Adrian.

"Fine, I'll give you some space." Niko sauntered toward the river. "Happy to."

"No, I mean you get out of here and you do not come back, and you stay away from me, and the Underworld, and Sophie, until I decide I want to lay eyes on you again."

Niko swung around. Derisive amusement twinkled in his eyes.

"Oh, you're banishing me from the Underworld? You have such powers, do you?"

"You have the rest of the world. That should be enough."

"You've said it yourself, Ade: you don't own this place. No one does."

"Well, I was here first." Adrian said it with deliberate clarity.

Niko snorted, but turned and strode toward the river. He paused once to call back, "You know, it wasn't even the only lovely surprise I had for you. But never mind. I suppose the rest will have to wait. Goodbye." He walked off.

The souls of Rhea and Sanjay, along with Sanjay's living widow, watched him go. They looked conflicted, but no one spoke to stop him.

"Adrian," Freya said. "He wouldn't have done it if he thought Sophie would eat the orange so soon. He acted rashly, yes, but—"

Adrian folded his arms. "I don't want to hear a defense."

"But I think you'll find," she said, "that he acted out of love, not malice. And it's going to be a good thing on the whole."

"Did he tell you?" Adrian asked her. "Did you know?"

She hesitated, and cupped one hand in the other. "Not until after he'd done it."

"At which point you still didn't tell me." Adrian swung away and walked toward Sophie. "Maybe you ought to go too." He tossed the words to Freya with cruel casualness over his shoulder.

Freya's sad gaze met Sophie's. Sophie only looked blankly at her, then stared at the pale ground. Rhea was dead, the orange was gone, Niko and Freya were not the great allies they had appeared to be, Tabitha was immortal, Adrian hadn't told her about Tab's past lives, Sophie had to find a new place to live, and she did not get to become immortal today. Nor tomorrow, nor for a couple of months, or however long it took for the fruit to grow. And who knew what Thanatos would try in the meantime?

All she wanted to do was sink to her knees and cry, or scream in frustration. But she felt the quiet, reverent gaze of the souls all around her, and even now, in her pathetic mortal state, she considered herself their honored representative—in some sense even their queen. A queen didn't behave like a whiny kid. She blinked as she stared downward, willing the tears not to rise.

"All right," Freya said. "We'll talk later." When Sophie finally glanced up, Freya had walked away. Her blonde head made a bright spot in the gloomy fields as she retreated toward the river.

Adrian stood before Sophie, head bowed. He looked up at her, and their gazes held a moment. Most of his anger seemed to have dissipated; he looked sad and preoccupied.

"Well," she said. "I guess I should go too."

His brows lowered. "Why? Aren't you staying the weekend?"

"I have a lot to do. Find a place to live. Talk to my best friend about how she's immortal, see how that's going. You know. Stuff." She knew she sounded cold. Too bad. She couldn't manage any kinder mood right now.

His shoulders drooped lower. "You were right. Is that what you want me to say?"

She stared at him in incomprehension.

"You said we shouldn't trust Niko," he added. "Just the other night. Well, you were right. What can I do now?"

"Like I said, take me home. I have things to do."

He shoved his hand through his hair, and paced a few steps away and back again. "A minute ago you were ready to spend eternity with me. Now you hate me. Why? Was I too rough with Niko? I'm sorry for that, but—"

"It's not that. I didn't like it, no, but I know he deserved it."

"Then what?"

"It would've been nice of you to tell me my best friend was Dionysos. What else haven't you mentioned?"

He drew in his breath, as if controlling another outburst. "That information—who everyone was, who they are now—it's dangerous. Surely you see exactly how dangerous it is, after everything Thanatos has tried to do to you."

"Yes! They're trying to beat me up anyway, even though I *don't* know everything. So why not go ahead and tell me? What difference will it make?"

"You'll remember it anyway. Quite soon. It would've been a—a lovely surprise when you realized—"

"A lovely surprise," she repeated. "Just like Niko was planning."

His eyes darkened. "Don't compare me to him."

Sophie looked away and stared without focus at an ash tree with violet-white leaves. She didn't apologize, and neither did he.

He sighed. "Look. It's been a rough week. Wouldn't you rather relax here a day or two, then go back?"

She calculated time zones. If they left now, it'd be the middle of the night by the time they arrived in Oregon. She'd have to sneak into the room where her treacherous roommate Melissa slept, and stay there. No, unbearable. Sleeping next to Adrian would be a challenge, but it was better than sharing a room with the girl who'd reported to the cult members of Thanatos about her.

"I'll stay here tonight," she said. "But I need to get back to the living world tomorrow, first thing."

He said nothing, and Sophie returned her gaze to his. He closed his eyes and lowered his face. "Fine. Whenever you're ready."

HE DIDN'T TRY to touch her when they climbed into bed. Sophie kept her back to him, beneath the black canopy in the chamber.

"Look, I'll answer whatever you want," he whispered. "Just don't shut me out this way."

She had plenty of snippy answers prepared, mostly regarding his not telling her important things like Tabitha being a god's soul. But those responses crumbled away when she reached for them, showing themselves the pointless, flimsy things they were. He was right. Telling her earlier wouldn't have helped much. It might only have caused her further confusion, in a time when her mind was already undergoing enough chaos. And she still would have learned about Tabitha eventually.

What made her withdraw into herself was a more basic and pathetic matter. She spoke the truth, in all its self-pity.

"It's not that I'm shutting you out," she whispered without

turning. "It's that I don't belong here. I'm mortal. I didn't want to be, but I am, so I still belong to the living world. I have to sort out my life there." The ache in her chest swelled until tears stung her eyelids. "I need a backup plan, because apparently I can't just join you here like I hoped."

Adrian latched his arm around her. His face pressed warm against the back of her neck. "You can, you always can. Please do."

"And do *what*? Drop out of college? Tell my parents I'm studying abroad at some place I can't give them an address for? Stare at the orange tree and wait for it to grow faster? And even when another orange does grow, *then* do I drop out and leave the real world? I don't know! I didn't think ahead far enough."

He sighed. For a minute or more he said nothing, only held her. She found his fingers at the center of her chest and laced hers into them.

"You're right," he said. "We're supposed to help the living world. That's been the point all along. And you do need backup, people there to support you and give you a normal life in case anything ever happens to me. Which Thanatos is doing their best to ensure it will."

She squeezed his hand. "Don't say that. We can't live in fear of them. That's...letting them win."

"Yes. Which is why you should ignore them as much as possible, and tend to your regular life. And be fantastic at it."

But he sounded so somber that she couldn't answer with any words of comfort or agreement. She said nothing, merely held his hand, and didn't sleep for a long while.

CHAPTER THREE

You say Kerberos ate one of them?" Persephone knelt and examined the small fruit tree. "And that's why he's so strong and healthy?"

"It's my best guess." Hades gathered up her hair and lifted it out of the way, then leaned down to nuzzle her neck.

"Mmm." She closed her eyes a moment. It had been ten days since the spring equinox, most of which time had been spent attending celebrations and moving Persephone's belongings to the Underworld. Demeter assisted in packing and carrying items, coolly as ever, but refused to take them all the way down into the cave.

Fortunately the new couple had other friends who were delighted to see them married. Hermes and Aphrodite had squealed like excited children and hugged them tight, and insisted on being the busiest helpers when moving Persephone's possessions and setting up furnishings for her in the cave.

Zeus and Hera threw them a grand feast, and all the immortals gave them gifts. Persephone's favorite was the crown Hephaestus made her: a slim gold circle with amethyst violets that matched the flower on her necklace. She had worn it for at least part of every day since.

Adonis, too, had been full of congratulations and embraces for her. He must have been relieved, Persephone thought in amusement: surely he had been as unenthusiastic about the idea of marrying her as she had been about marrying him. He hadn't made or accepted any proposals at the equinox festival, so he remained officially free and single for the time being—if you could call someone "single" who was as devoted as ever to Aphrodite.

Persephone and Hades' nights and private daytime moments, meanwhile, had been devoted to the kind of activity he was trying to engage her in now. She knew she'd give in soon. But she hadn't visited the orchard in months, and wanted to study her dear plants a bit longer first.

She plucked the only ripe fruit left on the tree, its skin a bright yellow-orange. "Let's see, then."

"I'm not doing a good enough job distracting you?" His hand stole into her tunic from the side and enfolded her breast.

Persephone elbowed his hand away, but she leaned back to press against his body. He murmured in gratification. She cut into the fruit's peel with her fingernail and sniffed the fresh aroma, then licked her fingertip. "Tastes good. Oh! It's blue inside."

"Didn't I mention that?"

"No. And look at the seeds." She squeezed one from the wedge she had pulled off. "They're shaped like starfish." The five little points protruding from the seed certainly differentiated it from the usual oval-shaped fruit seed.

Hades rested his chin on her shoulder. "I hadn't noticed. Strange."

Persephone bit into the blue flesh and sucked up the juice.

"Don't!" He swatted her hand down.

"Only tasting." She smacked her tongue. "It's safe, I'd say. No burning or stinging. Actually rather delicious." She tore off a small piece of orange, passed it to her other hand, and popped it into her mouth before he could stop her.

"Argh—no!"

She swallowed it. "Only a tiny bite. Relax. I've missed my orchards."

He pointed at her. "No more today. Not till you see how it goes."

"Understood." She fit the remaining piece of wedge back into the fruit and laid the peel on top of it. After wrapping the fruit in a cloth, she tucked it into her small bag and set it down. "What shall we do now?"

He settled forward onto his knees, crowding her backward in her crouch. He kissed her, and they sank until her back met the crackling leaves and sticks on the ground. She slid her hands up his back, beneath his cloak. "Won't we shock the souls, behaving like this?"

"They usually don't enter the orchard. You know that. Besides, it's nothing they haven't seen in a hundred lives already."

"True. I *have* daydreamed of touching you while we walked here together, all those times."

His mouth moved hot down her chest. "Touch me, then."

THAT EVENING, WHILE chewing on a bite of roasted pork, Persephone paused and stuck her tongue into a space between her back teeth. She and Hades were sitting on the beach outside the Underworld, beside a bright fire of driftwood.

When she set down the skewer of food and poked a finger against her gums, Hades glanced at her. "Something stuck in your teeth?"

"I think."

He broke off a toothpick-size splinter from his wooden skewer and offered it to her. She accepted it, and he returned to eating his own pork wrapped in its grape leaf.

But it wasn't meat stuck in her teeth. The space was where an upper molar had once been, pulled by Demeter when Persephone was fifteen. It had been infected at the root and causing her agony, and the removal of it had been torture. But after a few days of tenderness, Persephone had become used to chewing without that tooth and life had returned to normal.

The strange thing was that tonight the tooth seemed to be growing back. Those hard points felt like the surface of a molar breaking through her gums. Adults didn't regrow teeth. In addition, her injuries from the earthquake long ago—her crippled leg and the scars on her arm and face—had been tingling all day. Ever since eating that bite of blue orange.

The symptoms alarmed her, but she kept them to herself, reasoning that they were likely to go away as the fruit's properties worked themselves out of her system. If they got worse, she'd tell Hades.

"Kerberos!" Hades jumped to his feet. "Good lord. How in the world?"

Persephone looked up. Into the reach of the firelight Kerberos backed toward them, dragging a huge log with his mouth. In fact, it was an entire fallen tree, its trunk so big around that Persephone's arms wouldn't have circled it by half. Kerberos had his jaws clamped into one of the lower branches. The branches stretched far out on both sides, and scored deep lines in the sand as the determined dog hauled the tree along. Its top stretched out somewhere into the darkness of the beach. It would be one of the tallest trees around if righted. The wood was sun-bleached and bare, indicating the tree had fallen years ago, but it still surely weighed more than any normal person or dog could have budged.

Hades stopped Kerberos and pried at his jaws until the dog let go of his treasure. Hades took hold of one of the branches—he didn't even have to kneel, as the tree lying down rose as high as his head—and tried pulling the whole thing himself. It took some grunting and effort, but he did move it a bit. "How did you *do* that?" he asked the dog.

Persephone walked around the fire and crouched to stroke Kerberos' head. The dog panted happily, but didn't appear tired from his effort.

Persephone's hip no longer hurt, though it always used to when she crouched like this. Only the light tingling remained, which now was beginning to feel more like healing than harm.

And her lost tooth was growing back. And the scars on her face—she ran her fingers up them to check—were disappearing, smoothing away into her skin.

Her heart beat fast. She began to tremble.

"I think this dog is more than healthy," she said. "I think he's immortal."

PERSEPHONE AND HADES stayed up late. This time, rather than entwining and kissing, they were watching.

"They're definitely disappearing." Hades held a bright oil lamp near her cheek. "The scars were much clearer this morning. And you say when you walk...it feels better?" Even now he was too tactful to refer directly to her limp.

She stood from the bed and tested her weight on what used to be her weak leg. It felt sturdy and lithe, just like the other leg. She walked across the bedchamber with careful steps, unaccustomed to relying upon both legs equally. "No limp," she concluded, moving faster as she acquired practice in her new gait. She returned to Hades and lifted her tunic to the hip. They both examined the sleekly muscled line of her leg, so unlike the skinny and awkwardly angled limb she had lived with for so long.

Hades laid his palm on her hip in fascination. "What's happened to you?"

She giggled in sudden buoyancy, swooped down, and seized him. She lifted him off the ground and held him higher than her head, laughing anew at the shock on his face. He planted his hands on her shoulders and wriggled back to the floor without difficulty, but kept staring at her.

"I'm immortal!" She leaped on him. He caught her with a grunt, and staggered backward. "See? I was never strong enough before to knock you off balance. Let alone lift you."

"Darling." He set her down and cupped her face in his hands. "I married you as you were. I was prepared for you to age, to... to die eventually. You were prepared for it too. It's still all right if that's what happens. I don't want you to hang all your hopes on this idea."

"You're saying you'll still love me if it wears off tomorrow? Thank you, dear. I'll still love you too."

"I'm serious. What will you do if it wears off?"

"Eat another blue orange," she said. "And one every day after that."

"The tree doesn't have any more right now."

"Some green ones are ripening. And obviously we'll have to plant more."

Hades stroked her face on the side where the scars were vanishing. "You know I wish for a lifetime of health and strength for you. I always have. But we don't know how long this magic will last, for you or for Kerberos. It's late. Let's get some sleep and see how you feel in the morning."

"All right." She kissed him. Then, for fun, she picked up the large wooden chest where he kept a heavy assortment of weapons, clothes, and precious stones. She tossed it up over her head, caught it, and set it down again.

Neither of them slept that night with all that played upon their minds. But she felt livelier in the morning than she'd ever felt after a sleepless night. As they walked toward a nearby village to buy food, she danced alongside him, unable to contain her energy.

"You should try shooting an arrow through me," she said.

He looked at her, aghast. "No."

"I'll jump off a cliff, then."

"Are you mad?"

"Or perhaps Rhea's willing to stick a knife into me like she did for you."

"Why are all your ideas so lethal?"

"Because how else will I know I'm immortal?"

"Try living a long time without aging."

"As if I'm patient enough for that." She performed a running leap into a tree, where she caught a branch and scrambled up. Hades glowered at her, hand on hip. She jumped down, cloak flying, and laughed in delight when the hard landing didn't sprain her ankles—in fact, didn't even hurt at all.

"Here." He stepped in front of her and drew his bronze dagger from the sheath on his belt.

"Ah ha, you're willing to try it, then?" she teased, though her heart sped up in nervousness.

"Hardly." He turned her palm upward, and before she knew it, he had slashed a shallow cut upon her first finger. The blood welled up along the thin line. As she blinked in surprise, he sliced his own finger too, and pressed the wound against hers.

At last she understood. She wrapped her other hand around their joined fingers to hold them together. "Ah," she said. "Since you won't let me use the cloudhair seeds."

"Exactly." He put away the dagger with his free hand. "I'll be able to track you, which will of course be useful. But let's see if you can track me."

Their cuts stopped bleeding soon. Persephone licked away the smear of blood and watched the transformation on her finger. The cut joined into a white line, which then smoothed itself away into unbroken flesh, all within the space of ten or twelve slow breaths.

She took his hand and placed hers alongside it, comparing the healed fingers with triumph. "There. See?"

Hades only glanced at their hands. He was smiling at her with affectionate secrecy. "I can sense you." He slid his hands around her ribs, and laid his face on her neck. "You have no idea how long I've wished I could track you. Finally I can. Now I won't lose you."

Persephone embraced him in bliss and closed her eyes. "Then let me see. How does it work? I think of you... "

"Yes, think of me." He let go of her and moved backward. "No, keep your eyes shut."

She obeyed, closing them again, and stood still.

"Tell me where I am," he said. His footsteps traveled away and dwindled into silence.

Thinking of him, she did sense it: a hum, or a glow, or a vibration, some chord that meant *him* and no other. "You're off to my left," she called, keeping her eyes shut. "Now you're moving farther away, and behind me. Now—it's gone." Confused, she opened her eyes and turned around.

He stepped out from behind an oak tree far behind her. When he reappeared without the tree between them, the sense of his location leaped back into place in her mind.

"Ah," she said. "Oak."

He returned to her, smiling. "Then you can sense me."

"Oh yes."

He caught her up in a hug tighter than she had ever experienced. She returned it, squeezing him hard enough that she suspected it could break the bones of a mortal man.

He only laughed as he let her go. They resumed walking. "There is one more test, you know. Other than trying to kill you. Though I'm afraid it does require *some* patience."

"Oh?"

"Let's see if you can switch realms."

Chapter Four

Sophie opened her eyes to the perpetual darkness of the cave bedchamber, lit only by the dim blue of an LED button that sat on a wall ledge as their nightlight. She closed her eyes again in pain at the upbeat dream she had awoken from. Why did she have to experience that memory now, of all times? Persephone eating the orange, becoming strong and healed, embracing Hades as his immortal equal…it wasn't fair. She turned her face into the pillow, longing to sink back into the dream and not have to deal with the modern world today.

Adrian stirred alongside her, and moved to the other side of the bed. Soon another light sent its faint white rays across the stone walls—probably his cell phone, where he'd been checking the time. He slipped out of bed. She watched from beneath nearly-closed eyelids as he walked barefoot across the floor in his dark green boxer shorts and black T-shirt. He paused by Kiri's dog bed to pat her when she lifted her head, then he moved past into the bathroom.

When he returned to bed, his weight shifting the mattress, Sophie sighed and turned over toward him. But she felt too depressed even to slide closer or to meet his gaze. She stared across the rumpled blankets, her head heavy on the pillow.

Adrian rested on his side, gazing at her. "Been dreaming?"

She nodded. "Persephone ate the golden apple," she said quietly, in the ancient tongue. Golden apple: *chrysomelia*. Lovely word, really. Too bad she didn't have a damn golden apple of her own.

Adrian shifted onto his back to stare upward. "I wish Niko would come back so I could beat him up more."

Sophie exhaled a huff in place of a laugh.

They ate a breakfast of bananas, almond butter, and dry muesli, with Greek-style coffee Adrian heated over the fire in the bedchamber's hearth. What made it Greek style, Sophie gathered from his listless comments, was the long-handled pot you used to heat it over a fire or stove, and the foam that gathered on top as it boiled.

It should have charmed her, a modern detail of an exotic country to which she had ancient ties. Besides, ordinarily she liked coffee. But today the brew struck her as gritty and she missed the half-and-half she usually splashed in. Must everything be going wrong, down to the coffee?

"Still want to go back today?" Adrian asked after several minutes of silence.

She nodded and sloshed the gritty coffee around in the mug. "I need to call Tab. And do all that other stuff."

Her interest in life stirred again at the thought of talking to Tab, but it was a jealous interest. It would hurt to hear the glorious details of someone else becoming immortal. Still, she needed to hear them, because part of her was indeed happy for Tabitha, and also just to get the conversation over with.

Adrian splashed the remainder of his coffee into the fire, where it hissed on the coals. "Anytime, then."

Before they left, Adrian brought her to the fields so she could say goodbye to Rhea. He stood back several paces while she walked to the woman's soul.

Rhea must have heard they were coming; she walked forward to meet them. Compassion radiated from her translucent face. "I am sorry about Niko's trick. I'm sure he never meant to hurt you by it."

"Maybe not, but now I have to go on dealing with everything as a weak mortal."

"You're not weak. You've done a wonderful job so far. Please don't be discouraged, and take heart if your friend is immortal now. It means more hope for us all in the long run."

"I suppose. I just…feel betrayed. Or at least left out." In the pale grass, the buds of new red violets surrounded her sneakers. She thought of Persephone leaping without reservations into marriage with an immortal—as Sophie should have done from the start. But Persephone had fewer ties to the living world, many stronger ones to the immortals, and also, back then it wasn't so damn tacky to get married at eighteen.

"It's wise to leave room in our lives for the chaotic, the unexpected." Rhea chuckled. "Hermes has always been excellent at providing those elements. It's part of the reason I like him, despite the trouble he causes. Ultimately you will find he brings more good than harm."

Sophie lacked the eternal patience of the dead at the moment, and sourly felt her inadequacy. She considered muttering resentful words against Niko. But a resurgence of grief for Rhea's recent death swept back over her, and in a few seconds the red violet buds swam in a blur of tears. "I wish he'd been there to do some good for you," she said, her voice choked.

"Oh, my dear. My existence isn't over. It never will be. No one's ever is." Rhea stretched out her intangible, light-filled hands and traced them down the sides of Sophie's head and arms, as if sketching a line of blessing around her. "Do what you can. You don't need to be perfect and you don't need to rush."

Sophie blew her nose, nodded, and mumbled goodbye in the Underworld tongue.

Sophie and Adrian didn't speak as they climbed into the bus with Kiri and launched off. It reminded her of the first time she had come to the cave, that strange, unsettling visit when she had refused the pomegranate and he had tricked her into consuming it anyway. He'd been preoccupied and distant on that ride back, and this time he was even more so. Today, somehow, they had twice as many problems as they'd had a month ago, and they couldn't even find comfort in being together.

Over the Atlantic, cold, salty wind filled the bus. Adrian's arm around her was warm but felt like it belonged to a bodyguard, not a boyfriend.

She checked her phone messages. None from the newly immortal Tabitha, nor from Sophie's family. But she had a voice mail from someone with an Oregon area code. She tapped the button to listen to it.

"Sophie, this is Marilyn with the police department; we spoke yesterday. It's about eight a.m. on Saturday now. I need to inform you that the suspect Betty Quentin escaped from custody sometime during the night. Obviously we're investigating how that happened, but we also wanted to put you on alert, as the primary victim of her crimes. Our guess is she'll try to lie low rather than go after you or anyone else, but it's safest to consider her dangerous and to be on the lookout. So please call back with any questions, and we'll be in touch soon."

Sophie pulled the phone away from her ear and stared at it. "Shit."

Adrian looked at her. "What?"

"Quentin got out! She escaped. Already."

"Bugger." Clenching his teeth, Adrian steadied the reins. "Wilkes said she would. But I didn't think it'd be so soon."

"They say she's hiding out. They're looking for her. But—what if they can't find her? What if she finds us first?"

"Never thought I'd say this, but I wish I could track her." Adrian sighed in frustration. "Well—all right. She has to hide. She's wanted by the police now. That's good. That means if anyone even sees her, they can call the cops."

Terror threatened to undo Sophie's mind completely. She'd wondered how this week could get any worse, and now she knew. "But she's going to come after me! What the hell do I do?"

"I—I don't know! Look, maybe she won't. I mean, I did warn her I'd drag her into the spirit realm and leave her there if she made the slightest move against you, and if she's at all smart, she'll realize I meant it."

"Then she'll send someone else to do it. Like every other time." She was practically hyperventilating.

"Fine, do you want me to turn the horses around and take you back to the Underworld? You can hide out." He sounded upset, but hopeful—as if in truth he wanted her to do exactly that.

She hesitated, mouth partly open to answer. A short while ago hadn't she rattled off all the reasons she should keep her normal life in order and running smoothly? Didn't she already know Thanatos had people watching her, whether Quentin was locked up or not? She looked at her phone. "Maybe I'll call them back. See if they have any updates."

"Yeah." Adrian sounded tired. "Do that."

Sophie phoned Marilyn of the Corvallis police, and spent a few minutes collecting news. At the end of it, she hung up, still uncertain but less panicky.

"Okay," she told Adrian, "they haven't found her. They say someone came from the state police—or at least, they seemed to be state police—and brought Quentin out of her cell for questioning. Then there was a disturbance of some kind, another arrested guy freaking out and trying to grab a cop's gun, and everyone jumped on that. And when they settled him down, Quentin and the so-called state cops were gone."

"Clever. Planted a diversion. Niko could hardly have done it better." His lips tightened as he spoke the accursed Niko's name.

"So I'm supposed to be extra watchful, and they'll patrol campus and check in with me daily. And they say if I want, they'll post a guard overnight by the dorm. But…" She sighed. "I have to decide if I'm actually staying at the dorm tonight. Or ever again."

He nodded. "Where to, then?"

She pondered it only a few seconds, weighing scenarios. "Carnation. Home."

THEY EXAMINED THE GPS map on Adrian's phone, and Sophie directed him to land in the field behind her family's property. "It might be swampy, but nobody should be there."

27

A forest of something resembling maples stood there in the spirit world. He brought the horses down among the trees and the bus settled to a stop. Sophie leaned out to look around, comforted to know she was close to home, and curious what the wild version of home looked like.

"Even more trees than usual," she concluded, and climbed out.

He stepped down after her and tied the horses to a tree. Kiri leaped out and sniffed the ground.

Adrian walked to Sophie, his boots squelching in the wet earth. "Do you want me to meet your parents, or…?"

He sounded so unenthused that she smiled, though wearily. "Not today. I'm too shaken up to keep a good cover story going."

"Me too. I don't think I could even fake a decent American accent right now."

"So." She hitched her backpack onto her shoulder.

He wrapped his arms around her. She settled her forehead on the collar of his wool coat. Rather than switch realms, he held her in the embrace a moment, beneath the wild trees. "You'll want to stay with them the weekend?" he asked.

"Yeah. Suppose. Where are you going to go?"

"Maybe I'll go home too."

She shifted her face against his coat. Picturing the greater part of the Pacific Ocean lying between them made her feel more desolate than ever.

"You'll text me every waking hour?" he said. "Let me know you're all right?"

Sophie looked up and nodded. "You too."

He nodded back, then glanced aside. "Go run, Kiri. I'll be right back." He pulled Sophie into the living world.

The ground reshaped beneath them, meadow grass and mud squishing as their weight suddenly landed on it. The smell of the soggy meadow filled Sophie's nose with comforting familiarity, even in a chilly wind beneath dim gray skies. This was Washington. This was home.

But *this* was love, standing before her with unhappy dark

brown eyes. Adrian kissed her on the lips before letting her go. "Be careful," he stated, separating and emphasizing the words.

"You be careful too." She drew in her breath in the hopes that fresh oxygen would quash the ache in her chest. "Bye."

"Bye."

She walked away, navigating her sneakers around the biggest puddles in the high grass. The roof of the two-story farmhouse peeked over the trees ahead. One of the trees was an oak. Would Adrian not be able to sense her if he stood in certain places in the field while she was in the house? She looked back, strangely pierced by that thought of disconnection. He lingered there and watched her, the wind tossing his dark curls. He lifted a hand in goodbye. She waved back, and kept walking.

The next time she looked back, not half a minute later, he had vanished.

She trudged along the back fence to the gate, her heart so heavy that it felt it was residing in her damp shoes. But at the squeak of the gate hinges, and the click of the latch, the two family dogs started barking inside the house. Sophie smiled. Her step picked up as she approached the side door that let into the kitchen from the driveway.

Rosie's paws hit the door's window, her jowly boxer face between them. Beside her, Pumpkin leaped into the air, his small yapping head appearing and disappearing over and over. He was an orange-brown Pomeranian-terrier mix, and not nearly tall enough to see out the window unless he jumped.

Sophie laughed and pushed open the door. "It's okay, silly kids, just me." She knelt and wrapped one arm around each dog.

Yapping gave way to joyful whining and face-licking. Their tails whipped her hands and knees. She kissed each dog on the forehead, so unexpectedly glad to see them that she thought she might start weeping in happiness.

"What is up with you, dogs?" her dad called from down the hall. He appeared a moment later, eyeglasses on, light blue shirt tucked in and clean. Probably he'd been paying bills or answering email. When he spotted Sophie, he beamed and opened his arms. "Baby! This is a surprise."

"Someone was driving up this way, so I hitched a ride." She let go of the dogs and rose to hug him. He smelled like spicy aftershave and the worn leather of his favorite brown bomber jacket, which usually hung on the back of his desk chair.

"I am so glad to see you." He rubbed her back, then held her out to look at her. His eyebrows rose in the middle in concern. "You okay?"

After the other night, he meant. An attempt on her life, ending in a grenade explosion. That much he knew about, and it was more than enough to freak out any parent. But the other night also included a second grenade explosion in the spirit realm, which left some of her friends with severe if temporary burns; a discovery of the betrayal of her roommate; and the murder of their ancient mentor Rhea. Now, on top of those problems, she added her failure to eat an orange that would make her immortal, because Tabitha had already eaten it.

All of which her parents did *not* know about, and shouldn't.

Sophie nodded. "I'm okay. But I wanted to come home for a bit. Get some rest before going back and dealing with everything."

"Of course. Rest as much as you need." He grinned, his mustache stretching along with his lips. "I'm just so happy you're here. What a great surprise."

"Where's—" she began, but the question soon answered itself as footsteps thundered down the stairs, and her little brother skidded to a stop on the kitchen linoleum.

Liam was wearing his Avengers T-shirt and had acquired a green streak in his dark brown hair since she last saw him. He lurched forward as if about to hug her; then, apparently remembering he was cool now, being twelve, he stood back instead. He hitched his thumbs into his studded belt, flicked his hair out of his eye, and said nonchalantly, "What you doing here?"

"Visiting. Making sure you're not snooping through my room."

He snorted, as if to dismiss the notion that there could be anything he'd want in her stupid girly room.

Sophie looked out the window over the sink, toward the front of the house, where the produce stand's red and white striped tent stood. "Mom working the stand today?"

"Yep," Dad said.

A tremor of worry shivered through Sophie. Her mind flashed back to Quentin holding up a photo of the fruit stand on her phone. *Nice place. I should visit.* "By herself?" Sophie asked.

"Ross is with her."

Relieved, Sophie nodded. Ross was a high school senior, and a wrestling champion. He could surely defend Mom against Quentin if the old nutjob did show up. "I'll go say hi." Sophie set her backpack down against the wall.

"She'd be mad if you didn't," Dad said.

As Sophie walked to the front door to go out, her brother fell in step beside her, and began telling her about the smart-ass things his buddy had said in Spanish class the other day. Sophie smiled. Evidently Liam kind of liked having her home after all.

CHAPTER FIVE

FTER GREETING EVERYONE, COLLECTING ALL THE GOSSIP, AND helping herself to fruit salad and cheese from the fridge, Sophie went up to her room and shut the door. Such sweetness and luxury, having a bedroom all to herself again, filled with her familiar possessions from childhood and adolescence: tattered oval rug, TV-show posters rubbing edges with clippings about nutrition, a pom-pom in her high school's colors someone had thrown to her during a football game, the occasional hot guy in a magazine ad—none of whom looked as hot as Adrian did to her anymore.

But she only absorbed the atmosphere of her room for a few breaths before turning to the task at hand, the most important one. She sat on her bed, selected Tabitha's number, and called it. A text wouldn't do, not for this. Her heart throbbed against her throat.

"Hey, lady," Tab answered. She sounded her cheerful, vibrant self, but with something held back in her voice, a mystery that didn't match Tab's usual forthright openness.

"Hey." Sophie licked her lips, and switched to the language of the Underworld. "*Sounds like we have a few things to talk about.*"

Rather than answer with guilt or counter-accusation like Sophie had dreaded, Tab burst into sparkling laughter, not unlike Aphrodite's. "*So many things!*" she answered in the same language, then switched back to English. "When can I come see you?"

"Depends," Sophie said. "Can you switch realms and did Niko give you one of those horses?"

"As a matter of fact, yes, and yes." Now Tabitha did sound a touch guilty.

Sophie ignored the envy that prickled in her chest. "And you can sense me? So you'd know I was in Carnation even if I didn't tell you?"

"I can, and I'd figure that out, but I don't know why you're in Carnation."

"Come on over. I'll explain."

WHEN TABITHA SHOWED up—looking amazing, her skin and hair gleaming—they shut themselves into Sophie's room and settled down for a talk.

Sophie explained first, since her Greek god adventures had begun before Tab's had. She described her abduction by Niko, her introduction to Adrian, and her increasing attachment to him. She covered the scary attacks, which she had reported to Tab in their abridged versions earlier, but now Tab winced and nodded vigorously, helping fill in the Thanatos-related details that Niko had related to her. And when Sophie got to the orange she would have eaten last night, but which had gone missing, Tabitha gasped and covered her mouth.

She scrambled up from the pillow she'd been leaning back upon, and hugged Sophie with startling strength. "I'm so sorry. Oh, Soph, I had no idea, he didn't say a word! I swear, I will make it up to you. All he said was you'd been there with his friend Adrian, and you guys were Persephone and Hades, and honestly I still don't get all that, but—"

"Not your fault. Niko thought I was going to wait longer to eat it. He is still of course a sneaky douche." Sophie extricated herself from the hug. "And you'll start remembering about Persephone and apparently Dionysos pretty soon here." She realized she sounded like Adrian, reassuring her time and again that she'd remember everything soon. Sophie looked into Tab's blue eyes. "Now your turn. How did this all happen?"

"Well." Tab sat up straight on the bed and tucked her legs into lotus position. She'd never been so flexible before, and now that Sophie examined her, she suspected Tab had lost the ten pounds she'd always claimed she needed to lose in order to be perfect. Round, soft curves still defined her figure; she was certainly no twig. But now she radiated health and beauty.

"I don't remember *exactly* how I met him," Tabitha said. "I was a bit drunk at the time. It was at a party at someone's apartment. Tons of people. Lots of margaritas."

Though Sophie tended to remain sober at parties, Tab readily became hard to control after accepting a few drinks. Sophie sighed, and nodded for Tab to continue.

"But I know I ended up talking to this guy with crazy curly hair and, like, a full leather outfit," Tabitha went on. "I figured he was gay and planning to hit Capitol Hill and find himself a date for the night or something. Still, he looked familiar. Probably because you'd sent me that photo of him, the first day in the dorms. Remember?"

The day Sophie officially met Adrian. Of course she remembered. "The Eurotrash photo."

"Right. I didn't figure it out till later, though. I just kept saying, 'Don't I know you?' like a stereotypical drunk girl, and he kept going, 'Oh, you do, love.' But he wouldn't say how. Finally he was like, 'Hey, let me show you something,' and he asked if he could take me out onto the sidewalk and hug me. Dude, I'm in theater; we hug all the time. No big. So we step out and I hug him. And poof! World is gone."

"Other realm. Right."

"Right. It *rocked*. I made him take me back and forth a couple of times. Then I started singing and shrieking because it was so awesome."

"And because you were drunk," Sophie noted.

"That did factor in. Then I noticed his horse—his freaking *glowing ghost horse*. I mean, I had to check that out. I was sticking my hand through it and giggling, and he said, 'Let's go for a ride.' Which, to sum up, we did."

Envy stung Sophie again. She glowered at the colorful pompom on the wall. "All the way to Greece."

"Uh-huh. Via New Zealand."

Sophie looked at Tab. "What?"

"To pick up 'this girl I think you'll like,' he said. Well, he was right about that. Again, I'm fuzzy on the details, but—"

"What girl?"

"Zoe. I thought you knew. I mean, if you knew *I* was there—"

"Zoe? Adrian's Zoe?"

"Adrian's *and* your Zoe, if I understand it right." Tabitha licked her upper lip salaciously. "And so cute, oh my gosh."

Sophie's mind whirled. "My Zoe? Okay, what?"

"Well, Adrian filled her in on all the memories he was having back when, right?"

"Yes, I think so."

"So in a way, she already knew who she was back in these Greek god days. And again, I haven't even gotten to those, so when they tell me I'm Dionysos, I'm like, whatever; I'm immortal now! That's what counts."

"So who was Zoe?" Sophie asked.

"She said Adrian was her dad? Hek-something...what was the name." Tabitha studied the ceiling, then snapped her fingers. "Hekate. So we picked *her* up, and I gather she was blind, but she isn't anymore, because we shared the orange...you okay, lady?"

Sophie felt dizzy. "You both ate it?" Also, that name, Hekate, it was zeroing in on her brain, approaching, about to strike.

"Yep! Jeez, I thought you knew. Sneaky old Niko. Two new immortals, both hot gay women. The world is lucky, I'm telling you."

"He said he had another surprise." Sophie's mind slid toward Zoe, whom she'd never met and had only seen in photos on Adrian's phone. Adrian's child in a past life? Hekate?

Tabitha started talking again, but at that moment the recollection from Persephone's life burst upon her and showered details onto her mind, scattering them down like brilliant flower petals.

A young woman seated on the cave floor, decorating a mask

with bits of colored stone. The same young woman, or girl, standing face to face with Hades as he moved his hand level from his head to hers, finding them the same height; he then laughed in amazement and kissed her forehead. A younger girl, maybe twelve, lying in Persephone's arms, sick with a fever and dreadful sores while Persephone's heart fluttered in grief and terror. A little girl rolling down a grassy slope in the Underworld, laughing, while Kerberos bounced around her and yipped. A dark-haired baby girl, nursing from Persephone's breast, while Hades knelt at the bedside and gazed in adoration at them both.

Sophie gasped, filling her lungs with the air she'd forgotten to breathe for half a minute.

Tabitha stopped talking and stared at her in alarm. "Whoa. You okay?"

Her joyful tears made the room go blurry. Sophie blinked them away and laughed. "We had a daughter."

ADRIAN SOARED ABOVE the Pacific, speeding toward New Zealand and the gentle vibe that meant "Zoe." He was somewhere near the equator, and even with the speed whipping the wind against him and bringing the temperature down, the air was warm and humid and smelled of tropical salt water. Endless blue ocean surrounded him. The trip could have been viewed as a visit to paradise, but in his current mood it felt more like being lost at sea.

Sophie's immortality was delayed, and clearly the disappointment stung her, which alone would have made him punch Nikolaos. But it hurt Adrian too, not having her alongside him in equal power and strength. And no amount of beating up Niko would fix that.

Nonetheless, he had turned all angst-ridden King of the Underworld and banished two of his best friends, who had gone out of their way to help Sophie just the other night. He felt a bit ridiculous about that. But then, hadn't Niko and Freya acted sneakily? Was it really allowable for one party among the immortals to hand out the orange without consulting the rest?

Of course, he and Niko had approached Sophie without consulting the others. Rhea had been angry at him for that.

Rhea. There was another large component of his depression. The world's oldest living person, one of the world's oldest living things, now wiped out by thugs and reduced to merely another soul among the multitudes.

Adrian's hands tightened on the reins until the leather creaked and warped in his grip.

The world was horrible enough without a group like Thanatos. Why did they have to exist? And they would never quit. Every one of the members he'd spoken to in the Underworld, where they were souls and couldn't lie, made it clear: like so many other cult fanatics, they were crazily devoted to their cause, willing to kill or die for it. Now they had sprung Quentin, who would surely do her best to strike back at Sophie and himself. The vendetta had turned more personal than ever for her.

How could he keep Sophie safe, let alone himself and everyone else he cared about, with these people on the loose? He didn't know where his enemies were or even *who* they all were. He felt like a clueless loser, not a godlike immortal.

He tilted the reins to steer the horses toward New Zealand's North Island, which was at the moment only a fuzzy dark green line on the horizon. Perhaps seeing Zoe and his father would cheer him up, but he wasn't counting on it.

His father likely wasn't home yet. He worked full time at a railway office, where he arranged for freight shipments to find their way onto the right boats. Adrian wasn't sure of his hours today, and for both their safety, he never contacted his dad directly. They passed messages through Zoe. So it was to Zoe that Adrian steered his horses.

The spirit-realm twin of Wellington Harbor uncurled into view, its surface alive with the fins and flippers of sea creatures. It amazed him how full of animals the oceans were in this realm, and probably would be in the living realm, if people hadn't hauled them out by the billions in nets. He slowed the bus and glided a meter above the smooth harbor. A pod of porpoise-like animals breached the water beneath him, spraying him with mist from their blowholes.

He settled the bus on shore. Flowers speckled the ground and climbed into the trees on vines, their fragrance filling the air. Spring had recently arrived down here. Despite how the mythology had it, Persephone's seasonal presence was never truly gone from the Earth. It was always somewhere.

And their daughter was here too, now quite close to him.

Exactly how angry would Sophie be when she found out he hadn't told her about their child? He sighed in defeat, suspecting he had even more chilliness ahead to endure. But Sophie's mind was being blasted with such a torrent of memories already, he couldn't bear to pile on with more. She'd reach the life of Hekate soon enough. And all the wonderful and devastating details that went with it.

Arrived, he texted Sophie. *Off to see Z. xo.*

He whistled to Kiri, who bounded over from her olfactory inspection of a rotten tree trunk, and they began walking.

Sophie's answer arrived in a moment. *OK. Tab's coming over now. We'll talk.*

Let me know how it goes. Adrian put away his phone with a grimace.

Dionysos. Formerly known as Adonis. "Mixed feelings" would be an accurate way to put Hades' opinion of that soul. He hoped Sophie's influence could keep Tabitha on the better side of behavior in this reincarnation, especially now that Tab wielded immortal power and longevity.

Atop a hill, he stopped beside the stake that marked Zoe's bedroom. He sensed her nearby, perhaps in the garden or another room of the house. *Good day for a swim?*, he texted her, which was their code for drop-in visits.

She answered right away. *Yes!*

He felt her approach, waited until she was holding still, then picked up Kiri and switched realms.

The floor of the house stood nearly a meter above the natural ground. He got shoved upward and landed unsteadily on the carpet, knees bent, the dog squirming in his arms. He set Kiri down. "Hey, Z."

"Hey." Zoe stood in front of him, grinning, leaning with one hand on her desk. She wore a gray T-shirt and black capri pants, which barely covered the knees on her long legs. Her short, light brown hair was shoved messily to one side and tucked behind her ear, held in place by the sunglasses over her eyes.

Kiri trotted to her, tail whipping, and Zoe knelt to ruffle up her neck. "Hello, darling."

Adrian approached, and Zoe hugged him, her body strong in his arms despite her skinny frame.

"Been a while," he said. He pulled back to smile at the sunglasses covering her eyes. "Gone back to the sunnies, have you?" She'd worn them for a year or two in high school, but had discarded them after that.

"Yeah, makes things easier." She pulled them off and gazed up and down him—or at least, it certainly looked like she was doing that. It didn't resemble her usual gaze, the unfocused look of a blind person. Adrian peered at her, confused. She tilted her head. "That's a nice color on you, that navy blue."

He glanced down at his navy blue shirt, then blinked at her. "Um. How'd you know that?"

Zoe squinted at his head. "And what's in your hair, a leaf?" She reached out and plucked a scrap of something from his head, and examined it. "Seaweed or kelp maybe. How'd that get there?"

Adrian stared at her. She did look remarkably strong and healthy, not a blemish on her skin…and now she met his eyes directly, smiling. "Zoe?" he whispered.

"*Hello, Dad. Surprise,*" she said, in the tongue of the Underworld.

CHAPTER SIX

I T'S ONLY BEEN A FEW DAYS. MUM AND DAD STILL DON'T KNOW," Zoe said. They were sitting on the floor against her bed, a plate of sandwiches between them. She sent a furtive glance toward her closed bedroom door.

"Wow," Adrian said. "Thus the sunnies."

"Yeah. It's easy enough to fake being blind. I've got enough practice. But I'm starting to get sloppy. This morning I picked up a book and almost started reading it in front of them."

Adrian smiled, but the disgruntlement hadn't left him, even in his delight at her transformation. "So you can switch realms and all that?"

"Yep. Niko trained us. We even got to pick out a spirit horse, one for each. I keep mine tied up in the other realm here, near the back garden. You probably didn't see her. The sunlight makes them almost transparent."

"I guess." He fed a sandwich crust to Kiri. "You wouldn't eat the orange for me. Nor even the pomegranate. But you would for him."

"Ade. It wasn't really for *him*—though, yeah, he is quite persuasive."

For months now, Niko had been coming occasionally to New Zealand to check on Zoe and sniff round for Thanatos. It was safer than having Adrian do those jobs, since Thanatos or the neighbors would recognize Adrian, but didn't know Niko. Niko had gladly taken on the task. He liked Zoe instantly upon meeting her—not to mention he'd held affection for her in past lives. Zoe reported liking him too, or at least finding him amusing. But Adrian hadn't guessed Niko could persuade her into such a huge step. Especially without either of them consulting him.

He picked apart another crust. "Who was it for, then?"

"You. I mean, I was finally ready, is all, and the opportunity presented itself."

"But you didn't tell me. When it happened."

"I wanted to surprise you." She shoved at his knee. "I wanted this moment. Admit it. It was awesome."

Adrian glanced at her, then watched Kiri lick crumbs off the carpet. "Did it for Tabitha, didn't you."

She was silent too many seconds before answering. "No. I mean, I hardly know her. I didn't know her, that night."

"You had a few hours to chat before you got to the Underworld. The three of you cozily sharing Niko's horse."

The hint of ribaldry in her laughter stirred his irritation further. "That *was* interesting. And, okay, they did bring me a bottle of rum, and you know that's my favorite."

Adrian dropped a crust on the plate and pulled his hands away. "Right. He got the both of you completely soused, at which point you agreed, 'Yeah! I'll go halfway round the world at three thousand kilometers an hour on a bloody ghost horse, and eat some fruit in the land of the dead, which I wouldn't do for my best mate Ade even though he'd have got me there a lot safer—'"

"Oh, stop it. I feel bad, all right? I'm sorry. Really, Ade."

He lifted his gaze to the spring sunshine on the leaves outside the window. "I'm glad you're strong and healed and around forever, Z. You know that. It's only...I'd wanted to give that orange to Sophie."

Zoe pulled in her breath in a hiss of contrition.

"Niko didn't check with me," Adrian added. "I mean, he kind of did, but not really. I would have said no, or at least asked you to save a slice." He glanced at her in a flash of hope. "You didn't happen to save any?"

She winced and shook her head. "We were rather hungry by

then. It was a tasty orange. I mean, that and a few pomegranate seeds isn't a proper dinner…"

He sighed, and looked down at his hands dangling over his knees. "Of course. So. Only been a few days. In that case, you've not got to the Hekate memories yet, I assume."

Zoe shook her head. "Nowhere close. Nor has Tabitha." In answer to his questioning glance, she confessed, "We text each other now and then. Kind of a lot actually. It's a big experience to go through together, that type of thing."

"Yes, I'm glad you all bonded," he said dryly.

"But with me it's different, the memories," she said, apparently opting to ignore his condescension. "You've told me all about them, so I know the facts already, even if I haven't seen them in my own head yet."

"Getting to them yourself is very different from hearing about them." Concern took the place of his selfish hurt, and he examined her. "What are you going to do now? Fake your normal life a while, till you get caught out?"

"I suppose. It's safest, right?"

"I really, really don't want Thanatos targeting you. Please don't do anything stupid."

"I shall do my best. I might even do something smart. Something magical to help our side."

He considered it. "You were certainly good at that as Hekate. And in other lives, to a degree."

"In the ones I can remember so far, I did always try my hand at witchcraft. It seemed actually to work a few times." She scrunched up her nose. "And you weren't always my parent. Sometimes only my friend, like this life."

"Sometimes siblings."

"Never lovers."

He cringed. "Thank Goddess. How gross would that be?"

"Disgusting." She laughed. "So I assume Sophie doesn't know about me? Tab said she was going to keep it secret a bit. A surprise, and all."

"Well, she knows about Tab now, so she's probably finding

out about you." His phone rang at that moment. He looked at the screen. "And that's her. Bugger, hope she doesn't yell at me." He answered with a wince. "Heya."

"So I think I know what Niko meant by having another surprise for us." But Sophie didn't sound angry. She sounded more like she barely contain her excitement.

He smiled at Zoe. "Yeah, I think I know too."

"You're with her now?"

"I am."

Sophie laughed in wonder. "You did not tell me we had a daughter."

"We've got a bit to talk about, eh?"

SOPHIE'S CONVERSATION WITH Adrian was brief. She still had Tabitha there, and much to discuss with her. But after Tab returned to Seattle for the night on her ghost horse, Sophie phoned Adrian again.

He said he was camping out in the spirit realm in New Zealand, having just visited his father.

"How is he?" she asked.

"Doing well. Wants to meet you. He's a bit over the moon about my finally having a girlfriend."

Sophie lay back on her bed and smiled at her old posters. "That's sweet. I want to meet him too."

"You will sometime. And I suppose I'll meet your parents tomorrow. Officially."

"When you come pick me up? Only if you're ready."

"I ought to. I shouldn't have been a wuss about it today. Though, to protect them, I'll still have to lie about my name and other minor facts." He sighed. "So how's Tab?"

"Fine. I mean, she feels terrible about 'stealing' the orange from me, but it's obvious she loves being immortal. She's already got some plan for world domination. As far as I can tell it involves dropping out of school, becoming best buds with famous people, having parties every night, and sending hordes of fangirls to do her bidding."

"Oh my. We'd best stay on her good side. But you did warn her?" He sounded anxious. "She mustn't let it show, her being immortal, or they *will* work it out and target her."

"Yeah, I warned her, and she swears she'll be careful. But I can't make her understand. She thinks it's all fun. Or at least, ninety-nine percent fun."

"That's because she hasn't spent enough time with the memories yet. Nor has Zoe. They haven't even reached the ancient Greek stuff. Zoe knows the story, because I've told her, but I think it's the same with her. She doesn't quite grasp how much it all meant."

Sophie wedged her lower lip between her teeth as she remembered that moment just after Persephone's life: walking with Hades in the fields, both of them dead. *As long as she's all right*, they said to each other. She. Hekate.

A cold rope of dread slithered around Sophie's body. "Does..." she began, and swallowed. "I know we had to die. Obviously, if we were reborn. But how bad is it?" She cringed while awaiting his answer, afraid to search for it in her own memories. Perhaps he might say it wasn't too bad as deaths go...

He took a breath in and out. "For immortals, it always has to end violently. I haven't talked about it because I don't like to remember it. It...won't be fun for you. But it could've been worse. And like I said before, there's still so much good stuff before it. Please don't be scared of it. We're here now, together, alive. All of us."

Sophie let out her breath slowly. She spread her hand across the soft, worn comforter. "True."

"And going chronologically, you have years and years before... that. They're years full of important events. You'll want to explore them."

"Events like Hekate and Dionysos."

"Right. To name a couple."

She frowned and tried again to place Dionysos. "He wasn't our son or anything, was he?"

Adrian chuckled. "No. He was—um, do you want spoilers?"

Sophie deliberated, sliding her fingers back and forth on a loose stitch of the comforter. "I guess not. I'll let it be another fun surprise." She added irony to the words. "In the meantime, I have a hell of a lot to do."

"Finding new lodgings. Fun."

She groaned rather than select words to express how *not* fun it would be. "Tell you one thing," she said. "This time, no letting my roommates anywhere near my phone."

CHAPTER SEVEN

Zoe hadn't told Adrian everything. A person was allowed to keep some details to herself, after all. And he'd probably be happier not knowing, when he walked through the Underworld's fields, that Zoe and Tabitha had lain together under that particular clump of white trees with long gray-black leaves, while Niko took a few hours' sleep, sprawled upon his coat under the next tree over.

Adrian could live without picturing how Zoe and Tab had spread coats and scarves over themselves for warmth and privacy, and how, rather than merely sleep, they had started with a playful kiss, which had turned into more urgent kisses, which had turned into clothes being unzipped and unhooked and flesh being breathlessly fondled.

In the blur of lights and colors beginning to dawn in Zoe's healing eyes, Tab's golden hair and reddened lips were the first things in this world, this life, she had seen. It felt right somehow, since it was also the first time Zoe had touched anyone, or been touched, that way.

Snuggling drowsily with Tab afterward, her vision still a developing but fascinating blur, Zoe said, "I've never done that before. Probably obvious."

"Really? No, you did great." Tab chuckled against Zoe's neck. "I mean, as far as I can tell. I'm no expert myself."

Zoe circled her finger around a chunky cuff bracelet on Tab's wrist. "Had you? Done it before, with a girl. Or I suppose a boy."

"No boys. A girl…" Tab hummed in recollection. "Yeah. Once. Really, you haven't?"

"Never even kissed a girl till now," Zoe said. "A couple of boys. Even Adrian once—*before* his Hades memories—just because we were both curious and didn't have a lot of opportunities. But it didn't do a thing for me."

"Poor Adrian."

Zoe grinned. "Nah, didn't do a thing for him either. So who was your one girl? Not Sophie?"

"Nope, never Soph. I love her, but not like that. It was last year. Sophie and I went to a sci-fi-fantasy convention at a hotel, right? We were both dressed up. I was Merrin from 'Nightshade.' Naturally. Everyone's favorite lesbian character."

Zoe nodded. "Good choice." She watched "Nightshade" too, a supernatural-themed TV show. Well, not "watched" technically, but listened to and followed.

"We met this other girl, really cute, dressed as Baylia. I started talking to her, and later that night we danced at one of the parties…and she invited me up to her hotel room." Tab settled her head on the grass, her long hair still draped down Zoe's shoulder. "I finally got why people say 'One thing led to another.' I kept thinking she wouldn't go any further. Like she must only be doing this because we were in costume and playing. But somehow we didn't stop." Tabitha laughed softly, a rare sound of modesty, and stayed quiet a few seconds. "I never saw her again. Sent each other a couple 'Hey, that was fun' kind of texts, but that was it. So I guess I've had a one-night stand."

Zoe laid her hand over Tab's, which rested on Zoe's chest. "Sounds fun. I should try attending conventions."

Tab laughed again, sleepily.

Zoe added after a few minutes, "You could say you've had another now. Unless, I suppose…"

Tab hugged her from the side. "Hey, we'll be seeing each other for, like, the rest of eternity," she murmured.

Zoe accepted the answer and tried to get some rest, rather than pursue the question of whether Tab meant merely seeing each other or, you know, *seeing each other*.

Tab's friendly texts since then hadn't shed any light on the answer. Insecurity was starting to nag at Zoe, to be honest.

They did both have a heap of other tasks to sort out for the next few months, so she ought to be patient. But she wanted to know, to be reassured, to be validated. Or at least to be told, "Nah, that was it for now, bye," if such was the verdict.

But she knew better than to pin down Tabitha for an explanation too soon. No surer way to turn a person off. So she kept her thumbs off her phone and her lips zipped, and forced herself to wait.

In the meantime she also did not need to burden Adrian with her little romantic drama.

After all, he was kind of her dad now. Talk about weird.

BETTY QUENTIN STRETCHED her stiff legs, straightening one and then the other in the confined space of the car's front seat. "I'm too old for road trips," she remarked to her grandson Landon, who was driving.

"We'll stop soon for lunch," he said.

"No hurry." Outside the window, sagebrush blurred past beside the highway. The low, dry hills of eastern Oregon undulated out to the horizon, muted to a uniform brown by the gray clouds. Misty rain sprinkled the windows now and then, with occasional splatters of sleet.

"How long do you think we'll stay over here?" Landon's voice was steady, a bit on the high side, but he was keeping calm for someone who was willingly helping a fugitive escape and thereby breaking the law himself. He was a brave boy—a brave man, rather. He was twenty-six now.

"At least a couple of weeks. They'll be searching for me in places connected with Sophie, and around people connected with her. Also places I've been known to go. So we'll have to stay away from all those a while."

Landon's gaze remained on the highway, his long-lashed eyes hard to read behind his large glasses. He held his slender neck straight and stiff.

He was her only family—at least, the only one she counted as family. His mother, Betty's daughter, had always been too soft and silly a creature. She and Betty had clashed from day one. Betty hadn't been married for over thirty years now; she and her ex had divorced, right about the time she was rising in the ranks of Thanatos—all of which was kept secret from her husband, for his own safety. He'd died a few years after they split up. She had a brother she hadn't talked to in at least fifteen years. None of her family understood her or took interest in her philosophies and studies. None except Landon. How it cheered Betty's heart to see him take after his grandmother, even a little, and not after his mother. She almost hated to endanger him, though she appreciated his company.

"I'm not giving up," Betty added. "But you can go home if you like. After you drop me off somewhere safe."

He adjusted his grasp on the steering wheel. His old-fashioned gold wristwatch gleamed beside his shirt cuff. He shook his head. "I want to help."

"You'll be going into hiding too, then."

"Nothing to go back to."

His father dead, his mother nearly estranged from him, no job, no girlfriend—indeed, Betty suspected he was homosexual, but he had never admitted it—she saw his point. She thumped her hands on her thighs. "In that case, I have some ideas. And this time, I won't make the mistake of being so soft, even on people who are supposedly innocent." She cocked her head at him, though he still gazed forward. "Will that bother you? The possibility of collateral damage?"

Landon swallowed, his Adam's apple bobbing, but he kept the car traveling steadily down the highway. "Not if it's for an important cause."

"It is." She nodded and faced forward too. "You understand."

CHAPTER EIGHT

"I MMORTAL." DEMETER STARED, ROUND-EYED.

Persephone stood straight and proud in the garden outside Demeter's house. She had switched to the spirit world and back before her mother's eyes. She'd explained about the orange, shown her mother the vanished scars and the regrown tooth, and lifted the sheep's stone water trough in one arm.

At Persephone's request, Hades had stayed behind, leaving the two women alone for this conversation.

"I wanted to show you in person," Persephone said. "You're the first to know, besides Hades."

"But how do you know it'll last?" Her mother sounded anxious rather than joyous.

Persephone rolled her eyes. "You and him, you're a lot alike, you know. It's taken him all this time to start believing it too."

"Your scars, your strength—it's amazing." Demeter drew closer and touched her daughter's arm and the tip of her braid, as if even Persephone's hair was different now—which it wasn't, particularly. "I'll dare to hope, I suppose, but you must give me time." A smile surfaced on Demeter's face, rejuvenating her features. "Having you healthy is wonderful, though."

"I feel fantastic. You can't imagine the difference. Being strong, not having to worry about hurting myself or falling ill, it makes a person so much freer."

"Well, don't be too confident." Demeter picked up a clay jar and began walking toward the spring.

Persephone accompanied her. "You could forgive Hades. Since I'm one of you now."

"He committed his crime when you weren't one of us."

"It wasn't a crime! He didn't kidnap me."

"People are saying he did. The story's more lurid every time I hear it. The earth opening up beneath you and Hades pulling the innocent maiden under to rape her in hell."

"What nonsense. You know it isn't true. Aren't you setting them straight?"

"If I do," Demeter said, "I sound exactly like Hera defending Zeus every time he seduces another mortal."

"Hades is absolutely not Zeus."

"Perhaps not, but in their eyes, immortal men are all the same."

"You have to tell them it isn't so!" Persephone stomped on the ground as they walked. Her foot left a deep crater of a print, which she paused to stare at in wonder. Recovering the direction of her thoughts, she added, "Please. For my sake."

They reached the spring. Demeter lowered the jar and filled it. "Dear, I will try for your sake, but you must realize how ineffective it's going to be. We can speak the clearest words, explaining exactly how immortals live and operate, and what the differences between our personalities are, and the people will nod and bow and say, 'Yes, my lady, we understand now.' Then the moment our backs are turned, they begin spinning their stories. And by the time I meet them again, they're begging to hear about…" Demeter waved her hand impatiently in the air and came up with an example. "How a sea monster offended us by eating our favorite city in Egypt, so we killed it and threw it into the sky where it became a group of stars. Or some such insanity."

Persephone laughed, despite her irritation. "Gracious. We Greeks do enjoy our poetry."

"If word gets out that Hades has made you immortal, I can only imagine the stories they'll tell next." Demeter set the water jar against her hip, and gazed with a troubled expression at her daughter. "Oh, Persephone. I want to believe it will last. Yet I'm scared to hope."

Persephone took the full jar and held its weight easily in one arm. "You may as well hope. Hope makes life ever so much better. But that isn't our only concern. If the orange works for me, as it seems to have for the dog, then we have many questions to consider."

Demeter nodded. Her gaze grew distant. "Who else to give the fruit to."

"Who indeed." They turned back to the house. "Who deserves immortality? Who decides?"

"The gods." Demeter's tone was dry.

"The real ones? Or you—us?"

"Unless anyone's managed to contact the real ones, I suppose it's down to us."

As SOPHIE PREPARED and ate French toast on Sunday morning with her chattering family, she revolved Persephone's questions in her mind.

Last week, Niko decided alone who deserved immortality. But at least he had based his decision on who had once been immortal. Were Sophie on a jury, she would grant him some leniency on that point. But deciding who deserved the golden apple in the old days had indeed been contentious.

Sophie's brother interrupted her thoughts by demanding to know if she was coming back up for Halloween.

"It's only in a few days. I don't think I can."

"She's got to study," Dad reminded Liam.

"And move." Sophie sighed.

Her parents looked at her. "What?" Dad said.

"It is not working out with Melissa." Though Sophie didn't want to embark on the subject, it was time to warn her family and give them a piece of the truth. "She was feeding tips to Betty Quentin, that crazy cult woman who sent all those people after me. So we're through, Melissa and me."

Mom slammed down the glass bottle of maple syrup. "Why is everyone not arrested for all this?"

"The police are grilling Melissa. But I don't think she really knew what she was getting into. And they did arrest Quentin, but...she got out." Sophie set her fork down as her stomach twisted again.

"What the hell?" Dad said.

Sophie sent an entreating look at her family members. "Please be on the lookout, you guys. She could show up here. I don't know. Don't listen to her, don't believe her, call the police the second you see her."

"How are we supposed to know what she looks like?" Mom said.

"Can I taze her?" Liam asked. He had heard about Sophie getting to electrocute the intruder at the dorm, and had been quite taken with the notion of zapping someone.

"Not unless you're sure it's her," Sophie told him. "I'll find you guys pictures or something. But I'm serious, be careful. I don't know how I got on her radar..." Big whopping lie there, but she moved on. "But she's 911-worthy. The second you see her, call them, I mean it."

"Where are you going to live?" Dad asked. "What kind of place is safe enough?"

"I don't know. I have to look around. The Corvallis police said they're still going to offer me extra protection, so that helps."

Her parents exchanged frustrated looks. "Damn, girl," Dad said. "I thought I'd only have to worry about frat boys pawing you."

"*Them* I'll taze," she assured.

After breakfast, she packed up her clothes, and soon a text arrived from Adrian. *Be there in about 5 mins. Ready?*

Yep, she answered, though her palms went clammy in apprehension. She swung her backpack onto her shoulder, trotted back downstairs and said casually, "My ride's almost here."

"Do we get to meet this mysterious person?" Mom asked, looking up from a stack of invoices at the kitchen counter.

"Sure. His name's David." Sophie picked up a Golden Delicious apple from the wire basket by the sink and tucked it into her pack.

The knock on the front door came a minute later, respectful and proper.

Sophie's dad got there first. He swung it open.

Wrapped in his black coat against the cold wind, Adrian lifted his head and smiled. But to Sophie's trained eye he looked every bit as guarded as he had the day Niko hauled her into the spirit realm to meet him. Sophie's heart thudded hard, as Adrian's was likely doing at such a fraught reunion. *Hades, you remember Demeter?*

"Hi there." Dad stuck out his hand. "I'm Terry."

Adrian shook his hand. "I'm David. I, uh, gave Sophie a ride up here." As she expected, he faked an American accent, but it wobbled into strange vowels here and there.

Sophie tried not to wince. "Hey," she greeted, and pushed past her dad to join Adrian on the porch. "Ready to go?"

"Rushing straight off?" her dad asked.

"Yeah, it's kind of a long drive, and I have so much homework and apartment-hunting to do…"

But now Sophie's mom was in the doorway too. "Hi, I'm Isabel."

Adrian shook her hand. "David. Pleased to meet you."

"And you go to OSU too?"

"Yeah. I'm a geography major."

"What brought you up to Carnation?" Mom asked.

"I know some people in Seattle. I was visiting. Offered Sophie a lift."

"But we should go," Sophie repeated.

"David, can I get you some coffee or anything first?" her dad asked.

"Oh, no thanks. I've got some."

Dad frowned past him at the driveway. "Where's your car?"

"I parked it by the gas station back there. I fancied a walk."

Fancied? Sophie shot him a warning look. "It's fine. We'll stop for lunch somewhere. Love you, Dad!" She stepped up and hugged her dad to ward off any further interrogation. "Love you, Mom." She turned and hugged her too. "Bye, Liam," she hollered over Mom's shoulder.

"Bye," he shouted back from in front of his video game.

"Love you, honey." Her mom let go of her. "Good to meet you, David. And please drive safe."

Don't say "precious cargo," Sophie prayed.

Her mom rubbed Sophie's shoulder and added, "This is precious cargo you've got here."

Sophie shut her eyes for a second in resignation.

Adrian smiled, a hint of mischief coming alive in his face. "Indeed. I'll be very cautious. Good to meet you as well."

Several more waves and farewells later, Sophie and Adrian finally walked down the driveway and turned onto the path along the highway.

"Fancied?" she accused.

"Precious cargo?" he teased.

They passed behind a thick stand of maple trees, and he took her hand.

She glanced up and found him grinning. She smiled back, infusing the gesture with silent apology for all the anger and bitterness of their latest visit to the Underworld. "I wish you could get to know my family better. I think they'd like you."

"I'm not sure. That is Demeter's soul we're talking about, even if he doesn't know it."

"Demeter didn't always hate you. Just sometimes. But yeah, guess it's a good thing Dad doesn't know you're the father of my child."

Adrian squeezed her fingers. His hand warmed hers for a second before the wind whipped the heat away. "In many lives."

"True. I knew about a lot of them. But I was so much more... *invested* in the Persephone life, that learning about Hekate was..." She chuckled in wonder, unable to express it.

"I did want to tell you. If it would help, I would talk at you for hours, days, overloading you with every detail I can remember.

But it'd more confuse you than enlighten you, and life keeps giving us other tasks instead."

"It does. It really, really does." A car swooshed by on the highway. "Of course, I do want to know who the others are. Reincarnated, I mean."

"If you like." Adrian sounded reluctant.

"Zeus and Hera?" Sophie began.

"I can't trace either of them by the usual sense. We didn't exchange blood or anything. In fact, none of us can trace Hera. But Freya can sense Zeus."

"Of course."

"She says he's no one we've met. 'An unaccountably popular, licentious, good-looking arse, like always,' is how she put it."

Sophie smirked. "Poseidon, then?"

"Still a kid." Adrian looked away, into the field beside the road. "We reckon it isn't right to meddle when they're still kids."

"Suppose so. Athena?"

"Very high-powered career. Too busy to bother."

"How high-powered?"

"The president of Germany."

Sophie blinked in wonder. "Oh. Right. A bit busy. Um…Artemis?"

"Also quite high-powered and busy, though she's someone Sanjay was related to. She's in the Indian military or something. And she's married with little kids, and, well…after what happened to Sanjay, he doesn't even want us to approach her. Not for a while, at least."

"I see. How about Hestia?"

"Oh, she's in the Underworld. Was a nice old Chinese lady. Died a couple of years ago. Hanging around, waiting for her family."

"Ah. Hephaestus?"

"One of Freya's ex-husbands, in Sweden. She has a few. She's not terribly keen on making him immortal so far, but maybe we'll convince her someday."

"Then let's see, who else was there? Ares, I guess. Though I don't recall liking him much."

"Nor did I. Arrogant wanker. Happy to say he's some random loser from…Massachusetts? Missouri? I forget, something with an M. A woman this time, not much older than us. But I've no plans to bring her into the fold. The world can do without the god of war, if you ask me."

"I agree. So that's everyone, I think."

"Well. Not quite. But never mind, now we're entering 'overloading your brain' territory." He led her into the swampy field. They stepped from one mound of grass to another, then he took her in his arms and switched realms. The spirit-world forest materialized around them, dark and full of twisting branches and birdsong. "Your living situation," he said, still holding her. "Listen, I don't know if you'll go for it, but—"

"Can I move in with you?" she interrupted.

He looked surprised, then eased into a smile. "That's what I was going to suggest, yeah."

"I'll still need a front. Some place around campus I can have mail delivered to, somewhere I can show my folks if they come to town. But I don't want to sleep anywhere except in this realm, next to you."

He lifted her off the ground in an embrace. "Thank you," he murmured. "Yes, of course, it's all I want. I'd worry so much less." He set her down, repeated, "Thank you," and kissed her.

She grinned. "Well, don't thank me until I've snapped at you for leaving dirty dishes out, or whined about what a pain it is to do laundry. How *do* you do laundry?" His Airstream trailer, she knew, had no washer and dryer.

He shrugged. "Laundromats. Easy."

"But, really, would it be all right? I mean, living together, it's kind of a big step."

"Not near as big as eating a *chrysomelia*." He squeezed both her hands. "Which you were willing to do the other night, and which we will have you do, the second it becomes possible."

She nodded. "All right, then. Let's go home."

CHAPTER NINE

"I HEAR ADRIAN HIT YOU." TABITHA LAUGHED AND ROLLED BACK ON the grass in Volunteer Park.

"Didn't hurt," Nikolaos claimed. "And I hit him back. Harder."

"Then he banished you from the Underworld."

"Whatever. Like he can tell me what to do."

"So now they know about Zoe. Your cat's out of the bag."

He glanced at her. "No one ever knows about *all* my cats. But I knew they'd find out that one soon. So what are you going to do now?"

She sat up, dead leaves and grass sticking to her hair. The nearest streetlight in the park stood several trees away, but the light was enough for her to make out his curious look as he watched her. She turned to face the city skyline. "This is gross and selfish, but I kind of want to show off. Make people worship me. Make the douchebags from high school sorry they ever dissed me."

"Don't we all. I'm fine with that as long as you don't actually show off your immortality."

"Well, duh."

"So how will you acquire this worship exactly?"

"Theater was always my idea. Plays, musicals. Become the newest big name on Broadway or classical crossover, have cute girls begging me to sign their boobs."

"As long as I get to be there to help hold their shirts out of the way. How's your voice? Good enough for this fame plan?"

She pouted. "Not really. A month at Cornish with all the future divas of the world has been enough to show me how lacking I am." Tabitha had just begun her studies at Cornish College of the Arts, in the rushing heart of Seattle. "Plus the whole bullshit of auditioning, waiting to be called back, working your ass off in a restaurant or something while you're waiting—it actually kind of sucks. Or so I'm gathering."

"Then forget that. The parties are the choicest part of fame anyway. Skip straight to those."

"I'm remembering some. I just got into another life, in China, and dude, do you remember? I was this prince, and I seriously had a harem of women, and the parties I threw—"

"Oh yes, those were grand." He stretched his legs out in front of him. "But your parties as Dionysos, your festivals, now those were the days to be reckoned with. I'd scoot your memories along if I were you, and start recalling those."

Tabitha sent an impatient breath out her nose. "Sophie said the same thing. What I do not get is why some life three thousand years ago is so much important than what we can do *now*."

"On the whole I agree. But I make an exception for that life, because in that one, and only that one, we were immortal. Therefore it's instructive. Also it's sexy."

"I'll get there eventually." She pulled her long hair off her shoulders and twisted it up behind her head, sliding a stick through it to secure it. "So why'd you come find me? To make me the life of the party for eternity? Not that I'm complaining."

"I wanted you along for the ride," he said.

"And Zoe?"

Nikolaos looked up at the full moon, which shone through a shroud of autumn clouds. "Her too."

"Why us? You understand we're not going to have sex with you, right? I mean, if we live forever, I guess it's possible we'll come around to liking guys, but…"

He grinned. "I'll never give up hope. But even a perv like me does want friends. Ade and I aren't always the best match. Obviously." He pulled up his knees and folded his arms around them, considering the moon again. "I got on well with Sanjay—Apollo.

But they've killed him, and souls aren't the most exciting friends. You and I tended to be good mates. Drinking buddies, in most lives, though in immortal days we couldn't actually get very drunk. More like getting-other-people-drunk buddies."

"Right on. So, Zoe? She got people drunk with us, or what?" Tabitha realized she kept steering the conversation toward Zoe, and felt dorky about it. She did want to learn more about that tasty Kiwi, but hadn't decided yet if she wanted to be Zoe's girlfriend, or her friend with occasional benefits, or what. Living potentially forever with a person was a daunting prospect, and Tab didn't want to screw up their friendship, or relationship, right out of the gate. Thus the friendly but not totally affectionate texts, which she hoped weren't offending Zoe.

"No, her I brought back because…" Niko lifted his chin toward the moon. "She's magical."

"I get that, if by 'magical' you mean 'hot.'"

"I also mean magical."

"We switch realms and ride ghost horses. Aren't we all magical?"

"Yeah, but her more than most. You'll see."

Tabitha shrugged at the enigmatic remark, and squinted at him. "So, parties, you say. Hanging with famous people. How do we even do that?"

"I know a few and can introduce you. Your charm and charisma will do the rest."

"Not with my sucky wardrobe and small-town hair," Tabitha grumbled.

"Money fixes those."

She considered that truth, and remembered something he had said about diamonds and emeralds in the Underworld. "You said we can get money?"

"Already have it. Mountains of it. You're welcome to some. Immortal's salary, let's call it."

"Hmm. Then you're saying I can have some fun while I decide what to do with eternity. Enjoy the perks first."

Niko lay back, folding his arms behind his head. "The world is your jar of caviar, my dear."

ZOE LAY ON her back in the grass, gazing up at the feathery leaves of the titoki tree above her. She'd never actually seen the tree till this spring. All her life, in her parents' back garden, she'd heard its leaves rustling in the wind, touched its fallen seeds upon the ground, and sometimes thought she felt the tree's vibrant life force quivering through the Earth under her. To finally gaze upon it was a priceless treat.

And yet, closing her eyes worked best for sensing the magic. So she closed them. At once she felt the trunk stretching its roots like fingers into the soil. She sensed the mushrooms, mosses, worms, beetles, spiders, and every little quiver of life that added up to the symphony of Earth magic. It balanced the sky magic perfectly, the warmth of the sun and the rush of the wind as they poured across her.

She hadn't reached Hekate's life yet, though she was moving backward faster than Tab was, to judge from Tab's laid-back texts. But Zoe already understood how closely her own soul always linked itself to magic—witchcraft, if you wanted to call it that. And she already knew that in the Underworld, the Earth magic was of course immeasurably strong, but the huge mass of souls brought sky magic with them to balance it, and that was why they glowed.

Later, after going indoors, such thoughts never made much sense to her. But at the moment, lying with her eyes closed, her back against the Earth, spring's breath washing over her, it felt like the clearest, purest logic.

CHAPTER TEN

$\mathcal{T}$HE IMMORTALS SAT AROUND A FIRE IN THE SPIRIT REALM, EYES locked on Hades and Persephone as they told their revelation of finding the long-dreamed-of golden apple. Getting them all together in one place for a meeting on short notice had not been easy. It had taken a good deal of searching to find some of them in the first place, as plenty of them still couldn't track one another. But Persephone, Hades, and Demeter had urged the importance of the topic upon everyone, and insisted they come at once.

Demeter still wasn't speaking directly to Hades. Hades understood and tolerated it, but Persephone privately told him that her patience with her mother was wearing rather damned thin. However, Persephone seemed to be curbing her irritation for tonight and concentrating upon breaking the news to her aunts and uncles.

An immortality discussion was too dangerous for the mortal realm; they might be overheard. But several of the immortals still loathed venturing into the Underworld, so they didn't hold the meeting there either. Hades felt it was just as well, as he preferred to keep the exact tree's identity and location secret as long as possible. So they had gathered on a beach alongside the gulf near Zeus and Hera's palace.

After their explanation, Persephone stood and walked around the fire to show everyone her healed scars. She switched realms before their eyes and came back again. The other immortals murmured in astonishment or stayed silent in thought. Demeter looked perturbed, her hands clasped tight in her lap. But Aphrodite jumped up with a squeal of delight and hugged Persephone.

Meanwhile Hermes spun to shove Hades on the shoulder, and said, "Hades, you lucky sneak! I would have called dibs if I knew there was a chance."

"And I still would have said no," Persephone told him, but she grinned.

Ares, the soldier whom people were calling the god of war, studied Kerberos. "The dog too, you say?" He swayed a spear back and forth, its tip on the ground.

"It would appear so," Hades said.

Ares rose, and before Hades realized what he meant to do, he had done it. The spear flew and skewered Kerberos through the belly, emerging out the other side and pinning him to the sand. Blood splashed. The dog yelped a choked sound and went into spasms.

Several people shouted in protest, and Aphrodite threw herself across to seize Ares' arm, but he had moved too fast. Hades bellowed in rage and leaped upon him, knocking Ares' head back against the log he'd been sitting on. "What in the Goddess' name is wrong with you?" His hands tightened around Ares' throat.

A glance back showed Persephone and Demeter crouching by Kerberos. Persephone broke the spear and yanked it out, and she and her mother soothed the dog with gentle hands. Hades returned his attention to strangling Ares, whose neck was being crushed in satisfying fashion beneath his hands, and whose face was turning purple. But Aphrodite and Zeus and Poseidon hauled at him and clamored for him to let go, and since he wasn't going to succeed in killing the fool, he finally relented and did so.

Ares lay a short while gasping and rubbing his throat, then sat up and glared. "It's an important thing to test," he spat out, his voice croaking. "Would you rather I threw the spear at your wife?"

Hades lunged for him again, but his friends restrained him.

"He's recovering," Persephone called, her voice proud and cold. "You wish to see your test? Come look."

Though Hades and Ares exchanged glowers, they joined the group clustering around the dog. The bleeding from the spear wound was already slowing, and Kerberos was moving and breathing more easily, though he panted in pain. Persephone stroked his head, and Demeter used a handful of leaves to wipe away more blood and show the healing skin. Persephone sent her a grateful, chastened glance. A breath of solace softened Hades' anger—at least mother and daughter might be reconciled, if only temporarily and only where innocent animals were concerned.

Hades sat in the bloodstained sand beside Persephone, and drew the dog's head onto his lap. "Try that again and the spear goes in *your* belly," he said to Ares.

Ares answered with a mocking half-bow, and returned to sit on his log.

Hermes gave Aphrodite a pitying, probing smirk, as if to question her frequent dallying with Ares—a relationship (if one could call it that) that was no secret to anyone. Aphrodite sighed in response, with a look that seemed to beseech Hermes to tolerate a man less intelligent than himself.

Athena studied Persephone and Kerberos with her arms folded. "So the question is, do we give this fruit to anyone else?"

"Indeed, that is the question." Artemis still sat upon a rock, chin on her hand, watching the flames. She hadn't bothered rising for the scuffle. It took a lot more than such antics to alarm her. "You were nearly one of us already, Persephone. We all love you, and I'm sure we would all have chosen you as the first to eat it anyway. But who else deserves it?"

Persephone rose from her crouch. "We thought it only fair that all the immortals should decide as a group. Perhaps bring forth candidates and then cast votes. Anonymously, with a black stone to vote 'no' and a white one to vote 'yes,' as people do in some cities."

"Would a single black stone veto a candidate?" Hera asked. "Or does the side with the largest number of votes carry the day?"

Persephone glanced at Athena. "What do you think?"

Athena scooped up a handful of beach rocks. "There are now

fifteen of us. What do you all say to a two-thirds majority?" She tipped a few rocks into one palm. "If five or fewer say no, and ten or more say yes, then we acquire a new immortal."

"That seems fair," Rhea said.

The others voiced agreement.

"How many candidates may each of us present?" Poseidon asked quietly.

Hades, and probably everyone else, thought at once of Poseidon's situation: a wife and three daughters, all of whom he would surely wish to give the fruit to.

Persephone made the same calculation. "Perhaps four?" she said.

"Well, I know I won't be proposing any," Hera said. "All my children are long dead, and my grandchildren don't know me. I can't think of anyone I'd bother keeping around forever."

"We should definitely think about it a while," Apollo said. "This would be a bad time to be impulsive."

"Well, the next fruits won't be ripe for nearly a month," Persephone said.

"Then we shall give it another month," Athena proclaimed, "and meet again with the names of our candidates."

Again the group murmured assent.

"In the meantime," Hermes said, "aren't you going to show us this fruit?"

"I admit I'm dreadfully curious," Aphrodite agreed.

Hades caught Persephone's glance, and drew strength from it before answering on their behalf. "We're not sure that's wise."

"It isn't that we don't trust you…" Persephone began.

"Yes it is," Hades muttered, not looking directly at Ares—and, in truth, it wasn't merely Ares he distrusted. He shuddered at the idea of the chaos Zeus might create by immortalizing one lover after another, sneaking them down to the Underworld to find the fruit.

"Someone could easily become desperate to use it for a loved one," Persephone explained, "and might go so far as to take it without asking the rest of us. I'm sure we can all imagine a situation where we'd do that ourselves."

"But the two of you *could* do it without asking the rest of us." Hermes studied them, looking shrewd now rather than affectionate.

"The dog's and Persephone's immortality happened purely by accident," Hades said. "We live in the Underworld, with the ghosts, exactly as none of you wished to. You might find a similarly powerful discovery on the surface yet. You're welcome to look."

"It's the Goddess' wish that you should find it," Rhea said. She gazed at them from across the fire. "And that you should control it, at least for now. I respect your choice, and see its wisdom. I suggest we all do the same for the time being, and think instead about who among mortals is truly worthy to join us."

The others already looked absorbed in their thoughts, and nodded in acceptance. All except Hermes, who jumped up and tagged along with Persephone, Hades, and Kerberos as the meeting broke up.

"Honestly? You're not going to show it to me? After all I've done for you?"

Hades peered at him. "What exactly have you done for us?"

"I took your side! I wanted you two to get together. And I'm not afraid of your realm, the way most of them are. I happen to admire it."

"Hermes, we love you," Hades said, "but you rarely do as you're told, and you always do as you wish, and I haven't the slightest idea what you'd do with an immortality fruit, but I'm sure it would be both creative and disastrous."

Persephone laughed, and petted Kerberos, who was already well enough to walk and wag his tail.

Hermes pointed from her to Hades. "My revenge on you for *not* showing me the plant could be equally creative and disastrous."

Persephone let go of the dog, stepped up to Hermes, and slid her hands around his neck. "Someday, Hermes. But please wait *just* a little longer?" She added a gentle kiss on his lips, which looked sultry enough to stir a spark of jealousy in Hades.

She stepped back. Hermes remained silent, gazing at her with interest and gratitude. "Oh, very well," he finally said. "As long as that's how we greet each other from now on."

She grinned.

Hades rolled his eyes and latched his arm around his wife. "Come on, darling."

CHAPTER ELEVEN

SOPHIE UNPACKED THE GROCERIES ONTO THE TINY COUNTER IN THE Airstream's kitchen. Her head spun from her busy day, and she was glad when Adrian stepped outside to take Kiri for a walk. It gave her a few minutes to think in silence.

Though it was only 6:30 p.m., darkness had fallen outside beneath a cloudy sky. Dead leaves and twigs clicked against the trailer's exterior, flung by the October wind. Tomorrow was Halloween, and she had no particular plans for it, and no costume. That was a first. Halloween had always been a huge deal when she was growing up. The produce stand sold truckloads of pumpkins along with corn stalks and other "falloween" decor, as her mom called it. Sophie and Liam also helped with the neighbor's maze in the cornfield—they set up hay bales, scarecrows, and jack o' lanterns, and lurked in scary costumes to leap out at the kids navigating the labyrinth.

This year she had met lots of actual ghosts and was well on her way to becoming the queen of the Underworld, but for once she didn't have any Halloween plans. Strange.

She set out the butternut squash and Yukon Gold potatoes for the soup she planned to make tonight, and leaned back on the counter to check email on her phone. Her inbox held an assortment of messages from her parents, Tabitha, and others. Nothing looked important, and the sight of Tab's name still caused a twitch of jealousy, so she composed a message instead:

Hey guys,

I've found a room to rent in a house with a bunch of other students. Address is below. It's a short walk to campus and should be handy, and they're nice people. Got to deal with dinner—love you!

She addressed it to both her parents and Liam, and after a moment of hesitation, added Tab too, though soon she'd tell Tab her real living situation, of course.

The house was shared by five other students at OSU, one of whom was a grad student, the T.A. for Sophie's chemistry class. This morning, her brain fried from looking through the online housing ads, Sophie found herself rambling to the T.A. after class about needing to find a new place to live. All Sophie really needed, she confessed, was a place to keep stuff and a bed to pass off as her own if her parents visited, but in truth she was going to move in with her boyfriend, and she didn't think her parents would understand; hell, she wasn't sure herself if it was a smart move…

The grad student had jumped in with the assurance that she had done the same thing when she was starting college, and if Sophie wanted, she and her friends had a room Sophie could pretend was hers. In truth it was another girl's, who was similarly always sleeping at her boyfriend's, but Sophie was welcome to move in if she didn't mind sharing this front (and some closet space) with the other girl, and tossing in, say, a hundred dollars a month to help out with rent.

Sophie went with her to see the house, and decided it looked safe and genuine and totally unaffiliated with Thanatos. She shook hands with her new housemates whom she'd rarely see, moved out of the dorm (choosing a time of day when she wouldn't run into Melissa), split her possessions between the house and the Airstream, and changed her address with the student records department. Given her recent history of being the victim of attacks and intrusions, they were especially willing to honor her request that her information stay unlisted.

So here she was, shacking up in the spirit realm with the boyfriend she'd met about a month ago—though, of course, really they'd known each other for millennia. *See, Mom and Dad, that's why it's okay.*

For the last few days her mind had wrapped itself into knots. She worried she'd get on Adrian's nerves, or he'd get on hers, and they'd mess up the lovely relationship they had begun. The worry had even interfered with their physical relationship. Though she'd spent nights in the trailer before, and spicy ones at that, it felt different now that she had moved in. Her desire for him had hit a dry streak; or, at least, only extended so far before shriveling up as anxiety reabsorbed her brain.

"I'm sorry," she had mumbled to him the first night, when she withdrew from his probing kisses in the dark. "Everything's...I don't know."

He promised her it was fine, and let her fall asleep with her back pressed up against him.

Then it happened the second night too.

"It's not you," she lamented. "It's just, moving in together, it's so..."

"Domestic and boring?" He sounded slightly amused, at least. On top of being hurt, that is.

"No. Not really. I'm stressed, is all."

He lay back, not touching her except at the hip and knee, which the confines of the small bed required. "It's all right. Doesn't have to happen every day. Nor work perfectly every time."

"Do you want me to...I mean, I can..." But the reluctance came through in her voice, which made her feel twice as awful, because her distaste wasn't his fault. Such one-sided favors were the kind of thing she had begun doing for Jacob a few weeks before college began, as the relationship sputtered out. So although Adrian absolutely wasn't Jacob, doing such things when she wasn't in the mood still carried unpleasant associations for her.

"No, you don't have to." He sounded distant, and she sensed he was still awake, hours later as she finally fell asleep.

Yeah. Living together had its speed bumps, indeed.

But she did love him and wanted to stay with him. And in that case she had to be in this realm in order to stay safe. And until the next orange ripened, she had to keep relying on him to switch her back and forth between realms if she intended to continue her regular student life. Which she did, for now. A normal human life still mattered vitally to her. Thus she was, indeed, the mythic Persephone, commuting between the realm of the dead and that of the living, all because of a complicated link to Hades.

Funny how that worked out, as Adrian had said to her once.

She sighed and navigated back to her inbox, ready for a distraction. She opened Tabitha's email. It was a link to a video posted online, which, when Sophie tapped it open, turned out to be Tab at some party in an elegant room. Hundreds of small lights lit the living room or conference hall or whatever it was, some bulbs twinkling, some glowing steady, all in a spectrum of colors. Arrangements of flowers and potted trees gave the place an expensive feel, as did the sleek hairstyles and trendy evening clothes of the people in the crowd.

On the video, recorded on someone's phone, Tab wore a slinky, shiny emerald green dress Sophie had never seen before. Her hair had been set into perfect long gleaming waves, and she wore the kind of makeup only a professional could paint on. Beside her stood a scruffy-bearded guy, maybe forty or fifty years old, wearing a tux with a guitar strap over it. He looked familiar, but Sophie couldn't place him.

"So Grange," Tabitha was saying, "you confess you have a soft spot for some very silly songs."

Grange Redway, of course. One of the pioneers of grunge rock. Sophie opened her mouth in astonishment.

"I do," he said.

"And will you sing some for us?"

"Yes. Of course." Grange spoke with the lofty gravity of a certain stage of drunkenness. He swung his guitar into position and began strumming gently. "This is from a cartoon several of us watched when we were kids. Maybe you'll recognize it. Go ahead, sing along."

Adrian entered the trailer with Kiri as Grange began singing. "Hey," Adrian said. When Sophie didn't answer, Adrian moved up beside her and looked over her shoulder at the screen. "Is that Grange Redway? From Red Merlins?"

"Yeah." She stared at the video. "With Tabitha."

The silly song, performed with such seriousness and artistry, was hilarious. Sophie saw the humor even though she didn't laugh right now. Tabitha requested another, and Grange launched into a new one.

"What's she doing hanging with Grange Redway?" Adrian asked.

"I don't know. I mean, he lives in Seattle I think, but it's not like you can walk up to his door and invite him to your party. Or whoever's party this is. Even if you're immortal."

They kept watching. Tabitha urged Grange on to two more songs, each funnier than the last. At the end, the voice of the person recording threw in a few words of encouragement, and Sophie and Adrian groaned in recognition.

"Niko," Adrian said. "Of course. *That's* how you meet a rock star."

"Niko knows him?"

"He has a way of knowing people. The more rich and famous, the more he courts them. I'm sure none of them have any idea who he is, nor do they likely care, as long as he keeps bringing them whatever they want. Flattery usually, perhaps more money, drugs, fans..." Adrian gestured at the video. "A chance to show off."

Sophie lowered the phone as the video ended on a frozen blur of the final shot. "I could tell her we'd rather she didn't hang out with Niko. In fact, why *is* she hanging out with him? She knows what he did to us."

"I'm sure he offered whatever she wanted most. Fame, probably. Or at least parties with famous people. Besides, he's good at charming his way back into people's good graces. Oh, it doesn't matter. If we try to control them, they'll only misbehave worse." Adrian folded his arms and watched Kiri munch from her bowl of dog food.

Sophie reached through her memory, following those ripples that the name "Dionysos" caused. Still no definite recollections, only random images that could have come from mythology books:

outdoor parties under the moon, wine poured in abundance for everyone, all the attendees in animalistic costumes and masks... but also a sober bearded man in the daylight, crouching beside grapevines to tend them, with Demeter helping him.

Sophie dismissed the thoughts, accustomed by now to her memories not telling her all she wanted to know. "I suppose it'll make sense once I get to that part," she said.

"To the degree it ever makes sense." Adrian's gaze wandered across the floor. "I told Zoe, you know. 'If you did this for Tabitha, well, try to see beyond that. I realize I'm biased, having been your dad and for other reasons, but you're fabulous on your own and you don't need to impress any particular girl.'"

Sophie mulled that over. "Are you saying Hekate and Dionysos were...involved?"

Adrian swung his boot to tap a stray kibble back toward Kiri. "It's complicated."

Sophie considered Hekate, the child whose image was strengthening in her mind. She suspected it wouldn't be long before the dreams brought her a long-ago pregnancy announcement. "So if we had a baby, then evidently I convinced you to do a certain thing at least once."

Adrian unfolded his arms, and snaked one of them around her waist. His fingers slid up and down her hip. When he answered, his voice was markedly warmer. "Oh, it was rather more than once."

Sophie's body didn't respond in the wildfire way it would have last week. But there was a glimmer, a pleasant notch upward in heat.

However, as she contemplated that, and gauged whether she'd be able to follow through, Adrian seemed to remember her recent diffidence, and immediately pulled his arm away. He walked to the fridge, opened it, and stared inward, his face a carefully constructed blank mask.

CHAPTER TWELVE

A FEW DAYS AFTER PERSEPHONE AND HADES BROKE THE NEWS OF the immortality fruit to the others, they walked into the bedchamber in the evening to find a small bird darting around the stalactites. Birds didn't usually fly down into the Underworld, but occasionally one, lost or adventurous, swooped into the entrance and wound up fluttering around frantically in some part of the cave.

Persephone laughed. "Poor silly thing." She fashioned a net by wrapping a veil onto a long spear handle, and set about climbing the wall to catch the bird.

Using handholds of tiny ledges and lumps that took immense muscle strength and control to hang onto and wouldn't have sufficed for any mortal rock-climber, Persephone ascended easily, one hand free to hold the net. She swung the net through the air. The bird darted to avoid it, soared straight to the cold fireplace, and flew up the chimney—perhaps the way it had entered in the first place, and a good method of escape now.

Persephone and Hades laughed. She threw the net to the floor and picked her way back down the wall. Hades' hand closed around her bare foot to help her, and she turned and slid into his arms. Her legs straddled his waist; her tunic slid up around her hips. He moved his hands beneath it and stepped forward to press her against the rock wall.

Nearly every day since the spring equinox she had invited him to let her make use of those cloudhair seeds she kept around to avoid pregnancy. Every time he had refused, and redirected their desire to other tantalizing activities.

But it was increasingly clear Persephone was immortal. She had proved it by sensing him, by switching realms, and by feats of strength such as climbing this wall. As she kissed him now, her legs around him, she felt his resistance crumble, the evidence of her eternal youth finally conquering him.

Neither of them needed to speak a word of explanation. Persephone pulled his tunic out of the way. He shifted into position and pushed forward, and their bodies interlocked. A spark of pain gleamed inside her, and she caught her breath, then it lulled to a spreading warmth. He filled her; she surrounded him. They lingered a moment, breathing against one another's lips. Then Hades lifted her by the backs of her legs and moved her to the bed, and tumbled down on top of her.

Finally, I can do everything, she thought in bliss, moving with him. Not just everything Aphrodite could do with men, but everything anyone could do, anywhere. The world was hers.

Her increasing excitement scattered her thoughts beyond words, and she let herself only enjoy him.

Afterward they lay side by side, garments still half on, their hearts slowing back to normal. Persephone sat up and crawled over Hades. She reached across to the flat-topped stump he had brought down as a table. On it sat the cloth bag of cloudhair seeds and dried mint leaves. She untied the drawstring, poured a small handful into her palm, and tossed them back into her mouth.

A glance at Hades found him watching her, smiling gently. "Thank goodness," he said. "I wasn't quite ready to face *that* risk yet."

"Nor me." She grimaced. "Ugh! Aphrodite wasn't joking about the taste. Even with the mint. Bitter and oily. And the texture's like thorns." She swallowed, shuddered, and washed down the seeds with a swig of water from a jar.

"Sorry, love. If we ever find an herb that works for men, I'll happily take it, no matter how it tastes."

"I know you would. We'll keep looking." She settled into his arms, and wrapped his thigh between hers. "Worth it, though."

"Mm." His sigh was more of a groan. He nuzzled her throat. "I completely agree."

Sophie opened her eyes to the darkness of the trailer. Heat cocooned her. Adrian breathed in sleep, his head turned away. She had no idea what time it was, and at the moment cared nothing about such details.

She slid her hand under his shirt, reveling in the taut skin and the wiry hairs leading down from his navel. His warmth and scent captivated her. His breath hitched, his consciousness creeping back as she moved her hand inside his flannel pajama pants. She stroked one lean hip and then the other, and finally dipped between them.

He slid his arms around her and released his breath in a gratified moan.

She climbed onto him, knees planted on either side of his waist. He peeled off her shirt. She did the same to his, then lay down so their bare chests met. Without cloudhair seeds of her own, she wouldn't take it as far as Persephone and Hades had, but she could take pleasure in him, and give it back. At last.

She expected a question or a triumphant remark any moment, as they kissed and stroked one another. And she would have been happy, if shy, to relate the dream she'd awoken from. But he said nothing, smug nor otherwise; asked her for no explanation. He only breathed and groaned and touched and received. Goddess bless him.

OMG girl!! Zoe texted Tabitha when she got the video link. *You are a rock star ALREADY! FFS, invite me next time.* After shooting it off, Zoe wondered if she should have added a wink or something, to sound less needy. But then:

Ha, I wanted to come get you! Tab texted back. *But even with the horse it takes what, 3 hrs ea way to NZ? And I didn't think your folks would let you out so easy this time. Next time def!!*

Sounds great, Zoe answered, and this time added the smiling emoticon. *You're careful abt not showing your powers too much, right?*

Yeah & besides, I think I'll mostly be making things happen for others. Awesomest parties, coolest connections, cos we have the money, you know? Anyway, N thinks the weirdos don't even know for sure I'm connected w/ S. We're in different states now and all.

Zoe worked it out: N for Niko, S for Sophie, weirdos for Thanatos; but was that a safe conclusion about Thanatos' cluelessness?

Well, be careful. I'd hate to see my new favorite rock star get assassinated.

Aww, Tab texted back. *Can I count you as my new favorite groupie, then? ;)*

Zoe grinned, demeaning though the words might be if taken a certain way. *Absolutely,* she answered.

Chapter Thirteen

$\mathcal{D}$URING THE MONTH THAT PASSED BEFORE THE GODS WERE TO present the names of their candidates for immortality, Hades and Persephone examined the little orange tree with doubt. Only three oranges looked ripe enough to eat, and even if all it took was one decent-sized bite, that would probably translate into no more than twenty doses per orange. Sixty total. Persephone had opted not to choose anyone this time around to propose as a candidate, and when she asked Hades if he had anyone in mind, he said he needed no one except her.

But if each of the other thirteen immortals chose four, and if they were all approved, that would make fifty-two new immortals.

"Just enough orange, if we're lucky," Persephone concluded.

"But so many immortals." Hades gazed into the orchard, the shadows falling over his face.

But when the meeting came, again at night around the same fire pit, nowhere near fifty-two were proposed. Most of the immortals brought no names at all.

"No one for me," Hermes said. "It'd only tie me down."

"None for me this time either," Demeter said.

"I imagine someday I'll have a love I'll wish to bring into our circle," Apollo said. "But for now I don't."

Zeus, at his turn, seemed about to speak up at some length, but a stern glance from Hera shushed him, and he only said, "No one for us, either." A particularly beloved mortal woman would have been his suggestion, Persephone supposed, or one of his many illegitimate children. Perhaps someday he'd brave Hera's jealousy and bring forth some such person. But not today, thankfully.

The list ultimately came down to merely five candidates: Poseidon's wife Amphitrite; his three daughters, all grown but still young; and Adonis.

Aphrodite, of course, proposed Adonis' name. She spoke more timidly than Persephone had ever seen. She stood with her hands drawn close to her chest, in the pose of a child expecting to be chastened. Her long black hair, rather than tumbling loose as usual, was arranged in a tame braid draped over one shoulder.

"You've all met him at some point," Aphrodite said. "But he's a better man than most of you know. It isn't merely that I love him. I don't intend to marry him and he knows that. Marriage isn't my fashion. But he's patient and smart and well-mannered, and knows how to tend vineyards and make the best wine any of you have ever tasted. In fact, he's taken over the management of the vineyards almost completely, since his parents have grown so careless—"

"And therefore he should live forever?" Ares said with disdain.

"Let her speak," Athena said.

"I know he's young," Aphrodite said. "But he shows such insight and passion already—"

Ares snorted.

"Give him a chance, please," Aphrodite concluded, turning her face toward the others and ignoring Ares. She withdrew and sat upon her log.

"Five, then." Athena rose. "We adjourn to think these five names over, and meet here again three days from now after sunset to vote."

The voting day came. The immortals assembled as before.

Athena opened two skin bags, and began walking around the circle, handing out the contents. "Five white stones and five black ones for each of us. The jars will be upon that boulder." She glanced at Rhea, who held up one of five slender-necked amphorae standing at her feet. "We'll take turns going to them individually, and casting our votes."

She reached Persephone, who held out her cupped palms and received the ten stones, dropped in with meticulous measure. Athena moved to Hades and parceled out the stones into his hands.

Rhea, meanwhile, stood near the fire, and shook each amphora and tipped it upside down to show they were empty. Each candidate's name was written in charcoal upon a jar, in the angular lettering that had lately become common among educated Greeks. Rhea carried the five jars to the waist-high boulder several paces outside the circle, in the dark of the night, and set them upon it.

"Rhea, as the most senior member, would you like to vote first?" Athena asked.

Rhea nodded, picked up her white and black stones, and took them to the jars. With her back to the others, she dropped a stone into each. They clinked and bounced against the hard clay. She threw the unused stones out onto the dark beach, then came back and sat, her face impassive. The others all followed suit in turn.

At Persephone's turn, standing before the amphorae in the shadows, she dropped a white stone into each of the three jars marked with the names of Poseidon's daughters. They were kind young women, friendly the few times she had met them, and she heard only good about them. They were still young, only one married so far. But Poseidon said they all longed to become immortal and take the glorious path that their father and aunts and uncles had been given. Even the married daughter, he said, was not deeply enamored of her husband, and looked upon immortality as a chance at a happier life. Persephone was glad to offer it to them.

She also selected a white stone to drop into the jar with Adonis' name. He had never truly been a rival to Hades. Demeter had wished that match, not Adonis, nor Persephone, nor anyone else particularly. He loved only Aphrodite, and had never been more than a charming friend to Persephone. Aphrodite knew him best, and Persephone trusted her word. Besides, the male gods would likely vote against Adonis out of sheer jealousy, so he needed all the white stones he could muster.

Amphitrite's jar she left for last. She plucked a white stone from her palm, then hesitated. Amphitrite was a good, bright, caring woman; everything Persephone had heard about her, or seen with her own eyes, indicated this. But Demeter had once loved Poseidon, and might still. Would making his wife immortal make Persephone's mother miserable?

But then, Demeter had tried to keep Persephone and Hades apart, and the recollection chilled Persephone's sympathy.

Besides, if they all had eternity to exist together, Poseidon could easily come back around to loving Demeter, and Amphitrite could find another man. Or Demeter could come to love someone else.

Persephone dropped the white stone into the jar and returned to her seat.

Hades voted, and all the rest.

Rhea and Athena brought the jars back to the fireside.

"Ten votes in favor are needed for approval," Athena reminded everyone, as they leaned closer to watch the results. She lifted one of the amphorae. "Amphitrite." She tipped out the contents into a wooden tray. "Twelve white, three black. Amphitrite joins us."

Persephone smiled at Poseidon, as did nearly all the others. He drew in a deep breath and beamed, but gazed at the fire rather than meeting anyone's eyes. It must be difficult to adjust to, she thought, realizing the wife you had accepted to be mortal was in fact staying beside you forever. Hades would know best how that felt. Indeed, his arm slipped around Persephone, and he hugged her. Meanwhile, Demeter gazed at the fire with a carefully neutral smile. *Sorry, Mother*, thought Persephone. *You'll have to live with it.*

"Rhode," said Athena, naming Amphitrite and Poseidon's eldest daughter. She poured out the stones. "Thirteen white, two black."

Nearly everyone smiled now, and Poseidon's face grew more joyous. Keeping a child forever was surely easier to be glad about.

"Kymia." Poseidon's second daughter. Athena revealed the

count. "Thirteen white, two black." She cleared the stones away. "Benna," she said—the third daughter. She poured out the jar. "Thirteen white, two black. All three daughters join us."

The group drew a breath and murmured remarks, their tone delighted on the whole—especially Hermes, who raised his voice above the hum to ask, "Poseidon, once they're immortal and fully able to fight me off, I'm allowed a go at it, right?"

Smiling, Poseidon threw a shell at him.

Though the votes were meant to be secret, Persephone studied each face in the circle and tried to decipher who dropped in those black stones. Would Demeter have voted against Amphitrite, but not the daughters? Quite possible. Hera and Ares, she supposed, could always be counted upon for jealousy, and would disapprove nearly everyone. But she supposed the truth behind the votes could surprise her. Who knew another's heart, really?

Athena picked up the last jar. "Adonis," she announced.

The group went silent. Aphrodite clenched her hand around her braid.

The stones scattered into the tray. "Four white, eleven black."

A collective sigh whispered through the watchers. Aphrodite closed her eyes and bowed her head.

Pity moved Persephone to speak. "Couldn't she propose his name another year?"

"I don't see why not." Athena tipped the stones out onto the ground. "Circumstances may change, and with them our opinions."

"I doubt they'd change much." Hera's voice was dry.

Aphrodite rose, her back straight, grace infusing her limbs again. "We'll see. I grieve mainly to have to break the news to him. It will hurt him more than me." She turned away and stepped over the log.

"But you have so many ways to console him," Ares taunted.

She sent back a glare at him. "You needn't seek me out for a while, Ares." She stalked off into the darkness, her pale green cloak rippling behind her.

Ares scoffed and leered at his companions, as if to prove he didn't care.

Persephone guessed otherwise, however, and Hermes must have too. His eyes glinted with wickedness, and he adopted a concerned tone. "My friend, it's too bad you don't practice thinking as often as you practice throwing a spear."

Ares had no spear at hand—probably he knew better than to bring one, after the episode with Kerberos—but within a moment his arm flashed out and a knife flew at Hermes, its polished blade gleaming in the firelight. Persephone gasped, as did everyone around her.

But Hermes dodged aside and caught the knife by its handle. "You see," he said, "I knew you would do that." He flicked it into the sand beside Ares' feet before rising and strolling away.

Chapter Fourteen

ADRIAN BLEW ON THE SPOONFUL OF SQUASH SOUP TO COOL IT, then ate a bite. "It's good soup. Glad there was enough for leftovers."

Sophie nodded. She dipped a crust of bread into her soup bowl, and bit into it.

The wind sent dry leaves rustling outside the trailer, and she glanced at the window and sighed. Which she'd been doing all evening.

"Haven't said much on your blog lately," Adrian observed.

"Too busy. And why bother, if Thanatos is watching it to see if you comment?"

"I wouldn't comment anymore. No need."

Sophie shrugged, still not looking at him.

Adrian set his spoon down. "Something wrong?"

She left the crust of bread in her bowl and wiped her fingers on the paper towel in her lap. "It's weird, not doing anything on Halloween."

A spark of relationship panic flared to life in his chest, as if he'd forgotten her birthday. "Oh. It's…is it a big thing in America? It's not in New Zealand really, and I…didn't think. Do you usually do much?"

"We have a produce stand," she informed him, meeting his gaze. "We are up to our ears in pumpkins and Indian corn this time of year. We do a cornfield maze. We do costumes. We do trick or treating. Yes, we do a lot." She looked out the window again.

"You could have said. I…okay, do you want to go out?"

"We don't have costumes. We're too old for trick or treating now."

"Do you want me to take you somewhere? I'm sorry. I don't understand. I was gone all day with errands for the souls, and Halloween doesn't occur to me as a thing…"

She smirked, merely a puff of air from her nose, not truly a smile. "Doing errands for murdered souls is pretty Halloweenish. Guess you celebrate it every day." Ordinarily she was proud of the work he did. Tonight, her comment was more like snark.

"Er." He scratched his scalp, more bewildered by the second. "Tell me what you want to do, all right? We'll do it."

"I can't really."

"Of course we can. We can do anything."

She glanced at him and away, meeker now. He thought he detected a glimmer of tears in her eyes. "I want the holiday back, the way it was when I was a kid. I want…home."

He set his hand on top of hers, but tentatively, for she still held her back straight. And despite that sensual pounce last night, it was obvious he still had no idea whether she wanted his attentions, or indeed, wanted this life for good at all.

"I can take you home," he said softly.

She shook her head. "I'd still have no costume. No job in the corn maze or anywhere else. I'd be a creepy high school grad who comes back and hangs around for no good reason." She sniffled and drew a deep breath. "Besides, we don't know when Quentin or one of her people will show up. I can't be at home much anymore."

He lowered his gaze to his bowl of soup. "I know the feeling."

"Yeah." She turned over her hand beneath his, and folded her fingers around his thumb. "You can never go home. They say."

"Not often, in any case."

"Growing up sucks."

"Sometimes it does," he agreed.

"I'm sorry I'm so moody."

"It's all right. I get that."

"And sorry for…turning you down." Her mouth curved into a shy smile. "At least until last night."

He gave her hand a quick squeeze. "Last night was worth any wait."

"Those dreams. I tell you."

"Yeah." His heart sank a bit. It was obviously Hades, not Adrian, who tended to stir her up. *Could you be jealous of yourself?* "And what was Persephone up to now?" he asked.

"The proper deflowering. The day a bird got into the bedchamber."

"Ah. That is a good one." He pulled his hand back. "Do you want…" he started. "I mean. Should I grow a beard, or anything?"

Confusion and amusement morphed her eyes. "What?"

"It's just, the dreams seem to do it for you when I don't, and back then I—Hades—had a beard, and…"

She fell apart in giggles.

He allowed a smile. "Okay, sandals maybe? The cloak and tunic kind of outfit? You mentioned costumes…"

She laughed even harder. When she finally recovered her voice, she picked up her crust of bread and stirred the soup with it, grinning. "No. It's not about beards or sandals. You *do* do it for me. I just…sometimes have trouble processing this relationship. An immortal, the spirit realm, Thanatos. Greek gods. It *is* out there, you know."

"I know," he admitted, though his hopes sank again.

"I'm still trying to work out how to handle it. How much of my normal life to give up for it." She spoke gently and thoughtfully, watching a drop of soup fall from the bread crust. "But the dreams, the scenes like that…they remind me I should enjoy you. Maybe I do have to be an outcast, but at least I'm an outcast with you."

"You wouldn't have to be an outcast if it weren't for me." His brain told him to shut up, never to remind her of such things. But if she was unhappy, oughtn't they speak of the reasons why?

She ate the last bite of bread, and stood to take her bowl to the sink. On the way she kissed him on the cheek. "Thank you for making me laugh." But her smile was already gone, the pensive look in place again.

"Right. Anytime." He gazed at his spoon, marveling how he could live through millennia of lives, usually in love with the same soul, and still have no idea, some days, what she wanted.

THE IMMORTALS INITIATED the four women. Persephone and Hades invited them and the rest down to the Underworld for the event, since the orange's magic might not work elsewhere.

They still kept the tree's location a secret. While Hades picked the fruit, Persephone waited next to the river with the four women and the group of immortals, chatting with them to ease their nervousness about standing among ghosts. Most sent skittish glances around, and jolted when souls approached in curiosity to run an immaterial hand through their flesh. Ares, Persephone was smugly amused to note, seemed the most alarmed and least courageous of all. A taste for glory in war evidently didn't translate to peace in the presence of the departed. Perhaps he feared he'd encounter someone he'd last seen on a battlefield with his spear in their neck.

Hades brought the four sections of orange and handed one apiece to the women, who studied the blue fruit. Poseidon, Hermes, and other immortals sidled close to examine it too. But oranges didn't grow anywhere around Greece, so it was unlikely they'd recognize it, nor be able to identify which tree in the Underworld's vast and varied gardens it came from, especially with the telltale orange-colored peel missing.

Rhea, the most experienced at leading religious rites, had prepared a small speech to deliver before the women ate the slices. She invoked the "Fates" who decided the punishments and freedoms of souls, and asked them to embrace these women as immortal emissaries of the spirit realm. Fates were what the legends had called such forces, and the immortals had no other name for whatever was at work in the Underworld.

Amphitrite, Rhode, Kymia, and Benna ate their portions of fruit. Everyone smiled. A murmur of celebratory remarks began.

Persephone stepped up to the four and reminded them of the physical effects as she had experienced them, and how they probably would not feel much right away, but should indeed notice changes by this evening.

The joy radiating from Poseidon's face as he hugged his wife and daughters lingered in Persephone's mood after the others had gone home. She and Hades continued their work in the Underworld, sending out inquiries for murdered souls and listening to their stories to see if there was anything they could do to catch the culprit or ease the family's suffering. Meanwhile she kept thinking how one bite of that orange, at the right place and time, would have prevented all these tragedies. But it also would probably have overpopulated the world. Or did the Fates, or the Goddess, wish the immortals to have this realm—this entire other world— where they could act as stewards and emissaries for the living, as Rhea put it?

"It does make you wonder," she said that night after washing down another mouthful of cloudhair seeds. "We could have a child, I suppose. Eventually."

Hades, lying naked beside her, stroked her from underarm to hip. "A child who grows up in the Underworld? Unique soul that would be."

She settled down beside him and twined herself into his embrace. "Not for a while, anyway. But something to think about."

The blue orange took its expected effect. Persephone visited Poseidon's family and witnessed the strength and rejuvenated beauty of Amphitrite (suddenly young again), Rhode, Benna, and Kymia.

She didn't see Adonis, though she asked after him when one day she met with Aphrodite.

"He's being stoic, but it's stung his pride," Aphrodite said. "And wrecked his hopes for the future. Now he has to proceed like a normal man. Which wouldn't be any problem if I hadn't unfairly raised his aspirations." She twisted her mouth. "Not sure I'm doing him any favors, ultimately."

Persephone smiled. "I do know what you mean, but I doubt anyone on Earth would say you haven't done him any favors."

Persephone also checked in with her mother to see how she was coping with Poseidon's wife gaining eternal youth.

"I am sorry if it makes life harder for you," Persephone said over a tea of fresh garden herbs, in the house she used to live in with Demeter. Her tone was stilted despite her effort at sincerity. It was an awkward topic to bring up with your mother, especially when your mother had done her best to thwart your own marriage.

But Demeter shrugged in resignation. "I've been getting over that, in the past year or so. Even at the best of times, Poseidon and I were not an ideal match. It takes some admitting to oneself, but that's the truth."

Persephone's lungs expanded in relief. "Good. And you know, if you do find someone else, a mortal, even—well, now there's hope for a future there."

"Only if he's more popular with our friends than Adonis is." Demeter fished out a wet leaf stuck to the inside of her cup. "Poor lad. I rather like him, myself."

After leaving her mother, Persephone walked through the village, greeting and visiting the people she used to live among. She carried bags and baskets of plants from the Underworld and the spirit realm, and delivered medicines and treats to various households according to their needs.

An old woman tried to give her a block of cheese in return—one of the only bits of food in the house—but Persephone shook her head. "I'm not in need of anything these days. Just let me bring you what I can. The ointment should help your joints if you keep your hands wrapped for as much of the afternoon as you can manage, all right?"

"You're a good girl, Persephone." The woman smiled while Persephone applied the last wrappings of twine to hold the poultice in place. "Is it true you're immortal now?"

Persephone kept her smile in place, but an inner shield went up. The immortals, along with the candidates for immortality, were all sworn not to speak of the fruit. A different story had to be spread to account for their strength and youth. "Indeed, the Goddess has so favored me. Or so it appears. We'll see if it lasts."

"Marrying a god, then. Looks like that's what it takes. Know any who would take me?" The old woman laughed until she coughed.

But not everyone was so good-humored. Starting in Persephone's former village, and also in the seaside town where Poseidon and Amphitrite and their daughters lived, stories sprang up about the gods and their new ability to give out immortality. People had seen the rejuvenated women with their own eyes, women they had known for years, and thereby could swear the stories were true this time. The rumor spread swiftly to other villages and cities. It matched up with the fanciful tales people already wanted to believe, and became an instant mania.

When Persephone visited her former village again in a few days, she was thronged with requests.

"My son just turned old enough to become a soldier, and is leaving to help fight off the marauders," a woman said with tears in her eyes. "I fear he'll be killed. Please, isn't it a good cause? Can't you make him immortal?"

"My wife has begun having seizures," a young man said. "I'm afraid to leave her at home with the children. What if something happens? Please, she's a good mother. I don't even want to be immortal, but if she could be, like you and Poseidon's daughters, she'd be such a fine goddess."

"Look at my daughter," a mother said. The girl, maybe twelve, leaned on a walking stick and gazed humbly at Persephone. Her spine was curved, bending her neck forward, and one arm hung limp and shriveled. "She's been getting worse," the woman said. "How can the gods let a child suffer this way?"

Persephone emptied her bags and baskets of every medicine and small treasure she had with her. She pressed them into the hands of her supplicants, babbling instructions for healthy practices. She gave her cloak to a thin child, and her sandals to a pregnant woman, and pulled all the precious stones off the bracelet she wore and handed them around.

But as soon as she escaped and switched realms, tears flooded her eyes. Leaning her face against the saddle of her spirit horse, she sobbed.

When she returned to the Underworld, she followed her new homing ability to Hades. He sat in the fields, talking to souls and scratching notes onto a wet clay tablet. When he looked up to greet her, and beheld her miserable, tear-streaked face, his smile faded in alarm.

She dropped into his arms in a huddle. "What have I unleashed?" she wailed. "I should tear the tree out, burn it."

He murmured hasty apologies to the souls, and they withdrew. "What are you talking about?" he asked. "What's wrong?"

"Everyone clamors for immortality now. They all make good cases. There are children, mothers, fathers…I can't fix them all. But they want me to. I want to."

"Ah. Yes, Hermes tells me it's the same in all the places where they've heard of us. It was bad enough before, but now it's worse, with the rumors of us making people immortal."

Sniffling, she pushed her hair out of her face. "Shouldn't we destroy the tree? I can't bear to make such decisions. Who am I to choose?"

"We choose together, all of us."

"But the mere fifteen—nineteen—of us, who are we to choose?"

He slid the tablet out of the way and circled his arms around her. "I feel the same every day down here. How do I choose which of these souls to help? How can I ever help them all? How can I deliver every important message back to the living? I can't."

She nodded, ashamed at being so self-absorbed when he wrestled the same problems constantly. "Rhea would say the Goddess guides you to help the right ones. The Underworld, at least, does have its own thoughts or powers. But when I'm up there, among ordinary humans…"

"Doesn't the Goddess guide them too, and you as well when you're among them? Weren't you her priestess once?" He kissed her on the cheekbone. "No need to tear out the tree and destroy it. It's a blessing, and yes, like all blessings it's unfair that some receive it and some don't. But if we're wise, we'll see to it that it brings good to the world."

She tugged a handkerchief from her bosom, and blew her nose. "But people will hate me. They'll hate all of us. There could be revolts, riots, innocent people hurt or killed."

"Let's not worry about that until it starts to happen." He smoothed her unraveling ponytail back over her shoulder. "And anyone who hates you is missing out on one of life's loveliest features."

Chapter Fifteen

It had been a long drive back west into Washington to reach Carnation from the cabin in Idaho where Betty Quentin and Landon were staying. Landon offered to drive out alone, but Betty insisted on performing this errand herself. They did consider sending an anonymous letter instead, but both agreed it could be too easily traced and used as evidence against them.

Much better to stroll up to the Darrow family fruit stand, as she was doing on this frosty, clear November day, and speak to Terry Darrow directly.

Betty wore large sunglasses, and had the hood of her thick quilted coat pulled up around her head—all decent as a disguise, as well as keeping her warm on a cold day. She beamed like any cheerful old lady in search of a good deal on pears as she walked up to the middle-aged man.

Terry wore a brown bomber jacket and a battered Mariners baseball cap, and was unloading a crate of apples. His latest customer had just driven away from the gravel parking lot.

"Morning," he said to Betty. "Just got some great red pears in. And some gorgeous sweet potatoes."

"Marvelous." Betty leaned on her cane, picked up a sweet potato from its display case, and turned it over to examine it. "Your lovely daughter's not helping out here anymore?"

"Nope, she's off to college. Means I'm getting old." Terry stacked the apple box on top of the other empty ones.

"I've seen her a few times. Smart girl. But here's the thing."

She set the sweet potato down. "She's seeing a new boy. He's a dangerous article, Mr. Darrow."

Terry's smile vanished. Sharp wariness entered his hazel eyes. They resembled Sophie's, now that Betty looked at him. "What are you talking about?"

"Sophie's new boyfriend. Ask her about him. Ask her if his name's Adrian Watts, and if he's in the country legally. Because I can assure you that he isn't. He's from New Zealand, shouldn't be over here at all. Slipped in without going through the proper authorities. And he was involved in those attacks on your daughter." All true, though misleading, and in any case hardly Adrian's most dangerous features. Nonetheless, it would alarm any good father and might cause trouble for Adrian with law enforcement. Which was only fair, after he'd put her into similar trouble.

"How the hell—" Terry shut his mouth, and his posture stiffened. He stepped back. "Actually, you know, hang on. It's cold out. I'll find my gloves—I left them in the back room—and we'll talk. You stay here, all right?" He skittered toward the cash register. "Just wait right here," he repeated, and darted into the shed at the back of the produce stand.

Betty, of course, had no intention of waiting. The man was almost certainly dialing 911. Besides, she had delivered her message. She hobbled to the car and got in. "Time to go," she told Landon.

He had kept the engine running. Before she'd even clicked her seatbelt on, he hit the gas and they took off from the parking lot, and left Carnation behind.

"SHE SAID *WHAT?*" Phone pressed to her ear, Sophie stopped walking in the middle of the crowded campus sidewalk. Someone's backpack slapped against her and sent her sideways. She dodged around the other students and hopped up onto the steps of a lecture hall. "Dad. Did you call the police?"

"Course I did. Obviously it was the woman you warned me about, so I told her to wait right there and I'd come out and talk to her. Then I got into the shed and called 911. But she had a getaway car ready. Heard them peeling out a few seconds later. By the time I got out there to look, they were too far off to make out a license plate. Cops haven't found her."

Sophie clamped her teeth down against a selection of words her father wouldn't like to hear from her. "Did you get the make of the car?"

"Silver SUV. Think it was a Toyota. About the most common thing in the Northwest."

Sophie expelled her breath through her nose. Fear had caught up to her, and her hands were shaking. "But you guys are okay?"

"Yes, we're fine. No one laid a hand on me, and your mom and Liam weren't even there. But Sophie, you have not answered my question. What is this about some New Zealander named Adrian who isn't supposed to be in the country?"

She leaned back on the cold bricks of the building. "She's crazy, Dad. I have no idea what she's talking about." She wanted to sob already. Lying so blatantly, about something that mattered so much, to the father she loved dearly.

"It was weirdly specific, you know?" he said. "You can tell me. I want to help you. I trust you here."

"I really think she was only trying to cause trouble."

"That guy David we met. Where'd you say he was from?"

Uh-oh. "Um. Why?"

"Just asking. Where was he from?"

"He's moved around a lot. Some time in the South, also some here, in Oregon."

"His accent sounded a little weird."

Training Adrian on a better American accent: another item for the task list. "Yeah, probably from the time in the South," she said.

"Then, you two, are you…?"

"Oh. I don't know." She looked around, distracted, as if someone was at this moment about to stroll up and stab her. "It's, um—Jacob's still pretty recent, you know, so…"

"No, that's good. You're taking your time."

She rubbed her temples with trembling fingers. *No, I'm not,*

Dad, I'm completely rushing into madness. "But you guys are okay?" she repeated.

"Yeah, yeah, we're fine. And believe me, I'm keeping a baseball bat with me next time I'm manning the stand. And 911 on the speed dial. It's going to be required for anyone working out there."

"Good. I hope they catch her. And keep her this time. This is... it's scary."

"I know, honey." He sounded like her properly commiserating dad at that moment. He'd hug her if they were together; she could tell from his tone. Then he shifted back to suspicion. "But it's awful damn strange, all these attacks on you lately. I'm sorry, but I've got to wonder: is there something you got mixed up in that's causing this? Even if you didn't mean to? Something some friend was involved in, let's say?"

This. This was exactly what was bound to happen when you had a relationship with an immortal, and a family who actually cared and noticed what happened to you.

"They're a crazy cult, Dad. Who knows what they think or why they think it? I probably said something about...I don't know, being agnostic, or curious about Wicca, or something, where someone overheard me. Who the hell knows."

"You'll tell me if you figure it out, all right? We've got your back."

Oh, how she wished they could guard her back—and that she could guard theirs. But none of them were equipped to do that. "Okay. I love you. I've got to get to class."

"I love you too. Don't worry, baby."

After she hung up, she tapped out a quick text to Adrian. *Scared as hell. Q showed up at fruit stand and told my dad I'm dating you, then took off. I said it was a lie but what if they hurt my family??*

Before sending it, she navigated to Tabitha's number in the contacts, and added Tab as a recipient for the text too. She sent it off.

It was now a week and a half into November, ten days or so since Tab's first video with a rock star. Since then, she had posted two more. Two separate parties, two new celebrities, either singing for Tab or telling her an embarrassing story while at amusing levels of tipsiness. The celebrities themselves surely didn't even mind these things being posted; the videos made them look endearing and human. Each one had gotten over a hundred thousand views, and climbing. Tab was well on her way to becoming an Internet celebrity. Sophie couldn't imagine how she found time to study, and doubted Tab would want to do anything else serious either, such as protect Sophie's family. Still, Tabitha was her best friend, and turning to her in an hour of trouble was Sophie's instinct. It had felt wrong during that recent phase of getting involved with Adrian when she *couldn't* tell Tab about it. At least now she could, even if Tab wasn't able to help.

Sophie shoved the phone into her coat pocket and set out miserably across the muddy ground to her chemistry lecture.

Still, it was Tab who answered first, her text coming before Sophie took her seat in the lecture, beating out even Adrian's response.

Bastards!! Tab texted. *I am on this. Don't worry. We'll talk soon.*

CHAPTER SIXTEEN

Tab's idea of being "on this," it turned out, was to dash to Carnation on her ghost horse and casually check in on Sophie's family, then stalk around town looking for Quentin. "Didn't see the old bat," she told Sophie when she called that night. "But I'm going to go back every couple of days and check again, and make sure no one's acting shifty around your peeps."

"Thank you, Tab. Really." Sophie was moved, and Adrian grudgingly admitted, after she hung up with Tab, that it was a generous gesture, and no better than he could have done himself.

But Sophie's alarm level had only slipped down one notch, not all the way to "relaxed." Even with Tab prowling Carnation a few times a week, that left plenty of other times Quentin could send in her thugs. And if Tab did catch one of them and it came to a fight, she'd have to reveal her super-strength, and none of them wanted Thanatos to know about Tab's immortality yet. An imperfect solution it definitely was. But a perfect one likely didn't exist.

Tab did have one more gift in store, however. Sophie walked out of her communications class a couple of days later to find Tab awaiting her under a tree, wearing a new knee-length tan leather coat and gorgeous heeled boots.

They met in a squealing hug. Exquisite perfume wafted from Tab's hair; its scent mingled with the leather, and made Sophie think of crates of grapes unpacked on a fresh summer day.

"I have a surprise for you," Tab said. "Ready? I already cleared this with your boy."

Sophie laughed. "You texted Adrian?"

"Yep. Come on!"

Five minutes later, Sophie found herself on a saddled gray spirit horse, soaring through the chilly air toward Seattle, her arms latched around Tabitha's soft waist as if her life depended on it—which in fact it did. "Oh my God," she shrieked above the wind. She found herself laughing in spite of her fear.

Tab's long, loose blonde hair whipped across her own face and Sophie's. She grinned over her shoulder. "Haven't you ridden one of these puppies like this before?"

"Not in *this* lifetime. Dude, the trees are right there!" Beneath them, treetops blurred past, appearing to be mere inches away.

"Objects below horse are farther than they appear. Trust me."

Once they landed in Seattle, and switched into the living city, Sophie forgot her shaking knees and her thoughts of kissing the ground. Tab led her down a busy sidewalk and into a hotel—no, a convention center. People swarmed the room. Sophie spotted several wearing costumes from "Nightshade," one of their all-time favorite shows.

"What's going on? Convention?"

"Yup. I wanted to do this for you sooner, but it took me a while to pull all the right strings." They stopped at a velvet cord guarded by a muscular guy in a "security" T-shirt. With a few words from Tab and the flash of a laminated badge she pulled from under her shirt, the guy unhooked the cord and let them through.

They dodged through a hanging curtain, then Tab stopped behind a table where three people sat, signing items for the fans who approached. When Sophie recognized them as three of the central cast members for "Nightshade," a star-struck dazzle jolted her from toes to fingers. And she and Tab stood *behind* the table, *with* them.

The woman nearest them, who had played Merrin on the show, looked up at Tab. "Hey, you're back. Is this her?" The other two actors looked up and smiled at Sophie too.

"Yep," Tab said. "Everyone, meet Sophie."

They chorused "Hello"s and "Hey"s. Sophie stammered back, "Hi! I'm—wow—I'm such a—I love the—"

"Here, sit with us," the actor in the center said. He had played the actual character of Nightshade, the shape-shifter. He pulled over a folding chair and wedged it between his and Merrin's. "Hang out a while. It's cool."

Drifting in a glitzy dream, Sophie turned to Tabitha and mouthed, "Thank you!", then accepted the seat and hung out with the famous people a while.

How far back *have you got?* Zoe texted to Tabitha. She dug her bare toes into the smooth gravel on the shore, trying to enjoy the warm spring day rather than obsess about the rock-star American with the sexy voice. After all, said woman could have any bi-curious groupie she wanted, and was surely fast on her way to that, to judge from what Zoe had seen the other night.

Tab did invite Zoe as promised to the latest party, which was in Los Angeles. Zoe jumped at the chance. She threw all kinds of placating lies at her parents on her way out—staying with a friend overnight, bye...

It wasn't like her to leave and enter countries illegally. But then, it wasn't like Adrian either—he was so law-obsessed it was positively nerdy—and *he* didn't mind leaping all round the globe for convenience and romance, in technically illegal fashion. So Zoe indulged too.

The good part was being with Tab and soaking up the glamor of a posh party. The not-so-good part was they had no chance to be alone, what with all the social-butterflying Tabitha did. Tab gave and received kisses and hugs from beautiful celebrities all round the multi-million-dollar house they were visiting. From the playful growls and flirtatious grabs Tab exchanged with some women, Zoe had little doubt that invitations for dates were arriving regularly in Tab's texts. Unless everyone behaved like that in L.A.?

Meanwhile Tab had kissed Zoe in greeting and farewell. On the cheek. That was all. Bit frustrating.

Oh well, a crush was fun, and at least this time the object of Zoe's infatuation was actually gay too. That rarely happened.

Tab's answer came within a few minutes, though it was nearly 1:00 a.m. in Tab's time zone. Tabitha kept late nights, it would seem. *Memories? Not paying much attention. Still in India I think. 1800s.*

Go back faster! It's great stuff and we need to get to it. Think I'm almost to it.

But why rush, you know? Tabitha answered.

Zoe lifted her eyebrow. She deliberated whether to use the bribe she held up her sleeve, and finally couldn't resist, even though it meant throwing the spotlight on a different woman. *Did no one tell you who you shagged a lot back then?*

Uhhh no, who?

Years ago, Adrian had told Zoe about Adonis and Aphrodite, and Niko had confirmed it last time he'd visited her. In loyalty to Adrian and Sophie, Zoe had punched Niko hard on the arm for his blue-orange theft before settling down to enjoy a chat with him.

Before long, Zoe expected to remember meeting Aphrodite herself—though probably never as intimately as Dionysos had, back in his Adonis days.

Aphrodite, she texted.

THE Aphrodite?? Tab responded.

The one, the only. I'm jealous, mate.

OK yeah. I better get to those. How do you move the memories faster again?

Zoe pulled her knees up to sit cross-legged, and set about texting the instructions to Tab. To help her crush remember being a man who was madly in love with a woman who wasn't her.

It stung a bit. And could sting more before they got through it all. But by now Zoe knew her life usually went that way, one reincarnation after another: a sobering habit of ending up alone. A wise, stoic, inspiring type of alone, not a completely miserable alone. But Zoe would have liked a romantic "together" rather more often.

CHAPTER SEVENTEEN

$\int$T EASED SOPHIE'S WORRIES AT LEAST A SMALL AMOUNT TO HEAR Tabitha was accelerating her memories to learn about Dionysos—whom Sophie still hadn't dreamed about herself—although it had been an eye opener to realize she had also been Adonis. It might at least help Tab take the immortal business more seriously and do a more diligent job protecting herself and her friends. Rather than merely spending every night partying, and less and less of her time in college classes, which is how Tab's life sounded like it was going lately. Sophie couldn't really complain, given the cast meet-and-greet she'd been treated to—which had thrown a happy glow over her life for several days afterward. But as the glow diminished and real life resumed, her worries trudged right back in. Parties and famous people spiced things up, sure, but what good were they against murderers?

Sophie hurried to class through a near-freezing downpour, her ski coat's hood over her head. She gripped her new stun gun in her pocket, but doubted anyone would attempt an attack in the daytime on a crowded campus street, especially in such awful weather. November in Oregon was turning out almost as gray and dismal as November in Washington. Maybe it should have made her feel at home. Instead it served, as so many things did lately, to make her miss home.

When she walked the university sidewalks, or ventured into the Corvallis residential neighborhoods, homesickness rolled over her, brought on by the lighted windows at dusk and the smells of dinners cooking and the raked piles of leaves. Her rental house, which she visited a few hours a week, provided no sensation of "home" for her, though its inhabitants were always friendly to her. Adrian's Airstream came closer, since it contained him and Kiri, and she felt safer sleeping there than in the living world.

But it didn't fully measure up either. The other day she had wanted to bake gingerbread, thinking the activity and the sweet smell would ease her domestic longings. But Adrian had no spices in the cupboard except cinnamon, and no flour at all.

"Who doesn't own flour?" she had wailed.

He had scrambled over with cash in his hands, offering to take her to a grocery store at once; she could get anything she liked. But she hadn't bothered. It was too late at night to shop *and* make gingerbread. Another day, she'd said in defeat.

The cash. That was another issue. She told him she'd have to find a part-time job to cover her rental money and some of her tuition, as agreed upon with her parents.

"Don't be silly," he'd said, again producing envelopes of cash from inside one of the trailer's compartments. "Here. It's yours as much as mine. It's from the Underworld's gemstones. Come on, this way you can focus on your studies."

She had refused to take the envelope. She stared at it from a step away, embarrassed. "No!"

"Oh, don't think that. Look, it isn't like I'm...rather, I don't mean that you're..." He at least knew better than to bring out words like "mistress." Or "hooker."

"I can't take money from you."

"It isn't mine. Not really. You'd hate having some part-time job, and I'd worry about you the more hours you spent out there. Look, I give some to my dad and Zoe too, all right? It's not like any of us were rich before this."

They argued the topic for what felt like an hour. She ended up accepting the money, wearily acknowledging that her class assignments, combined with the Underworld drama and the family issues along with it, ate up every last second of her time already. But it still embarrassed her.

Then there were the animals. The spirit world teemed with them, some giant and carnivorous, as she'd found within her first few minutes there. All the animals, large and small, tended to keep away from Adrian and Kiri, and the trailer too, though if Sophie were by herself she was fairly sure she'd get attacked and eaten. And yesterday when Sophie and Adrian returned after dinner out, a fir tree was lying at an angle against the Airstream's roof. They shone flashlights upon the trunk and found it had been plowed over, its trunk splintered and broken after something strong rammed into it.

Picturing Tyrannosaur-like monsters, Sophie had gone dry-mouthed with terror. But Adrian shrugged. "Probably mammoths having a disagreement with one another," he said, and shoved the tree off the trailer. "I see them around from time to time." The shiny roof now had a dent and a few scratches, but none of the windows had broken. "Nothing to worry about," he said. "They wouldn't come round while we're here."

Right. Like she could sleep after that. All night her ears seized upon every strange sound, and she pictured herds of stampeding mammoths overturning the trailer and trampling them to a pulp. Or maybe some other-world version of rabies would infect one of those giant lions and make it unafraid of Adrian's immortal scent, and cause it to pounce upon them and devour them the second they emerged from the trailer one sleepy morning. Or what if a lightning storm swept through and stabbed a million volts through the metal trailer, frying them where they slept?

Nature was no better than Thanatos. Unfeeling rather than malicious, but still deadly. No wonder she longed for home. Home was the definition of safety. But Sophie couldn't go back to her old way of life now. She could only try to create a new security, a settled life of a different sort, if that was possible.

Even with her happy marriage to Hades, had Persephone missed the sweetness of her childhood home, and longed for more domesticity, more familial warmth awaiting her at a steady home she could count upon? She had. Sophie recalled it easily enough. In the past week she had let her memories carry Persephone's life along several months, enough to watch the joy in Poseidon and Amphitrite's family as they and their three immortal daughters spread inspiration and assistance throughout the coastal villages. A large happy family, in the sunlight and open air—it did appeal to Persephone with poignancy, even though she had traded that life for Hades and the Underworld, and wouldn't reverse her decision for anything.

That night, in her dreams, Sophie finally reached a certain important decision in Persephone and Hades' life.

They had been married nearly a year. On his way back to the Underworld, Hades dropped in on Persephone, who was visiting a young woman she had known in Demeter's village. The woman had given birth to a baby boy a few months earlier, and when Hades walked up, Persephone was carrying the baby around the garden, bouncing him gently on her shoulder as she talked to her friend.

Hades approached and smiled. "You look good holding a baby," he told her.

She hardly remembered the rest of the afternoon. That promising remark reverberated through her head, muting all else.

Later that evening, Persephone stood naked by the bed in the cave, tipping cloudhair seeds into her palm from the cloth bag. The light of the oil lamp flickered on Hades' body as he rested among the blankets, watching her.

She regarded the seeds, then looked at him again. "I could skip them."

A smile spread on his lips. The lamplight twinkled in his eyes. "You could."

Eager to see results, Sophie sped the memories ahead. She blurred past more suspicious and pleading villagers, more angry shouts against immortals, and more fawning worshippers who were calling her "their" goddess. It took a few months, and lots of skipped doses of cloudhair seeds, before the new moon came and went without Persephone's monthly blood accompanying it.

Not long after that came a morning when the prospect of bread and goat cheese for breakfast turned her stomach. Everything smelled too strong. Dried mud clung to Kerberos' fur from some romp yesterday, and he stank like a swamp. The smoke from the hearth was chokingly acrid. The cheese's odor was unendurable. Without a word to Hades, who was eating contentedly by the hearth and feeding Kerberos his scraps, Persephone walked out of the bedchamber. She seized a leashed ghost dog to light her way. She crossed the river on the raft alone, and sought out the only thing that sounded good: a pomegranate from the orchard.

Sitting against a trunk in the dark forest, she nibbled the sweet, crunchy seeds. Her head and stomach and breasts ached for the first time in a year. Soon Hades came after her, holding a torch, and crouched beside her. He stuck the torch into the ground. The flame danced, revealing hope and concern in his face.

They gazed at each other a long moment while she swallowed the seeds.

She drew his hand to her breasts. "A lot larger than usual, aren't they?"

His breath skipped out of him in wonder. "Now that you mention it. Then…"

"Considering I couldn't stand the sight or smell of cheese—and I could smell it from a league away—and considering the skipped period…yes. I think we can safely say yes."

Hades tumbled forward, collecting her enthusiastically but gently in his arms. He kissed her face, breasts, and belly until laughter and weeping overtook her at the same time. Absurd tears: yet another sure sign of pregnancy.

From her future perspective, Sophie knew both she and the baby would survive, but Persephone and Hades didn't know it yet. She was the first to try having a child after becoming immortal from the orange. Perhaps the fruit had limits? They tried not to worry, for in every respect the pregnancy was a normal and straightforward one—Persephone knew it from her training as a healer. But the concern lingered, especially in Hades, who now treated her with a delicacy that sometimes moved her and sometimes irritated her.

She worried too. All this Underworld-grown food she was

eating, what would that do to the baby inside her? Surely no infant had ever received nourishment like that in the womb before. Would it give the child unexpected powers? Or produce a monster, like ones from legends? When her dreams shut off past memories and let her brain produce its own fancies, Persephone dreamed of giving birth to a Minotaur, or a sea serpent, or a giant bat.

Demeter chuckled when Persephone told her about the dreams. "My sweet, every pregnant woman dreams such things." She was ecstatic at the prospect of becoming a grandmother, and assured Persephone the pregnancy looked absolutely fine, nothing to fret about.

Even so, Persephone suspected Demeter was only saying such things to calm her. Panic didn't help anyone, a pregnant woman least of all. She did believe she'd survive the childbirth itself, given her new strength and the fact that Amphitrite had survived her births even while mortal, with Poseidon as the father. But women sometimes bled to death afterward. And who knew what the baby's condition would be?

"These are the herbs to stop bleeding," she told Hades, every few days. "You mix them into—"

"Boiling water, and use enough leaves to cover the bottom of the cup, yes, I know."

"And if I'm not conscious enough to drink it—"

"The wet leaves can be used as a poultice. And Demeter and Rhea will be there. They'll know what to do."

Demeter still wasn't speaking to Hades, of course. Not the way she used to, at any rate. It drove Persephone into a heat of anger, and she marveled at the complexity of relationships with parents, how you could love and need them so much, and be so irritated by them at the same time.

Her worries reached their highest peak during her labor. When the pains began their rhythm, right on schedule with the moon cycle she had estimated, she had Hades take her straight to Demeter's house. Demeter sat with her while Hades rushed out to fetch Rhea, and soon brought her back too. Night fell and the pains worsened, and all Persephone wanted to do was make it stop so she could sleep. But Demeter kept urging her to walk circles around the garden, leaning on either her or Hades' arm.

What if she died? Hades and Demeter would hate one another forever, and all because of her. She'd reside in the Underworld and would be able to speak to them, but she'd be a dispassionate soul, ethereal, of little help.

Too exhausted even to cry, Persephone rested in her husband's arms. Her trembling legs barely held her up, and her huge, taut belly ached. "It shouldn't hurt this much, should it?" she said.

Demeter rubbed her back, and soothed her by pressing her thumbs into the places that ached the most, low on Persephone's spine. "It hurts like blazing hell, I know. But you're almost there. Don't worry, immortal women birth babies fast."

Rhea chuckled. She waited near them, holding a lantern. "It's true. Thank the Goddess for our strong muscles. And you'll recover quickly, too."

Hades only murmured, "You'll be fine, you're doing so well." He kept walking with her, and held her and fetched anything the other two women required. He showed remarkable courage, Persephone thought through her haze of pain, considering he must have been remembering his first wife, who had died in childbirth along with their baby.

That wasn't a useful thought for Persephone to be pondering, though, nor Hades either.

But Demeter and Rhea were right: Persephone's immortal muscles took over, and sooner than she expected, the other two women brought her into her old bedroom and told her to kneel on the blankets and cling to Rhea's arm. Then the pains dropped away and Demeter beamed and lifted a perfect, wiggling, crying infant to show the parents. "A girl! Well done, my darling, oh, well done."

Persephone forgot to worry about bleeding to death, and indeed hardly noticed the passage of the afterbirth at all. Demeter bustled about taking care of nurse duties, changing blankets and swabbing off Persephone's skin and tucking clean cloths between her legs, assuring her the bleeding looked normal. Meanwhile Persephone, like Hades, was entranced by the little girl in her arms. They cooed to her and laughed in wonder over her, and tried to teach her how to latch her mouth around Persephone's breast.

"Black hair, like you." Persephone stroked the baby's fine hair.

"A beautiful goddess, like you." Hades' curls were in a tangle; half of them had fallen out of the string he had tied them back with. Instead of the jewel-hemmed garments that usually proclaimed him lord of the Underworld, tonight he wore an old length of threadbare wool pinned over one shoulder, in preparation for the blood and sweat of childbirth. He looked perfect to Persephone: a glowing new father.

But the baby was the most perfect of all. Having swallowed a few pacifying gulps of milk, the little girl opened her green-gray eyes and locked a surprised-looking gaze upon Persephone's face. Persephone basked in the look while her companions crowded around her bed to view the baby.

"He's right," Demeter said. "She is a goddess."

Persephone glanced at Hades, who acknowledged the kindness with a grateful smile both to her and to Demeter.

"I shall inform the others," Rhea said happily. "But I won't let them come disturb your sleep. No one will be allowed till tomorrow afternoon."

"Thank you so much, Rhea," Persephone said.

Hades rose to thank her as well. Demeter gave him instructions on symptoms to watch for in mother and child, since she would be sleeping a while and he insisted on staying with Persephone and the baby during the night. Persephone listened without absorbing many words. She drank in the sight of her daughter, marveled at the softness of her cheek, and smiled in affection at how the baby grasped her finger when Persephone touched her palm.

After Demeter kissed her and the baby, and went to her own room to rest, Hades sat on the bed beside Persephone. She moved over to accommodate him. He stretched out alongside mother and baby. The little girl fell asleep atop Persephone's chest, in her wrapping of soft wool.

"There's something I haven't mentioned," he said, "because… well, in case anything went wrong. But her soul—I've been able to sense it for a while now."

"Of course you can. She's your child. I can sense her too."

"More than that. I know her soul from before. She was the baby I lost. The son my wife had, on Crete." While Persephone gasped in surprise, Hades continued, "I haven't tracked him before. I never really knew him, and there was no point getting attached. But now…it would seem he's been sent back to me. To us."

Persephone carefully moved one arm from beneath the baby and slid it around her husband. "I'm so glad." She kissed the side of his head. They gazed at the sleeping girl. "It's odd, isn't it. How sometimes parents' and children's souls find each other again, in the same arrangement as before, and sometimes they don't. When I was Tanis, Demeter was already alive, and I was someone else's daughter. What ever became of my mother and father from then? Or any other life? I might never know."

"Indeed. We only sense people if the connection's made while we're immortal. In all the mortal past lives, we've no way to find our loved ones, other than asking about them in the Underworld."

Persephone slid down and rested her head on the pillow. Moving with the utmost care, she set the swaddled infant between herself and Hades. "Maybe we're meant to love lots of people as our children, or our parents. Surely the world would be better if we thought of more people that way."

"I like that." He settled onto his side, regarding his daughter sleepily. "What shall we name her?"

"My mother's name was Hekate, when I was Tanis." Persephone rested her forefinger upon the baby's swaddled body. The tiny chest rose and fell in quick, regular breaths. "She was so proud of her daughter going off to become a priestess. And so devastated when I died. I like her name."

"Hekate," he echoed. "I like it too."

CHAPTER EIGHTEEN

ADRIAN ALMOST CRASHED THE BUS INTO THE SISKIYOU MOUN-tains when his dad called—using Zoe's phone—and told him the news.

"The police? And the *government*?" Adrian said. He steadied the reins with his free hand, smoothing the bus's turbulence. Thank the Goddess that Sophie wasn't with him, or he might have got her killed by that startle reflex.

"Someone gave them an anonymous tip, yes," his father said. "That you're out of the country, and traveling round the U.S., without clearance from either country to do so. They wanted to know if it was true."

"Anonymous tip," Adrian echoed in bitterness. Quentin probably had no idea he spent most of his working hours placing anonymous tips against dangerous people. By some twist of irony, she'd done the same thing to him—now not only with Sophie's father, but with the government of his home country. "You told them you didn't have a clue where I was?"

"Yes, the usual story. We've fallen out, he's out there somewhere, I haven't heard from him."

"Good."

"And of course the cult themselves has been sniffing round again."

A chill of fear traveled up Adrian's arms. "Oh? How so?"

"Eerie man showed up at work the other day. Skinny, tweedy bloke in his fifties. British, I think. Asking had I seen you lately, and did I know you were involved in operations that would end the world."

"What'd you tell him?"

"I said, 'Yes, you're completely right, he's on a path to sinful destruction and the mere sight of him makes me sick. Catch him and lock him away if you can.'"

"Oh, Dad. He believed that?"

"He did. I'm a better actor than you know. I told him you'd been seen up round Rotorua. Perhaps pursuing your Maori heritage or maybe just snowboarding. He got a gleam in his eye and took off straightaway."

"You shouldn't play double agent," Adrian said. "It's really dangerous. The kind of damage they could do to you if they found out…" He shuddered.

"It got him off my back, and threw him off your trail. Besides, he can't prove I *didn't* hear you were in Rotorua. So don't go to Rotorua, lest you were planning to."

"I wasn't." Adrian sighed, calculating his options. "Nor will I show up much in New Zealand at all, I suppose, if everyone lawful or not is looking for me. Oh, well. Wasn't as if I could have moved back home anyway."

"We'll still find a way. We'll sort this out." His father sounded anxious, and Adrian felt guilty for the empty-nest syndrome he was inflicting. Hard enough for his dad to get used to his formerly paraplegic son turning super-strong, and to accept the existence of an Underworld that clashed with his timid Christian upbringing. Quite unfair that not long after that, Adrian had to leap out of his home for his dad's safety, thanks to the killer cult on his trail.

"I don't know, Dad. I'm, uh, rather a lot different from normal people."

"You're better, you mean."

"Not exactly. My life can't quite fit with the living world."

Yet he was dragging the excellent and still mortal Sophie into such a life. What kind of monster was he?

ZOE WASN'T HAVING the best day when she finally uncovered Hekate's life.

Her job at a nearby college, helping other students with disabilities learn about the resources available to them, felt more and more disingenuous. Pretending to be blind behind dark glasses, running her fingers over Braille and leaving the computer's audible voice commands switched on, deliberately feeling round the edge of desks as she moved about the office, resisting comments on people's shirts or jewelry even when she wished to compliment them but wasn't supposed to be able to see them—ugh, it got harder by the day.

Then today the police visited. She was expecting them to come eventually, but the interview still made her sweat through her black shirt. She assured them, in concern and bewilderment, that she hadn't heard from Adrian in months and didn't know where he was. No, she had no reason to think he'd leave the country, but she wouldn't really know. They hadn't spoken lately; he'd been kind of an arrogant twerp, and acted too good for his old friends. So, no, she had no clue what he was up to. They thanked her, urged her to call if she did learn or remember anything, and left.

Goddess above. Lying to the police! A crime in itself.

All the changes to her mind and body after those fruits had shredded her life into brightly colored madness. She now saw why Adrian had become such a restless, distracted mess after eating that pomegranate.

But did she wish she'd never eaten it herself, nor the orange? No. She couldn't go so far as to wish that. Her expanded sight—both physical and inner—was too breathtaking to give up. It was only that she, like Adrian and everyone else who'd eaten those fruits, had increasing trouble fitting her ordinary life into this new giant canvas.

She hurried home and flopped onto the ground under the titoki tree in the back garden. The warm spring sun soothed her closed eyelids.

She reached back a little further, and there it lay: Hekate's life, a golden ancient tome, ready for her to blow off its dust and crack open its covers.

She stood back from it a while in her mind's eye, regarding it with wonder. Compared to her other lifetimes, longevity and power beamed from this one; it felt like the sun compared to distant stars. The prospect of opening it up daunted her. But perhaps it held the guidance she needed. She pulled the tome close in her mind and opened Hekate's life at the beginning.

THE VELVETY DARKNESS of the cave was Hekate's earliest memory, accompanied by her parents' affectionate voices and their hands holding hers, and the soft glow of souls—human, dog, horse, cat—illuminating the flowers in the fields.

Kerberos, the sleek brown immortal dog, was her sibling and playmate and protector. He followed her everywhere and slept on her bed. The smell of dog breath and the warmth of his tongue licking her skin formed a permanent part of Hekate's childhood. One day she fell in the river, and before her parents had time to do anything other than shriek, Kerberos leaped in, caught her by the back of her neck in his jaws, gently but securely, and swam with her to the bank.

She grew up around ghosts, people who had died. Her presence delighted them. She gathered it was a special treat for them to see a living child. She learned their language along with the upper-world tongue her parents frequently spoke, picking up both easily.

Pomegranates grew in the orchard, and they would have made her learn all kinds of other languages, but her mother and father wouldn't let her eat them.

"Not until you're older," her mother said. "No one's ever been down here so young before—not while they're alive, I mean—and we don't know whether it's a good idea for you to bring those memories into your brain yet."

Indeed, she was forbidden to eat any of the fruits or plants that grew in her mother's Underworld gardens. Her parents brought all Hekate's food down from the upper world. For, in addition to being a child, Hekate was mortal.

"We knew it as soon as you got your first fever as a baby," her mother told her several times. "It's what we expected. I was mortal too as a child, even though both my parents were immortal." Still, she always sounded worried when she said it.

"But you'll make me immortal when I'm bigger?" Hekate asked.

"Of course *we* want to, but we must make sure it's all right with everyone else." Her mother smiled and kissed Hekate. "So be nice to your aunts and uncles."

Of immortal aunts and uncles she had many, whom she saw now and again.

The immortals had established the ritual of meeting twice a year, at winter and summer solstice at the palace of Zeus and Hera, to nominate new initiates. Hekate usually didn't get to come along, and was left with a trusted mortal woman who had assisted her grandmother Demeter for several years, but she heard about the results of the voting afterward. The immortals had become cautious about awarding those white stones. It was no light matter, making someone live forever. It led to lots of arguments among Hekate's uncles and aunts. There was, for example, a man named Adonis whom aunt Aphrodite put forth a couple of times, and he kept getting voted down and making her angry at everyone.

But some candidates did get voted into the lucky group over the years. As she grew up she met several new ones: a man named Helios, a woman named Eos, two hardworking brothers named Prometheus and Epimetheus, a son of Aphrodite's named Eros—whom most people hadn't known existed until she brought him forward, all grown up—a son of Hermes named Pan (similarly unexpected by everyone), and a group of artistically talented women whose number gradually grew to nine. Hekate had trouble keeping their names straight, but they tended to be referred to in a group as the Muses anyway.

When everyone asked Hermes in curiosity where this son had come from, he blithely said, "A goat-herder's daughter, whose clan lives so deep in the mountains in Arkadia that it's a miracle I ever found them once, let alone twice. His existence was a surprise to me—I didn't even think she was pregnant—but he's a delight, truly, and he's definitely mine. Looks just like me, and nothing like the rest of the clan. And you should hear him play the flute." He shot Apollo a wicked smile. "He's better even than you, I think, Apollo."

Meanwhile, when Aphrodite was asked how she managed to have a grown son in another city without the others knowing, she smiled calmly and said, "In the last few months of pregnancy, loose garments and extended travel to avoid all of you. After that, wet nurses, who are easy to hire. As to his father, I'm saying nothing."

A longer story didn't appear likely to be got out of either of them.

Hekate's father and mother didn't propose any candidates. They told her she was the only one they wanted to keep forever. And in any case, they didn't know that many mortals, as they didn't deal with living people much, except in errands for the dead.

Hekate knew normal children didn't grow up in the Underworld. Most of them didn't live in caves at all; or if they did, they were caves close to the surface, where you could walk right out into the sunshine, and didn't need a ghost horse or a rope ladder to get out. And when those cave-dwelling children did go out, they were of course in the living realm, not the spirit realm. Most of them didn't even know the spirit realm existed, which struck Hekate as absurdly funny, equal to not knowing that wind existed, or that stars existed.

Hekate did travel to the living realm too, especially to visit her grandmother Demeter, but her parents didn't like to take her out much. The people grasped at them and begged and sometimes shouted threats, which made her mother and father worry about Hekate's safety. They all acted bizarre on the whole, those living people, when they saw an immortal. Hekate found them fascinating, but didn't mind staying away from them most days.

Hekate was also different in that she sensed magic, and could bend and control it a little. More and more each year as she got older, in fact.

Her parents didn't notice at first. When she prattled about a different "breath" or "warmth" or "tingle" or "glow" in one part of the cave or another, or during one season or moon phase or another, or while touching a certain type of plant or rock, they assumed she was being fanciful, pretending as children do. It seemed natural for an Underworld child to talk about sights and sensations rather differently than an above-ground child would.

But one day Hekate was walking with her mother through the Underworld's gardens, and winding a green braided rope around her fingers. She was nine years old. The rope belonged to her father; he sometimes used it as a belt, but had allowed her to take it and play with it today. Thinking of him, Hekate felt a sudden reviving warmth in the rope. "Daddy's coming back," she said.

Her mother pushed a handful of leaves into a bag, and studied Hekate. Confusion pulled her eyebrows together. "Yes, he is. But you can't sense people. Can you?"

"Not the way immortals can. I only knew because the rope told me. Since it's a piece of his clothing." It made perfect sense to Hekate.

Her mother only looked more puzzled. "I've heard of witches using such tricks to find people. But they have to say all kinds of spells and draw shapes on the ground and such. I've never been sure it really worked. It might only be luck when it does."

Hekate shrugged. "I ask the magic to help. In my head. There's a lot of magic down here, so it's easy. Don't you and Daddy do that?"

Persephone shook her head, and rubbed the leaves of a nearby olive tree between her fingers. "The magic we use is of a different sort. We don't feel it like that. We only see what it does when the plants contain it, after people eat them or use them."

"But you do use it," Hekate said. "When you switch realms. I can sense the wall—the gate sort of, the thing between this realm and the other—but I'm not perfect enough to get through it."

"Perfect enough?"

"Yes, immortals get through because their bodies are strong and perfect," Hekate said, impatient with her mother for not understanding something so obvious. "That's why I want to be immortal. One of a *thousand* reasons."

Her father arrived in the garden then, and called to them across the rows of plants. Persephone caught him up on this odd conversation. He frowned at his daughter, and they ended up spending the rest of the day testing Hekate's claims of finding people by holding one of their possessions and thinking of them. It worked fine when Hekate was in the Underworld, no matter where the person was, this realm or the other. It even worked fairly well, but with less certainty, when she was in the upper world. Her parents looked at each other inscrutably.

Hekate guessed her ability worried them. "It won't harm me," she said, exasperated. "The Earth knows we're helping lots of people every day. The magic won't hurt us if we don't use it to hurt anyone else. If we did, it would bounce back onto us, like if you threw a rock at a stone wall in front of your face. That would be stupid, wouldn't it."

Again her parents only stared at her in concern and astonishment, rather than agreeing with the obviously logical statement she had just made.

Another day, not long after that, she wandered up while her father and mother were talking about the caves of punishment. Hekate had seen those deep flame-lit caverns only once, and then only because she snuck down there without permission, with only Kerberos as company.

"But when I do want to find someone down there," her father was saying, "how can I? The souls can't speak to each other, each confined alone the way they are. No one knows where anyone else is."

"And walking along the cells, asking each one their name…" Persephone shuddered at the idea of the unpleasant, interminable task.

"Ask the cave to help you," Hekate told them.

They both turned and directed their sternest expressions at her. "Tartaros is no place for children," her father said.

"Even the cave knows that," her mother said. "Children's souls are never down there."

"But if you want to find someone, ask the cave," Hekate said. "Obviously the Fates are there, and listening."

Hades narrowed his eyes at her. "You haven't been down there again lately, have you?"

"No, just the one time, when you *made* me come back up. But the way the flames come on for you in the tunnel, and how the vines grow themselves and trap the souls—and how the souls have to go down there if they've been evil even though they don't want to go—it's all someone working magic. Spirits or Fates or something."

Her mother's olive-tan skin looked paler now as she regarded Hekate. She darted a glance at Hades, who was thinking with his frown cast toward the grass, then asked her daughter, "What do you think we should say to find someone?"

Hekate shrugged. "Take me down again. I'll figure it out."

She got her way after a bit more arguing. Soon they were descending the close, low tunnel, following flame after flame in the stuffy air.

They entered the stone arch to the chamber where the cave held the souls.

"Now what?" Her father folded his arms, his cloak wrapped around him as if to shelter him against the atmosphere of the place, though it was stiflingly warm.

"Who do you want to find?" Hekate asked.

Hades and Persephone exchanged another doubtful glance, but he finally answered, "Well, a husband and wife were found dead in Zakro, on Crete. It's been stirring up a lot of worry because no one's sure if they killed each other, or if it was a murder-suicide, or if someone else did it and escaped. I can't find them in the fields, so I suspect they're both down here and guilty of something. If I could bring an answer back to their neighbors, it would calm everyone down."

As she listened, Hekate trailed her hand along the stone arch's bumps and divots. She cupped her palm near a flame shooting out of the wall, as close as she could bring it without burning her skin. "What are their names?" she asked.

"Nopina and Drakokardos."

Hekate studied the chamber and what was visible of the tunnels. Flame and the specially twined vines—those were the living hallmarks of Tartaros. Best use those. She picked up a long scrap of willow-and-ivy rope that lay on the ground, and lit its end in the wall's flame, like a torch. "Fates who guard these souls," she said in the Underworld tongue, watching the flame she held, "guide us to the souls we seek: Nopina and Drakokardos, wife and husband recently dead, of Zakro on Crete."

"Hekate," Hades began, "I don't know if the cave knows or cares where Zakro on Crete is—" But he stopped, for a new flame burst forth with a whoosh.

They all looked toward the sound. The flame had emerged in the wall of one of the tunnels. Satisfied, Hekate dropped the makeshift torch, stamped out the fire under her sandal, and walked toward the tunnel.

It worked exactly as she knew it would. The flames led them to the separately confined souls of the wife and husband. Her parents stared at Hekate in wonder, almost forgetting to question the couple until Hekate reminded them.

The pair, it turned out, were guilty of two other murders together, before the husband killed the wife and then himself. Hades took the news back to Crete, settling the questions surrounding the deaths.

And Hekate continued to grow in her understanding of magic and how to use it, though every day she wished she were immortal so she could handle the magic even better. Her parents often brought her along on their errands to the living world, and made sure she impressed her immortal aunts and uncles with her insights. But everyone still held out on giving her the fruit of immortality—and still wouldn't tell her which tree it was—because they feared the fruit might freeze her in her child state, and therefore it was best to wait till she was older.

Then the plague came.

Chapter Nineteen

 OPHIE STEPPED OUT OF THE BUS INTO THE WARM, FLOWER-FILLED meadow. Blue mountains with snowy peaks stretched to the sky in front of her. The harbor lay behind her, its seawater-scented breeze sweeping inland and making the wildflowers bob their heads. A bird trilled a song from somewhere in a tree covered with fuzzy red blossoms.

The beauty moved her to extreme remorse. She turned to Adrian. "Oh God, I'm sorry! I've been making you hang out in boring corners of Oregon and Washington when your home looks like *this*."

He grinned as he wrapped the horses' reins around a tree with a palm-like frilly canopy. "No worries. Your Northwest is pretty too."

"You're just being nice. It isn't like this."

"It's spring here. Everything looks better in spring." He came over and latched his arm around her. "Shall we fetch her?"

Sophie nodded, her heart speeding up in nervousness.

Adrian sent Zoe a text, and said a minute later, "She sensed us. She's on her way."

Sophie regulated her breathing to normal, and nibbled her lower lip, which was sticky with lip gloss. She'd made greater effort than usual with her appearance today: makeup, hair products, a skirt and cute sandals instead of her usual jeans and sneakers. But it felt inappropriate now to have dressed up, even while it would have felt inadequate to have dressed down. How did you prepare for meeting your child? That is, the child you had in previous lives?

The wind rippled the meadow grass, then a young woman flickered into view and walked toward them. She was tall, almost six feet—taller even than Adrian—with strong bones framing a lanky body. Supermodel makings, Sophie thought, except Zoe came across as fully natural, with none of the artifice of a fashion model. She wore no makeup, and had short, light brown hair, unruly from neglect, it appeared, rather than by design. Her gray T-shirt and army-green cargo capris were well worn, as were the black high-tops on her feet. Her only jewelry was an ear cuff that glinted silver in the sun.

She and Adrian hugged as they met, then Zoe turned her alert brown eyes to Sophie.

"Hey," Sophie said, suddenly shy.

"Hey." Zoe's smile reflected the shyness, and she swung her arms awkwardly.

Should they hug? Sophie thought in a panic. Instead, she tried an explanation, though a totally unnecessary one, on topics they'd already covered in texts. "I'm finally remembering you—Hekate, I mean—and I wanted to see you, and New Zealand, and—and maybe Adrian's dad if we can arrange it, so…"

"Yeah, of course, I'll help with that. Can bring him to you if you like." Zoe had the same accent as Adrian, the Kiwi vowels twisting upward so half of them were like the "i" in "is." Sophie had tried to hear it in her mind, but Hekate's voice kept overriding it: the childlike tones, and the accent that sounded no different than Persephone's own.

"So you're—you know, remembering stuff now too?" Sophie asked.

Zoe nodded, stuffing her hands into her pockets. "I've got up to about age twelve, I think. Whole new set of parents. Bit weird, isn't it?" She sent Adrian and Sophie a crooked grin. "When we're all the same age now."

"You're older than me, even," Sophie said. Both Adrian and Zoe were twenty-one, while she was still eighteen.

"I'm glad you came." Zoe squinted past them at the harbor. "I wanted to meet you as well. Would've come seen you before long, if you weren't coming here to visit." Her glance darted to Sophie again, the awkward smile still upon her lips.

And in that glance, like a bright light being switched on, Sophie saw Hekate looking out Zoe's eyes; the soul of the beloved, brilliant child. Sophie laughed in amazement, her own shyness falling away. "It is *so* good to see you. Tell me everything. How's it going with your folks? How are you coping?"

Zoe's smile transformed into a frank grin, as if she were seeing Persephone at last in Sophie's face too. "Oh, it's been madness. Where to start?"

They strolled down the hillside as they dived into conversation. When Sophie looked aside at Adrian, who stayed quiet, she found him walking nearby with Kiri, head bowed, smiling as if perfectly happy.

"Nothing seems to be coming of our tip-offs." Landon prodded the fire with the poker, shoving an unburned log on top of the coals.

Betty Quentin adjusted her stiff leg and settled her foot on the hearth. "On the plus side, we haven't been found."

"True."

"The law takes a while to act," she added. "Especially when they can't find Adrian. And they wouldn't be able to hold him if they did find him, so all we're doing there is giving him and his friends headaches. Maybe it'll slow them down a little, at least." She gazed at the flames. Wind and rain beat upon the outside of the Idaho cabin.

Sitting on the hearth rug, Landon circled his arms loosely around his knees. "Do you think these are the first actual immortals Thanatos has found since...way back when?"

"I can't know for sure. But I'd say it's likely. There were others we've tracked down and eliminated, on the basis of longevity and strength and other boasts. But since they died pretty easily, I suspect they weren't the real article."

Landon kept facing the fire. His brows drew together. "Were those in your time, or…?"

"I've overseen a few. The rest I've read about in our records. Oh well. Unfortunate, if they were innocent, but it happens in war all the time. We're doing what we can. But this time is *very* different. We're seeing all the signs."

He nodded and drew his back up straight. "Those old tablets. Turns out the translation's accurate, then?"

"For a long time I wondered. I thought it couldn't be, or at least maybe it was allegorical. Talking about flying horses and oak wood and such. But now it matches up exactly with what Sanjay told Swami. So I'd say it's accurate. And therefore there's likely more we can learn from it."

The guru who had caught Sanjay for Thanatos had a long Indian name, but Betty and the others, to avoid such a mouthful of syllables, had fallen into the habit of simply calling him "Swami."

Landon wiggled his toes in his thick blue wool socks. "It's such an honor for you. To be head of Thanatos at the time the immortals actually come back."

"An honor and a challenge. Hand me the computer, would you?"

He brought her the laptop. She pulled up the photos of the clay tablets, their inscriptions so faint some of them resembled the mark of a leaf falling past the clay. Landon knelt by her armchair and gazed at them too.

"I first saw these in 1988, a couple of years after they were discovered," she said. "Heard they dug up some Linear B tablets that started out, 'O Thanatos, never forget.'" She traced the first few symbols on the tablet. "The archaeologists figured it was some kind of grave record, or maybe a poem or magic spell. Which it could've been. But I got a copy of the translation and photos of the tablets, just in case."

"So the records Thanatos had before 1988, the ones that kept the group going all these centuries..." Landon frowned. "What were those? Something from medieval times?"

Landon had only learned about Thanatos' existence within the last year. Betty had visited him and found him in need of a satisfying vocation and willing to shoulder important secrets and responsibilities. Perhaps the group wouldn't like her choosing her own grandson as her successor. But the choice was hers, and Landon had a certain conviction and intelligence. The rest of the group's members tended to be too short on one or the other, in her private opinion.

"Right," she answered. "Our Decrees were written by medieval monks, transcriptions of older scrolls, but we've never found those. Things got burned or lost all the time. We're lucky to have a transcription at all. But the Decrees, short as they are, do name some of the same details as these Thanatos tablets." She clicked her fingernail on the screen. "The immortals vanishing and reappearing from another realm. The powerful fruits in a garden of the dead. The names of Greek deities." She smiled at her grandson, pleased at the wonder in his eyes. "It's all true, Landon. I've seen the other realm myself now. I'm lucky to have gotten back alive, but that fiend gave me a gift by showing me it was real."

He blinked and swallowed. His gaze slipped back to the fire. "I almost want to see it. The other realm. But it's so dangerous. That kind of power could rip the world apart."

"That's why we've kept the Decrees alive all this time. To guard against such a day." She scrolled down, and read aloud what she had already memorized decades ago. "'There will be plagues and the immortals will celebrate while humankind dies, as we have already seen. They will strike us down at will, as we have already seen. They will seduce traitors to join them, and turn them immortal, as we have already seen. Then they will breed and multiply in their other world, and break through to ours and conquer us: weak humankind.' That's what we're seeing now. That's what we have to stop."

"Seducing traitors to join them," Landon said. "Like Sanjay. And Sophie."

"And who knows how many others. At least we know about Adrian. So he's the one to catch."

Landon sank back down on the hearth rug and pulled his knees up to his chest. "Don't you ever wish *we'd* been given immortality, instead of them?"

"Of course. It's a natural thing to wish. I could lose this bum hip, get my youth and vitality back, never worry about flu season. Everyone wants it. And that's precisely why it's so dangerous. Because it's such a temptation. Maybe you and I would handle immortality without tearing the world open, but what would other people do with it? No, it's a horrible scenario. Since it's not safe for anyone, nobody should have it."

He brooded over that a while, then asked softly, "When do we move in?"

She closed the laptop and folded her hands on top of it. "We'll need help. At least one more person. Wilkes would've been good, but now he's dead. Not everyone in the group is willing to fly out to the Northwest and…do what we might have to do. But I'm disenchanted with the street thugs we've gotten so far."

"What about the people who helped you out of jail?"

"They can help with parts of it." She glanced up at the rafters. "One of them owns this cabin. That helped. But they have careers, families. They were able to make a special trip that time, but they can't always be committing to such things. One of them lives in Oregon, and the other three came up from California. So if the job's in Washington, it's a longer haul for them. Some might make it, but…" Betty sighed. "It'd be nice to have someone who could properly join us, not drive in for one night and then go home."

"I've mentioned Krystal to you. My Internet friend." Landon cast her a shy, hopeful look. "She's not far from here. Lives in Montana. She's between jobs now, since she was working on a politician's campaign, but he just lost in the election."

"You say she's good with firearms?"

"Loves them."

"And she'd go with us on this?"

"I'm almost sure. I've sounded her out. Carefully, but enough to see she's interested. The secret group, ancient records, weird stuff happening lately—it all really intrigues her." He dropped his gaze. His long eyelashes swept his cheekbones. "Plus I think she'd do it just for me."

Betty chuckled. "Well, Landon. I may have misjudged you."

"Hmm?"

"Nothing, dear."

CHAPTER TWENTY

THE PLAGUE ENTERED GREECE FROM THE SEA. SAILORS WHO HAD been to Africa sickened first, and the disease tore through the islands and the mainland. Persephone and her family were among the first to hear of it, when a large group of deceased Kyprians of all ages arrived in the Underworld and told them about it. They were subdued as souls always were, but shaken enough that their consternation came through.

Persephone and Hades' mortal twelve-year-old daughter stood with them as they listened to the souls' account. Hekate's head brushed Persephone's chin now; she was almost grown. But not quite. Not tall enough or developed enough to count as anything but a child. Not old enough for the blue orange.

The plague had killed these people less than nine days after their first symptoms appeared. A terrible fever and thirst, rashes and sores, coughing up blood, and soon death—either by suffocating when their lungs filled with fluid, or by infection of their sores. Looking around at their numbers in the Underworld, the Kyprians estimated it had killed a quarter of the people in their village.

Cold sweat beaded all over Persephone's body. She clutched her daughter's arm, holding her here in this safe haven. When she glanced at Hades, he gave her a slight nod of assurance, but his face was tight with worry too.

That afternoon Persephone left Hekate and Hades at home and paid her mother a visit. As a healer, Demeter might have ideas regarding any precautions they might take. Demeter was already battling the plague in her village: symptoms had cropped up here too.

"A few concoctions seem to help. Feverflower and lady's mint boiled with green garlic—it reduces fever and lets them breathe a bit better. But I don't know. If it's as lethal as you say, oh, Lady help us." Demeter hurried around her hearth, chopping and boiling herbs and flowers as she spoke. Her hair had begun unraveling from its knot. She'd obviously been working among the people day and night.

Fear choked Persephone. Babies, young couples, gentle elderly, all the folk she had grown up with in the area...but the worst of the fear was for her daughter. "Hekate. How do we protect her?"

"Keep her out of the living world." Demeter looked at her with her sternest expression. "Not one visit, not for months if that's how long it takes."

Persephone tried to laugh. "Oh, mercy. The fit she'll throw at being confined like that."

"Too bad. It's her life at stake. And have her eat garlic and yogurt every day. They fortify the body against illness."

"I will. Is there anything I can do to help everyone else?"

"I don't know." Demeter sounded weary. "The people tolerate me well enough, at least around here, but they're starting to sound hostile indeed against immortals. They even say the plague is our fault."

"How in the world could it be our fault?"

"Oh, we control everything, don't you know? We invented it to amuse ourselves. Or to thin the ranks of mortals, of whom we're jealous because some of them are more beautiful than us. Or at the least, we could have stopped so many deaths and handed out immortality or magical cures, but we're refusing to, because we're too busy feasting and frolicking."

Frustration layered itself on top of Persephone's fear. "What kind of ingratitude—when they see how much you do for them, how much Hades and I do for them—"

"Yes, but you two have a fearsome glamour about you, being

gods of the dead, so they view you with dread in addition to respect. And in any case we three are exceptions." Demeter threw a handful of chopped mint into the pot over the fire. "Plenty of immortals do spend most of their time feasting and frolicking, doing more harm than good."

Persephone thought of Ares, Zeus, Hera...even her friends Aphrodite and Hermes, for that matter. She bowed her head, ashamed at her fine embroidery and jewels, and the clean perfection of her body. She remembered being mortal quite well, and understood the people's envy. "I don't know what to do," she said.

"Protect Hekate. That's all that matters."

TABITHA BALANCED HER latte in one hand while she ripped a sticky note off the door of her dorm room before entering.

You're missing a lot of class. Where are you? It was signed by not one but two of her professors. They were obviously conferring about her. Oh well, she knew as much from their voice-mails and emails. She hadn't been answering those either. Not a lot of time, between one party and another—but dude, she was meeting the coolest, hottest, most famous people.

A popular actor on a sci-fi show, who had five million followers on his social networks, had been at one of the L.A. parties she'd recently attended. He loved the impromptu interview she had filmed with a younger actress, complete with proud drunken singing, and he had posted the video link on his page a few days ago. Tab now spent her free time reading the comments—mostly appreciative; a few trolls, as always on the Internet—and answering calls from people she wanted to talk to. One was a national late-night talk show, inviting her to come on if she could get to New York.

Which of course she could. Speedily, in fact, and without having to spend a penny on airfare. She'd call them back soon and work out the details.

She knew she was neglecting Zoe. She hated the guilt that arose with that thought. But come on, they lived in different countries, and they'd have loads of time to get to know each other if they were going to live forever. These calls from New York TV shows, on the other hand, weren't going to go on forever. They had to be dealt with now.

But classes—ugh, who had the time?

In what was left of her free time, in those hours riding her ghost horse across the continent, or after crashing into bed drowsily at 3:00 a.m., she was pursuing the past. Following Zoe's urgings—and Niko's too—she was hunting down Dionysos, or Adonis, or whatever name he used. And that was confusing: those guys were two separate people, in the myths. At least, as far as she had found out from the Internet. But the actual past might tell a different story. So she hauled up each life, examined its temporal and spatial place in the world, and got distracted by its interesting features for at least a few hours each time before chucking it behind her and digging deeper.

Lately the past lives were seriously ancient. The concept of writing and reading grew sparse among the people she lived with. They grew crops and raised animals, but also sacrificed said animals and poured some of their wine or grain or fancy oils onto the ground for the gods.

Sometimes she was a man, sometimes a woman, but she always loved women. Apparently those kinds of traits and preferences varied from one soul to another. Zoe said she was nearly always a woman but had been sometimes straight and sometimes gay. Niko said he was usually a man, occasionally a woman, and always bi. And Sophie said she was usually a woman, but always preferred men even when she had been one.

As to where in the world she was in those primitive past lives, Tabitha often could only guess. People didn't know what globes or maps were back then, and considered their homeland the center of the universe.

But this morning she found the life she'd been looking for, and knew the setting at once. Greece. The incomparable blue of the

Mediterranean and cleanly elegant lines of the stone houses, the creatively arranged white or dyed tunics draped around everyone.

And she knew it for certain when the earliest memory of that life was her father—or rather, *his* father—bellowing, "Adonis!" accompanied by the crack of a wooden staff against Adonis' back.

Tabitha pulled in and let out her breath, and dropped her keys on her chaotic bookcase. She'd thought she had a rough childhood, what with her sexual orientation being outed in high school before she was ready, and her parents divorcing, and the general suckitude of a small town. Even college started out far crappier than she had hoped. Her dad lived in Bellevue, right across the lake from Seattle, where he was a real estate agent. In choosing a college in Seattle, she had pictured meeting him weekly for lunch—which would be far more often than she saw him during the last two years of high school. She envisioned impressing him with how grown-up and savvy she had become, and assumed he'd dash over to help her with any problem that might arise.

Instead, he always either answered, "Sorry sweetie, working," or, "Jamie and I have plans." Jamie was his girlfriend, another realtor, about ten years younger than Tab's mom. She wore way too much beige and reeked of over-sweet perfume. Though Tab was well aware of her mother's faults—most of them involving drinking—she couldn't stand to be around Jamie a single hour.

So Tab had seen her dad a grand total of once since moving into the dorms. Between that and being a state away from Sophie, she had felt depressingly isolated for her first month of college.

But holy shit, her life was a shower of rose petals compared to the glimpses she'd seen from the past. For example, Adonis. This one was going to take some quiet contemplation—a feature Tab rarely incorporated into life, but in this case it was important.

Tabitha's roommate was out. The girl spent at least five hours a day practicing cello, either in class or in one of the rehearsal rooms. Tab shrugged off her faux-fur-hooded coat and stood at the window, sipping her latte. Rain lashed the glass. The Seattle traffic three stories below, crawling up the steep street, looked like smears of dark paint and blurry lights. Tab had been up most of the night at a party in San Francisco (the three women who starred as secret agents in that summer blockbuster? Yeah, their party), and had gotten only a few hours of sleep on a couch in one of their guest rooms. Now that she was immortal, she didn't feel as tired on limited sleep as she used to. But, balancing that out, caffeine didn't really work anymore either.

She grimaced at the cup. "Why am I even drinking you? Oh yeah. You're creamy and tasty." She gave the latte one more gulp, then set it on her desk and dropped onto her bed.

So. Adonis. Time to learn some Ancient Greek.

CHAPTER TWENTY-ONE

In a half-dream, Tab moved fast through Adonis' early years. He was an only child, born to parents who were well off but weary. His mother had suffered several miscarriages before having him, and three after. His father, distressed by that and by the demands of the vineyards he owned, made life a torment for the family. He had a vision of creating the world's finest wine, better than Greece had ever tasted, wine fit for the gods.

According to the travelers and townspeople, he succeeded. His grapes were the finest, his fermentation technique the most masterful. But that only meant he had to keep up standards in order to meet everyone's demands for this wonderful wine, and he shoved Adonis into the vineyards to work almost as soon as he could walk.

It was for eating some of the fat purple grapes instead of placing them into the harvest basket that his father had beaten him with the staff. Well, that was one reason. Sometimes Adonis got beaten for sleeping in. Or for stepping in to defend his mother when his father beat her. Or for losing his temper and yelling back at his father, which showed a grievous lack of respect for one's parents, according to all the laws of gods and men. His father was perfectly within his rights to beat him, and to beat his wife. Adonis barely understood any other way existed in the world until he met Aphrodite.

She arrived at the vineyards one spring day when he was sixteen. Adonis was at work among the vines, crouching to examine each root for signs of pests, when he heard horses' footsteps on the rocky path. He stood up and beheld the most beautiful woman the world could possibly have produced. She slipped down from her horse, white and lavender garments fluttering. Flowers and jewels glinted in her sleek black hair and on her arms and hands. Other people surrounded her, a group of men and women, probably her servants and guards, but Adonis barely glanced at any of them. She captivated him.

"Well, well," she said in greeting. "If the wine is as delicious as the workers in the vineyard, then it shall match its reputation indeed."

Adonis blushed, smiled, and invited her to the house to meet his father and to taste all the wine she liked.

His father scented wealth at the first glimpse of the woman and her entourage, and donned his most complimentary behavior. Adonis assisted him, fetching and pouring all the jugs of wine they requested, and listened to their conversation. Soon he found out exactly who she was.

No wonder she had captivated him. She was an immortal. In fact, she was *the* immortal every man dreamed of and told tales about: Aphrodite, goddess of love. And worth every starry-eyed poem composed for her. She owned a small island not far off the coast nearest Adonis' house, and though he had heard roughly where it was, his family owned no boat, being confined to the hills and valleys of the vineyards. And Adonis' father would never have let him take time off to seek passage to such a place regardless.

But she saved him. By catching his enamored stares, and answering them with smiles and winks, she worked him into a state of tortured joy from across the room without even touching him. She bought several barrels of wine at the end of the afternoon, and Adonis, along with her own servants, lashed them onto the donkeys and carts she had brought. Aphrodite climbed onto her horse, then paused and asked his father, as if in a passing thought, "Would your son be available to come work at my palace? I like to choose only the most fetching attendants, as you can see, and I'm quite taken with his looks."

While his father opened his mouth in astonishment—for surely he had never seen anything in Adonis except his faults—Aphrodite added, "If it works out for us all, I'll happily pay the wages of another worker to replace him here on the days when he's with me. Two workers, even. I suspect he's worth that." She favored Adonis with another wink.

Shortly thereafter, Adonis' life was catapulted into near perfection. His father suddenly viewed him as a valuable asset to be sold and lauded, much like the wine. He sent Adonis to spend half of every month with Aphrodite, and spoke it far and wide that his son was the consort of the most beautiful goddess in the world, and his family and his wine were therefore blessed. He charged higher prices than ever for his wines, and people paid it.

That mattered nothing compared to how Aphrodite made Adonis feel. She caressed him and told him in quiet outrage that in civilized lands like Kypros and Crete, no one was allowed to beat their spouses or children. It was *not* the will of the gods. And she excited him to blissful frenzies he didn't know a man could survive. He hadn't done more than roll around drunkenly with a few girls at festivals before, and Aphrodite showed him how much he'd been missing, how truly there was an art to sexuality. He was completely in love, and felt loved, even though he understood she would always retain other lovers too. It was a strict rule of hers. The goddess of love couldn't confine herself to one person and lose the opportunity to educate and please so many others.

It meant he could never marry her. But he didn't care—at least, not at first. He already got to do anything with her he wished, and appear on her arm at festivals and feasts, and enjoy her gifts of fine clothes and jewels and foods. Why would anyone wish for more?

But he did wish for more as their dalliance stretched out to two years and beyond. He wanted to be everything she was—and everything the immortal men were, whom she still indulged in private visits that made Adonis fume with jealousy. There was no way to make him immortal, as far as anyone knew, but maybe marrying her would at least lift his spirits and his status.

However, she always refused—gently. And his parents, after those few pleasant years of letting him have his way, started losing their patience and urging him to marry. By the time Adonis was eighteen, his father was drunk and unreasonable most of the time, and his mother a wretched mess. They'd got it into their heads that Adonis marrying would fix their lives. Which it wouldn't, but they nagged and shouted at him about it anyway. If Aphrodite wouldn't have him, they said, then he must choose some other girl. How about that friend of his, Persephone? She was the daughter of an immortal—almost as prestigious. He should marry her. Aphrodite suggested it too, lightly, and promised she'd still be available to Adonis after that. Persephone would understand. Adonis hardly knew what to say to such a bewildering proposal.

Persephone's mother Demeter apparently wanted him in that marriage too. She visited the vineyards sometimes on days when Adonis was there, claiming she wanted to know all about how to care for the vines, and insisting that Adonis be the one to show her. She listened attentively and praised him for his knowledge. Though it made sense for the agriculture-inclined goddess to take interest in a successful vineyard, her visits also felt like the grooming of a potential son-in-law. But he saw no way to disillusion her of her notions. Even Persephone seemed resigned to the notion of marrying him, though clearly it saddened her, for she, like Adonis, loved an immortal instead.

When Persephone and Hades eloped at the spring equinox festival, Adonis' heart lifted to the skies. Not only did he delight in his friend finding her happiness, but now perhaps Aphrodite would see immortals could marry mortals, though she had already seen such evidence in Poseidon's family.

But no. Aphrodite applauded Hades and Persephone for following their hearts, but could not bend her own rule.

"Not even loving you as much as I do," she said, nestled against him in bed, smiling with sweet regret in the moonlight spilling through her window.

He loved her and he wanted to kill himself. All at once. Such was life as Aphrodite's plaything.

Then came the fabulous announcement. Persephone and Hades had found a way to confer immortality. Persephone herself had undergone the metamorphosis. And Aphrodite was going to put his name forward as a candidate.

"But only under the condition, darling, that you do not insist on marriage or exclusivity," she said. "Not even then. It isn't who I am."

"Of course, that's fine." Rapture made his future glow like the sun. He'd be immortal and with her forever, and could set up his mother on a comfortable private island of her own and leave his father to drink himself to death and never have to deal with him again...

But the other immortals voted him down. They, too, it would appear, viewed him as Aphrodite's plaything, not a man worthy of living forever.

The emotions of that evening dragged Tabitha in for a closer look, slowing the scene to the pace of actual life.

Adonis sat upon the beach outside her house and stared in shock at the cruel ocean. Beside him, Aphrodite stroked his arm in silence.

He clenched down his emotions, picturing, as he always did at such times, a thick bronze armor wrapped around his heart. He wouldn't let Aphrodite see him weep, just as he never let his father see him weep when his father struck Adonis or his mother—at least, he hadn't let his parents see such emotion since he was a little boy. And he had to look strong if he was to be a man worthy of the incomparably desirable goddess of love, who already honored him more than he deserved.

Sharing her he could have stomached if he got to be immortal. If he were immortal, she would look at him as an equal, the way she looked at Hermes and Ares and Zeus and Hades and all the others. Not like a beloved young pet, the way she seemed to view him now.

It was sweet, yes, how she caressed him, and how she said, "My darling, I'm so sorry. Is there anything I can do?"

But he only shook his head. He wasn't to be her equal after all. And he couldn't even indulge in the consolation of weeping upon her shoulder, because then he'd despise himself and have not even the last shreds of dignity in which to clothe his suffering.

Tabitha hauled her mind back from the scene, fleeing from the storm of pain. She opened her eyes and rolled onto her side. She focused on the shelves of alphabetized boxes in which her room-mate kept her sheet music organized. The mundane detail helped a little, but that agonized fire that was Adonis' soul still burned inside her.

In all the lives she had remembered till now, she had always rushed her memory past any sign of trauma, glossing over it until she got to a safe point from which to look back upon it. She had lived through enough humiliation and rejection herself. She didn't need or want to pry into anyone else's. And it did feel like prying, even though it was her own soul.

But her friends wanted her to see this, and now she had to admit: having tasted the glory of the Greek deities as they had actually lived, she was hooked. Even with the pain that came along with it.

She sat up and pulled her long hair over her shoulder, winding it into one thick rope as she stared at the window. She ached to learn more. She could pretend it was to find out where and how Adonis became Dionysos. But a more pressing and tantalizing possibility had flared to life in her head.

Aphrodite's soul was out there somewhere, alive again and immortal. Niko had said so. She was a gorgeous Swedish woman; that much had stuck in Tabitha's mind. And now that she could recall Aphrodite, Tab's immortal frame could sense her: far away, likely in Sweden or equally distant. But distances didn't matter much.

Tabitha could jump on her spirit horse and go see her. Now, today. Her feet were on the floor and she was reaching for her coat before uncertainty stopped her. Why hadn't this Swedish woman come to meet her already? She easily could have.

The likeliest answer was that she didn't want to, or wasn't comfortable doing so. She must know that Adonis was born a woman this life, and probably she herself was straight. That could be reason enough. Still, a friendly visit...why hadn't she come?

Tabitha slumped back on her bed. Knowing what happened in the rest of Adonis' life would be her best guide in answering those questions. But she sensed darkness ahead for him, flashes of bad things and worse things and truly horrible things, and she recoiled from the thought of lying here longer and remembering them.

Besides, it was past noon and all she'd had today was coffee. Time for lunch. Also, she thought as she pulled on her coat, time to call back the TV studio in New York and tell them that yes indeed, she *would* like to come on and chat.

CHAPTER TWENTY-TWO

EY, HONEY, SAID THE EMAIL FROM SOPHIE'S DAD. *WE ASSUME you're coming back up for Thanksgiving? Let us know if you need us to come get you. Handy if you can get a ride with someone else though.*

The Oregon police called me yesterday. They had questions about you and Melissa, to figure out where all these attacks on you are coming from and how much Melissa had to do with it. Obviously I don't have a clue. But if you do, this is really the time to be speaking up. I trust you and so do they. But this is a damn confusing case. They said as much.

Let us know your plans. Love you.

Sophie read the email on her phone as she stood in the corridor outside the chemistry lecture hall. Her mind still staggered from the midterm she'd just taken. How could it only be midterms of her first quarter of college? Hadn't she lived, oh, three thousand years or so since she arrived in this town?

"How'd it go?"

The voice in the silent hallway startled her. She turned. Adrian sat on the polished wood steps leading to the second floor of the building, rain glistening on his black wool coat.

She let out her breath in relief. "Stalker."

He rose and descended the steps to her, glancing toward the lecture hall she'd come out of. "I sort of miss exams. Exciting. If stressful."

"Yeah. I think I did okay. But there's this." She handed over her phone, the email still on its screen.

He read it. "Ah."

"The police keep asking me, too. How long before they figure out I'm hiding stuff? Stuff I can't tell them without sounding crazy? Will they ever just call it a weird, inexplicable case and give up?"

"They might. There are more unexplained cold cases in the files than law enforcement likes to admit. I'm still hoping they'll catch Quentin, though, and I'll be curious to hear how she explains herself."

"But isn't Thanatos doing everything they can to hide her? And to hide any evidence that she did anything wrong?"

"Of course. But obviously *someone* detonated a grenade on campus, and however mistaken Melissa might've been in feeding Thanatos information, I think the police can tell she isn't really the one behind it. So they need to decide whether Wilkes went insane and was acting alone, or what exactly."

Sophie rubbed the back of her neck, which had tensed up during the exam and was only tightening further at this conversation. "I don't know how much longer I can keep playing innocent. Sometimes I…I don't know."

"That's natural. I doubt whether I'm on the right path every day. I suspect everyone does." He sent her a reassuring glance, then returned to reading the email on her phone.

Yes, but he was immortal. Sometimes she doubted her strength to stick with this Greek-god involvement, was what she didn't dare say. She loved Adrian and stood in awe of the spirit realm and its powers and charms. She had enjoyed meeting Zoe, and Adrian's dad later that day—a soft-spoken man with gray streaks in his receding black hair, and a smile and stature like Adrian's.

At least Adrian got to tell his parents the truth about what he was up to. Sophie still had to hide it. And lately her knees felt ready to crumple from the pressure of keeping it all secret and endangering her family. A mere mortal girl couldn't be expected to take this all on.

"It's this other part I'm concerned about." Adrian scrolled up on her phone. "Thanksgiving. Another American holiday I don't quite grasp." He looked anxiously at her. "Do you go home for it?"

She took back her phone. "Yes. That one, everyone goes home for. Halloween not so much. Can you bring me home Wednesday night or Thursday morning, maybe?"

"Sure. Whichever."

"I should stay most of the weekend. I have a paper to write and studying to do, on top of helping Mom with the cooking." She took in his sad but affectionate gaze. "Where will you go?"

Adrian shrugged. "Errands for souls. The usual, I suppose."

Sophie pictured him zooming around the world, quietly resolving murder cases without a penny in payment or a word of official thanks for it, improving humanity's lot in the limited but unusual ways he could. Her love and admiration for him stirred again. But the wall separating her from the mighty immortals also looked higher at the thought. If she did become immortal and stay with Adrian forever, then she'd be on one side of that wall and her family would be on the other. And that notion, of course, also cast her down.

With her energy drained from the exam and these dilemmas, not to mention her recent scary dreams about the plague, she didn't even try to give him a brave smile. Instead she gazed at her phone and nodded. "Another weekend at home'll do me good."

THE PLAGUE HAD been killing its first victims in mainland Greece for only a few days when Aphrodite and Adonis came down to the Underworld. At the time, Persephone was speaking to the recently departed souls about the disease, while twelve-year-old Hekate grouchily ate a cup of yogurt and garlic at her side. Hades had gone out in search of healers on his home island of Crete, which was one of the most advanced civilizations around at the time and therefore should have the best ideas on how to contain a plague.

A murmur of news rippled through the souls, and soon two or three began telling Persephone at once, "The goddess of love is here to see you. Aphrodite. Adonis too."

Persephone thanked them and brought Hekate up to the top of the nearest hill, where they looked out toward the dark river. The solid white of Aphrodite's and Adonis' tunics stood out as they walked the path in the fields. Aphrodite waved to them. Persephone waved back, and descended to meet them.

"Who's with Aphrodite?" Hekate asked.

"Adonis. He's…her friend."

"One of her lovers?" Hekate sounded bored, and licked yogurt off her wooden spoon.

"Well. Yes." Hekate was getting old enough now to grasp such things, Persephone decided. However, she didn't imagine Hekate would wish to get married at an early age any more than Persephone had wished it. Nor would she have many opportunities to meet prospective husbands unless she spent more time above ground, which wasn't safe with a plague raging about.

They met Aphrodite and Adonis on the path. Persephone hugged each of them.

Aphrodite, of course, looked as ravishing as ever. So did Adonis. Persephone had seen him several times over the years, and his good looks had yet to fade. He was Persephone's age, and therefore in his early thirties by now, an age by which many men were losing their hair and gaining wrinkles and paunches, especially men with access to as much wine as Adonis possessed. But he was blessed with strong bones, a handsome face, still-thick hair that was all gold and brown, and a trim body. Likely he didn't imbibe as much as people thought. And he still wasn't married. He held out against his parents there, though surely they nagged him to choose a young bride every chance they got.

Persephone stole a glance at Hekate, who was meeting him for the first time. She looked surprised and interested, studying him while standing perfectly still, the cup of yogurt cradled in her hands.

"Adonis, this is our daughter, Hekate," Persephone told him.

He bowed toward her. "A pleasure, Hekate. You favor both your parents." Though he chose gallant words, his smile remained tight, and dark shadows lay under his eyes. He glanced around skittishly—the usual behavior of someone visiting the Under-world for the first time, but in his case his surroundings seemed only a small part of what bothered him.

"What brings you here?" Persephone asked.

"It's probably foolish." He sighed, and looked at Aphrodite.

"His mother and father," Aphrodite said. "They've both contracted the plague."

Persephone sucked in her breath, and instinctively drew Hekate back a step.

"My father can die for all I care," Adonis said, sounding tired rather than hateful. "And he probably will, with the poor shape he's in after his years of drinking. But my mother..." His gray eyes beseeched Persephone. "If there's anything you have down here, any ideas..."

"We've already been to Demeter," Aphrodite added. "She suggested some herbs, which we'll try. But she said her best guess for a miracle was something from the Underworld."

"Adonis, I'm so sorry," Persephone said, "but the disease is so new, and spreading so fast, honestly I don't have many answers. Of miracles, well, we only have one plant like that, and it...requires a vote of all the immortals." Her face heated in awkwardness as she recalled how many times he had been voted down for the immortality fruit. She turned toward the garden. "But I do have a variety of willow that works better than the usual at reducing pain and swelling, even when people use it in the living world. Here, come."

She hurried down the path. The other three followed.

"And, Hekate, can you pull up some of the biggest carrots, the ones with the red stone marking the row?" She looked back at Adonis. "Grate those and wrap them in the leaves I'll give you, and it makes a good poultice if the sores become infected. What else..."

Moving around the garden, she loaded up a basket of seeds, bark, leaves, and vegetables for him, and dictated instructions on how to use them. He thanked her with his gentle smile before leaving.

She and Hekate stood watching them cross the river on the raft. Adonis and Aphrodite climbed the opposite bank and soon disappeared through the entrance tunnel.

"His parents will probably die, won't they," Hekate said solemnly.

A shiver ran through Persephone. "Some people don't. Some recover."

"I hope *he* doesn't die." Now Hekate sounded anxious, an emotion that likely had the same cause as her oddly silent mood throughout Adonis' visit. Few young women ever saw such a handsome man as he, among the living or the dead.

Persephone smiled, and stroked her daughter's disheveled hair. Hekate said such unusual things all the time, it was actually odd to hear her say something typically adolescent.

"I hope so, too," Persephone said. "He's a good person."

CHAPTER TWENTY-THREE

T HAT VERY NIGHT, HEKATE DEVELOPED A FEVER. WHETHER THE sickness arrived with Aphrodite and Adonis, or with Hades from his visit to Crete, or some other way, they didn't know. She stopped eating, and only accepted water. Persephone saw her own fear reflected in Hades' eyes.

"They had no better ideas in Crete?" she asked him, though she'd already asked when he returned earlier.

"Not really." Kneeling by Hekate's bed, he met his daughter's dark-eyed gaze and tried to smile. "But you're a healthy girl. Magic all round you. Right?" He stroked her forehead.

She nodded, but soon closed her eyes and lay shivering.

Within three days, she was coughing up blood. Two days after that, sores bloomed on her body. The fever raged, spiking high and falling a little sometimes, but not enough. Hekate became too exhausted and disoriented to speak. Persephone raced back and forth between the Underworld's gardens and Hekate's bedchamber, a small cave just off theirs, bringing medicines and attempted cures.

Hades had abandoned his duties among the souls, and stayed beside her day and night. Sleeplessness darkened the hollows around his eyes. He looked up at Persephone as she brought in the latest infusion of herbs, steaming in a wooden cup. "People have recovered, even from this stage, haven't they?" The anxiety racking his voice tore at her heart.

But sharing her panic wouldn't help him, nor Hekate. She

cleared her throat. "I think so. It's...hard to predict. Here, hold her up and we'll see if she can drink this."

They both knew the pattern now as well as anyone: about one-quarter of the people who contracted the plague died. The illness didn't pick off any particular age group more than another. Those with weaker constitutions did die more often, but they heard a lot of stories of strong, healthy youths dying too.

Hermes showed up that afternoon, and sucked in his breath at the sight of Hekate, her skin sweaty and marred with brownish-red sores. "I heard a rumor to this effect, but..." He glared at Persephone and Hades. "My gods, you two. Why aren't you giving her the orange immediately? We'd all forgive you!"

"She's twelve!" Persephone said. "What would happen if someone became immortal when they weren't fully grown? What if she stayed twelve forever? Her mind—her body—I don't know!"

Sternness still glowered in Hermes' green eyes, but now uncertainty flickered there too. He took a slow breath, nostrils flaring, and let his gaze slide to the girl lying limply in bed.

"I'll do it anyway if we must," Hades said. He remained seated by Hekate's bed, his hand on her arm, his eyes never leaving her.

They listened to Hekate's wheezing breaths. The girl's skin was now flushed red around the sores, and her lips had taken on a blue tinge. Terrifying symptoms. Persephone laid her fingers against Hekate's cheek. The fever burned higher than ever.

"Hermes, will you fetch my mother for me, please?" Persephone whispered. "Quickly."

He nodded and sprinted out of the cave at such speed that he seemed to vanish in a flutter of his cloak.

Persephone sat opposite Hades and took Hekate's other hand. He met her gaze. It was like looking into a mirror, she thought: in his face she saw a thin crust of courage and fortitude covering a deep well of terror. If she looked any longer, she'd burst into sobs, so she turned again to Hekate.

"Grandmother's coming, dear," she said. "She'll help you feel better."

But as they waited, Hekate's breathing became wheezier and

more irregular. And a bit later, as Persephone tried to adjust Hekate's position on the pillow to assist her, Hekate began convulsing.

"Gods—what—" Hades pressed her arm to the mattress, as if to stop the seizure.

"No, don't hold her down! Go. Get the orange."

"I don't want to leave, I don't want to be gone if—if—"

"Then hurry!" Persephone wailed.

He raced out, bare feet pounding the stone floors.

Kerberos whined, pacing back and forth by the end of the bed. Dogs did that sometimes, sensing death just before it happened, Persephone thought in despair. Tears spilled onto her cheeks. She drew her convulsing daughter onto her lap, doing her best to shield Hekate from biting her own tongue or striking the hard wood frame of the bed. *Please, Goddess, this cannot be how you mean to end her life, and destroy ours,* she prayed. But countless parents lately had sent up the same prayer and still ended up burying their children.

Sandals slapped upon the stone tunnel floor outside. Demeter ran in, and handed a torch to Hermes, behind her.

"Mother," Persephone entreated.

Demeter sat on the bed next to her daughter and granddaughter, taking in Hekate's appearance. "You should have called me sooner."

"I thought…we…" Words failed Persephone. She stared at her mother in anguish.

Demeter turned a sharp gaze upon her. "Fetch the orange."

Persephone nodded. "Hades is. He's—"

His footsteps raced back toward the chamber, and he rushed in with an orange.

"Give it here." Demeter reached out.

Hades handed it over and knelt by the bed. He stroked Hekate's black hair. "But how will she eat, if she's like this?" he said. Hekate still convulsed, her jaw clenched shut.

Hermes, looking pale, stepped up and rested his hand on Hades' back. Hades didn't even glance up.

Kerberos whined again, closer now, and bumped his muzzle

against Hekate's hand. Persephone petted him, but moved him out of the way.

Demeter ripped the peel off the fruit. The fragrant orange curls fell to the floor. "We'll have to try our best." Holding a wedge of the blue fruit, she crawled closer to Hekate. "Open her mouth."

"I'm trying. I can't," Persephone said. Hekate's whole face was blue now. The world thundered in Persephone's ears, about to end. If she died in the Underworld, at least her soul wouldn't have far to go. They'd see it separate from her body, right before their eyes, and she'd still be with them, but they'd never hold her again, never see her quick living passions...

"Let me try." Hades climbed up too, and pried at Hekate's locked jaw. "Come on, darling, come on. I don't want to break her jaw—"

"She has to get this in her mouth!" Demeter snapped.

Kerberos howled, and nosed forward again, his head bumping Hekate's limp hand.

"Kerberos—I'll take him—" Hermes began, but then Hekate's hand twitched and reached for the dog.

Persephone noticed the motion. "Wait, let him."

Kerberos set his chin on the bed, and Hekate's hand rested upon his furry head. At that moment, her jaw relaxed its hold and she took a calmer breath. They seized their chance: Demeter squeezed the orange's juice into Hekate's mouth.

"Swallow that, dear," Persephone said.

Hekate swallowed it, coughing and choking, but the juice stayed down.

"Now eat this little bite." Demeter tore off a morsel of the orange wedge and placed it on Hekate's tongue.

"Chew that and eat it," Hades said, still stroking her hair. "That's right, darling."

Persephone placed her hand over Hekate's, atop Kerberos' head.

Sliding her fingers back and forth in the dog's fur, Hekate weakly chewed the orange morsel and swallowed it. The convulsions died down and she lay still. The wheezing sound faded, and her breath steadied. With eyes still closed, she licked her cracked lips and squeaked, "Tastes good."

Demeter smiled tenderly. Persephone wiped tears off her cheeks. Hades sank his face into the blanket, shoulders trembling. Hermes heaved a sigh of relief.

"Have another, dear." Demeter fed Hekate the rest of the orange slice. "It'll make you all better."

Hekate ate the blue morsel. The torch in Hermes' hand flickered and crackled, suddenly the loudest sound in the calm chamber. Kerberos resettled his large head on the mattress, his nose bumping Persephone's leg. Keeping one arm around Hekate, Persephone reached down with her other and stroked the fur on the dog's neck. Possibly he had transferred some kind of magic to Hekate that revived her enough to let her swallow the juice, the sort of power she claimed to feel when she touched various objects and creatures. At the least, his presence had grounded the girl. Whichever it was, Persephone felt even more grateful for the dog today than when he had hauled her out of the river years ago.

Hekate stirred. A healthy sweat shone on her skin, and she pushed off the goatskin blanket. When Persephone touched her lips to Hekate's damp forehead, she found her temperature descending back toward normal.

"I'm thirsty," Hekate mumbled.

"Here." Hades scrambled aside to fetch the jug of water.

Hekate sat up unsteadily and took it and drank, then examined his tear-streaked face. She looked around at all of them. "You weren't that worried about *me*, were you?"

Persephone beamed, but still couldn't speak past the lump in her throat. Neither, it seemed, could Hades.

Hermes stepped up to tap his finger against her bare toe. "We were, and with good reason, you imp."

Demeter folded the blanket onto the end of the bed, and rose. "Sweetheart, would you like to sleep now, or eat?"

Hekate took another drink of water, and coughed, but the cough sounded less lung-racking then it had a short while ago. She yawned and handed the pitcher back to her father. "Sleep."

She wriggled free of Persephone's arm and flopped onto her side, eyes closed. But now, even with the sores still red upon her skin, she looked more like her old self, the child comfortable and cozy in bed, not the trembling, sick patient.

Persephone kissed her fervently on the ear before standing up. "We'll be near if you need us."

"Mmf," Hekate answered, her usual response when she was ready to be left alone to sleep.

Kerberos hopped onto Hekate's bed and curled up at her feet—his customary spot, and tonight no one would contest it. The adults withdrew outside her chamber. They looked at each other, shock and tentative joy on their faces. Persephone's legs wobbled beneath her.

"So we see what happens," she said.

The others nodded, gazes flicking to Hekate.

"It wouldn't be so bad, being twelve forever." Nonetheless, anxiety wavered in Hades' voice. "She seems to enjoy it usually."

"She'll be fine if that's how it goes," Hermes assured. "A new type of immortal. The child goddess."

"She's nearly grown," Demeter said. "Some girls marry at twelve. I wouldn't worry. Now, you two get some rest. I'll watch her."

"But if—" Hades began.

"Yes, of course I'll wake you instantly if anything's wrong." Demeter's annoyance rose to the surface again. "Go."

Hermes stayed too, and made up a bed of extra blankets against the wall of Persephone and Hades' bedchamber. He fell promptly asleep. Beside Persephone, Hades settled into a quiet rhythm of breaths. But Persephone couldn't sleep. Every time she slipped toward relaxation, her mind fluttered awake again, attuned to her child, listening to each rustle or murmur. It was like the night she'd spent after giving birth: exhausted, but unable to rest, concerned her child would need her, worried she would miss something important.

And what kind of girl was being born into the world this time? What had they done? Even while thanking the Goddess ardently for allowing Hekate to live another day, Persephone pleaded that Hekate wouldn't hate her parents for transforming her into—into what, Persephone didn't even know.

CHAPTER TWENTY-FOUR

ZOE RECOGNIZED THE FEELING OF WAKING UP AS AN IMMORTAL, THE first morning it happened to Hekate. It had happened to her as well, after all, not so long ago. In Zoe's own case the change had come with a wondrous brightness. Her eyesight had reasserted itself slowly upon eating the orange, some of it not entirely healing until she slept. When she opened her eyes the next morning, lying next to Tabitha in the Underworld, the world suddenly loomed everywhere, colorful, detailed, confusing. Dazzling.

With Hekate it was almost as bright and amazing a change, Zoe now recalled, shampooing her hair before work while her mind wandered in the ancient world.

Though Hekate's eyesight had been fine to start with and wasn't much changed, the difference between the bodily aches and dizziness with which she fell asleep and the sweet, vibrant freshness in which she awoke was—well, a miracle. That was what the orange accomplished.

But Hekate didn't even know, when she awoke, what she had eaten or what it had done.

Persephone woke her when she quietly pulled aside Hekate's blanket in the bedchamber to examine her legs. Hekate squinted at her, then sat up, curious herself, and tugged up her tunic to show more of her skin. Persephone hadn't brought a lamp with her, probably not wishing to wake Hekate, and the only light came from a torch burning outside the chamber in a wall sconce.

It wasn't much to see by. But it was obvious the sores were completely gone, on her legs and everywhere.

"Huh," Hekate remarked. "Well, I feel much better. I guess this plague isn't so bad after all."

Persephone smiled, looking both anxious and relieved, and sat to push Hekate's hair out of the way and feel her forehead. "The plague is definitely bad. We fed you a special medicine, which has apparently worked." She tilted her head at Hekate and blinked, as if finding her appearance odd.

Hades stepped into the little chamber, carrying an oil lamp, his hair unruly and escaping its twine ponytail holder. "Look who's up." He came forward and kissed her, but he looked anxious too.

Hekate narrowed her eyes at her parents. "What's wrong?"

They exchanged a quizzical look.

"She's grown," Persephone said to Hades.

Hades examined Hekate, frowning. "Quite."

"What are you talking about?" Hekate demanded.

"Can you stand, dear?" Persephone asked.

"Of course I can." Hekate swung her legs out of bed and stood on the stone floor. Then she swayed in confusion, because although she felt fine, she was higher than she should be.

Hades lifted the lamp, sending bright rays of light across her. Her parents gazed rapt at her. She looked down at herself, running her hands up and down her body, and gasped in astonishment to encounter hips and breasts beneath her wrinkled tunic.

She glared at her parents. "How long have I been asleep?"

They broke into grins. "Only a night, darling," Persephone said. "We...had to save your life, so..."

"We fed you the orange," Hades said. "The immortality fruit."

Hekate slowly reached out to touch the stone wall. The Earth magic so alive in the Underworld flooded into her fingers, potent and scintillating. Yes, it was hers now, she could tell: the bodily perfection she had craved.

"I'm immortal," she said.

"Yes," her mother whispered.

Hekate touched her tall new body, then turned and seized her polished bronze hand mirror from the wall niche where it resided. Its reflection was always a bit fuzzy, especially in only the light of an oil lamp. But it was clear she had changed. She had become a woman.

"So apparently," her grandmother's arch voice said, "that's what the fruit does when you give it to a child. You look well indeed, Hekate."

Hekate looked at the entrance to her chamber. Demeter leaned there, hand on her hip, smiling.

Hermes darted into view too, and stopped to stare. His eyes expanded in pleased surprise. "Now that," he said, "is much better than staying twelve forever." He bowed to her. "Good *morning*, Hekate."

Hades grimaced at him. "Only you could make 'Good morning' sound so disgusting."

Hekate looked in the mirror again, then back at Hermes, who was looking her up and down in a way she'd only seen men look at grown-up women. Was that how men were going to look at her from now on? Rather exciting. If strange.

"She's even lovelier than you, Hades," Hermes remarked, "and you know how much I fancy you."

"Must you be here?" her father asked him.

Hekate smacked the mirror down. "I'd never fancy *you*," she retorted to Hermes. "And if you ever try to kiss me, I'll—I'll keep a snake hidden in my clothes and make it bite you. On the lips. And on both ears."

"See, your threats are still age twelve," Hermes said. "I'll help you work on that."

"Hermes," Persephone said, a laugh rippling her voice, "will you please carry the news to the others? I'd like them to hear it directly, before rumors spread."

"Happily."

"We may have some irritated parties to deal with," Hades said, "but on the whole I think they'll be pleased." He strolled up to his daughter and reached for her.

The love on his face melted her. She leaped into his hug. He grunted, falling back a step. "Yes, you're certainly stronger. And taller." He let her go and set his hand atop his head, then moved it straight out, where it brushed the top of hers.

"She's as tall as you," Persephone said in wonder.

Hades laughed, amazed, and kissed Hekate on the forehead. He had to tip his face up to do it.

"Will you all *please* let me bathe and have breakfast now?" Hekate complained. "I'm starving. And my robes are disgusting."

They obliged. Everyone kissed her one more time before dashing off. Only Persephone and Kerberos stayed, and accompanied her through the tunnels on the way to the rivers. The cold stone floors tingled against her bare feet. The stalagmites sent up sparks at the brush of her fingertips. All of it invisible, of course, but she sensed the magic like never before. It roamed the air like shreds of mist, and thrummed in the earth and rocks.

She threw off her sweat-stained tunic and climbed into their designated bathing spot, a pool in a small tributary to the main river. The current moved gently here and the water was only shoulder-deep. Or at least, last time she had bathed, it had been shoulder-deep. Today it was only waist-deep. Hekate smiled in surprise at that, and folded her legs to sink down and rinse her hair while her mother collected her discarded tunic and carried it downstream to wash it.

The Underworld's water magic had always shimmered around Hekate in this bath, wrapping her in comfort despite the chill. Today the shimmer became almost an audible song. Tipping her head to watch the reflected torchlight waver on the stalactites, Hekate swished her arm back and forth beneath the water, finding the currents and aligning them into a vibrant thread.

Persephone paused in squeezing out the garments, and lifted her head. "That sounds like bells. Do you hear that?"

"It's the water. I'm making it sing."

Her mother listened with a frown to the chiming jingle. It danced at the edge of hearing, within the chatter of the water. Hekate demonstrated with an extra flourish of her hand, which caused a louder surge of bells.

Her mother looked at her in astonishment. "Have you always been able to do that?"

"No. Not until today." In joyous harmony with the world, Hekate closed her eyes and floated.

WALKING FROM THE bus stop to the university office where she worked, Zoe glanced aside from behind her sunnies at a stretch of grass between buildings. A mother and a little girl peered up into a tree, the mother tugging at a string. Above them, wedged between branches, was their kite, green and frog-shaped with a long yellow tail.

"I know, sweetie, but I don't want to break the string," the mother apologized to the little girl.

Zoe slowed beneath the tree and stretched her fingers out to the trunk.

The tree's magic hummed there, pliable and aloof. She detected the currents of the wind too, gentle today but easy to pull together and direct into a new gust.

With the tiniest expansion of her fingers, she seized the magic and twisted. In one northerly gust, coinciding with a cooperative bend of the twigs, the tree released the kite. The frog swooped out and nose-dived harmlessly to the ground. Mother and child cheered and ran to collect it.

Zoe walked onward, smiling.

HEKATE CLIMBED OUT of her bathing pool and dressed in clean garments. Her parents approached from the direction of the fields, and Persephone handed her a pomegranate. Magic throbbed from within its tough red skin. Hekate knew at once it wasn't a usual fruit, and must be from her mother's orchards.

"If you're going to be grown up and immortal," Persephone said, "then you'd best eat this. It's the quickest way to make your mind catch up." She smiled, though her eyes remained solemn. "I'm happy for all the knowledge you'll gain, but sorry we had to abandon your childhood so quickly."

Excitement pulsed in Hekate's chest. She sliced into the pomegranate with her thumbnail. "But this'll give me memories of lots of other childhoods, won't it?"

"It will," her father said. "Plenty of unpleasant memories too. It's why so few of the others have wanted to eat it."

"They're cowards, then." Hekate ripped free a section of fruit. Seeds fell loose and bounced off her wet bare feet. She shook some of the red gems into her palm, tipped them into her mouth, and chewed and swallowed. "Mm. These are even better than the ones from above ground, Mother."

"Now you can eat them whenever you like, I suppose," Persephone said, still wearing her poignant smile.

"When does it start working?" Hekate asked.

"Probably not until later today, or tonight," her father said. "Not till you sleep again, and dream."

"Oh well. I'll explore other magic today, then." She ate another handful of seeds. "Who else has eaten the pomegranate? Hermes, I know."

"Him, and Aphrodite too," her father said. "Athena and Rhea did as well. Prometheus said he'd like to, but he hasn't come down here to do it so far."

Prometheus and his brother Epimetheus were fairly new immortals, both brave and honest as far as Hekate had seen, but Prometheus did strike her as the more inquisitive of the two, the likelier to seek wisdom such as these seeds could give.

"None of the others yet," Hades added.

"Cowards," Hekate echoed, in playful sing-song.

Her father smiled, transforming his somber bearded face into that of a young man's. "Compared to you, most people are indeed."

Her parents returned to their duties of speaking to the newly dead and bringing messages above ground, and also kept looking into any assistance they could offer against the plague. It still raged up there, killing people, while Hekate roamed safe and alive—in fact immortal now—in the Underworld.

She spent the day exploring the fields and orchards in a strange mix of sadness for the plight of others and delight at her own for-tune. Persephone told her she still shouldn't eat anything growing in the Underworld without asking first, but she was allowed to touch the plants now and see what magic might lie within them, if Hekate could indeed read such things.

She certainly could. Touching all the different fruits and leaves and roots that day was like opening a box of paints in colors she had never seen before. It was too much to comprehend in one day. Mastering all this magic was going to take loads of practice.

But when she reached the graceful tree with the glossy leaves, and closed her hand around one of the orange-skinned fruits, the newly strong blood in her veins pulsed in recognition and harmo-ny. This was it, then: the fruit of immortality. She had suspected it already. Her mother had always been vague about what this tree did, saying it had "a type of healing medicine," but never picking it and using it on patients, as far as Hekate ever saw. She smiled to have discovered the secret, then left the fruits alone and wandered off, Kerberos trotting beside her.

She strolled out of the orchard and onto the path that took her around the hills. When the river's edge came into view at a bend in the path, she stopped.

He was back. Adonis. The beautiful man. Hekate's heart began thumping as if she'd been running, though she stood perfectly still. Didn't poets, and the dead souls too, talk about that kind of reaction when they described love?

Hekate couldn't love Adonis. She barely knew him. But her heart smacked its silly rhythm against her ribs all the same, and she had to acknowledge a certain magic in that reaction too—a magic any human could experience.

She studied the cause of this madness as he stood before her.

As before, Aphrodite had come with him, her arm linked in his. Adonis looked weary, shoulders drooping beneath his dark green cloak. He spoke to the soul of an older woman, and periodi-cally wiped his eyes on a scrap of cloth. Hekate walked forward quietly. As she drew near she saw that not only was he crying, but he was ill. The same sores that had flamed all over her own body yesterday stood out now on his bare arms, and he coughed, and winced when he did so. She winced too—she remembered the knife-like feeling of that cough in her chest.

The older woman, now dead, had fair hair like him, and his serious, splendid eyes. His mother, then, hadn't survived the plague despite Persephone's medicines.

Aphrodite spotted Hekate, and after a squeeze of Adonis' arm, she left him with his mother and walked over to take Hekate's hands in greeting. At her touch, Hekate felt a surge of goodwill—the love and joy Aphrodite spread through the world. Maybe she left envy and longing in her wake rather too often, but her intentions were good; Hekate felt sure of that.

Aphrodite gazed at her. "My dear. You're enchanting—you're tall! Is it even you? How did this happen? Some new magic of your mother's, I assume."

"The immortality fruit," Hekate said. "I would've died last night, they said, so…" She shrugged. At the moment, she really didn't care much about being immortal. But being grown up and shapely—would Adonis notice that about her? Her gaze slipped back to him. No, he wouldn't today, nor for a while yet. He was plunged in grief. Her heart ached for him.

Aphrodite glanced over her shoulder at him, then returned a grave look to Hekate. "Both his parents died. His father three days ago, his mother last night. I promised to bring him to see her."

Hekate looked around. "Where's his father?"

Aphrodite's voice turned acerbic. "The other place, I suspect. He was not a good man."

"Oh." Tartaros' magic was much too strong for Hekate to break; that she knew. She couldn't release a soul locked there, not before the Fates' assigned time. She studied Adonis, who was nodding miserably in response to something his mother was saying, as if trying to be brave for her. He coughed again. "He's ill too," Hekate said.

"Yes. I'm keeping a close eye on him." Worry lowered Aphrodite's dark eyebrows as she surveyed the masses of souls. "I've lost nearly all my mortal friends and servants. Some have died and the others I've let go to be with their ailing families. It's a nightmare up there, Hekate."

"If he gets really ill," Hekate said, "bring him here. Please. Don't let him die."

Aphrodite gave her a complicit nod. "That was my plan. I'll plead for him with your parents."

"I'll give you the fruit myself if I have to. I know which one it is."

Aphrodite smiled, a sparkle of teasing lightening her features. "Why, you *are* growing up, if he's affected you so. Do come and see me when all this horror has passed. We'll discuss men and what to do with them. If your parents don't mind."

"I ate the pomegranate. I'll start remembering things like that soon."

"Ah, but there's an art to love, and not everyone learns it, even in a whole lifetime." Aphrodite turned aside on the path. "I'd better return to him. Don't worry." She sent Hekate a kind smile. "We won't let him die, will we?"

CHAPTER TWENTY-FIVE

So THE PLAGUE ENDED UP OKAY," SOPHIE SAID. "SORT OF."

"To the degree plagues ever do." Adrian opted not to add anything more pessimistic, though he certainly could have.

It was Thursday morning, Thanksgiving, and they were soaring north in the bus toward Carnation. Heavy gray clouds socked in the entire Northwest, and frigid temperatures kept Sophie bundled in the wool blanket. The wind lashed at Adrian through his hat, scarf, coat, and gloves, though the cold wouldn't harm him, of course. Nor would spending a few days and nights mostly away from her, camping out and doing his grim errands.

But he did worry Thanatos might try to pounce on her. Thanksgiving, he gathered, was the kind of occasion when you could count on uni students returning home. Quentin would know where to look, and had already shown up at Sophie's house. So snooping around the area looking for the old villain, fruitless though his search was likely to be, was partly how he planned to spend his weekend. Which sounded dismal.

"Adonis didn't die," Sophie added.

Adrian drew his mind back to the plague that had rendered their daughter immortal. "Yeah, he pulled through." That wasn't how Adonis had received his ticket to immortality. That came later.

"But people started hating us. I mean, some already did, in places. But after the plague…" Sophie clutched the black blanket around herself, frowning at the cracked dashboard. "They blamed us. We were 'the gods.' We must have made it happen."

He nodded. She'd remember the next part any second now.

"Thanatos," she said, right on cue. "That was when they officially formed. Mortality for everyone."

"We didn't take them seriously at first," he said. "So they were bitter and angry, so what? Everyone was. We were doing all we could to help people. It wasn't as if they could kill us."

"Except they could."

"Yeah. They didn't find that out for a while, though. Nor did we."

"Guess I get to that later." Sophie leaned her head back against the seat, eyes closed. Same pose she had taken, and same overwhelmed look she had worn, when he first carted her off to the Underworld. Two months ago now. They'd come so far in just two months.

But undergone such damage too. He thought of Rhea. Of his father, seeing him less and less, puttering around the house, lonely without him. Of Zoe and Tabitha, their lives evolving into madness. Of Niko, whom he'd kicked out, and Freya too. Of Bill Wilkes and his fellow assassin, dead and probably mourned by someone somewhere. Of Sophie's family, worried by the attacks on their daughter and the police's questions. And above all of Sophie herself, trying to stand firm beneath the weight of past lives, Thanatos, a new supernatural boyfriend, and university coursework. She was crumbling. He could see it.

She needed this break, and he'd do whatever he could to keep Quentin away from her during it. Not to mention for the rest of her life. Or forever…

They landed near her family's house, in the marshy forest of the spirit realm. On this cloud-dimmed day, it was dark as twilight under the tangled trees.

He switched her into the living realm. The trees vanished, but the clouds and swampy ground remained.

"Try not to obsess about Thanatos," he told her. "Not their origins and not what they're up to these days, either. Just for a few days, forget them if you can. Enjoy your family. Think about nice things."

"I'll try." She kept the stoic mask on. Weariness and exams had put shadows under her eyes and given a paler cast to her skin.

"Will you be seeing Tabitha?" he asked.

"Probably. Though I wouldn't be surprised if she's got some parties lined up to jet off to."

"Well, if you do talk to her, be careful about discussing things where people can hear you."

Sophie nodded.

They kissed goodbye. She turned toward the farmhouse. He watched her walk off, and wished with all his soul that, since he couldn't give her a blue orange yet, he could at least give her happiness and peace. Just a few days' worth, enough so she could rest.

Perhaps there was a spell for that.

Hmm.

Once she was indoors, he hopped back into the spirit realm and texted Zoe. *Can you do magic to give Sophie a nice weekend?*

It was still five in the morning in New Zealand, so Zoe would be asleep, and he wouldn't get an answer for a while. He put away his phone.

Kiri barreled over to him, splashing mud. He crouched to pick dead leaves off her fur, and began plotting where to look for Quentin first.

A couple of hours later, as he wandered around the town of Carnation, failing to find anyone suspicious-looking, Zoe texted him back.

You mean like altering her mood? Not cool, without her consent.

Suppose not, he responded. *How about protection then? Is that ok?*

She called him.

"Hey," she said. "Protection's all right, but what do you need it for? What's up?"

It started raining. He took shelter under the faded wooden eaves outside a grocery store. "The usual. Thanatos. She's visiting home for a few days, and they might try to attack. I don't know, I'm being paranoid."

"A spell would be hard from over here. Where is she? At her parents' house, you said?"

"Yeah. Carnation. Little town east of Seattle."

"Seattle." Zoe sounded more interested now. "Well. I could take a sick day and come over."

He lifted an eyebrow, suspecting Tabitha's presence in Seattle had something to do with that proposal. But if it meant magical protection for Sophie, so be it. "Cheers."

"See you in a few hours. I'll track you down."

THE FARMHOUSE'S OVEN radiated comfortable heat throughout the kitchen. The smell of roasted turkey mingled with the scent of the spiced cranberry sauce Sophie stirred on the stovetop. Sophie's mom was manning the stand with their high school employee and both dogs (and a baseball bat), keeping the business open a few extra hours so people could buy their last-minute apples and potatoes.

Sophie's dad wore a red apron and sang along with the Perry Como tunes blasting from the speakers on the counter while he chopped potatoes. Sophie and Liam teased him and each other, and debated what kind of pie was the ultimate best and which Christmas movies the absolute lamest.

In short, she felt surprisingly good. She'd been here only a few hours, but home was already working its restorative magic.

So now, of course, she missed Adrian and felt bad that he was wandering around outdoors in the cold while she was preparing a feast in a cozy house. She'd have to sneak him out some pie and turkey later. And as many hot water bottles as she could find.

She went to the sink to fetch a paper towel, and wiped the steam off the window to peer outside. She stopped, squinted, then whipped out her phone.

CHAPTER TWENTY-SIX

ADRIAN'S PHONE BUZZED. HE WIPED THE SALT OFF HIS HANDS AND read the text.

What are you doing creeping around in the field? And who's with you?

"Ah, she's spotted us," he told Zoe.

He waved at the house, and saw an answering blur of movement in the ground floor window.

Zoe stayed crouched in the tall grass, pouring out the line of sea salt from the paper bag she held. "Well, you insisted in doing this in broad daylight. Say hi to her for me."

Zoe's putting a protection spell around your house so Thanatos won't ruin your Thanksgiving, he responded to Sophie. *She says hi.*

Aww. Thanks! Tell her hi.

Will do. He slid his phone back into his pocket. "She says hello." He followed Zoe down the line of salt that wound its way through the mud and high grass. "What if a dog digs up the salt line or something? Does that break the spell?"

"Nah. I used ordinary Earth magic for most of it, and some of their rain magic too since they've got so much of it here. The salt only shores it up a bit."

"Okay." She used to talk like this as Hekate. It made just as little sense to him then.

She edged along, crouching crabwise, pouring salt. The wind messed up her short hair, and water dripped on her blue parka from the tall wet grass. Zoe grimaced up at the slate-gray sky. "Grim here, isn't it?"

"In autumn, yeah. Or winter. Sophie says November here counts as winter. So this'll protect them?"

"Well…" Zoe turned the corner behind the fence, and kept pouring out the salt. "It works best against malicious magic, and as far as we've heard, Thanatos is dumb as a box of hammers when it comes to magic. But they do use brute force, which sometimes bangs its way through. As brute force does."

"Couldn't you—I don't know, send a spell to confuse Quentin a while? Or make her drive off a cliff?" Adrian muttered the latter suggestion, but Zoe heard it and shot a warning look at him.

"We don't harm others with magic, Ade. Bounces back on us threefold."

"But she deserves it! Come on. Surely the universe understands that."

"It does, and that's what Tartaros is for. Also law enforcement. But magic to protect a loved one, that's all right. Your first instinct was the best." Zoe emptied out the salt bag, joining the line to its starting point. She stood and squinted at the farmhouse. "There. This'll help, I think. Feels good. "

They had managed to draw the line all round the property, mostly in the field. The section in front of the produce stand had been the trickiest. Adrian had to pretend to be browsing pumpkins while Zoe snuck past pouring out salt along the curb. As far as he could tell, Sophie's mum hadn't noticed, being busy talking to other customers.

"Thanks, Z," he said. "Really. Coming all this way."

"No worries. Think I'll visit Seattle while I'm over here."

"Say hi to Tab for me," he teased, slightly accusatory.

She hugged him with a calm smile. "Will do."

I'M OFF TO look round some more, Adrian texted Sophie. See if I can turn up anyone evil.

Ok. Be careful! Sophie answered. I'll save you some food tonight.

She peeked out the living room window at him. He had worked his way around to the other side of the house in his mysterious spell-casting with Zoe, who had left. Adrian looked in Sophie's direction, and she waved at him.

He waved back and picked his way through the field toward the highway.

"Who you waving at?" Her dad was right behind her all of a sudden.

She tried not to jump noticeably, though adrenaline jolted through her. "A friend was walking by."

Her dad squinted after Adrian. "Isn't that the guy who gave you a ride that time?"

"Yeah. David. This time too." She tried to sound offhand, pretending to read a text.

"Could've invited him in. We have punch and pumpkin bread." Her father sounded indignant. Inviting in every friend you could shout at from the front porch on Thanksgiving to partake of cranberry punch and pumpkin bread was practically a legal requirement in his eyes.

"That's okay. He's got plans." She slipped past him toward the kitchen. "Oops, I better turn off the heat under the sauce."

The afternoon consisted of a parade of visitors, friends of her parents or of Liam's. Soon Tabitha arrived too, bringing Zoe, to Sophie's surprise.

"Friend of mine. She's from New Zealand," Tabitha said, introducing her to Sophie's dad.

"Hi, nice to meet you." Zoe shook hands with him, and accepted a cup of punch.

Sophie widened her eyes in a warning flash at Tabitha. Sophie's dad was already suspicious about anything to do with New Zealand thanks to that tip-off of Quentin's, which apparently Tab had forgotten. But Terry was smiling and exchanging small talk with Zoe, and before long he stepped aside to answer the door for another visitor.

Sophie herded Tab and Zoe into the hot kitchen, where they

leaned on the counters. Food, plates, and napkins covered the table and every other surface in preparation for dinner.

"She came to see me, since she was up here doing magic for you," Tab said with a grin.

"Shh!" Sophie glanced toward the living room. "Don't talk about magic. But thank you, Zoe, really."

"My pleasure," Zoe said. "Mind you, it isn't bulletproof, but it should help."

"Are we talking actual bullets?" Sophie asked anxiously.

"Well. Just an expression, but I guess in the case of some people, yeah." Frowning, Zoe sipped her punch.

Sophie exhaled a long breath. She'd been instructed not to think about Thanatos. Holiday; enjoy it. Okay.

She asked Tabitha how her weekend was going. Despite being an Internet celebrity now, it turned out Tab was still having Thanksgiving dinner in Carnation with her mom.

"Then my dad tomorrow," she said, rolling her eyes. Splitting Thanksgiving in two would indeed suck, Sophie reflected. Such was the toll of divorce.

She thought of her own folks, who were at least sparing Sophie and Liam that fate by allowing an open relationship. Not that Sophie wanted to think about that a second longer than she had to.

"Are you staying for dinner?" Sophie asked Zoe. "You're welcome to, if you like." It made her nervous, anticipating a meal full of her parents grilling Zoe about New Zealand, but the invitation was the least she could extend.

Zoe glanced at Tabitha, whose sleeve pressed against hers. "I'm going along to her house for it."

"Oh good!" Sophie said, relieved. "That'll be nice."

Tab nudged Zoe's hiking boot with her own knee-high, three-inch-heeled leather boot. "Thank God. Buffer zone between me and Mom and awkward silence."

Sophie watched the nudges, the flashed intimate smiles, and wondered how far this little friendship had gotten. Now she had loyalties on both sides, and didn't wish for either one to break the other's heart.

Tab turned to Sophie. "Are you saving food for Adrian?"

"Shh!" Sophie hissed.

"Don't say the A word," Zoe reminded Tabitha, grinning.

"Yes I am, but shush," Sophie said.

"I need to meet him," Tabitha said. "I've only seen photos. He looks really cute." Tabitha picked up a second slice of pumpkin bread and bit into it.

"We could go find him," Zoe suggested. "Want to?"

Tabitha looked at the clock on the microwave and sighed. "Can't now. We better get to my mom's house."

They hugged Sophie and thanked Terry for the punch and pumpkin bread, and trotted down the front steps into the chilly air.

"New Zealand." Terry watched them go. "That's odd."

"I know, right?" Sophie turned to the kitchen again. "Almost dinner. Let's clean up the table."

"So THIS IS interesting," Landon said.

"What's that, dear?" Betty Quentin looked up from the newspaper.

"Krystal and I have been searching through people Sophie and Adrian know, on social networks and stuff, to see if there are any leads to other unnaturals. Krystal just sent me a bunch of links. Looks like Sophie's best friend from high school, one Tabitha Lofgren, is suddenly hanging out with celebrities and showing up at expensive parties. Maybe hosting them in some way—that isn't clear."

"Money and power. Definite warning signs. Did she have money before?"

"I don't know, but I doubt it. She was from that same little town as Sophie, which doesn't look exactly rich."

Betty folded the newspaper up and regarded him. "And is she near Sophie? Protecting her, maybe?"

"Doesn't look like it. She's at school in Seattle now, and these parties are all over the country. L.A., New York, San Francisco. A lot of travel."

"Travel's easy if you have their forms of transportation."

Landon looked dubiously at her. "Ghost horses?"

"I know, it's crazy. But Sanjay said so, and the old records did too, and obviously they have some way to move around fast in that other realm." Betty set aside the newspaper and heaved herself out of the chair to prepare turkey sandwiches for their low-key Thanksgiving dinner. "Well. Perhaps we can find someone in Seattle willing to get a closer encounter with this Tabitha."

"See if she's immortal?"

"If she is, we'd best know sooner rather than later."

ADRIAN HAD FOUND nothing all day, zero. He hoped that meant Thanatos wasn't in town, rather than meaning he'd managed to miss them. Of Carnation's small stock of cafes and stores, most were closed due to the holiday, so he had to remain outdoors in the near-freezing air and intermittent drizzle.

At dinnertime he checked in once more with Sophie, then admitted defeat and flew back to the Airstream in Oregon to warm up with a hot shower and a meal. Then, unable to bear the idea of sleeping a whole state away from her when he didn't have to, even with the protection spell in place, he returned with all his warmest camping gear and parked the bus in the spirit realm outside her house.

In the back of the bus he set up the tent on top of a thick blanket—warmer and drier than the ground—and got inside it with a lantern. He wrapped Kiri up with him in a down-filled sleeping bag and read a book until Sophie texted him at 11:00 p.m.

Got your food. Come to the side door.

When he tiptoed up to the house, all was silent within, and without too. Only an occasional car swooshed past on the highway.

Sophie opened the door and stuck her head out. Adrian climbed the two wooden steps to meet her. She slipped out, shut the door quietly behind her, and handed him a heavy paper plate covered with foil. The food's warmth radiated through the bottom into his palm as he took it.

"Thanks," he whispered. "You didn't have to. I've got food."

"Yeah, but you have to taste my pie."

It was asking too much to resist that double entendre. He murmured, "Yes, I do," and leaned in for a deep kiss. She caught his face in both hands and indulged him. Her spice-flavored tongue fenced with his until he had to pause to catch his breath.

A scrabble of toenails rattled inside the house, and a small dog started barking furiously. Its head popped into view over and over in the door's window.

Sophie sighed. "That's Pumpkin. Pumpkin, *no!*" She pushed Adrian toward the stairs. "You better go."

"But..."

"I can't tonight. Tomorrow. Go!"

He obeyed, stepped up to kiss her once more, then jumped off the stairs. He dived into the spirit realm in mid-air before landing on his feet on the wet ground, carefully cradling the plate so the food wouldn't get smashed.

Back in the bus, tucked under half a dozen blankets plus the sleeping bag, he texted her.

You like those memories sometimes, so...there's one from about a year after the plague. We were at Zeus & Hera's for a feast. Hekate didn't come. She was with Demeter that night. At the table you put some olive oil in your hand and...well, try to remember. See you tomorrow. ;)

Oh reeeally? she answered in a few minutes. *Ok, off to look for some olive oil in my dreams. Night. ;)*

Enjoy. And that, he thought, snuggling down with a smile, was as close to sexting as he dared get for right now.

But maybe he'd go further, depending how she liked that memory.

CHAPTER TWENTY-SEVEN

DAMN, ADRIAN, SOPHIE TEXTED HIM THE NEXT MORNING. *GOOD choice.*

She had found the memory easily enough in her dreams, and, as she told him in their ensuing flirtatious text conversation, it kept her volcanically warm all night.

She wandered through her lazy post-Thanksgiving Friday. She munched leftovers, helped her mom at the produce stand, did homework, and napped on the sofa while her dad watched football. But she kept replaying the hot evening in ancient Greece in her mind. It was more than a little distracting and slowed her studying down to a crawl.

When she was with Adrian, she missed home. At home, she wanted Adrian. The flowers were always prettier on the other side of the fence. Was that what it meant to be an adult and move out of the house? You had to slice your heart in half and place it in two receptacles that couldn't be joined? Probably. She could see how that'd be a normal enough situation for anyone. Maybe that's what the story of Persephone's kidnapping and half-a-year arrangement with Hades meant to people long ago: in part, it simply reflected the sadness of leaving your parents and getting married.

But for the record, that Hades/Persephone marriage was still in excellent shape thirteen years after their daughter was born, if their sex life was any indication.

As Adrian had recounted, Persephone and Hades had attended a feast at Zeus and Hera's palace, while Hekate, now thirteen though still looking at least eighteen, spent the night with her grandmother. Both Hekate and Demeter disliked the grandstanding of Hera and Zeus' parties, and were happy to give Persephone and Hades a night out.

The palace overflowed with treats and the happy chatter of the immortals and their chosen guests. The plague was finally gone, several months behind by now, and after a period of exhausted quiet, everyone was reviving to new life. While their friends conversed around the table after the meal, in the light of oil lamps reflected in the jeweled metal bowls and plates, Persephone found herself entertaining the notion of showing Hades how glad she was for his company. She tipped olive oil into her hand from a small bowl, and slid her hand up Hades' thigh, beneath his tunic, under cover of the tabletop. No one else even noticed, as far as she could tell—except perhaps Hermes, who at one point gave them a particularly knowing smirk from farther down the table.

The situation, to sum it up, had escalated deliciously all evening and culminated in a dark glade in the spirit realm as soon as they left the feast.

With that scene in Sophie's mind, by bedtime on Friday she felt she was going to spontaneously combust if she didn't see Adrian soon.

Finally her parents and Liam went to bed. The house fell quiet. Sophie coaxed Rosie and Pumpkin into the study on the first floor, where their cedar-stuffed dog beds lay, and shut the door so they wouldn't bark if she snuck someone into the house.

She texted Adrian around midnight: *Everyone's asleep. Think you can come visit?*

Sure, he answered in a minute. *Side door?*

Yep. See you.

When he arrived, she was ready by the door, shivering and barefoot. She let him in. Tonight she wore her sexy robe rather than her everyday terrycloth. The sexy one was made of dark red silk with a pattern of roses, and stopped at mid-thigh. Beneath it she wore only a pair of cream-colored silk panties. Thus the shivers. But she was sure to warm up soon, with what she had planned.

Her heart thudded as Adrian's gaze traveled from the robe to her bare legs and back up again. His expression morphed into gratified surprise. "Hey." He kissed her, his lips chilled by the November air. He stroked her waist, his hands equally cold even through the silk. Luckily he'd be warming up before long too.

"How was your day?" She snuggled up against him. "Said in your texts you got some errands done."

"Yeah, the usual Underworld stuff. Looked some more for Thanatos; couldn't find anyone. Nothing to report really."

"Ah well. Come on up."

They tiptoed upstairs and shut themselves into her bedroom. She leaned back against the closed door, pulling him to her in a longer, wetter kiss.

He chuckled. "Miss me?"

"Mm," she agreed. "I've been enjoying that memory."

He sucked in his breath, and released it in a warm rush against her neck. "Oh, good." He kissed her throat. "Hoped you might." His body pressed against her, legs to shoulders.

"Olive oil. Naughty."

"You kept rubbing and teasing me whenever you had the chance, working me up…" He untied the knot on her robe and let it fall open. When he slid his hands inside it, she found they were indeed warmer now.

She set her feet farther apart to brace her melting weight while he caressed her. "You kept whispering in my ear what you were going to do to me later," she said.

He touched his nose to hers, grinning. "Filthy mouth I had on me back then."

"I liked it."

"I remember you did." He sank, kissing her breasts and then her navel. "That's not all my mouth can do, you know." Within seconds he'd whisked the silk panties off.

She stepped out of them and trampled them under one foot, and closed her eyes, leaning her head back against the door.

He lifted her smoothly, not even disengaging his mouth as he carried her the few steps to her bed. This, she thought in bliss, was why it rocked to have an immortal lover. He could lift you like a paper plate, support your back in one hand and your rear in the other, all with no effort and while keeping his mouth wonderfully, sublimely busy.

He laid her on the bed and paused a moment to take off his warm hat and boots. Then, still in his coat and all the rest of his clothes, he knelt over her on the mattress, stretched one hand up to her breasts and spread her thighs with the other, and got back to work.

She undulated against his tongue, trying not to make a sound, trying to make it last. But the memory had wound her up so fully that soon she was gripping his shoulders and riding out the waves that overtook her. His mouth and fingers stayed with her until she settled to a stop—and that mouth and those fingers did technically count as magic, or at least should, she thought in satisfaction.

He rose on his knees, grinning, and wriggled out of his coat. "I was just getting warmed up." He dropped his coat on the rug, and crawled to lie on top of her in his hoodie and jeans and socks.

"Stay warmed up. Your turn." She pushed at his chest to move him onto his back, and climbed on top of him, straddling him in nothing but the open robe while she unfastened his belt buckle and jeans.

His gaze drank in the sight, traveling up and down her. He folded his arm behind his head. "Bloody hell, could anything be as hot as you?"

She smiled. "You are. And were, in those memories." She unzipped his sweatshirt and pushed up his T-shirt.

He pulled both shirts off and lay back, naked from thighs up. "I am ever so glad I fed you that pomegranate."

"The dreams must have tormented you, before you came and fetched me." She ran her fingertip down the length of him, enjoying how it made him twitch.

"Very much. There were, um, things I had to take care of basically every morning when I woke up. If the dreams hadn't done it for me."

"Mm. I would've resorted to that tonight too, if you weren't coming to see me."

He breathed faster as she played with him. "You'll have to show me that sometime."

"In this life, at least. Obviously I have before." They exchanged intimate smiles. She reached for the pump bottle of hand lotion on her nightstand. "This may not be olive oil, but…"

The dollop of lotion on her hand warmed quickly as she wrapped it around him. Adrian's sudden gasp and groan was loud enough that she leaned down and clapped her other hand onto his mouth.

"Shh," she reminded him.

He nodded, eyes blazing in desire.

She settled back, freeing his mouth, and kept stroking him. Lotion squished up between her fingers; she'd perhaps used too much, but he didn't seem to mind. Quite the opposite.

"Thank you," he whispered. He eyes fell closed as he rocked up into her touch. "Oh, thank you…thank…" Then he couldn't speak anymore, and jolted hard enough that the old iron bed frame creaked in protest.

After cleaning off with a hand towel she'd stashed beside the bed, they stretched out in a tight hug on the mattress and pulled up the comforter. They stroked each other's skin in sleepiness and arousal and love.

"You're wrong, you know," she murmured.

"Hmm?"

"It wasn't filthy, what you said to me. It was lovely."

He slid his lips back and forth against hers. "Agreed."

They engaged in an increasingly lazy, heavy string of kisses, then she laid her head on that gorgeous warm place where his neck, shoulder, and chest met, and closed her eyes. Just for a minute, she thought. It'd be nice to rest together like this before he had to leave, just for a bit.

CHAPTER TWENTY-EIGHT

A SCRAPE OF FURNITURE BEING MOVED WOKE ADRIAN. HE BLINKED at the room in confusion—ah right, Sophie's house—then his heart jumped nearly out of his body in terror.

Her father was in the room. Barely a meter away, glaring straight into Adrian's eyes. Terry had pulled out the wooden chair by her desk—probably the sound Adrian heard—and was sitting in it with his feet planted wide and a baseball bat across his knees. His face was arranged in a look exactly as murderous as you'd expect on someone who finds a near-stranger in bed with his teenage daughter.

Shit.

Adrian glanced at the alarm clock. 1:42 a.m. He considered diving directly into the spirit realm. But disappearing before Terry's eyes wasn't the best idea, nor would it be kind to leave Sophie to face the consequences alone.

Adrian attempted polite reparations, staying where he was, bare-chested with Sophie asleep on his shoulder. "H-hi," he stammered. "I'm David."

"I remember. Or is your name Adrian?"

Fuck.

To gain time, Adrian frowned as if confused, and gently moved Sophie aside so he could sit up. She stirred, starting to awaken. "I'm sorry," Adrian said to Terry, surreptitiously fastening up his jeans under the blanket. "It was late, and Sophie invited me up… but um, I should go. Soph? Wake up, I've got to go."

"You stay right there," Terry said. "The police are on their way and you can tell all your interesting stories to them."

Now the swear words piled on in several languages in his mind. Adrian scrambled for a response. "That's—no, I promise there's no need..." He still had no shirt on, and he quickly pulled the blanket up to Sophie's shoulders so her open robe wouldn't show. As if it wasn't totally obvious what they'd been up to.

Sophie awakened fully and blinked up at him. Then her gaze shot across the room and she gasped. She clutched her robe shut, rising up on her elbow. "Dad. What are you doing?"

"I got up for the bathroom," Terry said, "and Rosie was downstairs whining. I let her out of the study—thought it was pretty weird how the door was closed there—and she came running straight up and started sniffing at your door. So of course I opened it to make sure nothing was on fire. And look what I found."

"Okay, I'm sorry, it was late. You guys were asleep. Dad, you remember David."

Adrian was impressed. Sophie sounded shaken but patient, far more convincing with her lies than he usually was.

However, her dad wasn't buying it. "Yeah, if that's his name. I'm thinking maybe it's Adrian. And that he's from New Zealand. Got any ID on you that says different, son?"

Adrian swallowed against his dry throat. "Not on me, no." Which was true. He was smart enough not to carry incriminating documentation. But maybe a fake ID would've been smarter. Crap, why hadn't he got Niko to do that for him? Why had he thrown someone useful like Niko out of his life?

"This is ridiculous," Sophie said.

"Is it? I heard Tab ask you about 'Adrian' earlier. And sure, it says 'David' on your texts, but you do call him 'Adrian' in at least one of those."

"You looked at my texts?"

"When you were asleep on the couch."

"Dad!"

"I am not proud of it. But maybe someday you'll have kids, and someone will be breaking into their dorm room and blowing up grenades near them and worrying you sick. And other people will be giving you weird hints about what your kid's up to and who they're seeing, and then I'll ask you what you would've done."

"I'm eighteen." Her voice seethed with outrage. "You don't get to act this way."

"I find someone in my house who's suspected of being in the country illegally, not to mention being connected with the people who attacked you, and I don't get to call the police? Gosh, here's me thinking I could. So I did. They're coming now, and if this guy's clear and innocent, fine. My apologies and I owe him a real nice dinner."

Sophie sat up straight. "You did not call the police."

"See that?" Terry gestured to the window, where blue and red lights flashed, brightening and moving nearer. "Guess they're here. I told them I unlocked the front door, so they'll be right up."

"You do not know what you're doing." Sophie furiously tied the robe around herself, and shoved the blanket off her legs.

Adrian took the opportunity to put on his T-shirt and sweat-shirt, and leaned down to put his boots on too.

"Tell them you made a mistake, and send them away," Sophie hissed at her father.

"You are acting real suspicious, girl," Terry said. "I don't want to make them interrogate you too, but if it's for your own good, I will."

"Do you want me to *ever* come back here again?" she said.

"Oh ho, being like that now, are we?"

The front door opened downstairs. "Police. We're coming up," a man called, sounding oddly mild.

Terry rose and leaned out the bedroom door to beckon to them. "Hey, Roger. Up here."

Small town, Adrian thought fleetingly. First-name basis with the police. He looked at Sophie.

"Escape. Switch realms," she whispered, in the Underworld tongue.

He nodded and grabbed his coat. She threw his hat to him. Just as Terry turned around again, Adrian caught the hat and leaped into the spirit world.

The house disappeared. Darkness surrounded him, punctuated by the gibbous moon, which he had a split second to glimpse before he plummeted to the ground from the height of the second floor. His legs and arms smacked against tree branches on the way, knocking him one direction and another. With a bone-jolting thud, he landed on his side on the muddy forest floor.

Thank goodness for immortality, he thought, grunting and pulling himself to a sitting position against the tree's trunk. He rested and breathed deeply a minute, wincing at his scratches and bruises, waiting as the pain gradually faded.

He whistled for Kiri. She barked from not far off. The tread of her paws bounded through the forest toward him.

"Well." He caught the sides of her head and let her lick his nose. "That was rather an awkward date." He sighed as Kiri sat beside him. Her fur warmed his arm. "Poor Sophie. What have I left her in the middle of?"

SOPHIE'S DAD STOOD gaping at the space where Adrian had stood a moment earlier. "Where'd he go?"

"He left," Sophie said.

Two police officers entered the room, both male, one young and stout, one middle-aged and thin.

"Evening," the middle-aged one said. His name was Roger. Sophie's dad knew him in high school, and still attended Seahawks games with him. Roger had been eating pumpkin bread in the living room at one point yesterday. "Terry tells me you've got an unexpected guest." Roger glanced around the room, looking puzzled at not finding any such person.

"He wasn't unexpected. I invited him." Sophie felt less feisty and more cowed now. She didn't like defying the law any more than Adrian did.

Terry marched forward, dropped to his knees, and looked under Sophie's bed. He climbed to his feet, glowering. "He was right here. Then he disappeared like some Vegas magician."

"Closet maybe?" The younger cop wandered over to Sophie's half-open closet door. "Okay if I look in here?"

"Yes," Sophie said.

"Yes." Terry stormed over and opened the closet all the way.

The police officer moved aside a few of Sophie's hanging clothes with his flashlight, then shrugged at Roger.

"He left a few minutes ago," Sophie said. "Look around if you want, but he's not here."

Her dad pointed at her. "That is not true. He was here *seconds* before you guys came in."

"You know, Terry, it's late." Roger's voice was placating. "It's easy to get confused, drift off for a minute. Make a mistake."

"Damn it, that is not what happened!" Terry glared at Sophie. "Let's ask her. Who is he, then, huh?"

She curled her hand tight in the top of the robe, holding it shut, feeling exposed with the cool air on her legs. "You know his name is David. You've met him."

"Your dad was thinking he might be someone who's not supposed to be in the country?" Roger still sounded pleasant and kind, like always.

"Dad's mixed up. He didn't like finding me asleep with... someone he didn't know was here." Sophie's face burned with shame. "But that's for him and me to talk about. There was no need to call the police."

The younger cop peered out the window, checked its latch and screen, and shone his flashlight around outside. Evidently he saw nothing worth mentioning, since he looked at Roger and shrugged again.

Roger looked at Terry. "I got to say, I think she's right."

"I'm telling you, Roger, you did not see—"

"Terry, I came here as a friend, because I trust you. She had someone over when you didn't want her to, okay, I get that. But if I can't find him, I can't ask him who he is or what he's up to. And if she says she invited him, and he wasn't breaking in or hurting anybody, there's really not a lot I can do. She's eighteen, man. It's not a crime."

"What if he's an illegal immigrant?" Terry said. "Or—or illegal tourist, or whatever the term is?"

"Without knowing *who* he is, I can hardly prove anything like that. Besides, that's more an issue for the feds. I can give you a number to call if you find any proof."

Isabel, Sophie's mother, stepped into the doorway, in her pale blue nightgown that covered her from shoulders to ankles. She squinted in disbelief at the tableau before her. "What's going on?"

"Nothing," Sophie told her emphatically.

"Sophie's dating Houdini," Terry said to her. "Did you know that?" He swung back to face the cops. "Go look for him. I'm telling you, he could not be far."

"And I'm telling you," Sophie said, "he's gone, and there's no need to look."

Roger exchanged a glance with the other officer, then looked at Terry and spread his hands in helplessness. "It's true what she says. I don't really have much reason to go after the guy here."

"Dad, let them go home," Sophie said. "We'll talk about this."

"I think that's the best idea," Roger agreed.

Her dad curled up his fists and hunched his shoulders, drawing in a long breath. Finally he expelled it. "Fine. Yes, we are going to talk, Sophia. And I will be calling you again if I see the need," he added to Roger.

"Great, fine," Roger said mildly. "That's what we're here for."

Terry tromped downstairs with the two policemen. Sophie looked in apologetic weariness at her mother, who came forward and draped her arm around her. "What's all this about?" Isabel asked.

"David came to see me. Dad found us asleep."

"I see. And he took that tip-off from the crazy woman a little too seriously?"

"Sort of. I'll explain in a minute." Sophie leaned in gratitude against her mother, then edged away to put on warmer pajamas, flannel with full-length pants and sleeves. Her mother went out into the hall to peer down after the police. Sophie tossed the sexy robe into the laundry hamper, along with—furtively—the hand towel she and Adrian had dropped on the floor.

Having changed, she came out of the room, and she and her mother crept down the stairs. No sound came from Liam's room, opposite Sophie's. He evidently still slept the sleep of the pre-adolescent, and had missed all the excitement, or at least the opening act of it.

The police had left. Terry stood with his arms folded in the kitchen, facing the range. The hood light above the stove glowed in the dark room.

"So where'd you hide him?" Terry asked without turning. "How'd you do that? Did my ancient eyes in fact deceive me?"

"No. He isn't here anymore." Sophie pulled out a kitchen chair, with dented chrome legs and cracked turquoise vinyl cushions. She sat in it and folded her hands on the table. Her mother did the same.

Sophie considered, for the last time, prolonging the cover story. But now it collapsed in her mind like a tower of cards every time she constructed it. The disappearance witnessed by her father, the incidents of people attacking her, Quentin's tip-off, the mystery of this guy she was dating...her parents weren't going to be fobbed off with a simple lie this time.

"How'd he disappear, then?" Terry asked. "*Is* he some kind of Vegas magician?"

"Why do you keep saying he disappeared?" Isabel asked.

Terry turned around. "Because he did! There one second, gone the next. Right before my eyes. I do not know what the hell I saw up there, but it was weird."

"He's not a Vegas magician," Sophie said. "He's...a Greek god. Kind of."

Terry snorted. "Of course."

Sophie took her phone from the pocket of her pajama shirt. "I'll have him come back and show you. That's easiest."

Time to bring my parents in on it, I think, she texted. *Can you come back and prove it so I don't sound crazy?*

"What do you mean, a Greek god?" Isabel asked.

"He has…abilities. And he's kind of immortal. That's why the cult leader woman and her friends are after him."

"Kind of immortal?" Terry said. "Oh, I am *not* listening to this."

"You saw him disappear. What's your explanation?" Sophie asked.

"I—" Terry tossed his hands in the air in surrender, then dropped them, and pulled out a chair. He plunked down into it.

A text bounced in from Adrian. *Sigh. Suppose you're right, if they'll be calling the police on us otherwise. OK, see you soon.*

"He's coming," Sophie said.

"So that woman who warned me about him…" Terry said.

"Betty Quentin."

"She thinks he's immortal, too? And that's why she's going after you? Because you're dating him?"

Sophie nodded.

"Honey," her mother said, "someone who claims to be immortal, and who's got people trying to kill him…look, he seemed nice, but that doesn't sound like the kind of person you should be seeing."

"I am wondering about the mental health issues here," her dad agreed.

Sophie shrugged, tired. They'd see soon enough.

The knock sounded softly on the side door. Sophie got up and let Adrian in. She peeled a dead leaf from his coat collar, and frowned at the mud smeared on his jeans. "What happened to you?"

"I do not recommend switching realms from anything higher than ground floor." He sounded tired too. His gaze slid to her parents, who watched them from the kitchen table.

Terry glowered, but said nothing.

Rosie and Pumpkin scampered in from the study, yipping in excitement. Adrian crouched to let them smell his hands and clothes. They quieted down, intent on sniffing, fascinated by the scents of Kiri and whatever else they picked up on him. He stroked their heads and said hello to them. They wagged. Rosie licked his hand.

Sophie smiled. Her dad always said dogs knew how to recognize good people.

Indeed, Terry glowered even harder at this show of affection from his faithful animals toward the intruder.

Isabel rose. "Come sit down. Is it…David? I'm sorry, I'm confused."

They approached the table. Adrian questioned Sophie with a look.

"No, it's Adrian," Sophie said.

"Adrian Watts, from New Zealand," Terry guessed.

Adrian nodded, flashing a glance from one parent to the other. "Wellington, specifically." Then he shut his mouth and looked again at Sophie for direction.

"Actually," Sophie said, "don't sit. Come outside."

"Why?" Terry said.

"This is the kind of thing you have to show someone. Telling doesn't cut it."

"Going to *show* us how you're immortal?" Terry said, deeply skeptical.

"He's going to show you how he disappeared," Sophie said.

"Fine." Isabel came around the table. "I'm curious. May I get a coat?"

"Sure. Of course," Adrian murmured.

Terry grumbled, but he got up too and fetched his coat.

They shut the dogs inside the study, with orders to stay quiet, and tromped out into the gravel driveway. The motion detector light went on, casting its bright glare across the front and side of the house. Frost glittered on the herb garden.

"Right over here's good." Adrian led them to a spot near the garden hose. "No trees in the way."

"Trees?" Isabel glanced around.

"You'll see," Sophie said.

"So, um, I suppose I'll go alone first, to demonstrate." Adrian backed up a step, awash in the security light. Then he vanished in a puff of air.

Isabel sucked in her breath with a squeak.

"That." Terry pointed at where he'd been. "That is what I'm talking about."

Adrian reappeared in the same spot, startling them anew.

"Okay, Mr. Watts, you got my attention," Terry said. "How do you do that?"

"I guess now I bring you along." Adrian glanced at Sophie.

"Can you even take three at once?" she asked.

"Well. Bit awkward, but, yeah. Here. Do kind of a group hug, you three."

Sophie nodded to her parents, and drew them in so they both hugged her.

"Now this is ridiculous," Terry said. "What kind of drugs are we talking about here, honey?"

"Just hold still please." Adrian stepped up and got his arms most of the way around the huddled group. Then with that familiar wobble and tug, the world darkened and the ground shifted, and he released them. "Perfect. There we are."

Sophie's parents released their hold on her. They stepped back, turning to stare at the dark forest and patches of meadow.

"Where the hell...?" murmured Terry.

It was so dark here after the glare of the security light that Sophie could only see her parents as black silhouettes. Stars twinkled overhead; the clouds had cleared. Night insects and animals clucked and chirped their eerie sounds all around.

"How did you do that?" Isabel asked in a hushed voice. "Where are we?"

Sophie turned her head toward Adrian, whose arm still brushed against hers. "You want to take this one?"

CHAPTER TWENTY-NINE

T HEY SAT UNEVENLY ARRANGED AROUND THE RECTANGULAR kitchen table. Sophie and Adrian stayed close together near the two sides of one corner, Terry dominated one long side, and Isabel the other end.

Adrian still felt Terry was likelier to kill him tonight than Quentin was, from the resentful glances he kept flinging. But at least now Terry and Isabel were starting to believe him.

They covered all the necessary territory, Sophie patiently supporting him and sharing in the explanations. His disability in childhood, his mum's death, his first encounter with Rhea and the Underworld, his introduction to the past and its assemblage of Mediterranean immortals, his bringing Sophie into it, Thanatos and the truth surrounding the attacks, and the complications of Sophie not being able to become immortal yet because Zoe and Tabitha had eaten the last ripe fruit. It also explained why Tabitha kept cheerfully but oddly showing up just to "see how they were doing"—not that Tab's efforts were keeping Quentin from coming round on other days with her own check-ins.

The "bringing Sophie into it" part was what drew the most resentment from her parents, of course—notably her dad. Her mum tempered her worry with fascination, and asked more questions than Terry did.

They wanted proof, as any sane people would. Switching realms impressed them, certainly, as did the ghost horses. Adrian drove the bus away from them and back again to demonstrate its high speed, but Terry and Isabel refused to get in and experience it. Still, those didn't absolutely prove anything about past lives, immortality, or the Underworld. Sophie and Adrian both trotted out the foreign languages, which Terry did his best to verify with online translation pages. Adrian dealt his arm a shallow cut with a kitchen knife so they could watch it heal. And upon getting the nod from Sophie, Adrian handed over his phone with the video of Sophie's grandfather on the screen.

As he watched his father speak kindly in a message to Sophie from the Underworld, Terry pressed his hand over his mouth, his eyes aggrieved, much as Sophie had looked when she first saw the video.

Isabel watched over his shoulder, then sent a keen look at Adrian. "It's an actor, isn't it? How'd you find someone like that?"

Adrian shook his head. "It's him. I can take you there tomorrow—later today—if you want."

"That may be the only way you'll really believe it," Sophie said.

"Would we go in that bus?" Isabel asked, and winced when Sophie nodded. "Oh, dear. That looks a little scary."

Terry cleared his throat, his gaze upon Adrian's phone, where the video had ended. His voice sounded soft and hoarse. "I'd be able to talk to him? See him?"

"Yes," Adrian said.

Terry pulled in a shaky breath and tapped "play" on the video again. He and Isabel watched it in silence.

"It really looks like him," Isabel murmured as it ended.

Terry set the phone in the center of the table. "All right. I'll go with you, Mr. Watts."

Adrian wished he had the confidence to say, "Please, call me Adrian." Lacking it, at 3:30 in the morning after being caught mostly naked in this man's daughter's bed, he only answered, "All right."

"The pomegranate?" Sophie asked Adrian.

He nodded. "I suppose, since you both know everything, you're welcome to your past lives as well. When you're there, you could eat the pomegranate. As to the immortality fruit—well, I don't have that, or Sophie would've eaten it by now. But there are always plenty of pomegranates."

"I don't know." Terry sat with hands in his lap, still staring at Adrian's phone. "I'm...not quite ready to mess with my head that much yet."

"I'd like to do it," Isabel said.

Terry frowned at her, and she shrugged. "I'm curious," she said. "Plus I'd love all those extra languages."

Terry sighed. "You've always been more adventurous than me. Guess that's where *she* got it." He shot a glance at Sophie.

"Last question for tonight," Sophie said. "Liam? Should we tell him?"

"I'm thinking no," Terry said.

"I agree," Isabel said. "I mean, he'd love it; it's like something out of those comic books he reads."

"Graphic novels," Sophie corrected.

"Right," Isabel said. "But he could be tempted to say something about it to a friend, and if word got out...if these cult people are really that dangerous..."

"Oh, they are," Sophie said.

"Then let's wait on telling him. Yes."

It was nearing 4:00 a.m. They agreed to adjourn to bed and meet again after lunch to work out a plan for visiting the Underworld. Before saying goodnight and heading upstairs, Isabel and Terry each shook Adrian's hand.

"I still am not going to claim I like this," Terry added after the conciliatory gesture, and pointed at Adrian's face.

Adrian swallowed. "Understood. Completely."

Terry shook his head and followed his wife to the stairs. "Goodnight."

At the kitchen door, Sophie took Adrian's hands and gazed wearily up at him. Her forehead wrinkled as she lifted her eyebrows in an apologetic cringe. She wore buttoned-up flannel pajamas with her hair wrapped back in an elastic band, a different picture from the woman with the loose wild curls and the open silk robe sitting on top of him a few hours ago. But equally lovable.

Adrian kissed her forehead to smooth the wrinkles away. In an undertone he said, "I think I felt closer to being murdered when I woke up and saw him there than I did when Wilkes shot me."

Sophie grinned and hid her face against the front of his coat. "God. Not how I planned this weekend going."

He slipped his arms around her, savoring the warm flannel-clad curves. He debated a moment internally, then decided. "Listen. Regarding Liam…"

She lifted her face in question.

"Just between us," he said. "Well. You haven't liked it when I've kept things from you, so…remember how I said Poseidon was still a kid?"

Sophie froze, then her eyes widened. The dim kitchen light caught and brightened the green in them. "Liam is Poseidon?"

Adrian nodded.

She stepped back, out of his arms. "Wow. How much else are you not telling me?"

He glanced unhappily at the clock over the stove. "How late do you want to stay up?"

Arms folded, she gazed across the tile floor. "No, I know. Encyclopedias' worth of information, I'll remember it eventually, blah blah blah."

"Is there—are there any other questions you want to ask right now?"

She looked at him. "Who was my mom?"

"I've told you, I honestly don't know. Not everyone we know was an immortal. People can still be our loved ones in this life, or any life, even if we never knew them before."

She sighed through her nose. "You knew about Liam, all this time."

"What would it have changed, if I'd told you?"

She shook her head, avoiding his gaze, as if finding him impossible.

"Do you have any other questions?" he asked again.

"Way too many, and I need to sleep."

He gave up. She kissed him with nearly as much coolness as you'd kiss your grandmother, and they parted.

Zoe found the text from Adrian waiting for her when she switched on her phone Sunday morning.

Z, I don't mean to complain, but wtf kind of protection spell was that? Her dad caught me in bed with her and called the police. Yeah, you can laugh. I got away. But we ended up having to tell her parents everything. They're in on it now.

Zoe did laugh in shock, covering her mouth. Still in bed, she pushed off the blankets and scratched her head, finding her hair sticking up all directions, as it always did in the morning. She texted him back.

OMG. Wow. Well, the spell protected against outside forces. He was inside the house, yes? And if you got away, then it sort of worked. Also, LOL. Details pls. Not gross ones of course.

While awaiting his answer, she rose, picked up the sunglasses from the desk, and put them on before heading for the bathroom.

How much longer could she go on deceiving her parents? She almost envied Sophie, coming clean about what she'd been up to, sharing the wonders of the spirit realm with two of the people she loved most in the world.

At the notion of love, Zoe's mind slid right where it wanted to: toward Tabitha. Oh, she didn't love Tab, not yet. They didn't know each other well enough. But it had felt too good, dreadfully sweet, to share Thanksgiving dinner with Tab and her mum, to watch Tab's awkward side emerge, as everyone's did when their embarrassing relatives met their friends.

Tab's mum drank too many glasses of wine, and got maudlin and nosy by the end of dessert. Tab and Zoe improvised excuses for Zoe to leave soon after, and in the frosty driveway Tab had apologized for her mum's behavior, looking humble and ashamed. Also gorgeous—all warm sleek blonde hair and velvet-covered curves, and lips that probably tasted like pumpkin pie at that moment...

Not that Zoe got to kiss them. No, she got a hug, but then Tabitha's phone sang with its five thousandth text message of the night, and they stepped apart and Zoe flew home to New Zealand. Alone again.

If only Tab weren't so obsessed with another. Not Freya—though surely that would be an issue soon too. No, the faceless goddess Fame was the more dangerous one contending for Tabitha's worship right now.

It wasn't safe, Zoe reflected, washing her hands in the bathroom and emerging again. Seeking fame was outright stupid for any immortal. Someone would notice Tab wasn't aging, if the fame kept up long enough. And why would anyone want to be pestered everywhere they went, anyway? But then, adoration and Adonis-Dionysos went hand in hand.

Spells existed to alter someone's affections. Wasn't hard. She could tweak Tab's mind a little, make her care less about fame, more about her friends…

But along with not using magic to cause harm, you didn't use magic to mess with a person's brain or body without their consent. Except in dire circumstances such as to save their life, or prevent them from harming someone else.

On the way to the kitchen, a new text from Adrian arrived. Zoe paused to read it, lowering her sunglasses in the shadows of the corridor.

Reading his shortened text version of the evening took a minute, then she tapped in her reply.

When she lifted her face after that, her heart seemed to stutter to a halt. Her mum sat in the armchair in the front room, in full view of the corridor, laptop on her thighs but with her gaze fixed on Zoe. She'd seen it all: Zoe reading the phone with her eyes after moving the sunnies out of the way, and replying via the on-screen keyboard in a way a blind person simply couldn't do.

Zoe gazed back.

"When were you going to tell us you could see?" her mum said.

Zoe already knew the first word she'd be texting back to Adrian now.

Fuck.

CHAPTER THIRTY

*H*EY, DO YOU HAVE FREYA'S NUMBER? TABITHA TEXTED TO NIKOlaos. *And do you think she'd be up for meeting me?*

I do have it, but that depends, he responded. *How clingy do you plan to be?*

I am never clingy!

You rather were in the old days, is all. At first. She'd be cautious because of that.

Whatevs. I can always just track her without calling first, you know, Tab texted.

Yes, because that doesn't look stalkery or anything.

Adrian did it to Sophie.

I rest my case, answered Niko, which made Tabitha grin.

Well, will you give me the number? she texted.

How about I talk to her for you. I'll let her know you've reached those memories and are keen to see her.

Thanks. Tell me how it goes. Soon!

Tab put her phone down and scowled at the football game her dad was watching on TV. He called this bonding? Whatever. At least his girlfriend Jamie wasn't here. Tab could spend the rest of the game brooding about Aphrodite and not trying to make excruciating "girl talk."

It had hurt so much, and felt so good, that feeling of love that had tortured Adonis. Tabitha had never known anything quite like it in her own life.

And the torture, she lately recalled, had expanded one day to levels you could truthfully and chillingly call suicidal.

ADONIS SAT ON a boulder and stared into his fifth or maybe seventh or eighth cup of wine that night. Revelers at the late-summer bonfire festival sang and wavered around him.

Shock stunned his mind. Aphrodite had ended their relationship.

How long had it been? Eighteen years? She'd found him and brought him into her bed when he was sixteen, and now he was thirty-four and his shoulders got stiff more quickly when he worked outdoors, and wine made his head ache sooner and longer, and though his hair was still brown and golden, it did have a few threads of gray. She had stolen his youth. Taken over his life during all of it. He would have given her the remainder of his years too, but she no longer wanted him.

It wasn't because he was aging, she said. She loved his maturity, and still found him as handsome as ever. So she said, and she looked miserable—but never actually wept. Had he ever seen her weep, in fact?

"I'm holding you back," she had said. "You can't live like this forever, when you have the vineyards, and a good life to give a family, if you only would. Your mother wants you to marry, have children. You know she does."

His mother had been dead almost a year now, but yes, thanks to Aphrodite, he still got to visit her.

"You've always taken me to the Underworld. Who would take me if you wouldn't?" he'd asked, pathetically.

"Hermes would. He likes you well enough. Obviously."

Adonis hugged himself, grimacing at certain memories. "We only did those things together because you wanted us to. I don't want anyone except you."

"Maybe *you* only did it to please me, but he truly likes you."

"He taunts me."

"He taunts everyone. Look, as to the Underworld, if no one

else could take you, I still would, as a friend. But…" She wrung her hands, and stepped back to evade his embrace. "You have to learn to stand alone. And you have to learn to share me, or you can't have me at all."

Adonis had kicked furniture over, broken vases, shouted that of course he got jealous; who wouldn't? Did she love him or not? How could a mere mortal (he'd sneered the words) learn to share with gods?

They'd hashed out the argument many times before. But tonight his words didn't move her, nor did the tears he finally surrendered to.

She told him it was over, then brought him to the festival and left him, after placing him in the care of a sweet girl who always sent moony gazes at him. The girl was nearly two decades younger than him and he couldn't remember her name. After his first two cups of wine, he had chased her away with a snarl, declaring he wanted to be alone.

Alone he was. Quite alone.

The bonfire, burning high as a house, swam sickeningly back and forth as he blinked at it. The dancers swirling around it looked like moths, or strange animals from the other realm.

He refilled his cup from the barrel of wine provided for the festival—from his own vineyards, which were mostly kept by his trusted overseers and workers these days, with only the slightest input from him.

His workers wouldn't care if he died. No one would, much.

How much more wine would it take before it poisoned him and stopped his heart? Or at least gave him the courage to walk into the ocean and let the waves close over his head? Not the fire—he knew nothing could make him brave enough to jump into that, and anyway, someone would drag him out before he died. The ocean was good and dark, out there at night. A cool, quiet death. Its surf beckoned to him at the edge of hearing.

Did suicides always end up in Tartaros? He should have asked Persephone one of those times he was visiting the Underworld. Oh, well. Even Tartaros couldn't hurt this much. And he'd led a good life mostly, hadn't he? He'd avoided hurting others, tried to be of use, tried to please everyone. It hadn't worked, but he had tried. Surely the Goddess would only place him in the caves of punishment a short time, if taking his own life did offend her. And after that he'd be free to walk the fields as a placid soul alongside his mother.

While he gathered his strength, planning to stagger down to the ocean, an arrogant laugh cut across his thoughts.

Ares strolled into view between Adonis and the bonfire. He wore an immaculately white tunic, clasped over one shoulder with a gold pin. His skin and short dark hair and even his bare feet gleamed with health and vitality in the firelight. Three young women walked with him, clinging to his arms, stumbling and giggling. Ares supported all three easily and teased them.

Rage returned Adonis' spine to him. He rose, letting his wine cup fall on the ground and spill. He stormed forward into Ares' path.

The immortal soldier stopped and lifted an eyebrow. "Oh, it's Aphrodite's puppy. He's lost." Ares looked around, pretending to be solicitous. "Anyone have a leash?"

The girls giggled again.

"She never loved you," Adonis snarled. The words didn't sound as clear as he wished, but Ares obviously understood them, from the anger hardening his eyes. Adonis kept on. "She thinks you're pathetic. She only takes you into her bed because she pities you."

Or was he actually referring to himself? Adonis was confused now.

Ares shrugged off the young women and stepped forward. "You're not worth a single flick of my knife, pup, though that's all it would take to kill you."

"You all think you're so magnificent," Adonis slurred. He spat at Ares, pleased to see the wine-colored spittle stain the white tunic.

Fury contorted Ares' eyes, and his foot lashed out and caught

Adonis in the stomach. The kick sent him rolling across the rocky ground toward the fire, gasping and gagging.

Another kick bruised Adonis' ribs. Adonis groaned and kept his face in the dirt.

"Had enough?" Ares asked.

Adonis said nothing.

Ares turned away, evidently satisfied.

Adonis pushed up onto his hands and knees, grabbed the end of a branch that stuck into the bonfire, and yanked it out. He jumped up and whirled the flaming tip toward Ares' back.

Warned by the screams of the girls and other onlookers, Ares spun around and knocked the burning branch to the ground. Then his hand was at his belt, and something gleamed in it, in the firelight, and he rushed at Adonis.

Pain scorched deep into Adonis' gut. He lost track of time for a bit, then refocused. He found he was lying on his back, the taste of vomit in his mouth, his whole body sticky and bruised and racked with pain, especially his belly. The bonfire sent sparks high into the night sky. People screamed and shouted around him. Someone familiar knelt above him, with neck-length curls and a handsome face topped with a gold-winged crown.

Hermes turned in anger. "Perfect, you fool. That's exactly what we need, to kill harmless mortals in front of the whole world."

"He attacked me," Ares' annoyed voice said. "With fire."

"Oh, save your breath, Ares, I saw the whole thing."

Adonis tried to make sense of it. "Killing" harmless mortals? Then he was dying, as he had wished? With very difficult movements, Adonis transferred his hand to his belly. He found, instead of his smooth skin, a ripped mass of blood and flesh. Oh, indeed. People died from knives to the gut. Fairly fast. Gods, but it hurt. He could hardly breathe.

"Get out of here!" Hermes shouted—at Ares, Adonis supposed.

Then Hermes lifted Adonis carefully, keeping him as flat as he could. The fire and the revelers and the noise all vanished. "You poor bastard." Hermes sounded shaken, but gentle. He sighed and lifted his face to the stars, as if lost and searching for direction among them. Finally he looked down at Adonis again. "Shall I take you to Aphrodite?"

Adonis nodded and closed his eyes. Hermes lifted him higher.

Adonis had the impression of swift movement, then he tumbled out of consciousness.

CHAPTER THIRTY-ONE

So," Zoe said over the phone, "Sophie's parents know now, and so do mine."

Adrian stopped walking. "What?" Sophie and her parents moved along ahead of him, crossing the field toward the farmhouse after their visit to the Underworld.

"They caught me using my eyes. I considered the whole 'miracle medical cure' explanation, but they would only want to talk to the doctors involved, and I couldn't produce them, so..." Zoe sighed.

"How'd they take it?"

"Oh, they think it's fab. They were flinging questions at me left and right. 'How strong are you? Can you lift a car? How about a bus? Can you fly? How fast do the horses go? Can you kill someone with magic? Can you conjure up spirits just to, like, freak someone out?' I mean, I knew my parents were geeks, but wow. I didn't realize how far it extended."

Adrian grinned as he thought of her parents: both of them stout and unruly-haired, her mum a software engineer and gamer, her dad a security systems expert and also gamer. "They probably hope you wear some cool superhero uniform. And have special weapons to carry round."

"Ick. So not me."

"Nor me. Let's make a pact. No uniforms."

"The good part is, now they can help cover for us," Zoe said.

"They're totally into using all their tech tricks to do that, and will even help track down Thanatos if they can."

Adrian felt the same chill that had shook him when his dad reported acting as a double agent. "Tell them to be careful. Thanatos people aren't always smart, but they're violent. I'd rather not get any of our families mixed up in it, if we can avoid it."

"Says the guy who just took Sophie's parents to the Underworld."

He turned to see them talking to Sophie by the side door. "Touché," he said, defeated.

"How'd that go?"

"Fine, basically. They saw Sophie's grandfather, and an aunt of her mother's who died a while back. So they believe it all now. Also, Sophie's mum ate the pomegranate. That'll be interesting."

"Indeed." Zoe sounded impressed. "Not her dad?"

"No, he's not reached that level of trust with me." Adrian turned away from the house, and watched Kiri nose around in the garden. He lowered his voice. "He got me alone at one point and confronted me on the strength issue. Whether being unnaturally strong meant I'd accidentally break Sophie when I touched her."

"Oh, Goddess," Zoe said wryly.

"I gave him the whole kitten analogy—"

"The kitten analogy?"

"Yes. You know. Like when you play with a kitten, you don't worry about breaking them really, because even though they're so delicate, you know that and you've adjusted the way you deal with them. It's second nature." He grimaced. "But I think he only came away with the impression that I molest kittens."

Zoe laughed. "As long as he's stopped calling the police on you."

"For now. They say they'll defend us against Thanatos, even. But same with your folks, I don't like them taking a stand when it might get them...hurt." *Killed*, he didn't dare say. Though of course it could. What wouldn't Quentin authorize, if she sent suicide bombers after innocent uni students?

"We'll be careful, Ade. I promise." Zoe sounded confident. She hadn't seen it firsthand, the explosions, the flesh and hair burned off the assassin, off Niko too…

Ugh, he shouldn't have ejected Niko.

"How are the memories?" he asked, to pursue a less difficult topic.

"Good. Or dramatic, at least. I've got to where Ares stabbed Adonis. Hekate wasn't there, but saw the aftermath." She added a garbled shuddering sound.

Perhaps she had seen grisly sights firsthand, come to think of it.

"Never a dull moment. Then or now," he said.

"Never," she echoed.

HEKATE SAT UPON the rocks above the cave's entrance, gazing at the full moon in the dark sky. Its magic flowed over her, cool and fresh as spring water. Kerberos prowled around, sniffing the earth, perking up his ears at the occasional howl or screech of a night animal. Arriving souls streamed past and dived below ground. Hekate smiled at them and spoke welcomes.

Kerberos lifted his head, his ears rising to full alertness. He barked a hopeful greeting. Hekate turned to look that direction, and soon she spotted the horses speeding toward them, carrying riders whose solid bodies and rippling tunics caught the moon's rays differently than souls did.

Immortals. Hermes and Aphrodite. She rose to watch them approach.

Aphrodite held someone across her lap, a cloak wrapped around the person to secure him there: a full-sized adult but evidently unconscious. Hekate barely caught a glimpse in the moonlight before Aphrodite plunged into the cave with her passenger.

Hermes noticed Hekate, and pulled up his spirit horse to hover beside her. He stretched out his arm. "No time to dally, love. We have a dying man."

With a tremor, she guessed who the dying man was. "Adonis," she said.

Hermes nodded. Large splotches of blood stained the front of his tunic. Not his own: though he looked more somber than usual, he wasn't hurt as far as she could see. Someone else's blood.

Adonis. Dying.

She grabbed Hermes' arm. He swept her up in front of him onto the horse. Kerberos barked and bounded over, and leaped up to join her. She and Hermes caught the dog. Hekate held him in both arms. Hermes snapped the reins, and the horse shot forward and down, plummeting into the cave's mouth with the other souls.

"She brought him hoping for a miracle." Hermes reined in the horse as they settled to the entrance chamber's floor. "From you or from Persephone. But I don't think there's any hope."

Hekate slid off the horse. "There might be. I need to see him first."

They hurried through the tunnel along the river. "Your magic," he said. "Can you ease someone's pain?"

"A bit. If nothing else. But I hope I can do more for him than that."

"I wasn't thinking of *his* pain, love." They emerged across from the wide, glowing fields to find Aphrodite kneeling in tears beside Adonis. "I was thinking of hers," he said softly.

Hekate rushed forward.

Adonis lay on the black rocks, eyes closed and face pale, his clothing a nightmarish mess of blood, vomit, and other bodily fluids spilling from a rip in his belly. Persephone knelt near him, speaking rapidly with Aphrodite.

Hekate fell to her knees, trying to ignore the frightening stench coming off Adonis, and carefully took his hand. She closed her eyes in pain at once. Dying, without a doubt. The life was flowing out of him, its sparkle dwindling with each heartbeat.

"There are poultices I can try." Persephone unwrapped the bloodstained wool from Adonis' torso. "But oh, Goddess, a knife wound like this…"

"There isn't time!" Hekate leaped to her feet and scrambled to the raft. "I'll fetch the orange."

"Hekate, we can't make a decision like that," Persephone said.

"Can we vote?" Aphrodite's voice shook. Tears had left tracks down her cheeks. "Are there enough of us—can we get enough?"

"Hades is out tonight," Persephone said, "but even if he were here, no, that isn't enough of us."

"They keep voting him down." Hermes paced beside them with hands on his hips. "What good would it do to vote again?"

So Hermes hadn't voted him down, or at least not every time, Hekate thought briefly. She steered the raft across the river and darted up the other side. She paused to call across, "I'm fetching it!", then sprinted into the orchard. She ran easily in the near-darkness, familiar with the paths and logs and rocks.

The glossy tree's crown rose higher than her head now. She halted beneath its branches and snapped a ripe fruit off. With it in hand, she raced back and crossed the river again, and dropped to her knees at Adonis' side.

Persephone had uncovered his wound, and poured river water over it to clean away the blood and fluids. She winced as she probed his flesh. "No. When the intestines are cut through like that, infection sets in so fast, and—"

"Yes, he's dying!" Hekate interrupted. From the choked sound of her own voice, she realized how near tears she was herself. "And we can't let him." She tore into the fruit. "Remember, Aphrodite? We can't let him."

"I don't want to," Aphrodite wailed. "This shouldn't have been how it happened. But—"

"But nothing. This won't be how it happens." Hekate pulled off a section of the blue fruit and squeezed its juice onto his unresponsive lips.

"Hekate!" Her mother pulled her hand away. "We can't choose this."

"Who would find out?" Aphrodite's voice trembled.

Persephone stared at her, then up at Hermes, who lifted his eyebrows with a permissive shrug.

"How *wouldn't* they find out?" Persephone asked.

"Say if he left the country," Aphrodite said. "Disappeared a while, took on a new identity. Then at least it'd be a long time before they did find out. Their anger would cool."

"We're saving a life," Hermes added. "Worse not to, isn't it?"

"Yes," Hekate said, and yanked her arm free from her mother's grip. She placed one hand against Adonis' face and held the orange to his lips with the other. She pulled every scrap of energy left in his body toward his mouth, willing him to open it, to accept the piece of orange.

If the Fates wished him to die, then of course he would. He'd be a soul here and she could talk to him, as long as he wished to stay, but that was nowhere near the same as talking to a living person. She couldn't touch him; he'd never fall in love with her. Souls didn't fall in love with new people. They only relived the love they had felt in life.

But if she brought him back to life, gave him immortality, he'd have a reason to be grateful to her forever. He would live and love again. So if the Underworld's powers didn't mind her saving him...

His lips parted. His breath slipped inward. Hekate wedged the orange between his teeth. "Eat," she said. "Swallow."

His jaw moved a few times, crushing the fruit, then his throat pulsed in a swallow.

She slid her fingertips down to his neck. His energy picked up strength, heartbeat by heartbeat. The glow and warmth filled back up inside him. Hekate breathed freely at last.

The others looked at her. "Did it work?" her mother asked.

Hekate nodded. "He'll wake up soon."

"Are you sure?" Aphrodite gasped as his eyelids fluttered. "Yes—look."

Hermes crouched and peered at the knife wound. "The bleeding's stopped. He's healing."

Adonis' face crinkled in pain. His hand moved to his belly. The torn skin there twitched, beginning to pull itself together. "It's..." he breathed. "What..."

"Shh, it's all right, dear." Aphrodite stroked his hair. New tears ran down her cheeks through her smile.

"It'll hurt while it heals," Persephone said. "He'll need to rest."

"Let's get those clothes off him and put him in the pool." Hermes slid his arms beneath Adonis' shoulders and lifted him. "He won't want to look like *this* when he wakes up surrounded by beautiful women."

CHAPTER THIRTY-TWO

ADONIS OPENED HIS EYES. THE STALACTITES OF THE UNDERWORLD hung above him, glistening in the glow of souls and torches. That he expected. But he was naked in a chest-deep pool of cold water, and still appeared to have flesh and a heartbeat and chattering teeth, all of which he did not expect.

He wiped water off his eyelashes to clear his vision further. Someone held him around the chest from behind, sharing the pool with him and keeping his head above water. He twisted around to look.

Hermes smiled. "Hello. Feeling better?"

"How did…" Adonis splashed free of him and stood, shivering and looking from Hermes' naked body to his own, not sure whether to be offended or grateful.

"The water's cold, isn't it?" Hermes said. "But Hekate thought staying in it would help heal you faster. Something about magic. You know how she is."

Adonis had no idea what he was talking about. Chilly water dripped down his chest from his wet hair, which hung loose over his shoulders. Hermes or someone had bathed him to wash off the blood, he supposed.

He splayed his hand over his smooth belly, frowning at it. Where was the wound? And considering he'd been staggeringly drunk, why didn't his head pound nor his mouth feel like it was scoured with wool? Why did he mostly feel…fine?

Hermes leaned back against the pool's edge, arms spread along the rocks, and studied Adonis. "I remember when you looked like that. Not a giant change, mind you. You were aging gracefully. Still, it's noticeable."

"Now we look the same age," a woman's voice said.

Adonis swirled in the water, startled.

Hekate walked up, carrying folded white cloth over her arm and a torch in her hand. The large immortal dog padded beside her.

"He's confused," Hermes confided to Hekate. He addressed Adonis again. "To sum up, the good news is you're immortal now. The bad news is Aphrodite still broke up with you, and you have to leave and go away so no one finds out we made you immortal, at least for a while. We went a bit over the heads of the usual council, you see."

"So I heard," a man said.

Hekate turned to look at Hades, who stepped forward from one of the tunnels and glowered at the scene in front of him. "Hello, Father," she said sweetly.

"Hades. Join us?" Hermes invited from the pool.

Hades leaned against a limestone column and rubbed his face. "Persephone went to Zeus and Hera to tell them Ares mortally wounded Adonis. We're allowing them to think, for now, that he died. They'll advise Ares to leave the country a while. He usually listens to them, so he'll do it. But people will be panicking, shrieking about how the gods not only released a plague, but now are stabbing mortals for fun too. It's the kind of thing those mad speech-makers love to say against us."

"We could show them he's not dead," Hermes said, "but then we'd have to explain how he survived such a wound."

"And a miraculous recovery won't help the rumors," Hades said.

"Would only make them worse," Hermes agreed. "He's known to be Aphrodite's lover. Special favors bestowed by the gods to bring him back to life, when we 'let' everyone else die? No, the mortals wouldn't like that."

The mortals, Adonis thought. A class he had belonged to, so

bitterly and inescapably, until just now. How strange. He flexed his wet hand, noting how a scab that had been on his thumb several days was now gone. He lifted the strands of brownish-blond hair draped over his shoulder to see if his threads of gray were still there, but the torchlight was too dim for him to tell.

"By the way, you should be able to track us now," Hermes addressed him. "The four of us—Aphrodite, Hekate, Persephone, and I—gave you a small cut and all gave you drops of our blood while you were recovering, and we got a drop of yours too. Well, Hekate and Persephone did. Aphrodite and I could already track you, of course." Hermes widened his eyes in a roguish flash.

Adonis thought for a moment, and realized that indeed, even blindfolded he could have pointed in the direction of each of those people and estimated whether they were near or far.

Aphrodite, for example, was far. Or at least, farther than the Underworld. Probably back on her island.

Adonis nodded. "I do feel it."

"Good," Hermes said. "That will help you come back to us eventually."

"So he'll have to leave." Hekate sounded sad. "Become someone else."

"For a while," Hermes said. "That'd be my advice."

Adonis looked about to find the three of them watching him, awaiting an answer. He cleared his throat. "I...had no plans. Anything you think is best."

"Then let's get you dressed," Hermes said, "and train you on a spirit horse. And on how to switch realms."

THREE DAYS LATER, after grasping the art of switching realms, and after several practice flights upon a spirit horse—which he had ridden before with Aphrodite, but never alone—Adonis was ready to depart the Underworld.

Persephone had returned. She had informed his workers at the vineyards that he had been mortally wounded, and that Aphrodite had taken his body to the spirit realm. By custom, in the absence of an heir, the vineyards would pass to his chief overseer. Adonis hardly cared about that anymore. Anyone who wanted his troublesome lands and vines was welcome to them. Several of his workers, though, had been kind to him and counted as friends or almost family, and he felt touched to hear they grieved for him and would be holding a funeral, even without his body. Persephone reported they had already begun planning it, and intended to make Aphrodite the chief goddess to whom sacrifices would be dedicated.

Wasn't that ironic, Adonis thought at first. The goddess who caused his would-be suicide receiving the honors at his funeral. Then again, maybe it was fitting. In the logic of worshippers, making sacrifices to Aphrodite after such an event might keep her from bringing doom down upon them next.

In the fields, he said goodbye to the soul of his mother for the time being. Her pride at seeing him turned immortal almost returned cheer to his heart. Almost.

Persephone and Hades packed him a bag of extra clothes, food, knives, and other useful items for a traveler.

He hadn't seen Aphrodite since she left him that night. They told him she had brought him here, had made it possible for his life be saved—with the help of Hekate's magic—but she evidently still didn't want to face him. He could sense her now, but to follow that sense and show up against her wishes would do him no favors. He would have to live with knowing where she was and doing nothing about it. The ache in his heart grew at the thought. Immortality did nothing to ease loneliness or rejection, it would seem.

"Here." Hekate ran up, holding a pomegranate in a small cloth. "You should eat this. For the languages, if nothing else. Someone traveling can always use those." She flashed an anxious look at her mother, who nodded in assent.

Adonis accepted the fruit and pulled it open, catching its wayward seeds and droplets of red juice in the cloth. He ate the seeds, recalling that Aphrodite had eaten this fruit too, when most of the immortals hadn't. He would become her equal in as many ways as he could.

None of this could be happening, he still thought. It was likely a dream while his body lay dying by that bonfire. For if it were real, and he had to abandon his home country and take on a new identity, then what next?

Hades stepped closer. Adonis glanced cautiously at him. Hades had always intimidated him with that fierce unsmiling gaze.

But now he looked more resigned than fierce, and he pulled a bronze knife from his belt. "I might as well track you too. Let's have your arm."

Surprised, Adonis held out his arm. Hades dealt the quick cuts to Adonis' wrist and his own, and pressed them together.

"I once left my homeland too," Hades added, "letting everyone think I was dead. It's a strange journey. But you'll get used to it." He let go of Adonis' arm.

Adonis pressed the pomegranate-stained cloth to the cut. "Thank you." He looked around at the others. "All of you. I…hope I'm worthy of this gift."

"You're worthier than some who were born with it," Hermes remarked. "And who continue doing nothing to deserve it. Certain rock-brained soldiers come to mind."

They walked with Adonis to the entrance chamber. He led his new spirit horse along by the reins, a white mare with gray mane and tail. Strange how it felt like leading a live horse, but when you reached back to pat her on the nose, there was no tangible nose to be touched.

"Where will you go?" Hekate asked.

"I'm not sure. Where was Ares going?"

"He'll head west, from what Zeus said," Persephone answered.

"Then I'll go east." Adonis had been to India with Aphrodite a couple of times. He wouldn't mind spending longer there, wandering around. Deciding who to be now.

He climbed upon his horse. The others bade him farewell. He shot into the sky and eased up on the reins to let the horse go faster and faster. It was nearing sunset now; the red and orange rays stained the sea. Only three days had passed since she had thrown him out. Three days, but everything in his life had changed.

He flew out over the sea, low enough to feel the spray of a surfacing dolphin or whale on his ankle as he whipped past.

The sense of Aphrodite pulled within his chest, and his hands steered the horse toward her island. Just for a last look at the land, he thought. He wouldn't even switch realms to see her. He landed, wondering if he'd be strong enough to stick to that decision.

No building stood here in the spirit realm, just rocks and wild olive trees. Her palatial home with its white columns existed only in the living world. Nonetheless, he and she had lain right here many a time, upon this beach, in this realm.

He slid off his horse and picked up a diamond-shaped piece of lapis lazuli from the ground. One of Aphrodite's tunics sported a line of these blue stones stitched to its hem. It must have fallen off on some visit. She might not even have been with Adonis at the time. She could easily have been with someone else. That was the trouble. Too often, she was with someone else.

He tucked the stone into a small bag at his belt, and walked forward, following his sense of her. Then he stopped, for she was approaching. She remained in the other realm—somehow he could tell that without looking—but she drew right up to him until the shimmer of her presence sang in his ears.

She didn't switch realms, nor did he. They lingered with the wall of the realms between them, hesitating. Emotions and smothered declarations pulsed inside him.

What words could they add to the millions they'd already spoken? Didn't he already know what she would say? Wouldn't it only hurt more to hear the rejection again, or even to see her again?

He lifted a hand to caress the air where she would be, if they shared the same realm. Silently, he thanked her for delivering him to the Underworld, to salvation. Apologized for the jealousy he couldn't control. Vowed to be worthy of her the next time they met, whenever it might be.

Then he backed away. She didn't move, didn't appear. He

climbed onto his spirit horse, snapped the reins, and vaulted away eastward at the speed of a shooting star.

CHAPTER THIRTY-THREE

THE YOUNG WOMAN FIRED TWELVE SHOTS FROM THE HANDGUN, knocking down each of the soda cans she and Landon had set up on the fence posts between the pine trees. She swung the gun down to her side, relaxed her stance, and turned to Betty Quentin with a smile. The cold sunlight gleamed in her long orange-red hair and brought out the pale freckles on her white skin. Landon smiled too, and his gaze moved anxiously from the young woman to Betty.

"Impressive," Betty said.

"That's at fifty yards." Krystal's voice was as cold and brittle as her name—or the Idaho ground this late November morning. "I can usually hit about half that at a hundred yards."

"Close range will be more important. I'm not likely to need a sniper, but we'll see." Betty shifted her weight, leaning on her cane, careful to avoid any of the large pinecones that littered the dry ground. "Courage and dedication are the important things. Plus a strong stomach. To do what needs to be done."

"Someone asked me once if I could be an executioner." Krystal slotted the gun into its shoulder holster. "You know, actually pull the switch on the electric chair. I said, for murderers? Terrorists? The only people who ever get the death sentence? Of course I could." She squinted at the fence posts. "The person who asked was surprised. Guess not everyone feels that way."

Betty nodded and hobbled closer to Krystal. "And the people who help them? Harbor them? What about them?"

Krystal flicked her hair over her shoulder. "Sounds like treason to me."

Betty glanced in approval at Landon. "She gets it."

Landon smiled, looking relieved. Silly boy, Betty thought affectionately. As if she wouldn't have accepted Krystal after spending most of yesterday indoctrinating her into the history and purpose of Thanatos, not to mention letting her sleep under their roof.

"So. A two part operation, like before," Betty told them. "Only, we hope, with success on both fronts instead of just one."

"First the test attack on Tabitha Lofgren," Landon said.

"To distract and divert them, and find out what we can about her. And shortly thereafter, the elimination of Adrian Watts."

"Using Sophie's family," Krystal added. They'd filled her in on the latest players, too.

"Exactly," Betty said. "If they won't help turn him over, well…" She nodded toward the obliterated soda cans. "Guess they're traitors."

The three returned to the car, to drive back to the cabin.

"Best we don't stay at the cabin much longer," Betty remarked. "We're lucky no one's found us so far, but the longer we stay, the greater the chance someone will."

"We'll want somewhere closer to the traitors anyway," Krystal said.

"Oregon?" Landon asked. "Or Washington this time?"

"That may depend on whether Sophie's parents choose to be on our side," Betty said. "Let's move west. We can find a place to stay. And we'll deliver them a reminder."

"So HOW DID this happen?" Ben Zarro asked Tabitha. The stage lights blazed upon his stiffly swept-back hair and navy-blue suit. "How did you start hanging out with all these famous people? Did it require a pact with Satan, or…?"

The audience laughed, as did Tabitha, throwing back her silky blonde hair. "I'm good at networking," she answered, crossing her legs in their shimmery wine-red tights. "I met Grange Redway at a party in Seattle, and he knew someone else, and they knew someone else..." She shrugged.

Zoe watched from the second row of the studio, surrounded by strangers in the other seats. Pride and excitement tingled inside her, at being in New York City with a date who was a guest on "Late Night with Ben Zarro." And this time Zoe didn't even have to lie to her parents about where she was going.

"We'll cover for you," they'd said. "We'll keep it secret." And they'd winked and touched their noses in weird gestures of complicity, all set to stand guard for the immortals. They were sweet.

Tabitha soared through the quick interview, flirting with Ben Zarro and delighting everyone with saucy, hilarious gossip about the celebrities she had partied with.

"Finally, I hear you're good at selecting wines," Ben said toward the end of their allotted time. "And other drinks. Is this true?"

"Yes."

"How? How is that? You're not even old enough to drink."

"I've helped my mother with catering gigs, and she allows me to taste drinks. I have an excellent palate." Tabitha smiled.

Zoe grinned as the audience—largely college-aged—hooted and clapped.

"All right, so a modern holiday dinner," Ben said. "Say, turkey and a risotto. Pumpkin pie for dessert. What should I drink with that?"

"I would try a dry Prosecco with dinner. Or if you want something stronger, a gin cocktail, maybe one with apricot brandy. And I'd say sherry with dessert."

Ben gaped at her while the audience cheered again. Zoe laughed and applauded along with them.

The catering answer was only part true, of course. In all of Tab's past lives she'd been a connoisseur of feasting and entertaining, which contributed a great deal to her knowledge.

"Well, now I'm hungry," Ben concluded. He shot out his hand to shake hers. "Tabitha Lofgren, everyone! Internet sensation. Tabitha, a pleasure."

Zoe maneuvered through the jumble of people on the sidewalk outside the studio afterward, following her sense of Tab's location. Soon Tabitha emerged from the crowd, and her warm arms engulfed Zoe.

Finally, as easily and naturally as picking up a chocolate and biting into it, their lips met again in a kiss.

They stood entwined on the frosty pavement, skyscrapers twinkling above, taxis honking on the street, scarf-wrapped pedestrians strolling around them. Zoe rested her nose on Tab's cheek. All she needed was falling snowflakes and an ice-skating-in-Central-Park scene for the perfect ridiculously romantic New York evening.

Then Tabitha's hold went limp. She turned to look behind her. Zoe looked too, and though she saw nothing yet, she suddenly sensed it: a familiar soul drawing near at a walking pace.

Tabitha slipped out of Zoe's arms and stepped toward the arriving immortal. A knot of pedestrians strode past, and in their wake, the figure appeared. Freya walked toward them, in a quilted ski parka, tight jeans, suede ankle boots, and a sea-blue fleece beret. With her curves, graceful walk, stunning face, and bob of golden hair, she looked utterly fabulous. It was possible she wore lipstick and mascara, but also possible her lips were really that full and rosy, her lashes that dark and thick. Men and women both sent her second glances as she passed.

Zoe, as usual, wore no makeup and had done nothing about her hair except cram a knit hat on top of it. She'd reckoned her all-black outfit—jeans, jumper, fleece, sneakers—was up to the fashion standards of Manhattan, but now she felt dull and colorless.

Freya smiled in greeting at Zoe, who only stared. Then Freya's gaze moved to Tabitha. Tab leaped forward to meet Freya on the sidewalk, and threw her arms around her, kissing her full on the mouth, with those same lips that had just been on Zoe's.

Zoe fell back two or three steps, feeling the blow like a kick in the chest. And Freya, rather than evading the kiss, embraced Tab and returned it for an endless stretch of seconds.

They broke apart and spoke their hellos. Zoe couldn't hear

the words. Her body kept trying to spin around, turn her away from this scene, send her walking, sprinting, flying out of North America. But that would be over-dramatic. They all had eternity now, or at least a bloody long time, to learn to live with each other. And didn't she at least owe Freya a hello, having not met her in this lifetime yet, and having been usually, sort of, friends with her in other lives?

Fighting the pressure to flee, Zoe forced her legs forward, hauled up a smile and said hello, and agreed they should all go out for pizza, yes, and drinks, and bring all these random audience members who were crowding round to say hi; yes, absolutely, good idea.

THE NEXT EVENING, back in New Zealand, Zoe sat in a chilly sea wind with her hands folded around a paper cup of mocha. "She just kept staring at her," she lamented. "Like I wasn't even there. I shouldn't care, we have forever to work it out, but…"

Nikolaos drank from the bottle of Lemon & Paeroa he'd bought at the cafe. He smacked his tongue, examined the label, then took another drink. "The trouble with lesbian love triangles is you can't tell which 'she' and which 'her' we're talking about."

"*Tab* kept staring at *Freya*, of course. And vice-versa. No one was staring at me." Zoe scowled at the lights of a ferry crossing the strait. "Well, except that one bloke from the audience who kept wanting me to say things in 'New Zealandese.'"

Niko settled back on the rock. He stretched out his leg; its side touched hers. They had hopped across Cook Strait on their horses, and now sat atop one of Arapawa Island's rocky bluffs, looking toward the vast North Island in the twilight. "I can tell you one thing, which you already know," he said. "No one ties down Aphrodite. Nor Freya. Nor any other person she's been."

"And I can tell you Tab's soul has always been obsessed with Freya's, regardless of not being able to tie her down. That's likely *why* she fascinates people."

"Quite so."

Zoe tilted the cup back and forth, disillusioned even with the mocha tonight, which tasted too sweet and fake. "I don't know. I'm *one* of the people Tab kisses and flirts with, and I should settle for that. It's more than her soul ever gave mine in some lives. Maybe someday, in the future, it'll work out, or I'll stop caring. But last night…it hurt, that's all, and I wanted to talk to someone." She glanced at him sheepishly. "Thanks for coming all this way."

He watched her with a curious smile, close enough she could see a mole behind his ear and the fuzzy texture of the hair growing back on his shaved head. "Why talk to me, and not your best friend?" he asked.

She smirked and returned her gaze to the receding ferryboat. "My best friend's also my dad now, in a way. Makes things a bit weird when discussing romance."

"So you don't want to hear about his and Sophie's sex life either?"

She shuddered. "Ew! Stop."

He laughed, full-throated and carefree. Then he hugged her around the waist, and planted a kiss on her temple. "For you, I'll always come halfway round the world."

"Thanks, mate." She breathed in the salty air and released it.

And suddenly the vapors from the timeless ocean, mixing with Niko's warm touch around her middle, delivered the knowledge as clear as a text message: Hermes had loved Hekate. And now Niko loved her. And so it had gone in many, many lives in between.

She hadn't reached the memories yet that would tell her what, if anything, had happened between Hekate and Hermes. But she did know, from memory-instinct as well as magic, that he didn't expect her to reciprocate. Happiness, in fact, emanated from his touch, as if he was content just to know her. For someone famed as a callous trickster, the secret sentiment was remarkably sweet.

"Wow." She turned her face to the sky.

He looked at the stars too. "Hmm?"

"Hermes loved Hekate who loved Adonis who loved Aphrodite. We're a bloody Shakespeare comedy."

If it embarrassed him to be called out on his feelings, he didn't show a shred of it. She doubted whether he'd ever been embarrassed in any of his lives. Instead he quipped, "As you like it, darling," and offered her the bottle of L&P.

CHAPTER THIRTY-FOUR

AFTER ADONIS LEFT, HEKATE TOOK TO EXPLORING THE LIVING world more often. Her parents did too, attempting to quell the rumors and panic among the mortals. They explained, over and over, that the immortals had no intention at all of slaughtering people; nor of introducing a new plague, which they had no power to do anyway; nor of breeding a race of superhumans to conquer humanity. The tragic fight between Ares and Adonis had been nothing but a spat over a woman, the kind of thing that happened everywhere, and Zeus had punished Ares with banishment.

Of course, the truth was none of them could control what Ares did; Zeus and Hera sending him away was more of a strong suggestion that he was good enough to comply with. In reality he could come back whenever he pleased, and furthermore, a certain subset of mortals wanted him to. He loved war and was an asset in battles, and marauders and barbarians did periodically attack the cities and coastlines of Greece and the islands. For those involved in fighting, Ares was a favored god indeed, provided he fought on your side.

It was all quite complicated and tedious, Hekate gathered as she wandered the towns and listened to the arguments. Which side deserved the help of the immortals? Should they assist in wars at all? She and her parents and her grandmother Demeter would rather protect the people than attack anyone, but sometimes protection did require active defense. At least she could sense the times when the magical powers would flow willingly to assist her, versus the times when she would be forcing them into an unjust action and they would rebound upon her. But most people couldn't sense that, and for them, making life's decisions must have been like navigating in a fog. No wonder the living world roiled in such stress and chaos.

Still, something in the chaos called to her. She found laughter, beauty, kindness, and cleverness among the people, even in the midst of worries about invasion or illness. They wrote poems and songs, crafted musical instruments, fashioned masks and costumes, grew gardens and cooked delicious foods, adored their children and lovers and pets. They told stories about the immortals, some of which were true while others were total fabrications. But even the latter tended to be captivating, and Hekate suspected most people didn't quite believe any of the stories anyway. They were all for entertainment. Yes, those mad wandering preachers seethed with anger against the real immortals, and they were gaining a small but loud following. But most Greeks loved life, and found ways to savor it.

For example, the festivals! All the regions held them regularly, usually one on every full moon, but details varied from one area to another: which gods or goddesses were honored (sometimes real immortals, other times only legends), what processions or rituals were required, who would preside and what everyone should wear, which foods and objects were to be brought, which animals or items sacrificed. Each participant took the rituals seriously and adhered to the rules.

And the rituals worked, in their way, despite the variations from place to place. When Hekate attended, usually staying modestly in the background, she sensed the magic flowing up from the Earth and down from the full moon and through the joined hands of the participants. Their devotion and cooperation brought it forth, and though they didn't have the power to direct the magic into anything startling, they surely sensed the beneficial boost it brought them.

This had been Adonis' world, she kept thinking in her explorations, though she tried not to dwell upon him so much. He had come from this tumultuous imperfection, and had somehow kept his beauty and grace and loving devotion, though the devotion hadn't been returned the way he wanted. Hekate couldn't comprehend why Aphrodite would throw out such a treasure. But that was another interesting thing about people, even immortals: they all wanted different things, when you got down to specifics.

Some evenings, Hekate followed her sense of Adonis—faint and distant, but usually traceable—and climbed to the top of the mountain ridge that ran the length of their peninsula. There she faced east and looked out across the land. His essence beamed to her from far away, like an evening star, and she longed for the day when he'd return with his heart healed, his purpose in life refreshed.

Did he ever think of her, reach out for her essence? She had no magic to find out that answer, not from this distance. And knowing his mind might only hurt. She could guess which immortal woman he spent most of his time thinking of.

Though she kept silent about having brought Adonis back to life, Persephone and Aphrodite one day conferred and decided to confess what they had done.

They did so at the next meeting of the immortals, several months after Adonis had left. Hekate came along, as she sometimes did, though she usually said nothing, reckoning the others wouldn't listen to the input of a fourteen-year-old, even one who looked older.

Tonight the glares from the rest of the immortals would have cowed her into silence anyway, at least at first.

"This is true?" Zeus demanded of Hades and Persephone. "You made someone immortal without asking the rest of us?"

"It is true," Persephone said, her hands folded meekly before her. She, Aphrodite, and Hades stayed standing while the others sat around the beach fire. Their position gave the impression they were on trial.

"Bleeding Goddess," Zeus said. "We all overlooked it when you did it for her." He waved toward Hekate. "A child dying, and one we would have approved anyway—no one minded. Much. But this? What are we to do with you?"

Hermes stood too. "I was there. I gave my consent and encouraged them."

"But it was my doing," Aphrodite insisted. "You all know I've tried to bring Adonis into the circle before. I didn't like to do it without consent, but he was dying, and—"

"I did it." Hekate had leaped to her feet and spoken almost before thinking. Everyone stared in surprise at her. Her legs weakened at the sudden attention, but she added, "It was my idea. I ran and fetched the fruit, even when my mother told me not to."

"Hekate," Hades began.

"It's true!" She turned to him. "You weren't there. But that's exactly what happened."

"We don't care exactly how it happened," Hera retorted. "The trouble is it did happen. The damage is done, a new immortal walks the Earth. What are we to do about it?"

Fear chilled Hekate from head to feet. Did they propose to kill Adonis all over again?

"Oh, you'll like him well enough when you meet him next," Hermes said, in his casual, confident way. "He's becoming leagues smarter, you know, thanks to that pomegranate. Oh, right—most of you haven't eaten it. Well, that's a shame, as it does vastly increase intelligence."

Hekate almost laughed, though part of her now feared they'd kill Hermes, too.

The others only continued to glare, however.

"A man unconscious," Rhea said, "who didn't steal the fruit and didn't even know it was being given him, can hardly be punished for having it pushed into his mouth. And we all agree Ares shouldn't have killed him—or tried to—in the first place. Adonis needs no punishment. But you four? Or rather, five?" She included Hekate with a nod.

"We have ideas," Aphrodite said. "We thought, for instance, if we allowed everyone else one additional candidate at the next round of proposed immortals…"

"That hardly helps," Hera said. "Most of us don't propose anyone, and if we do, it's rarely more than one at a time. We don't even need the four we're allowed."

"How about if the five of you," Zeus said, "are not allowed to propose any candidates for the next year?"

"Five years," Hera said.

"Two and a half," Athena murmured, seeking the diplomatic middle ground.

The five glanced at each other. Hekate had only just started being given a vote on immortal candidates at all, and had never proposed anyone. She wouldn't feel any loss at giving up the privilege. But the others looked relieved too, and nodded.

"Fine with us," Hades said.

"Yes," Aphrodite said.

"Should we revoke their votes on the new candidates as well?" Hera asked Zeus.

Hades and Persephone glanced around the circle, where everyone still sent them decidedly annoyed looks. They exchanged another nod with their co-conspirators.

"We willingly relinquish them," Hades said. "For two and a half years."

"And it should go without saying," Zeus said, "that you will not administer that damned fruit of yours to anyone, ever again, without asking the whole council."

All five of them nodded. "Absolutely," Persephone said.

The meeting moved on to other topics, and the pressure upon them lessened. As the group broke up for the night, Hermes clapped Hekate and Hades on the backs, one with each hand. "We didn't even get banished!" he said in quiet glee. "Fantastic luck, friends."

Another two years slipped by. Hekate practiced her magic. Hades and Persephone kept at their tasks of delivering messages from the dead to the living and back again, especially where murders were concerned. And the immortals learned that Ares, having become happily established as a new war god on the Italian peninsula, had participated in a sea attack upon the Greek coast.

Rumors and anti-immortal panic leaped up again and spread like brushfire through the land.

"Yes, that town is run by a usurping bastard and deserved to be attacked, but *still*," Hermes complained.

Several of the immortals were gathered at Zeus and Hera's palace to discuss the situation. Hekate attended with her parents, though kept quiet as usual, and spent most of the time petting Kerberos, whom she had brought.

"That's how we should phrase it, of course," Hera said. "He wasn't attacking the Greek people. He was liberating them from a tyrant."

"Killing plenty of Greek people along the way," Hestia said.

Zeus shrugged. "It's war. It happens."

"Would you care to come down to the Underworld and say that to the souls who died?" Hades spoke in the quiet, incisive voice he only used when especially angry.

"Hades." Zeus, in turn, used the smiling, ingratiating voice he employed to win people over. "Naturally you sympathize with the dead, but do remember we're here to serve the living, primarily."

"What have you done to serve them lately?" Hades inquired. "How does coddling their murderer do them any good?"

Hera spoke up again. "You know very well we protect this city and give its inhabitants a much better life than the average Greek gets."

Hades sat back, lips tightly shut. He did know it; everyone did. Still, it wasn't the full picture.

"You mean you reward them for worshipping you," Hekate said quietly.

Hera gave her a mocking smile. "Would you rather I had them worship the moon?"

Hekate remained silent and stiff-backed like her father, but sent a pointed glance around at the riches surrounding them in this court alone. Gold, silver, bronze, jewels, animal skins, oil lamps and vases, potted trees and flowers, and brilliantly dyed fabrics vied with each other for space in an ostentatious display of wealth. Yes, Hekate would most certainly advocate worshipping the moon over worshipping such vanity.

"We'll try to rein Ares in," Zeus said. "And we'll tell the people he, like us, means only to deliver good to humankind."

"Another festival should placate them," Hera added, frowning at the gold-threaded edge of her cloak, as if it might have a minuscule flaw. "They do love their festivals."

The group dispersed without having come to any more useful conclusion. Hades stormed ahead on the way out while Persephone lingered to exchange quiet words with Hestia.

Hekate and Kerberos followed Hades, but she paused outside the palace gates and looked down the slope into the city. Lute music rose from somewhere near, and the smell of sweet incense and drying autumn leaves curled into the darkening sky. Her feet moved that direction, the domestic magic of a mortal city pulling her in.

"Coming home, dear?" Persephone called to her.

"In a little while," she answered.

"Don't be late." Her mother sounded anxious. "If anyone starts shouting at you, or threatening, just…"

"Switch realms. I know." Hekate waved goodbye and started down the slope, touching walls and sniffing the air. Kerberos trotted beside her.

"Sometimes Hera and Zeus are enough to make you wish you could get drunk," said a pleasant voice near her shoulder.

She turned. Hermes strolled up alongside her. His gold-laced sandals glittered in the twilight. "Agreed," she said. They walked down the road together. "So full of themselves. Oblivious to real life."

"Always have been, since I've known them." He nudged her with his elbow. "You're wiser than they are, since you've eaten the pomegranate. Which they never have and say they have no need of."

"Yet they're viewed as the king and queen of our kind." Hekate wrinkled her nose in disgust. "What is *wrong* with people?"

"Zeus and Hera have political charisma. They're willing to be seen frequently and worshipped, to live in an absurd palace in the mortal realm, with mortal servants. To get involved in local issues and bestow favors. To throw riches and prizes to the fawning masses. All that rubbish that would make most of us want to fling ourselves off cliffs if we spent all day doing it. In addition, it's usually from their mouths that the mortals hear the decisions of our little council. So, yes, they come out looking like our royalty. And really, does it matter?"

"Hm." She shot him a grudgingly impressed glance. "You're smarter than you look."

"Why, *thank* you. Such a charmer, you."

She grinned. "What are you doing here tonight, in the city?"

"Following you."

"Yes, but what else?"

He shrugged. "Feasting, whoring, gambling. You know me."

"You always say that when I see you out at night."

"Because it's true."

"Why do you try to make me think the worst of you?"

"So you can only be pleasantly surprised when I turn out not to be thoroughly awful."

"Wise plan."

"Well, go on. Show me something," he requested.

She took his hand, found a ring on it with a large clear quartz stone, and demonstrated the latest spell she'd been practicing. Soon light began shining within the stone, making it glow like a lamp.

He whistled in admiration, and splayed his fingers to gaze at the light. "Doesn't even feel hot."

"No. It isn't fire. It's only drawing in light from the sky and pooling it in one spot." She let go of his hand and the light dimmed, but still glowed. "It doesn't work as well if I'm not touching it, and it goes out when I stop concentrating on it." She did so, letting the magic drop away. The light in the ring went out. "I need to work on that part."

"Nonetheless," he said, "that's fabulous. It's why I come find you whenever I can. I love these tricks of yours."

"I still think you could do some of them, if you concentrated."

"Oh, I'm sure I couldn't."

"Couldn't concentrate, or couldn't do the magic?"

"Either." He grinned. "Surely your being conceived and raised in the Underworld has a lot to do with your abilities."

"Yes, but the rest of you did learn to switch realms, so with a little focus…oh, never mind. Most people would only use magic for the wrong purposes anyway."

"I definitely would," he agreed.

She smirked and changed the subject. "Aphrodite looked well." She had been at the meeting at Zeus and Hera's too; quiet for the most part, but composed and relaxed.

"Delicious, lovely, nothing new."

They drew nearer to the lute player, an old man sitting in a doorway. "Any news of Adonis?" Hekate asked.

"Well…" Hermes looked aside at the old man, who abruptly stopped playing and jabbed his fingers in an odd gesture at them. Hekate felt the harmless but tense ripple in the air: an attempt at warding off evil. Them? He thought them evil?

"Messengers of the dead, get back from me!" the old man said in quavering, angry tones.

Hekate blinked in surprise.

"Oh, you recognize us, then?" Hermes said, and laughed when the old man jabbed the gesture at them again. "Here, my good fellow." He pulled the quartz ring off his finger and tossed it underhand to the man's feet.

Hekate sent a placating ripple of energy back in his direction, along with a smile, and they walked on.

Nonetheless, the ring came bouncing past them on the packed ground a moment later. Hermes left it behind. "A gift for the next traveler," he said.

"In Zeus and Hera's own city, people hate us?" she said, perplexed.

"There's a mad one in a corner in every city. The preaching lunatics are gaining popularity. It's the stylish thing to do lately:

be pro-mortal and anti-immortal, and generally anti-fun as far as I can tell."

She nodded, and considered whether she dared repeat the question that hadn't been answered yet.

Fortunately he seemed to read her mind, and returned to the topic himself. "As to Adonis," he said, "Aphrodite hasn't gone to see him, but I did last month."

"Oh?"

"He's well. Learning. Exploring. A bit aimless, but he'll be all right."

"I wonder what he'll be when he returns." Hekate glanced back in the direction of the old man, whose lute started up again. "And what he'll return to."

Hermes threw his arm around her. "I can tell you he's prettier than ever. But still not as pretty as you, so don't worry. My heart remains yours."

"I'll sic my dog on you if that hand gets any lower."

"Ah, your threats have improved," he said, and kept his arm comfortably latched around her shoulders.

CHAPTER THIRTY-FIVE

$\mathcal{S}$OPHIE HAULED HER TIRED BODY AND HEAVY BACKPACK UP THE library stairwell while her mind turned over the two notable pieces of weirdness in her day so far.

One had been an email from Melissa, her former roommate.

I want to tell you I'm sorry, officially. They aren't sentencing me to jail time, but I'm getting court-ordered counseling, and part of the therapy is I need to acknowledge I was reckless with your safety and privacy, and didn't show you enough respect.

There's still a lot I don't know and would like to know in order to understand everything that happened. So let me know if we could talk, because that would help give me closure.

The first paragraph was memorized and recited, sounded like; an assignment by her counselor. But the second was surely another bid to get in with the Greek gods. Which was not happening. Sophie answered only with *I appreciate the apology. Merry Christmas.* And she pushed the emails into the archive folder and resolved never to have further dealings with Melissa.

In the second piece of weirdness, her mom had called to laud the "stupendous," "fabulous," "incredible" memories the pomegranate had released in her mind. She and Sophie compared notes and verified that in the life before this, when Sophie had been a woman named Grete in Germany, Isabel had been her favorite older cousin. But in the life before that, they hadn't known each other; nor in the one before that. Isabel hadn't gotten farther back yet, but it did appear that their thread of association hadn't begun until recently.

"But that's so strange," her mother mused. "You and Adrian go back thousands of years, and you and your dad too, but you and I only a few decades?"

"I know," Sophie said, oddly disappointed about it. "But…it's like Adrian tells me. Our loved ones are still our loved ones, no matter how many lives we shared with them. Maybe we'll have a thousand awesome future lives together, now that we're linked."

"I'm sure we will." Isabel, for her part, sounded optimistic rather than poignant. "Oh. And in case you've wondered, I'm not seeing Sam anymore. You know. The man I mentioned."

"Oh. Right." The other man, whom her parents' companionate marriage allowed her to date. Which Sophie tried never to think about.

"I broke up with him yesterday." Isabel sighed, though again sounding upbeat on the whole. "Somehow he didn't fit in anymore. With all this to occupy my mind…I don't know. It's hard to explain."

"No, I get it." Indeed, Sophie had broken up with Jacob soon after acquiring her pomegranate memories. She could relate. "That's good. I mean, if you're good with it."

"I am. This is…it's all wonderful, Sophie. Thank you so much for bringing us into it."

Even with Thanatos on the scene? Sophie had wondered wearily, though she didn't say it. Her parents had already been warned, and had plenty else to deal with in daily life. As did Sophie.

Case in point: next week was finals.

On the third floor, she thumped her backpack down beside a computer, and grimly dove into her research.

HOURS LATER, SOPHIE rubbed her eyes and considered texting Zoe to see if she had a spell for making term papers write themselves. Stacks of thick, boring books on science in media, her chosen topic, shared the table with her while she took notes in an attempt to pull together a respectable final paper for her communications class. In addition to this project, she had another paper due for her writing class, a statistics final to study for, and a serious bitch of a chemistry final.

Why? she wondered for probably the thousandth time. Why persist in a bachelor's degree and a normal career? Wasn't the spirit realm a much more instructive, and cheaper, place to learn and reside?

It was. But deadlier, too. And even if she became immortal, maybe she wouldn't wish to drop out of the living world fully. That still seemed too momentous a step to take, even now that her parents knew about her secret life.

Where would she and Adrian and the others be without the living world, after all? They wouldn't have cell phones or the Airstream or its generator, or groceries or Internet service or jeans or sneakers or movies or TV…no, she loved too much of the real world to distance herself from it, and so did Adrian. He constantly talked about how he missed it.

So at least for now, given she was still a mortal, she had to participate in the world like a normal citizen. That meant writing term papers and taking final exams, even though the rise of Thanatos, in ancient days as well as modern ones, pounded like a sinister drumbeat in her mind.

It was dinnertime. Hunger twisted her stomach. The bland words of the book in front of her ceased to make sense. She groaned and rested her head in her hands, elbows planted on the book's pages.

Quiet footsteps approached on the tiles. Her heart skittered in panic. She shoved her hand into the pocket of her coat to grip the stun gun. The third floor of the library, between the stacks, with no other students in sight, would be a choice location for a cult assassin to kidnap or murder her.

But the dark-coated, black-haired person who turned the corner at the end of the stacks and approached her was no one to fear. Only the king of the Underworld. She let out her breath, dropped the stun gun back into the pocket, and lifted her face to receive Adrian's kiss.

"Hey. Ready to eat?" he said.

She nodded.

Outdoors, fog filled the cold air. It was the first week of December, and the sky had been fully dark for at least two hours even though it was only a bit past seven o' clock. Twinkling lights and wreaths on dorm windows and streetlight posts did lift the gloom a little, when she was near enough to see them in the fog.

They bought take-out burritos, and ate as they walked toward one of their switching-over spots. Sophie's mood slowly ascended as her blood sugar rose.

"They said it might snow," Adrian said between bites. "I'm excited."

"Couldn't you see snow anytime? Just hop up to the nearest mountain."

"Yeah, but for Christmas. Actual snow in December, like in the movies. That's new for me."

"Southern Hemisphere freak." She smiled, and sank her teeth into another bite of tortilla-wrapped rice, beans, and pico de gallo.

In the shadow of a maple tree beside the student parking lot, he caught her around the waist in one arm and hauled her into the spirit realm. The fresh air blew around her, the smells of a wild forest taking over the campus smells of food, cars, and trampled grass. But the other realm wasn't as dark as usual, and she blinked in delight as she realized why. The Airstream, a few paces ahead, wore a string of white holiday lights around its top like a crown, each bulb sending a bright reflected streak up and down the trailer's shiny exterior.

"Like it?" The lights sparkled in his hopeful eyes as he glanced at her.

She laughed. "You really are excited about Christmas."

He pushed away a fallen branch with his foot. "Well, I wanted it to feel a bit more like home. For us both."

"You and Kiri both?"

He reproached her with a second glance. "You and me."

She knew that. She stepped closer and hugged him with her free arm, cradling the burrito in the other. Their breath formed clouds between them. "It's pretty. I do like it."

The Airstream wasn't *home*. Not yet. Creating a new home would take a lot more than a string of lights. It probably required a settled family situation, and a plan regarding what she wanted to do with her life, for starters. But tiny white lights glowing outside the trailer's windows tonight would improve her world at least a little.

ONE MORNING IN winter, a few months after that contentious meeting at Zeus and Hera's palace, Persephone walked out from the Underworld's living quarters to find a crowd of souls waiting in the fields. They called and beckoned to her.

"What is it?" she asked across the river. She hugged her cloak around her, fearing news of another plague or something equally dreadful.

"Come across," an old woman said. "Zeus and Hera are here."

Persephone looked at the raft, puzzled. It idled on the shore nearest her. If any living visitors had come, and were out in the fields, they likely would have taken the raft across and left it on the opposite side. But perhaps its rope hadn't been tied tight, and it drifted back.

Hades and Hekate had gone into the living world today to visit one of the northern Aegean islands. Persephone would have to work this out alone. She stepped aboard and grasped the soaked rope to pull herself across.

In the fields, she asked the cluster of souls, "Where are they?"

Zeus and Hera weren't among those Persephone could trace. The couple had generally dismissed the need to keep close track of the others, and hadn't performed a blood exchange with anyone. Zeus, of course, could surely track a large number of people, once you counted all his lovers and children, but only the immortal lovers would be able to track him. Hera had never taken any other lovers, as far as Persephone heard.

"They're in the deeper caves," the old woman said. "They couldn't stay. But they wanted us to tell you they were here."

"Why are they visiting the deeper caves?" Persephone asked. Hera and Zeus disliked the Underworld in general, and to her knowledge they had never descended to the caves of punishment. Perhaps they urgently wished to talk to some lately deceased murderer?

But the souls looked grim. "They had to," the old woman said. "They couldn't stay here."

The chill spreading deep inside her marked the start of understanding. "They were souls?"

The woman and the other souls nodded. "They said it was important to tell you. They've been killed."

The word sank in, and Persephone broke into a sprint toward the back of the cave, hitching up her wool robes above her knees. The distance between the river and the far wall seemed impossibly vast. Alarm spurred her on, a hundred fears and questions swarming her mind. Foremost was the simple and terrifying chant: *We can die.* If Hera and Zeus could die, she could die. Hades and Hekate could die. Everything would change.

She was panting and sweating by the time she slipped into the narrow tunnel. She hadn't brought a torch, and didn't want to bother weaving a vine and capturing a ghost dog to bring down. So she felt her way down the tunnel alone in the dark, hand upon the rough wall, scraping her ankles on rocks, until the first blue-and-orange flame burst forth deep down to guide her.

In the entrance chamber to the honeycomb of caves, where the constant fires flickered red, she picked up a vine and lit it in one of the flames. She beseeched in a trembling voice, "Fates that guard these souls, I seek Zeus and Hera, immortals. Former immortals." She shut her eyes in having to add the "former," and hoped the cave wouldn't respond.

But the whoosh of a flame bursting forth signaled an answer. In dread, she turned and dropped the burning vine, which went out in a curl of smoke. She followed the sinister beacons down the passageways, past soul after tortured soul.

At last she stood before her father. He lifted his face from the study of the small flame on the floor, and regarded her with handsome, sad eyes.

She had never thought of Zeus as her father really, nor had he ever made any move to act like one toward her. But from a distance she had viewed him with the knowledge of her paternity, and noted similarities between herself and him: thick dark hair, full lips, boldness and curiosity. Now grief and sympathy swelled in her chest to see him here, another lowly soul serving his punishment.

Down the tunnel, five or six cells away, burned another flame, indicating Hera's location. But Persephone could only speak to one of them at a time, given the separation, and she chose Zeus.

"What happened?" she asked.

"An uprising." His voice carried its usual timbre, but with a hollowness behind it. Whether this was from being bodiless or from being distressed, she didn't know. "Those mortals who preach and rile up the crowds. The ones who chant 'mortality.'"

Thanatos. Mortality. She had heard that chilling chant. Someone shouted it after her in a village a few days ago, not far from Zeus and Hera's palace. "But how?" She reached into the cell to pass her hand uselessly through his arm. "How did they even do it?"

"We didn't think they could. That was our downfall. They stormed our house in the middle of the night." His gaze fell to the flame again. Misery shadowed his dark brows. "We were arrogant. We stood and fought rather than fleeing to the other realm. We thought we could punish them for their insolence. We did kill several, but...they were too many. They caught and held us, and before we knew it, we were pierced through with spears, and couldn't switch realms. Then we were souls, in the spirit realm, and flying here."

Persephone gazed at the little flame too, her breath shallow, clammy sweat prickling her back. "But even stabbed," she said, "we should survive."

"We'll hear soon what they did. I suppose they ripped us to pieces, too many to come back together. Or burned us. Or both."

"I can ask. If you killed some of them, they must be here, and I can ask."

"Yes." Zeus said it without expression, lost in the flame's pale light. "Forearm yourselves with what you can learn." He lifted his eyes to her again. "I don't want them to do the same to you, daughter."

It was the first time he'd ever called her that, and tears stung her eyes. "We'll find out," she repeated.

His gaze dropped back to the flame, and she hesitated, not liking to leave him alone. She didn't wish to ask what he saw in the flame, why he and Hera were down here, though she had plenty of good guesses.

He spoke instead, without her needing to ask. "There were so many we killed, or helped to kill, in all those wars. We didn't look deeply enough into it, to see whether we were in the right. Too many innocent victims. And the women, all those I left pregnant, they usually died. We thought we were helping in wars, I thought I was giving the women a treat as a lover, and surely we did help a great many, but…no, on the balance, we tipped too far this way."

Persephone's mouth was dry. "I can't free you. I'm so sorry. There's no magic, no way to do it. With any luck you won't be held long, but it isn't up to us. Please know that."

He nodded, not looking at her. "I know. It's all clear to me now."

Quick rhythmic footsteps pounded behind her. Hermes raced in, torch in hand, his face grim and gleaming with sweat.

Persephone leaped to him in a frightened hug, then pulled back to look at him.

"I've been there," he said. "Heard them crowing about their victory. It's…" His sigh shook with fury or grief. He stepped forward to look into Zeus' cell. "Give me a little while with them," he said softly to Persephone, his eyes upon Zeus. "Then we'll collect everyone—in the spirit realm, where it's safe—and go over what we know."

CHAPTER THIRTY-SIX

THEY WERE BASHED WITH CLUBS AND ROCKS," HERMES SAID QUI-etly to the assembled group in the cave, "then thrown onto the fire. Evidently that does it."

Hephaestus stared at the small fire they'd built. "I suppose if the flesh isn't given a chance to heal, if it's destroyed and scattered before it can…" He trailed off.

Silence and unsteady breaths rustled in the air as the group contemplated it.

Hekate felt the fear running through everyone like a winter flood, herself included. She shivered and lifted her face to the pale gleam of sky at the cave mouth. Outside, cold rain poured down, lashed along by wind. Thunder rolled between the hills. The weather magic exuded power today, and struck her as utterly indifferent to humans, immortal or not.

The group had taken refuge in a spirit-realm cave for their meeting, halfway up a mountain near Athena's city. Not the Underworld itself: that location unsettled too many of them, especially now.

Not everyone was here. Adonis was still far away in the east, for one. Still, he needed to know this news, and Hermes had promised to track him down and tell him soon. Three of the women known as the Muses were away on travels too, as were Eros and Pan. But the oldest original immortals were all there, along with many of the younger ones who'd been turned immortal by the orange. Ares attended as well. Hermes had fetched him back.

"If they're reborn," Prometheus said, turning to Persephone and Hades, "would they be immortal again?"

"We don't know," Hades said. "It's never happened, as far as we've heard. We can hope."

"Do we know who the butchers were?" Ares asked, jaw clenched.

"The leaders, yes," Hermes said. "I could point out the ones who were boasting and speech-making about it at the gathering I saw."

"Then we kill them."

Artemis answered Ares with a nod, her face stony. The point of her bow and the feathered tips of arrows stuck up behind her back.

But most of the others only gazed at the fire, and Aphrodite said wearily, "No."

"No," Hades echoed.

"I would agree we don't fall upon them and massacre them like barbarians," Apollo said. "But surely we capture them and turn them over to the city's judges, given what they've done?"

"That's fair," Persephone said. "We do that anyway with murderers."

"We'll never get all of them," Hestia said. "Even if their leaders are tried and executed, plenty of people who helped in the attack would probably still be walking free. And executing a few might only stir up outrage and make the rest more violent against us."

"Killing the leaders sets an example," Artemis corrected coldly. "It's the way of war."

"War?" Rhea said. "For the Goddess' sake, none of us wants a *war* with the mortals."

"We'd win if it came to that," Ares claimed.

Hermes scoffed. "Even I wouldn't gamble on that."

The collective sour mix of bloodthirstiness, terror, and grief surged too strong for Hekate to take. She rose, her stomach churning, and clambered to the cave mouth. Covering her ears, she leaned against the cold rock entrance, and took gulps of the fresh outside air.

The debate raged all afternoon. She couldn't bear to be a part of it vocally. Instead she wove an invisible rope circling the group, both of its ends out in the storm: destructive emotions channeling out, where they became lightning and thunder, and cleansing energy from the rain flowing inward to soothe and clarify. The little river traveled around the arguing immortals, and their words eventually turned from insults and defenses to compromises and ideas.

Hekate slumped at the cave mouth, exhausted and shivering, her head against her knees, her tunic soaked from the windblown rain.

The other immortals decided upon two pieces of action. One was to pursue the three leaders Hermes could definitely identify, and insist upon a trial for them if the people hadn't already rounded them up. The other was to meet with as many local leaders in Greek towns and cities as possible, make clear the good intentions of immortals toward mortals, and request peace on both sides.

The sky and rain and earth still felt indifferent to Hekate. No assurance their resolutions would succeed, no hint of their failing. Still up in the air, as life usually was.

Her father's hand fell warm upon her shoulder. She knew him by his energy even before she looked up. "We'll need your help, if you can placate the people the way you've done for us," he said.

"You knew I was doing that?"

"I've learned to detect a thing or two, even if I can't perform it the way you can." He helped her up, and kissed her forehead. "Thank you."

"There's one more thing we should do," Rhea said, lifting her voice above the murmurs of conversation. "While we're all here, and all together. Let's join our blood, each with every other, so we can never lose one another again."

"I suppose that's wise," Athena said. "In case anything happens."

They all consented. Knives came out, and the immortals lanced fingers or arms, and pressed their blood together. The crowd mingled to make sure each met with every other. Hekate found strength in the exercise, fascinated by the unexpected tints or flavors threading through each person's essence. She had sensed such feelings before, faintly, when touching their flesh, but the blood exchange gave a far brighter, stronger impression. An iron will she hadn't expected in Hestia, a soft modesty in Artemis, a shimmer of anxiety in Ares, and a love almost innocent and pure in Hermes.

No, the future held no guarantees of cooperation. Too many conflicting wills, too many changing circumstances, too many souls. It was far beyond Hekate's skill to weave that kind of peace. But she would try. And as Rhea had said, at least now this little group of flawed but beloved companions, this family of sorts, wouldn't easily lose each other again.

TABITHA SAT IN the cold night air on top of her dorm, absorbing the sparkle of downtown Seattle and its roar of traffic. She wasn't supposed to be up here, but had easily leaped onto the fire escape ladder and ascended. Getting on top of buildings without having to worry about falling: another plus of immortality. For what that was worth.

Zoe hadn't texted her in several days. Tab supposed she should contact her, check in, see how she was doing. But her mind kept wandering before her thumbs could do the actual typing.

Freya. Hell. Freya wasn't even Tab's usual type—Zoe was, all lean and natural and short-haired and boy-wardrobed. But Freya wasn't the goddess of love for nothing. She fascinated everyone; she got a hold on you. She haunted you.

Freya didn't love Tabitha. At least, not in a way that would've put Tab above all other contenders. But such *chemistry* zinged between them. So many hotly burning flames in the past. Not just as Adonis and Aphrodite, but in other lives too. Tab had the disturbing impression that once her soul had gotten a whiff of Freya's, life after life, the obsession had eclipsed all other lovers, though many of them would have been healthier for Tab, in her previous incarnations, to pursue.

Even as Adonis managed his slow metamorphosis into a god, hadn't it largely been with the secret aim of impressing Aphrodite? Or at least becoming good enough for her?

Also, he had wanted worship and respect from as many people as he could get. Life had been grievously lacking in those for the guy.

Tabitha had a symphony to listen to and a paper to write about its technical details, but screw that. Her report card was going to suck balls this term anyway. Nothing she could do it about it now. So she wandered into the distant past, following the itinerant Adonis.

HERMES ARRIVED WITH the sobering news about Zeus and Hera. Adonis was in western India at that point, having started at the southeastern coast and roamed his way along, usually on foot, though he kept his spirit horse tied near in the other realm in case he needed her. The news did make him reflect that he should be more careful, but it didn't shake him the way it apparently had the others. Not long ago he'd been ready to die, and had nearly succeeded. It still felt a bit unreal to have survived. Now he reckoned, once more, that he probably would die some day, but at least he would enjoy strength and mental clarity until then.

India fascinated him, with its exotic array of gods and animals. In both the living realm and the spirit realm, the animals were different than the beasts in Greece. In the spirit realm here, he'd found reddish elephants, wildcats with stripes and spots on the same coat, hellishly huge crocodiles, small hoofed beasts with wings, and delicate butterfly-like insects in every color imaginable. He loved the animals. Sometimes he captured one and brought it into the living realm to astonish people.

He only sometimes bothered mentioning he was immortal. The language barrier was part of the issue. He didn't speak the Indian tongue in any of his past lives, so he had to learn it the usual way, by listening and practicing. And mostly he liked to listen, and to experience new flavors. He approached wine-makers and other alcoholic drink creators, and talked to them about their techniques, learning from them and sharing what he knew.

Aphrodite still burned in his heart. But the ache lightened a bit with each passing month. He allowed himself to be seduced at Indian festivals, first by a young woman and later by a man, and although they couldn't measure up to Aphrodite's skill, their sweetness and avidity flattered him, and that helped heal him too.

After India, he trekked slowly westward, visiting deserts and mountains and warm seas. He learned new languages, and new methods of cultivating grapes and turning them into wine. He adopted a pet from the spirit world, a big leopard-like cat he raised from a kitten. He named her Agria, the Greek word for "wild." She padded tamely along beside him like a dog; the sight of her terrified some people and delighted others.

He witnessed a thousand varieties of worship and revelry, and heard countless religious stories. One recurring in several areas was that of the dying and rising god, a person who was tragically killed and then brought back to life as a god. People worshipped the cycle of life through him, comparing him to the plants decaying into the dirt and then shooting up green and new again in spring.

Adonis related to the resurrection story rather literally, since such a thing had happened to him.

The dying and rising god had as many names as he had towns in which he was worshipped. But in Crete, when Adonis finally got there, the people called that god Dionysos. They honored him with wine and grapevines and animal masks, among other offerings. It seemed fitting.

Adonis discarded his old name. Henceforth he would be Dionysos.

Chapter Thirty-Seven

ERSEPHONE STROKED THE SMOOTH SIDES OF THE CLAY JAR ON her lap, gazing into its empty black interior. Beside her on the ground burned an oil lamp.

Hades walked into view, down the path between the orchard's pomegranate trees, a leashed spirit dog lighting his way. Kerberos and Hekate followed, Kerberos nipping playfully at the spirit dog's tail, though his jaws snapped shut on nothing each time.

Hades and Hekate sat on the ground near Persephone, the fallen black leaves crackling under them. The lamp shone in the middle of their triangle. Persephone set the empty jar beside it.

"Who do we assume would find such a thing, if we bury it here in the Underworld?" Hades asked.

"Only someone important and clever enough to get into the Underworld," Persephone answered. "Which is how it should be."

Hekate nodded, chin on her hand, gazing at the jar. "People will always remember us, of course. Once they become souls."

"But souls can't touch the jar or the trees or anything else," Persephone said. "And if we're all destroyed, they might not remember in the living world after a while."

The three contemplated that idea soberly.

Hades murmured, "Grave goods. Before we're dead."

"More like a record," Persephone said. "A gift. We could write something down, but writing may fade, or the language could become undecipherable. Whatever we put in it might not last, either. But after what happened to Zeus and Hera…"

"We should try," Hekate agreed. "I'll seal it with magic, to give it a better chance at surviving and being found someday."

Persephone looked in gratitude at her beautiful, tangled-haired daughter.

Hekate returned the glance with a bright smile. "So what do we put in it?"

They settled on a number of items: small cuttings of their hair (including Kerberos'), a whole pomegranate that was beginning to dry up, an amethyst from one of Persephone's jeweled belts, an emerald from one of Hades' cloaks, a piece of a favorite rock of Hekate's that had a strange magic of its own and attracted iron to it, a few clay figurines that worshippers had given to them or left for them, a scrap of the red cloak Persephone had been wearing when she eloped with Hades, a scrap of the blanket Hekate had been wrapped in upon birth, a twist of the willow-and-ivy reins from the chariot, and a single whole orange from the tree of immortality.

Persephone picked up the jar, rattled the items around, then grimaced at her daughter and husband. "Who's going to make sense of all this, other than us?"

"But it might be us, someday," Hekate pointed out.

They went soberly quiet again.

Persephone fit the stopper onto the jar and sealed it with beeswax. Hekate set her hands around it, doing nothing that Persephone could see or hear, but after a moment she declared, "Done."

Persephone opened a small jar of dark blue paint, and picked up a paintbrush. "How should we decorate it? Something related to death? No, that's a bit morbid."

"The night, then," Hades said.

"Bats?"

"Owls," Hekate said.

Persephone nodded. "I think I can draw owls better than bats anyway." She dipped the brush in the paint and touched its wet tip to the jar.

AND OVER THREE thousand years later, Sophie thought as she awoke, a wheelchair-bound boy named Adrian Watts remembered that jar after eating the pomegranate seeds Rhea gave him. Rhea carried him into the narrow passageway to the spot where the jar was hidden, deep behind rocks in a crevice in a wall of the Underworld, and the soul of Hades uncovered and beheld the jar painted with owls. Inside they found the star-shaped seeds of the long-dried-up orange, and replanted them, and they grew. Thus immortality was back in season again after all these centuries.

Just not, quite yet, for Sophie.

NEARLY FOUR YEARS after Adonis' near-death, Hekate thought of him one spring morning, and stopped mid-stride in the Underworld's fields. He was near, much nearer than he had been in all this time.

She ran with Kerberos to the river and crossed it. Her mother knelt in the entrance chamber, weaving a harness for a spirit horse.

Hekate seized her horse and unwrapped its reins from the stalagmite. "I'm off for a ride. Perhaps I'll visit the market. See what's in season." She wasn't sure why she was lying about her purpose for leaving. Because crushes were embarrassing, she supposed.

"Choose one of the friendly villages," Persephone warned. "You know the ones to avoid."

"Yes." Hekate picked up Kerberos and leaped onto the saddle with him.

"And switch realms instantly if there's any trouble. Even if you have to leave Kerberos."

"Of course. I know."

Persephone sent her a worried smile, and waved goodbye.

For the past two years Hekate had been traveling with Hades or Persephone or another immortal envoy to one village after another, doing their best to spread the truth about immortals and to combat the vicious rumors. On the whole, people were glad to receive them and hear their assurances, and most promised they had no intention of participating in an uprising against the gods.

But in nearly every town, they did find some who glared fiercely or shouted "Thanatos" at them. It didn't help that Hekate and her parents couldn't deny that some immortals *had* killed mortals in battle or self-defense, or that Ares had stabbed a mortal rival over Aphrodite.

"We're humans too," Persephone tried to explain in one town. "We have passions and moods, and at the worst of times, such things happen. But we do wish to abide by your laws and do no harm."

"If you're human too," a man growled back, "you ought to be mortal like us. *Thanatos!*" The chant was picked up by others, and Hekate and her mother retreated swiftly, protected—that time— by a circle of kind mortals who escorted them out of the village and apologized for their fellow citizens.

Not every time would go so smoothly. Hekate could see that. It was partly why she usually only went out at night, if she wasn't on a diplomatic mission. The moon and stars cloaked her in serene magic, and the darkness hid her from easy recognition.

Today, shooting upward into the sunny sky, she worried more about how Adonis might be received if he strolled into some town and announced himself as an immortal. Hermes had warned him, apparently, but Adonis might not realize the extent and determination of the angry faction. He could find himself stabbed all over again.

Hekate landed in a wildflower-filled field, tied up her horse, and switched realms. She knew the location: a large coastal town on the southeastern peninsula, where the sea was a clear, light green-blue. The island of Kythira lay as a low blue shape on the horizon. The spot where she switched over was the customary place for immortals to do so around here, marked by a lightning-split tree in the spirit realm and a pile of stones—a cairn—on a path outside town in the living world. Cairns or small shrines had sprung up in several of these crossover spots, built by adoring mortals, those who still loved the immortals.

Hekate now found herself before an old woman trudging up the hill with a bundle on her back. Upon seeing Hekate swirl into place with Kerberos in her arms, the woman beamed a toothless grin and raised her hands with a joyful, "Ah! Goddess!"

Thank goodness Hekate ran into someone who did worship them, she reflected. Perhaps using these customary switch-over spots every time wasn't so wise. Thanatos-crazed enemies could lie in wait by the cairns with spears and bonfires at the ready.

But so far that hadn't happened. Perhaps the good worshippers chased away any such idlers, or perhaps the murderous group was too small and thinly spread to assign watchers to many points at once. For now she dismissed the concern, distracted by the prospect of seeing Adonis. She set Kerberos on the ground, and with a bow and smile to the old woman, she and the dog ran downhill.

Finding Adonis would have been easy even without her immortal sense of him. People jogged and hurried toward the market square in the middle of town, calling with excitement to each other.

"A new god!" was the call she heard most often, along with, "The god Dionysos," which intrigued her. Dionysos was from old stories. Her father had told her of sanctuaries to Dionysos on Crete, and a festival for him that involved drinking wine and wearing animal masks.

When she pushed through to the front, her Adonis-sense singing brighter and clearer, she saw why they might have begun calling him Dionysos, and she laughed in delight.

He sat upon the low stone wall surrounding the spring, speaking conversationally with the excited crowd that clustered around him. He wore a long purple cloak and a sandy-yellow tunic fastened over one shoulder, with no jewelry that she could see, but exquisite embroidery of grapevines curled all round the hems of his clothes. He had grown a thicker beard, and his hair was gathered into a loose ponytail of gold and brown waves. He looked both exotically wild and resplendently elegant. The old feeling of breathlessness punched her lungs once again as she beheld him.

At his side lay a giant wildcat, as large as he was himself. She wasn't sure what to call it. It was rather like the leopards in Africa, but brown with yellow spots rather than yellow with black, and certainly bigger than Greece's wild cats. Likely he'd captured it from the spirit realm. It drowsed in the sun, blinking lazily while he stroked its fur. The people kept their distance, staring at it and tittering nervously.

But they had many questions and comments for him, coming from all quarters, and they addressed him as "Dionysos."

On his other side sat a large clay jug, and he invited people forward to fill their cups from it. Wine, she deduced, glancing into someone's cup. The heady fermented grape scent perfumed the air.

He must have sensed her then. His gaze moved straight to her, and he smiled and held out his hand. "A familiar face. One of my saviors."

She stepped forward and took his hand to squeeze it in greeting. "Welcome back. Dionysos." She tried out the name aloud. She decided she liked it.

His gray eyes twinkled at her a moment, then he turned to the crowd. "The goddess Hekate," he introduced. "You know of her, don't you?"

They mostly murmured "yes." She and Hades had visited here a few months ago.

"She has powerful magic. She helped to raise me up from a dying, miserable mortal man to a god."

"The Fates did you that favor," Hekate quickly corrected, for it wouldn't do to spread the word that she could make people immortal. The orange's secrets had to be guarded closely, and the rumors were already persistent enough. "You've been traveling a while," she added, to turn the subject.

He nodded and began talking about a festival he'd seen in Egypt, which drew further questions from the increasingly tipsy listeners. Most were soon laughing and pressing closer, jostling Hekate aside.

She climbed onto the wall on the wildcat's other side so she could stand higher and look for any sign of an anti-immortal siege. But nothing looked amiss, and in any case, the mood of the crowd felt jubilant and silly, no malice that she could sense. All the same, she sat and placed her palms upon the circular wall, infusing it with protective energy, which should give them a chance to escape before anyone harmed them. She also had a job keeping Kerberos away from the cat—he growled with hackles raised, and the cat opened her eyes a slit and hissed in answer.

As Dionysos chatted with the others, Hekate only listened, smiling to be near him, but feeling out of place. He had a way with the people, a charm she lacked. She could sense energies and adjust magic and sometimes save lives with it, and she admired the colors and vibrant life of the cities, but she had never fit into them. A girl conceived and raised in the shadows of the Underworld carried that dark imprint forever. Dionysos, in contrast, had begun life among the mortals on the surface, and had always strived to please them through beauty and enjoyment.

Soon they were imploring him to honor them with his presence at their own Dionysian festival, later in the month. He cheerfully accepted, and glanced at Hekate. "You'll come, won't you?"

Her face warmed, and she chuckled, glancing at her feet. Dionysian festivals involved the most public nudity, drunkenness, and general madness of all the rituals out there. "Well. Perhaps. Just to watch."

He nodded approval, then turned to answer someone else.

CHAPTER THIRTY-EIGHT

EKATE WAS ACCUSTOMED TO FESTIVALS TAKING PLACE ON A single night, corresponding to the full moon. So it surprised her to learn that this village's Dionysia would last three days.

She showed up the first day at sunset to watch the procession. She didn't advertise being an immortal. She left Kerberos in the Underworld, and tried to be nondescript in the crowd in her dark blue cloak and loose, unadorned long hair, with a light wrap of magic around her to dissuade unwanted attention.

Apparently Hermes saw through her spell, though, for his presence soon zoomed close to her and in the next moment he was weaseling in beside her. He was barefoot and wore a lightweight red tunic, with a yellow narcissus stuck behind his ear. He was clean-shaven, as usual, and his brown curls fell loose to earlobe length, making him look about fifteen years old altogether.

"You've heard of his rousing homecoming, then?" Hermes said.

"I came and said hello when he arrived. He does have a way with them." She glanced about at the milling crowd. The procession wasn't ready to begin; its officials scurried around in purple robes, bringing baskets and masks and food behind the draped-off staging area inside a house.

"He'll be the next great immortal sensation," Hermes said. "Mark my words. The herald has spoken."

She smirked. "Herald you may be. Not the same as an oracle."

He lifted an eyebrow at her, pleased, and opened his mouth

to banter back, but a blast of horns and drums rolled out from the draped house. The crowd answered with a greeting cry. All turned toward the house and fell silent.

The drape tumbled to the ground in a ripple of purple. From the house the procession marched forth, all its members cloaked head to toe in purple linen. Their masks were blank cloth covering their whole heads, nothing upon them except small holes for eyes and mouth. The horns and drums played a wild, lamenting tune. The marchers touted grotesque animal masks upon poles, with a large mask of a bearded man at the head of the procession. Behind, others carried baskets of grapes or bread, and jugs that probably contained wine, water, or oil. Hekate also spotted sexual symbols on some poles—oversized and stylized male and female body parts, though male ones were the more numerous, since this ceremony honored a male god.

"Ah, they clearly used me as the model for those," Hermes whispered to her.

She elbowed him, which gained her an "Oof" and then silence.

After the last cloaked marcher passed, the crowd fell in behind and followed. Hekate and Hermes joined them. They traveled out of the town, up the hill past the cairn, and into a rocky hollow studded with conifers, where a cliff rose up as a backdrop.

The leader stuck the pole with the god's mask into a crack between rocks, then climbed onto the boulder next to it. He rolled up his cloth mask only enough to display his mouth, and began his oration.

As the sunset faded to an indigo sky, and torches were lit below him, throwing stark dancing shadows upward onto the cliff, he performed the tale of the dying and rising god. "Performed" was much more the word than "told." Even Hekate, who knew the tale was largely poetic invention, felt goose bumps rise in thrill upon her arms as he lamented the death of the betrayed youth. The crowd shrieked their grief in genuine-sounding agony.

"Death is woven into our life, eternally," mourned the masked speaker. Around Hekate, people wept and sent up the wails they customarily only used at real funerals. Even Hermes looked impressed, and stayed quiet. "But behold, my sisters and brothers!" The speaker swung aside to display the mask of the god. "He is born again! For life is woven into the fabric of death, as well. He shall live again, tonight!"

A cry of hope arose from the crowd.

"We must summon him," the speaker said, in his most sepulchral tone. "Friends, we must bring about the appearance of the god. Summon him now by name!"

"Dionysos!" people began shouting. The drums beat hard and loud in accelerating rhythm. Soon everyone called the name in unison. "Dionysos! Dionysos! Dionysos!"

Hekate chanted it along with them. The magical thrill swirled around her and shot through the crowd, though she knew all it would do was push them to higher ecstasies rather than actually summon Dionysos. She sensed him behind her, though couldn't see him—he was likely another of the masked folk, hiding among them until it was time to make his appearance.

Which evidently was now. Her sense of him changed: he was switching realms and rushing forward.

Then, in a sudden flare of light, new torches burst into being before the mask, and a breeze rocked all the flames, sending the light slanting crazily back and forth. There he stood, masked like a leopard, bare-chested, with a short cloth draped around him from waist to knees, torches in both hands.

This must be what it felt like to stand beside a strike of lightning, Hekate thought. In the triumphant roar of the crowd, and the sudden blazing appearance of the god, the people's amazement and devotion nearly made the Earth tremble under her. Indeed, many of the worshippers fell to their knees as if bowled over, while their shout of victory rose to deafening levels.

Then everyone threw off their masks, revealing colorful face paint. The horns struck up a lively, happy tune. Meanwhile Dionysos stood holding the torches, a regal smile upon his lips, as the people cheered and danced. An attendant brought his leashed leopard forward, and the cat prowled possessively around Dionysos' legs.

"He does know how to make an entrance," Hermes said to Hekate, leaning close in the noise.

Hekate agreed, laughing, and accepted an ivy wreath from an attendant, which she put upon her head the way everyone else was doing.

But in her own body, the worship for him throbbed and rushed around, as strong as any of these mortals could possibly be feeling it. It made little sense for an immortal to feel this way, especially one so closely connected already with the mysteries and magics of the Underworld. It wasn't his immortality or the mystery thereof that she wished to worship, the way it was for them. It was him, bodily; and his mind that she couldn't fathom yet, but wished to; and most of all, the emotions and thrills he stirred up in her and in nearly everyone he met.

HEKATE COULDN'T SAY she liked every part of the festival. Dionysos' many duties kept him busy, and throngs of people vied to be close to him, leaving her no chance to wander up and talk. Though he did kiss her in greeting, he did that with everyone, so she couldn't take it as a special favor.

She also didn't care for the official opening of the wine jugs, because it led to widespread inebriation—among the mortals only, of course—and she ended up fending off too many drunken attempts at seduction and witnessing too many bouts of vomiting. As for the theatrical performances, some moved her, but others left her more baffled than entertained.

And the evening of the sacred marriage was her least favorite.

Dionysos honored the hosting city by "marrying" a local noblewoman in a non-binding but realistic ceremony, after which he swooped her up and raced off with her into the dark wilderness. The people cheered and shouted lecherous suggestions.

Hekate asked Hermes, "Does he actually…?"

Hermes plucked a cup of wine from a stumbling passerby and stole a sip. "If he wants. If she wants. And why wouldn't they both want?" He offered her the cup. "Don't suppose *you* want?"

She glanced at the wine, as if he meant that, though she was sure he didn't. "Not now, thanks."

CHAPTER THIRTY-NINE

DIONYSOS RESOLVED NOT TO SEEK OUT APHRODITE. HE HADN'T seen her in four years, though he heard she still lived upon the same island, an easy spirit-horse jaunt from the mainland. Even two years ago, he would never have been able to keep away. She would have drawn him like those magical rocks that pulled iron up against themselves. But now he did resist, and when he thought of seeing her again, it caused only a flutter of a disturbance within him, not the full cold sweat and longing it would have before.

But the true test, he knew, would come only when he did see her. Which finally one night he did.

It was a few days after the first festival. He was on the road with his nine newly hired attendants—the people he liked best who had performed offices in the festival, and who were willing to leave town and wander with him to celebrate the rituals in other parts of the land. They had made camp for the night and begun to cook their supper in a sheltered spot between grassy mountain slopes. A glitter of distant sea peeked between the hillsides, shining in the sunset.

When he felt Aphrodite approaching at immortal-horse speed, his hands stilled in opening a jug of wine. He looked toward the sea.

Wild goats bleated. One of his new friends played a flute while another sang a poem. The fragrant smoke from the campfire billowed up into the clear sky. Then the smoke swirled about in a puff of wind as Aphrodite broke through into this realm, standing dangerously near the flames, one sandaled foot touching the end of a burning stick. His friends yelped in surprise; the flute and song stopped abruptly.

Aphrodite started and leaped aside to the grass. Dionysos jumped to his feet, wine jug still in hand, to take her arm. "Careful!" he said.

She stamped her feet and rippled her pale green gown, looking down to make sure she wasn't on fire. Upon finding she wasn't, she exhaled dramatically and lifted her face to him with a laugh. "Goodness. Not my most graceful entrance."

"You're accustomed only to setting others aflame, not yourself," he teased.

Her laugh tempered to a fond smile as she looked him up and down. Even in the wake of an awkward appearance she managed to look exquisite: tumbling waves of black hair, slim and flattering gown, artfully placed flowers and jewels on her hair and body, and in every curve the kind of beauty he thought he'd overestimated in his memory. Now he saw she was every bit as breathtaking as he had remembered.

But this time he could look away, smile at his companions, and speak with self-possession. "My friends, we are honored indeed. As you can surely tell by looking at her, this is the goddess Aphrodite."

His followers were a familiar and enthusiastic lot, not the somber and pious type. Rather than drop to their knees and go into an awed hush the way some worshippers would, they sent up a joyous shout, and began rearranging the camp to make her comfortable. They pulled over the best blankets for her to sit upon, praised her, kissed her hand, served her wine and bread and honey, offered to invent a new song for her, raced out into the dusk and back again with fresh wildflowers to strew in her lap. Both she and Dionysos were soon laughing at their attentions.

Of course, it meant he and she couldn't speak in private for some time. The feasting and chatting had to be taken care of first, and his companions did have a thousand and one questions for the famous Aphrodite. Between her answers, he sometimes exchanged a gaze with her in the dancing firelight, and discovered a respect upon her face that he'd never seen before when she looked at him.

It gave him the confidence to set down his wine cup late in the evening and stretch his hand to her. "Will my lady take a ride with me?"

She smiled and took his hand. They said goodnight to his followers, who merrily sent them on their way.

Holding hands, they switched into the spirit realm. Her white ghost horse gleamed in the starlight. She glanced about. "Where's your horse?"

"I'm traveling in the living realm, with them," he said. "Hermes has agreed to bring my horse to the next festival. I'm without her a few days."

Facing him, Aphrodite laced her fingers into his other hand as well, and held out their arms at both sides to draw their bodies closer together. "Then you didn't intend to take a ride? I can't imagine what you did intend."

Dionysos wound his arm around her, lifted her up, and maneuvered her legs around his waist. She laughed in delight. He knew he was showing off, displaying the immortal strength she'd never witnessed in him before. He'd been able to carry her when he was mortal, but not this easily, especially not with just one hand.

Apparently she liked it. "It's wonderful to see you this way." She ran her palm down his jaw. "Strong and bearded and followed by worshippers."

"It shames me how weak I must have seemed to you before."

"You were young. Now you never have to be weak again." She tightened her legs around him, and tilted her head to kiss him.

He savored the taste of her mouth, the feel of her, all the sensations he had missed with a physical ache for the past four years. He sank to his knees on the wild mountainside and lay on top of her, reveling in her heat as the cool wind swept over them. For a few poignant moments, he was Adonis again, seventeen and so in love and lust with a goddess that he would have traded the rest of the world for her.

But he wasn't Adonis anymore. Nor was he obliviously young, not since eating those fruits from Persephone's gardens.

His ardent kisses slowed.

He could have his pick of anyone, at any festival. These days it was easy. And yes, Aphrodite meant a great deal to him, the way a long-time lover would for anyone. But she was...he sought the appropriate word. Typical? Ordinary? Those didn't seem right to apply to the goddess of love. She was *the* quintessential female, what every seductive woman aspired to be.

"Darling?" Aphrodite stroked his ear as he stilled.

Perhaps that was the problem. Yes, she excelled at seduction and beauty. But lots of people's skills and looks came close, and in any case, seduction and beauty weren't enough. They added spice to the ribald parts of festivals, and he would always enjoy indulging in them. But having entered into the spirit realm and studied its wild beasts and landscapes, and having wandered the world and his own past lives all these lonely years, Dionysos wished for something deeper now when it came to love, something more extraordinary.

And one thing he did not wish to do was tumble back into old destructive habits.

"What?" Aphrodite purred. "Is there something else you'd like?"

He drew back. He sat upon his knees and smoothed his tunic into place. "Yes. I'd like to get some sleep."

She sat up too, draped her gown over her legs, and examined him shrewdly. "If you're turning the tables on me by trying out a rejection, I quite understand the maneuver. But I'm offering a reconciliation, you know."

"As one of many lucky immortals who share you." He said it gently.

"Indeed, I'm still not offering exclusivity." She, in turn, sounded cold. "But I did love you, and wish to remain on intimate terms with you. Especially now that you're..."

"Immortal? Respected? Worthy?"

"Adonis…"

"Not my name anymore."

She looked away.

He huffed a soft laugh out his nose. He stood and offered his hand.

She rose without taking it.

"We'll always be friends," he told her. "But now my life is different indeed. If we do become lovers again, you'll have to share *me*."

"I always did," she pointed out. "I wasn't the one who had a problem with that."

"Then why are you the one who sounds annoyed right now?"

She folded her arms and turned to face the wind. The moon was rising over the crest of the mountain, painting her gown with beams of silver-blue. "Forgive me," she said. "I must need sleep as well."

"Nothing to forgive," he said mildly.

He walked with her to her horse.

"Do come to a festival if you can make it," he added. "You're welcome anytime."

"As are you upon my island," she answered, but the declaration sounded formal, the way she might invite a king she had just met.

He waved farewell and watched her fly off, his heart unquiet and confused. With his new personality and lifestyle, he *was* in some fashion a king she had just met. A king without a country, and without a queen.

But with subjects, at least. He trudged back to them, hoping their company would cheer him.

CHAPTER FORTY

ONE BY ONE, OR IN PAIRS OR SMALL GROUPS, SEVERAL OF THE other immortals came to see Dionysos.

"Hekate said we should come," Rhea told him, smiling, during a festival in summer. "Exchange the blood with you, say hello. It will be less awkward for you to attend the meetings of the immortals if we've welcomed you beforehand."

"I do appreciate it." He felt truly honored to be approached by the oldest immortal on Earth. "And, er, I apologize for the... informality of these festivities."

Rhea looked about at the carousing crowd, several of whom were naked except for animal masks. She laughed. "As if I haven't seen wilder things in my time. Come, serve me this famous wine of yours."

Not all were so comfortable. Hestia, Athena, and Artemis attended together, giving off forbidding waves of modesty and uneasiness—Artemis in particular. But they did prick their fingers to exchange blood with Dionysos, and spoke in a friendly enough manner with him before departing. When Demeter attended another night, she surprised Dionysos by chatting with several farmers about the growing of grapevines, and laughing with abandon at the bawdy theatrical performances.

The immortal men who showed up—including Poseidon, Pan, and Apollo— generally had no trouble accepting masks and cups of wine and joining in the festival. They left after exuberant assurances to Dionysos that he was now among their favorite friends.

But it did jolt Dionysos' nerves when he turned around during a festival in late summer to find Hermes leading Ares to him. The soldier bristled with disgust as he beheld Dionysos in his vines, flowers, body paint, and skimpily cut animal skin. Given the heat of the evening, it was all Dionysos was wearing, and more than many of his followers wore.

"Ares?" Hermes prodded.

Ares glanced aside, and his mouth flattened in resentment. "My apologies for the dishonorable attack."

Dionysos bowed. "And mine for the drunken insults. I assume Aphrodite has smoothed them over."

Ares' lip curled in a sneer. "Oh, yes. Many times over."

"She's generous that way," Dionysos admitted, satisfied he could remain so calm on the topic of Aphrodite now.

"We're all on the same team," Hermes said, and turned to Ares. "The same army, to put it in terms you'd understand." While Ares narrowed his eyes at him, Hermes went on, "So shall we seal this pact in blood and wine?" With a flick of his hand, a knife spun up into the air. He caught it without even looking, glancing instead between Dionysos and Ares with his troublemaking, charming smile.

Ares rolled his eyes, but held out his arm.

Dionysos held out his too. "You're welcome to as much wine as you can drink, Ares."

"Little good it does us." Ares flinched as Hermes cut his finger and Dionysos' and pressed them together. But his wince quickly smoothed as he watched two bare-breasted women stroll by. "Am I welcome to your worshippers as well?"

"If they'll have you. Force yourself on anyone, though, and the cat gets to gnaw on your anatomy." Dionysos nodded to Agria, who prowled around the crowd. "Those are the rules."

Ares smirked, and wiped off his bloody fingertip as Hermes released their hands. "No problem there. I'm very persuasive."

Hermes shook his head at Dionysos and mouthed in comical exaggeration, *No, he's not.* Dionysos grinned.

Ares didn't notice. He snagged a cup of wine from a man passing by with a tray full of them. "See you at the next gathering. Time to try my luck." And he swaggered off in the direction of the two women.

IN THE FOLLOWING year, Hekate heard the Dionysia were held in one area after another, month after month. Communities found reasons to adjust their usual festivals to incorporate Dionysos: the planting season, the grape harvest, the sealing of wine into jugs for the winter, the official opening of the jugs, and other bits of yearly life that warranted celebration. Dionysos traveled with his attendants to preside at as many of them as he could. Attending all of them was impossible; the festival became so popular that it often took place simultaneously in several villages and cities, and those were only the ones he heard about. But he was always on the move, it seemed, and Hekate frequently took a night or two off to fly her horse to wherever he was, and watch the festival. Hermes was nearly always there, too, never one to miss a grand party.

Hekate only saw Aphrodite attend once. Aphrodite dressed modestly enough by her usual standards, but still outshone every woman there. The way she and Dionysos greeted one another, with a calm kiss on the cheek, made Hekate think they'd reunited before tonight. The thought dejected her. Although he didn't select Aphrodite as one of his "concubines" or "brides" or whatever they would be called that night—indeed, Aphrodite left too soon for that—his manner seemed both wilder and more preoccupied for the rest of the night.

Hekate wished she could get drunk that time. She tried, boldly entering into a drinking contest with a burly local man. But she won much too easily, feeling only a slight and temporary warping of her sense of gravity and judgment, while her opponent crashed unconscious to the ground. The people cheered and awarded her extra garlands of flowers and spices. She felt no victory, only guilt for having used an unfair advantage. She sat by the unconscious man and held his arm between her hands a while, sending magic through him to chase out the noxious alcohol and leave speedy healing in its wake.

"I don't quite understand what Dionysos is doing," Hades said to her one day in midwinter while they walked through a village market. "Just traveling and being worshipped?"

"It isn't only that. He visits vineyards whenever he can and advises them on growing grapes, and on any problems they've had."

"Like your grandmother in that sense, then."

"Yes. But with rather more taste for playfulness and madness than Demeter."

"The things I've heard about those festivals." Hades shook his head, and glanced aside at a donkey passing them, loaded with bags of barley. "I'd forbid you to go, but I don't think I'm physically able to stop you." He tossed her a half-smile.

She grinned and dropped her gaze. Would it help to tell him she was, in this body, still a virgin? No, she was old enough now for it to be none of his business. And he'd still worry anyway. "The festivals, the masks and craziness," she said, "think of it as his being an ambassador for the immortals. Showing mortals we do want them to have a good time. Reminding them life renews after death. Really, we Underworld folk could hardly do a better job delivering that message if we tried."

"Good, because I'm not sure I'd look at all handsome in a jackal mask," Hades said dryly.

The jackal mask, long-nosed and tall-eared, was one of the three she had crafted to bring to the Dionysia. She had made it in honor of Kerberos, who sometimes looked like a jackal when his ears perked up. The second mask was a simple cloth one that covered only the top half of her head, with pieces of multicolored stone fastened to it with tree sap. The third was a large bark mask, blackened with charcoal, with white bits of shell stuck to it to suggest the face of a skull. To judge from how people drew back a step when she wore it, it gave off a fearsome aspect indeed.

She told her parents she kept attending the festivals because she enjoyed the variations each area created, and because it was good to see an immortal earning adoration from the people instead of resentment. She didn't tell them she hoped to weasel into a sacred marriage with the god some night. Or even be one of his "concubines" on a non-marriage night—for his followers adopted whimsical titles for themselves, based on the roles they temporarily played for him. Some called themselves "minions," "executioners," or "slaves," though no one was literally being killed (except the goats in the sacrifice, so everyone could eat); and while his followers came from all social classes, the title of "slave" could apply to anyone who took the role. But comely youths of both sexes were fastened to his sides at every moment, whether during the festivals or on the road between them, and she saw no way to intrude.

Besides, he treated her differently than he did the others. With her, he displayed gallantry and respect, as if still thanking her for saving his life.

She would have preferred a more physical form of thanks.

He did at least take interest in her magical abilities. At the next festival, he brought her a cup of wine and drew her further under the large tent cloth they had tied up between tree branches. A summer rain shower had just begun sprinkling everyone. Loads of other revelers crowded under the tent too, bringing their musical instruments and still playing them while others danced the ground into a muddy swamp.

"Hermes tells you can control the elements," Dionysos said in her ear while the music blared.

"Some of them. And only within limits."

"Can you make the rain go away?"

She lifted a palm, testing the air and the raindrops. "I could, I think." She grinned at the dancers. "But they seem to be enjoying it."

He grinned too. "Then can you make it rain harder?"

She looked at him, and her breath caught at the beauty of his gray eyes and easy grin in the smoky torchlight. She lifted her hand higher, and tipped her head back. Darkness obscured the sky, but she could feel where the clouds were, and they moved about easily as she sent out her magic to prod them. She gave the winds a twirl, squeezing the rainclouds tighter above the revelers. The rain poured down in a gush, doubling or tripling in strength.

Everyone shrieked—mostly in joy—and the dancers stomped more enthusiastically than ever. Dionysos laughed. "That's marvelous. What else can you do? Summon beasts?"

"I can, but I rarely do. There's not much reason to. Other than calling my own dog."

"You'd be an asset to hunters."

"Ah, but for hunting it wouldn't be fair," she said. "The score's already about even: hunters with their weapons versus animals with their speed and strength."

He saluted her with a lift of the wine cup. "You are a just soul. I commend that."

"But if you merely want to *see* some animals…" She turned her gaze outward, and let her mind's feelers stretch through the nocturnal forest. A little rustle of energy sent up into one treetop did the trick: within moments, a flapping rush zoomed toward them, and a cloud of small bats arrived. They circled over the heads of the dancers, in the midst of the pouring rain. Another cry of wonder rose from the crowd. The bats wheeled and darted out again into the darkness, where they vanished.

"Amazing." Dionysos turned to her. "Utterly wonderful. Can you work any magic on me?" He held out his arm in invitation. His smile became a touch wicked, his eyes sparkling.

Desire spread warm in her belly like a swallow of the strongest wine. She *could* touch him and give him a jolt of lust. But that didn't seem like playing fair, and he might not like her for it afterward. So instead she offered, "Shall we make your hair the color of your grapevines?"

His eyebrows lifted in surprise. "You can turn people green?"

"Your hair, at least. Temporarily. It would fade long before sunrise."

"Then yes, do it." He opened his arms, and closed his eyes with a comical cringe like someone expecting a splash of water in the face.

She slid her hand over his warm shoulder, along the edge of

his wildcat-fur tunic, and grasped his wavy ponytail. His golden hair already nestled comfortably against its wreath of bright green grapevines, which made it easy to convince the color to spread out. In a quick shimmer, the gold all turned to spring green. "There." She released his ponytail.

He eagerly drew it across his shoulder to look at it. His face lit up, and he whooped a laugh. "You're extraordinary. Simply extraordinary." He kissed her on the forehead, then leaped out into the rain, and called, "Friends, behold! I am become one with the grapevine!"

And though his magically tinted hair was the spectacle of the rest of the night, he never divulged that Hekate had caused the magic—for which she was grateful, if regretfully so. Secrecy was the best approach in matters between mortals and immortals, even if it meant less adoration for her.

The last night of that festival, she slipped up close to him during a wild dance in the torchlight, with everyone masked, including herself—the pretty colorful cloth mask this time. But he knew who she was, of course, and laughed. "Dear Hekate." He twirled her in the dance, his arm deliciously tight around her waist. "Now, you are one I don't dare tamper with."

"You can if you like." Excitement and anticipation filled her chest until air barely had room.

"One whose parents rule the Underworld? I can't imagine anything more unwise." Still, he wasn't letting go of her.

She wrapped her arms around his neck, savoring the heat and sweat of him, and the tangy smell of the grapevines in his hair. "I do what I wish. They respect that. And it isn't as if I would tell them."

Behind the holes of his leopard mask, his eyes fluttered downward in flattery, and he laughed again. He sounded a bit breathless too. He squeezed her closer, caressed her rear, then let go. "I think you're putting a spell on me," he teased, sweetly enough that she couldn't be angry, only dismayed; and he turned about to catch up a new dance partner.

CHAPTER FORTY-ONE

$\mathcal{B}$ETTY QUENTIN AND HER TWO COMPANIONS SWUNG INTO THE parking lot of the Darrow family produce stand. On this December afternoon, a mix of rain and sleet gushed down from heavy clouds. The weather had driven everyone indoors. Perfect: no other customers. And as far as Betty could see from her foggy passenger-side window, only Terry Darrow worked inside the stand today, unpacking some fruit or vegetable into its display case.

To cover the license plate of the silver SUV, Landon had attached fake dealer plates on it, along with a holiday evergreen wreath on the front. After this little visit, they'd pull over somewhere and remove the wreath, change their hats and glasses, and switch to yet another set of plates. Landon and Krystal had it all planned, clever kids.

"Leave it running," she told Landon.

She opened the door and heaved herself out. Leaning on her cane, she hurried across the uneven gravel into the stand. The cold wind whipped about beneath the tent roof, rattling the tattered edges of the canopy. She kept her thick scarf wrapped around her neck and head, and glanced about, shaking raindrops off her coat. A string of multicolored lights lined the inside of the tent, and some 1950s crooner sang "I'll Be Home for Christmas" from the speakers. A teenage boy in the back room was busy moving crates around, and didn't notice Betty.

Terry did, though. He looked up from his box of yellow onions, and froze. Anger or fear rippled through his face, then he steeled it with a mask of calm, and said, "Afternoon."

"Afternoon, Mr. Darrow." She hobbled forward a couple of steps. "Do you remember we spoke several weeks ago? About Sophie, and Adrian."

The mask stayed in place. "I remember." He set down the onion he held, and rested his gloved hand on the far edge of the wooden case, watching her. He didn't question the name "Adrian." Perhaps he knew by now, then. Likely he had confronted Sophie last time, as Betty had hoped, and learned a few disturbing things, though likely not *all* the disturbing things.

"He isn't what a father would want for his daughter, is he," she commiserated.

"I admit he wouldn't have been my first choice." Still keeping a guarded gaze on her, Terry rolled his upper lip under his teeth, making his mustache wiggle.

She picked up a green pear and sniffed it. "It would please me if you could help us catch him. You're in a good position to do so."

"Sorry. I trust my daughter. And I trust Adrian, at least for now. I'm going to have to pass."

Betty set down the pear and smiled at the little lights decorating the tent. "Cute place you've got here. I'm sure you'd hate to see anything happen to it. Or to your family."

Fury flared in his eyes. He plunged his hand down behind the display case and yanked a baseball bat into the air. With a quick swing it was pointed at her, gripped in both his hands, and he advanced with slow steps. "Ross, call 911 *now*," he bellowed without looking away from Betty.

The boy popped his head out, dumbfounded. "What? Why?"

"Do it! We have an intruder."

The boy nodded and scrambled off.

"You," Terry said to her, "are done harassing my daughter. And hell if I'm going to let you threaten me and the rest of my family."

She edged backward, keeping pace with his advance. "Terry, I give you this last chance to cooperate. You will not like the consequences if you refuse."

"You stay right there. We're going to see how well you like jail."

"Drop it, sir," Krystal barked in her brittle voice.

He looked past Betty and his mouth opened in shock.

"Drop it now," Krystal added.

He let go of the bat, which smacked to the gravel, and lifted his hands. Resentment burned in his gaze.

Betty glanced with a smile over her shoulder. Krystal, in black-haired wig and tinted glasses, pointed her handgun at Terry from the opened window of the back seat. Betty looked again at Terry. "You'll cooperate and help get Adrian for us, won't you? So we don't have to ask Sophie again, I mean."

Terry glowered. "I may not totally like the guy. But he's right about one thing. You're evil."

"A subjective word. You may live to regret saying that." She limped to the car and opened the door. "Or maybe you won't. Live, that is." She climbed in and shut her door. "Let's go."

Landon peeled out. They didn't even hear sirens yet.

"Too bad about her family," Betty said. "But it's what I expected."

"Traitors," Krystal said with scorn, and tossed her wig onto the floor.

PLEASE COME FIND me, Sophie's text said.

Adrian's heart kicked up in fright. As a test, he answered in an English-lettered version of the Underworld language, *Daughter's name?*

Hekate. It's me, safe for now, just bad day. She used the Underworld words too.

Still, someone could have been forcing her to answer. And "safe for now" didn't reassure him. He leaped out of the Airstream into the night. Clouds overhead smothered every star. In the beam of a flashlight, he and Kiri sprinted across the wilderness toward Sophie's location. Mud splattered him on the way, and he had to clamber over three huge fallen trees and innumerable smaller logs.

Adrian drew up close to Sophie's living-world location, ordered Kiri to stay, and switched over.

To his relief, she was alone; and to his surprise, they were in a restroom of some campus building—likely the women's room— standing outside one of the stalls. But he forgot his uncertainty about being caught in here when he saw the tears in her eyes and the panic creasing her forehead. He drew her into his arms. "What, what happened?"

She clutched him. "Switch us over."

He obeyed. They thudded a few centimeters down to the wet ground in the darkness. Kiri barked a happy hello.

Adrian stepped back to sit upon one of the fallen trees, pulling Sophie onto his lap. With her face on his shoulder, she spilled out a flood of words. Her father had called; Quentin came and threatened him again, this time at gunpoint; the police didn't get there in time; Quentin got away and still hadn't been found. As she spoke, cold anger and resolve pooled within him, edged with panic.

"All I want to do is hide." Sophie was trembling, as she had been since he first fetched her. "Hide here forever, never go back. Except I need to hide everyone else too. My family, my friends, *your* family, Zoe's...everyone I might ever care about. And they wouldn't go. Dad doesn't want to hide, he said so. He's mad instead of scared. He wants to 'take a stand,' even though he knows how dangerous they are. How can we convince them to—I don't know, join the Witness Protection Program or something?" She lifted her head. "Is that even a real thing? The Witness Protection Program?"

"Um. Well, yeah, it is, but I don't think we could easily explain our case to the U.S. government. Hiding out here's a better idea. It's just, as you say, I don't think we can convince them all to do it. I didn't want it to come down to a war against Thanatos, but..." He sighed. "We have to stop them."

"Can we? How?"

He kicked his boot heel against the tree a few times. "Okay, suppose I swallow my pride and apologize to Niko."

She nodded instantly, sitting up straighter. "And Freya. They were awesome last time. I've been wanting to text them myself."

"Fine. Let's do it." He got out his phone. Its screen lit up their patch of wilderness. "Maybe with more of us searching, we'll at least find out where Quentin's hiding."

Selecting Niko's number, he gritted his teeth and texted, *I apologise, mate. We need you back. Q's threatening S's family again. She's probably in Washington. New assassins with guns. Help please? Name your price.*

He sent it off.

Sophie kissed his cheek. "Thank you."

Adrian tapped his camera app. "Hey, got something to show you. Dropped by the Underworld today for an errand. Look." He turned the screen toward her, displaying the close-up shot he'd taken.

Two tiny green fruits gleamed in the flash of the photo, glossy leaves around them, dried-up flower petals still stuck to their tops.

Sophie drew in a breath in rapture. "The oranges."

"Merry Christmas."

She took the phone and gazed at the picture. "How long till they're ready?"

"Took three or four months to ripen last time."

She studied them. "At least one bite for me and one for Liam," she finally said. "If Liam wants."

"Absolutely. Reserved for you two, no exceptions this time."

His phone buzzed. "Ah," she said, and handed it back to him. "I think Niko responded."

Adrian opened the text and snorted. "God. Wanker."

"What's it say?"

"'*My price? A blow job. Then I'm at your service, mate.*' But he did add a smiley face, so…"

She chuckled. "I think we have him back."

He resettled her across his lap and hugged her.

She wasn't trembling anymore. She tilted her head and pointed above them. "Stars coming out."

Adrian looked up at the stars twinkling between drifting clouds. "Yeah. Nice."

He'd suffer Niko for her, gladly. And he had already texted Zoe to ask her to fly to the Underworld when she had time and put a health-and-protection spell upon the orange tree to guarantee its successful harvest. But what could he possibly do to make up for what Thanatos inflicted upon her and the people she loved?

In addition, she'd dream of Persephone's heartbreaking end soon. Very soon, the way she was speeding ahead to follow the ancient adventures. He should warn her, tell her to brace herself.

But he didn't have the heart, not minutes after a new scare from Quentin. Besides, she probably had at least another night or two before reaching that part. So he hoped. Then she could always go back into the good parts again, slower, and savor them as many times as she liked, the way he'd been doing for three years now.

Adrian shivered and hugged her tighter.

"Cold?" she asked, eyes still upon the stars.

"A bit. I'm fine."

BEFORE GOING TO bed, Sophie received texts from Niko and Freya. Freya's said, *Thinking of you, dear. Sorry Q has troubled your home again. Been lovely catching up with your Tab, and I'll soon come see you too, if it's all right?*

Niko's said, *Hello sugar. I've missed you. Can I squash some enemies for you?*

She sent back grateful acceptance to both messages, but remarked to Adrian, "He didn't actually say 'sorry.'"

Adrian pulled off his shirt and tossed it into the pile on the tiny closet floor, then wriggled into the long-sleeved T-shirt he wore to bed. "That's him all over. Doubt he's apologized to anyone in the last three millennia."

He switched off the lamp and climbed into bed beside her. They intertwined under the covers, holding close and shivering while they warmed each other up. The Airstream had been getting progressively colder in the last few weeks. Some mornings when Sophie awoke, she could see her breath in the air. She hated to ask that he use up more generator fuel by setting the thermostat higher, and it seemed wrong to start the new generation of immortals off by polluting the air of the spirit realm. They'd discussed it, though it made them roll their eyes at themselves for being such environmental-guilt-ridden Westerners. She compensated by bringing extra fleece blankets to pile on the bed, and he looked up how to add weatherproofing to the trailer's windows. Meanwhile, since the mattress still tended to be chilly when you first got into bed, they performed this body-heat exchange nightly.

It usually led to more specialized touches and higher heat. But tonight, likely because her dad's call had sent her flying like a scared bird into Adrian's arms, he only held her. And when she kissed him, he hesitated.

The dim orange nightlight from the bathroom glowed around his silhouette. She touched his cheek in question.

"The dreams," he said. "Thanatos is doing damage there too, you've said. And...well, you already know the immortals don't live forever."

Dread washed over her. "Zeus and Hera have been killed already, like I told you. But...you mean us."

"Us and nearly everyone eventually. I don't know if you'd get to any of that tonight, or even tomorrow, but I feel like I ought to warn you."

Tonight or tomorrow. So soon. The chill swept through her again, even though they were talking about events that happened over three thousand years ago. She scooted closer until she felt the beat of his heart against her arm. He was alive, here, now. So was she. That was what mattered, as he'd said. "It's kind of like hearing your favorite character on a show is going to get killed off, isn't it," she said. "I mean, you know it doesn't matter really, but in another way it totally matters. It feels real."

"It was real," he said softly. "But we did come back. Try to hold onto that."

CHAPTER FORTY-TWO

ERA SHOWED UP IN THE FIELDS, A FREE SOUL AGAIN, ABOUT A year after her death, and Zeus a few months after her. Persephone gladly ran to greet each of them when the other souls sent out the word. The formerly royal pair bore a subdued gratitude now. Time in Tartaros tended to do that to souls, leaving them cowed but thankful, with a habit of finding as many of their former victims in the fields as they could and apologizing to them.

Since they had only spent a year or so in the caves of punishment, evidently the Fates did recognize the large amount of good the pair had performed in life to help balance the bad. Those who were truly murderous and remorseless often got held for a span of time equal to a whole human life—thirty, forty, sometimes fifty or more years. Even the thought of one year in such confinement shot a chill through Persephone. To her memory, she had never been sent there between any of her past lives. But would she in future? Would she die at all?

Death, at least, was looking more likely. Thanatos became only more determined with each passing month. Three more immortals, in different and far-apart attacks, had been captured and killed in the year since Zeus' and Hera's murder.

Benna, Poseidon's youngest daughter, was first, turned upon by the village she had lived in for years. A good woman who would never have merited the caves of punishment, her soul had appeared in the fields at once. Her two immortal sisters fled to shelters in the spirit world. Lately Poseidon and Amphitrite visited the Underworld often to talk to Benna, and bring her news of the rest of the family. The grief on the immortal couple's face at seeing their daughter among the dead brought tears to Persephone's eyes every time. It was too easy to remember almost losing Hekate, and to fear losing her again in this new and horrible way.

The vicious fringe group also captured and killed one of the Muses, a sweet poet named Euterpe; and similarly, Epimetheus, Prometheus' brother, who never suspected his living-world neighbors would betray him.

At least Zeus and Hera had enjoyed over a century of immortality. These latest three had only tasted it for a modest span of years, and ended up living no longer than the average person.

Fear and rage spread through the immortals. Several withdrew to the spirit world to build homes there and ventured only occasionally into the mortal realm, the way the Underworld gods already lived. But, as Persephone knew, residing in the spirit realm felt unnatural and lonely, even with souls, wild creatures, and other immortals for company. The immortals were meant to be stewards of both realms—she sensed it, and Hekate, more in tune with the forces of nature, confirmed it when Persephone mused aloud about it to her. But how could you act as steward and helper for those who might try to kill you?

Living among others always involved danger, she supposed. Earth held treachery. Death and life were joined, eating each other's tails like sacred snake bracelets. Anyone familiar with the Underworld knew that.

But mortals hadn't been actively trying to kill them before, not until lately. And it didn't help that some immortals, Ares and Artemis foremost among them, had struck back in revenge, treating it as war. They hunted down and slaughtered several of the mob leaders, exactly as the other immortals had warned they shouldn't. More meetings followed, more shouting at each other. Neither Persephone nor Hekate could take much of it. Hades, at least, seemed to get perverse pleasure out of reminding Ares how Tartaros had claimed Zeus for similar behavior.

"Your record's worse than his, in fact," Hades had said at their last meeting, "and that's only the deeds of yours I know about. I doubt you're doing good works in your spare time to balance it out. You're building yourself a lovely thick rope in the afterlife indeed."

"Assuming the afterlife can ever catch me," Ares had retorted. "I don't plan to be stupid enough to get killed."

"Oh, are you finally trying not to be stupid?" Hermes had said, in optimistic tones. "What good news."

Most mortals didn't wish to harm the immortals, and the itinerant Thanatos speechmakers even got run out of town in some places. Most immortals, in their turn, devoted the majority of their time to improving the living world in some fashion. Gratitude and prayers in the form of written tablets or offerings of food appeared in sanctuaries that had sprung up all over the mainland and islands. Persephone had visited some, heard of others, and had no idea where every last one was or how many there were. She tried to reassure herself with that knowledge: the immortals had plenty of allies, more than they knew.

Still, she had trouble sleeping every time Hekate jaunted off to another region, especially if her purpose was to join the Dionysia. Yes, Dionysos was especially well loved among mortals, and his followers particularly vicious against intruders. At a Dionysia up near Mount Olympos recently, three Thanatos fanatics, two men and a woman, had infiltrated the party and leapt upon Dionysos during a dance. Hekate had seen it all, and related it to her parents. The attackers stabbed him with knives while he fought back, all four tumbling on the ground in a whirl of blood. But the struggle lasted mere moments, because then his followers pulled the three off him and did to them exactly what Thanatos had done to Zeus and Hera: they ran them through with blades, tore them apart, and threw them on the fire.

Hekate was horrified, as was Dionysos. Persephone and Hades found the three in Tartaros, and confirmed the story—it had gone just as Hekate and the rest described. The king of the nearest city, which governed the revelers and the would-be killers, listened to the account told to him by Dionysos in person. It sounded like perfectly fair self-defense, the king concluded. He even apologized for the shocking rudeness of his citizens violating a religious ritual, and said he hoped the sacrifice of the three would bring the blessings of the gods back to his shamed countryside.

None of the immortals knew how to answer such a thing. It was good to have allies, especially kings, but hard to explain that supernatural blessings were not so easily lost, obtained, or understood. It was as Demeter said: the stories sprang up and grew on their own, with no basis in reality. People loved their poems and legends better than they loved truth.

So Persephone and Hades naturally went right on worrying about Hekate participating in the Dionysia, despite Thanatos' failure there. What if the killers tried harder next time, with a greater force? What if they targeted Hekate instead of Dionysos? The crowd wasn't as likely to protect her. She wasn't the central focus of the festival.

"They usually don't even know who I am," Hekate assured her. It was a few days before midsummer. She was sitting on the stone floor of her bedchamber, using sticky sap to refasten some of the colored stones that had fallen off her cloth mask. "I don't call attention to myself. In fact, I use magic to deflect it. You needn't worry."

"I'll try." Persephone folded her arms, lingering in the doorway. "But need I worry about you coming home pregnant with some unknown reveler's child?"

When Hekate answered with a sharp laugh and lifted a half-amused, half-offended expression to her, Persephone added, "It's all right. I love you and trust you and I want you to enjoy yourself. But…you might wind up rather unhappy if that happened."

Hekate arched a black eyebrow, an expression inherited straight from Hades. She returned to her stone-sticking. "Some unknown reveler? No, of course not."

"Well. That's a relief." Persephone felt this conversation was uncomfortably like her long-ago exchange with Demeter—when Demeter had asked her straight out if she was in love with Hades.

Hekate rose with the completed mask. "Besides," she added as she slipped past Persephone, "there's magic to prevent pregnancy, you know. Too bad not everyone can do it that way. Cloudhair seeds, ugh."

Persephone stared after her daughter's retreating back, her mouth falling open. Then she murmured to herself, "Indeed, too bad. That'd be convenient."

Q's in the Seattle area, said Sophie's text to Tabitha. *Threatened my dad. Be on the lookout just in case.*

Tab frowned and spent a minute figuring out who "Q" was, then recalled it. *Let the bitch try*, she texted back. *My followers rip people apart.*

Ha. Yeah, I remember. Srsly though, be careful. They might check out anyone who's close to me, such as my BFF.

Thanks. YOU be careful, babe!

Tabitha sent the text and sat back against the cafe bench seat, earbuds blasting the class-assigned symphony into her ears without her registering a note.

Crazy cult people? That seemed a lame thing to worry about. Not when she had tasks on her list like planning the next party—lined up for it she had The Luigis, *the* current number one band popular with hipsters. Also on the to-do list: deciding how best a girl should enjoy boundless riches and secret immortality. Niko and Freya totally got that. They were enablers that way. But honestly, why didn't Sophie and Zoe—and apparently Adrian—realize the amount of fun they could be having, and weren't? Gloomy Underworld types. She switched the symphony off, and clicked instead to The Luigis' album on her iPod.

Annoying thing was, she sort of did see their point of view. With great power comes great responsibility, and all that Gandalf-advice shit. Hell, Dionysos could be considered one of those Underworld types, with his dying-and-rising-god routine. So maybe that meant Tab was one too. But it was sure more fun to hang with Freya or Niko.

Especially Freya. Damn, that woman had her technique

down—mainly the "I'm flirting madly with you but I promise nothing" technique. Now that Freya was hanging around the West Coast to help search for Thanatos, Tab saw her more often, and got lots of doses of alluring confusion.

"What are those for, those kisses?" Tab asked her the other night, when Freya kissed her goodnight after they'd had dinner.

"Old times' sake," Freya said.

"Sophie said you slept with Adrian for old times' sake, too. She didn't seem way happy about that."

Freya only laughed. "Sophie has nothing to fear from me. She knows that."

And somehow she'd left without Tab feeling any the wiser.

Meanwhile that attraction to Hekate-Zoe stayed rooted in her brain, bugging her at inconvenient times. What was up with that? Why was that so hard to trust or resolve?

She thought of Zoe's steady, unnerving, wise stare, which made Tab feel about five hundred years younger than Zoe instead of three years, even though age shouldn't matter between two immortals with access to past-life memories. She thought of Zoe—and Hekate—doing her amazingly cool tricks, waving magic about with the ease of blowing bubbles. In comparison, she felt unworthy, a raucous and immature partier. Zoe wanted something deeper, and Lord only knew why she'd look for it in Tab.

Plus she honestly kind of wondered if Zoe had thrown a spell on her to make her keep thinking about her, same as Dionysos had wondered it about Hekate.

She scowled at her open computer on the cafe table. Final exams, cults, relationships, magic spells? Who had time for this crap?

She turned up the volume on the music, and tackled the much more delightful task of planning the next party.

CHAPTER FORTY-THREE

NIKOLAOS SAUNTERED UP TO THE TRAILER IN THE FROSTY MORN-ing air, where Adrian stood waiting. Niko wore clothing that was dark-toned and unobtrusive, for him, aside from the red and white striped scarf and matching hat.

Adrian sipped his coffee. "Oh good, I've finally found Waldo."

"I thought perhaps the chances of you licking me were greater if I looked like a candy cane."

Adrian snorted. While he tried to decide upon the most insulting comeback, Kiri hurtled in from the field. She greeted Niko with a yip of joy and darted round and round his legs, her tail whipping back and forth. She was too well trained to leap onto him without permission, but clearly was having trouble restraining herself.

"Yes, it's all right," Niko assured her. "Come give me a hug." He knelt, opening his arms.

"You'll regret that," Adrian said.

Kiri planted her paws in Niko's crouched lap and licked his cheeks. He grunted, wincing. "Muddy dog."

"Told you."

After gratifying Kiri with fur-ruffling and compliments, Niko rose and tried to wipe the mud off the front of his clothes.

Adrian opened the trailer door. "Come in. I've got dog towels."

Inside the Airstream, Adrian toweled off Kiri's muddy feet while Niko took another towel and cleaned his coat and jeans.

"Sophie off studying?" Niko asked.

"Yeah. Final exams coming up. Had a study group to meet at the library."

"None of them in Thanatos, one hopes."

The familiar anxiety twisted in Adrian's stomach. "I don't even bloody know. I don't think so. None of them are acting as suspicious as Melissa used to. But...argh."

They sat opposite each other at the table.

"Well," Niko began, "I do still have access to the guru's email. And through that, I've read what Quentin's emailed him. But it isn't much. Mostly she assures him she's in a safe location, doesn't say where, and they ponder the possible meanings of ancient documents that talk about immortals. They do seem to be matching it up with what they learned from Sanjay, and piecing a few things together that are actually true."

"Such as?"

Niko took off his hat, and scratched at his scalp. He already had an inch or so of hair grown back after shaving it in the wake of the grenade fire. Adrian hadn't seen him in well over a month, he now realized. "Oak, for instance," Niko said. "They're finally understanding Sanjay claiming he could sense certain other people, and that oak blocked it. Apparently in their ancient chicken-scratched tablets and scrolls, there's a similar mention of gods finding one another by a magical sense unless oak stands between them."

Adrian frowned and wrapped his hands around his cooling coffee mug. "I don't much like them knowing that."

"Curiously, I don't like anything they do. Except when they get suicidal impulses. I approve of that."

"If only they didn't keep taking others down with them."

Niko nodded. "Good news is, I haven't yet found any mention of Freya or myself, nor Zoe or Tab. I don't think they know about any of us, though they do suspect there are others. Or that you'll convert others soon."

"Then tell Tab to keep a bloody lower profile," Adrian muttered.

"Yes, we do remind her, but the dear thing's having such fun, she forgets."

Adrian grumbled inarticulately.

"However," Niko added, "I still haven't managed to hack into Quentin's account itself, to see what else she's sending, and to whom. That'd be convenient. I don't suppose she's handing out new business cards of people we can stalk, the way we did with Wilkes?"

Adrian shook his head. "Not that we've heard. Instead she's walked right up to Sophie's dad in person, and did the whole Mafia threat." Adrian attempted an Italian-American movie gangster accent. "'Nice family you got here. Real shame if anything happened to them.'"

Niko smirked. "It's old-school and clichéd, but it does get the point across."

"Obviously they're going to go after Sophie again, or someone in her family, and hold them hostage in order to flush me out." Adrian clenched the mug to keep down the tremor developing in his hands. "What else could that threat mean?"

"Indeed." Niko frowned out the window. The pale December sun lit up the green of his eyes. "Or it's a diversionary tactic, to get us to look one way while they do their real dirty work elsewhere. Or they'll do both, the way they went after Rhea and you at the same time. Whatever it is, I do suspect it's you they're trying to eliminate."

"Naturally." Adrian pulled in another deep breath. The smell of the coffee now nauseated him instead of soothing him. Yes, all he needed to do to protect his beloved was offer himself up as a sacrifice, and join the dead in the fields of souls. No problem. That'd make everyone happy.

What truly chilled and depressed him was the whisper in his head that said, actually, that would be best. Sophie would be better off, even if losing him grieved her in the short term. She'd have her family, she'd have her life back…

He shuddered, shaking off the horrid thought. No, Thanatos couldn't be right. They could never be.

"So we look for them," Adrian said, "and we guard Sophie and her family whenever we can."

Niko nodded. "Freya's helping. We'll make a habit of lurking round Carnation. And I'll keep up my hacker tricks to see what other intelligence I can turn up. Oh, and I've brought you some new disguise pieces. Just because that amuses me."

"Cheers." But the nausea lingered within him. For right this moment, no one was guarding Sophie, and as Niko had lightly suggested, one of her study companions could be in Thanatos.

Adrian got up and dumped the rest of his coffee in the sink. "Well, I'm off to meet Sophie."

She still had a few hours of study group left, in truth, but he'd find a table near hers and keep watch. And if Thanatos wanted to attack today, great, because he'd love a good excuse to throw someone out a library window, plate glass shattering and all.

No ONE IN Sophie's study group was in Thanatos. She honestly didn't think so, and chuckled when Adrian told her he was guarding her in case of that possibility. He'd lurked at a table next to theirs for two hours, and she had to pretend not to know him. What with the studying for tomorrow's chemistry final, and the huge paper she'd just finished writing, she was too tired to laugh in a full-bellied way at his appearance, though his new disguise was decidedly laughable. The orange and black Oregon State hat with earflaps would have been bad enough, but paired with the oversized sweater in blue and white block stripes, and the fake goatee, it was a wonder she kept a straight face.

She pulled the hat off him as soon as they got into the spirit realm. But she touched the goatee, loosened up his hat-squashed black hair, and regarded him. "Yeah," she said. "With facial hair, you are indeed very Hades."

"Fancy that." He left the goatee on for now, and walked with her through the dark spirit-world night. "And how are Hades and Persephone, in your memories?"

"Fine. I mean, unsettled about Thanatos, and about Hekate always going off to the Dionysos festivals. But all right otherwise."

He nodded without looking at her. With a twinge of unease

in her belly, she remembered, as she did several times a day, that they would *not* be all right pretty soon now.

She drew in a breath of the cold night air. Ice was forming, its crystals crunching underfoot in the meadow grass and fallen leaves. Sophie glanced at the sky and found it heavily clouded, as it had been in the living realm.

"Might get your snow tonight," she said.

He glanced up too. "That'd be nice."

In the chilly trailer bed, before sleeping, they embraced and sought comfort in kisses and intimate strokes. But tonight it seemed to her that Adrian's touch carried desperation, a clinging to her, as if someone was about to pull her away. She clung to him too, in anxiety and love. But she still didn't know how she would respond if someone were to say, *Choose. Adrian or your family. Adrian or the rest of the world.*

Why can't I have both? she lamented in silent answer, and held him tighter.

CHAPTER FORTY-FOUR

HEKATE SWUNG HER KNAPSACK OF CLOTHES, MASKS, AND OTHER items onto her shoulder. She found her mother in the fields, and waited until Persephone was done talking to one of the souls.

"I'm off," Hekate told her, and gave and received a kiss on the cheek.

"Three days, as usual?"

"Yes. In Argos, or just outside it, at least."

Hades walked up with Kerberos, and Hekate kissed her father too. "I'm leaving Kerberos with you this time."

Persephone's brow crinkled. "We feel safer when you bring him."

"I know, but he hates it. The drums scare him, and the drunk people keep trying to play with him and put costumes on him."

That made them grin. Hades took hold of the scruff of the dog's neck to keep him back. "All right, let him stay." He pointed at her, the grin fading. "But be careful."

"I will. Goodbye!" She strolled across the white grass, feeling its soft coolness under her bare feet, while her mind already raced ahead to the possibility that this time, this festival, Dionysos would do more than just dance with her. The way he'd looked at her and held her against him in the dance at the last festival, half a month ago, sent hope and desire surging up in her chest.

She crossed the river on the raft, and on its opposite side she turned to wave at her parents. They were two small figures among the masses of souls, but easy to discern from the solid gleam of

Persephone's white and red clothing and Hades' white and purple. They waved back. Kerberos darted around Hades' feet, in the attitude of having brought a stick to throw, and planted his front legs down flat in front of Hades in invitation to play. Hades knelt and took the stick, and teased Kerberos with it, making the dog dance from side to side in a frenzy. Persephone and Hades both seemed to be laughing.

Hekate smiled too, walked away through the entrance tunnel, and flew her horse to Argos.

"No FEARSOME WATCHDOG of the Underworld today?" Hermes greeted her when she arrived at the gathering spot at the city gates of Argos.

"I allowed him to sit this one out," Hekate said.

"In that case, I'll protect you." He hooked his arm into hers and waggled his eyebrows.

She laughed. "I wonder about your definition of 'protect.'"

The festival took place outside the city. Starting at sunset, a procession led deep into a sea of olive trees at the base of a broad, dry hill. Night fell early, for this was the winter solstice. Hekate was glad for both her woolen cloak and for the grove of trees that sheltered the group from the cold wind. Like most of the worshippers, she wore fur-lined leather boots instead of going barefoot or sandaled, and a wool shawl around her head in addition to the jackal mask.

Torches, drums, the masks and symbols upon poles, the oration about the dying god—these features usually remained consistent from one Dionysia to another, and tonight's was no exception. But extra torches and bonfires burned in the spaces between the olive trees, for warmth as well as light.

Dionysos, when he appeared, had a gorgeous leopard pelt around his shoulders in addition to a long wool tunic, and skin boots with gray rabbit fur. An ivy wreath decorated his head. He looked every bit the king of the winter night, becoming the part as splendidly as he became king of the languorous summer in the hot months.

An idea came to Hekate as she listened to his speech about the return of life and light, his words tailored to match the solstice. Could she manage the spell from here, without touching him? She'd been working on it, and thought it worth a try. Concentrating, she pulled in and directed the energies, and focused her thoughts upon the leaves of his ivy wreath.

Little glowing lights burst to life, hovering at the tips of the leaves, a crown of stars the blue-white color of moonlight. The people gasped and cried out in wonder.

"Oh, nice touch," Hermes complimented, beside her. He had figured it out at once, of course. He'd seen her perform such tricks before.

Dionysos faltered in his speech, confused at the people's reaction, then gathered it had something to do with his crown. He took off the wreath to examine it. The magical lights came with it, a hovering circle of twenty or more shining sparks, and he stared in surprise a moment before breaking into a smile and looking straight at Hekate in the crowd.

She beamed at him.

He inclined his head toward her, like bowing for a noblewoman, and replaced the glowing wreath on his hair. Ever the adept improviser, he continued his speech, adding words about how the stars themselves had come down to light the people's way back to spring. The poetry at his command—she loved that too. She sensed and understood nature, and could control it to a limited degree, but he could speak of it in silver-tongued words, inspiring others in a way she never could.

When the feasting and dancing began, adorers mobbed Dionysos, as ever. But he hadn't designated anyone as his festival brides or concubines yet. Hekate wasn't sure if this city's version of the Dionysia included such a thing. Sexuality was explored somehow in all of them, but in some it was more a matter of free experimentation among the crowd, with less emphasis placed on Dionysos himself as a participant. Still, he did always seem to wind up kissing or fondling someone, or at least letting himself be kissed and fondled. If he did more than that, it wasn't in the public eye. She did wonder, with pangs of jealousy, what exactly took place on the occasions when he disappeared with some woman or man.

Tonight, though, he maneuvered through the throng to catch Hekate's wrist in one hand and Hermes' in the other. "My friends, I seldom get to talk to you. Sit by me this time."

So, to her surprised joy, she found herself next to Dionysos during the feast, on cushions and skins that insulated her from the cold ground. While they sat and ate roasted fowl with sweet raisins, his attendants built a large tent around them, stringing up draperies between trees and poles so that soon the better part of the group was enclosed on three sides. A hole was left in the top through which the smoke escaped, and the front of the tent stayed open for people to wander in and out. But with so many torches and fires, the light stayed bright enough to be cheerful, and the air inside the tent lost its chill. Granted, Hekate's warm comfort might have had something to do with Dionysos, who had draped half his leopard skin around her, and sometimes slipped his arm around her too. Meanwhile his wildcat Agria snoozed on the ground directly behind them, giving them a warm living cushion to lean back upon.

Dionysos spoke to her throughout the feast. He praised her for the light magic she had worked, and suggested they think of other impressive ideas to dazzle people during rituals.

"I'm happy to," she said, "but then word might get out that I'm an immortal. And a terrifying Underworld one, at that."

"More of them already know it than you think," Hermes said, from Dionysos' other side, between bites of a drumstick. "You've visited quite a few cities with your parents. People remember you."

"Hm." She frowned into the crowd, and did indeed catch a few people staring at her. But then, everyone tended to watch whom-ever Dionysos was with, out of curiosity or envy. "I wonder why no one's given me trouble."

"Something to do with people being torn apart last time," Dionysos murmured, his face grim.

"Indeed." Hermes picked a scrap of food from his teeth. "That and your scary immortal dog."

She smirked. "Kerberos isn't scary."

"Not in reality, no. But from the stories they tell about him, he is."

After the feast, Dionysos got up to introduce and judge the performances, which tonight took the form of people competing to tell the most tragic tale of jilted love. All the stories were supposed to be true, their veracity sworn upon the River Styx.

"Is that our river, in the Underworld?" Hekate asked Hermes. "We never named it."

He handed her a cup of wine. "The River Styx is from old stories, but sure, you've got an underground river in the fields of souls, so why not say it's the Styx?"

While the competitors delivered their drunken tales of woe, to roars of laughter and moans of sympathy, Hekate's gaze kept sliding to Dionysos, who stood near the well-lit performance area. Tonight, more than a few times, he looked across the crowd to where she sat, and let his gaze linger in hers for a few moments.

"You know," Hermes said in her ear, "I've spoken to him about you."

Nervousness stiffened her spine. "Oh?"

"He's quite attracted to you. But even for him, it's a daunting prospect, debauching the powerful daughter of the gods of the dead."

She scoffed. "He should know better. They don't *control* death, or have any powers over it."

"No, but he has great respect for both your parents, and doesn't wish to do anything that might offend them."

"Absurd." She swigged her wine. "I'm grown up. It's nothing to do with them."

"True. But it's difficult to convince him. So I was thinking…" Hermes scooted closer to her on the piece of fur they sat upon, till their arms and legs touched. "What if I showed him *I* wasn't afraid to toy with you? And that you didn't mind toying with me?"

Her ears began ringing in shock as she listened.

"Then once everyone was…warmed up," Hermes continued, his low-pitched voice tickling her ear, "I could transfer you over to him."

She swallowed; her throat was strangely dry. A quick glance at Hermes was all she could manage at the moment. But he did look particularly handsome, tongue flicking the inner edge of his lips as he watched her, green eyes keen and interested. "You'd only get 'warmed up'?" she asked. "That doesn't seem satisfying. For you."

He chuckled. He wove his fingers into hers, against the luxurious fur they sat upon. "Believe me, love, merely warming you up would be unbelievably satisfying for me."

His tone as he said it was what convinced her. She didn't have much experience in this life with suitors, but she had plenty of memories and had witnessed lots of other attempted seductions at all these Dionysia. Comparing Hermes to those, she found herself impressed. He didn't seem arrogantly confident like the men who viewed women as a land to conquer (Ares came to mind), nor did he sound like a pathetically besotted adolescent who would gladly slit his own throat if she requested it. Instead he sounded as if he were letting her in on a delightful dirty secret, or offering her a forbidden treat. That was how it should go, in the absence of true mutual love, she supposed.

After all, most of the people fondling each other at these festivals weren't in love. They had merely found an attractive partner for the evening, perhaps a friend they could trust. Aphrodite served as such a friend for lots of people—which had been a source of heartbreak for Dionysos once, but surely a great convenience for others. Including Hermes.

And in order to get to Dionysos, if Hermes' invitation was what it took…

She turned her hand over and laced her fingers more snugly with his. "Let's try."

His eyes darkened as his pupils widened in thrill and amazement. But only for a moment. Then bawdy merriment returned to twinkle in them, and he set aside his wine cup and hooked his arm around her waist. He moved her hair aside and planted a long kiss upon the side of her neck, which made her catch her breath more deliciously than she had expected. Excellent technique. Aphrodite had taught him well.

"I'll ask your consent before each move," he murmured. "Just so you won't hit me with some awful, painful spell."

"And I could, you know." Smiling, she tilted her head farther in invitation. "But that was all right. Go ahead."

CHAPTER FORTY-FIVE

TABITHA LEANED HER ELBOWS ON THE BALCONY RAILING OF THE Nectar Club in downtown Seattle, and watched the caterers set out tablecloths, plates, and glowstick-filled vases for the party. On the stage, techies ran sound-checks and crawled around adjusting amps and lights. People were lining up on the street, waiting to be let in, but it wasn't time yet. The Luigis were supposed to be here by now. But then, performers were usually late. She wasn't worried.

She checked her phone again, though of course Freya hadn't answered to say whether she could come or not. Last Tab had heard was this morning's *I'll try. Boring spy work to be done first!*

Some shit about scouring the city for Thanatos. Lame. You couldn't go worrying about a few random terrorists and letting it ruin your good time.

But the nagging feeling that Tab was neglecting Zoe, unfairly and even egregiously so, was ruining Tab's good time too.

She was about to text Zoe, invite her to fly over and catch the end of the show at least. But then the band arrived in a burst of greetings, guitar cases clunking against the walls, and Tab hurried down the steps to say hello.

Yeah, she had to figure out her relationship with Zoe someday, and yes, she remembered Dionysos getting over Aphrodite and wanting Hekate with an accumulating urgency. But he'd had years to figure that out and find his place in the world. He'd been older and wiser by then. Tab was still only eighteen and had only been wobbling around in her new immortal high heels for a few weeks.

And getting to meet the goddess of love and desire, who was still incredibly hot, and knowing that Freya-Aphrodite had, at various times, desired Tab, and might possibly be up for some kind of sex again now? Yeah, that was distracting in a major way. Even more distracting than the parties with celebrities that had distracted her from Zoe in the first place.

Ugh. Too much drama. And too much of it having to do with Greek gods in ancient freaking prehistory. Tab had things going on now, tonight. End of story.

Not that the story ever ended, did it. That was the damn problem.

Dionysos' blood heated and chased itself faster through his veins as he watched Hermes mouth the side of Hekate's neck. She closed her eyes, black eyelashes sweeping down to her cheekbones, their shadows thickened in the torchlight.

Hermes had talked to him about her a few days ago. "You could have her, you know," he told Dionysos. "She wants you. I'm almost totally certain."

"I'm too old. She's too young."

Hermes scoffed to show how much he valued that statement.

"I suspect she cares too much," Dionysos elaborated. "I don't want to hurt her. Not physically, I mean, but—"

"I know what you mean," Hermes cut in. "And are you sure *you* aren't avoiding caring too much for anyone? It hurt you a great deal last time, I know. Isn't it likely you're steering clear of that happening again?"

"From you I'm hearing this?" Dionysos laughed. "Your lack of commitment is the stuff of legend."

"It may be. That doesn't mean I don't love." Hermes looked stormy for a moment, staring at the distant hills. Then he added, "I want her to be happy. Don't you?"

"Of course. What I'm not sure is that I'm the right person to achieve that."

His reasoning felt perfectly sound at the time. Now, in the sparkling winter night amid the wild revelry, watching his two friends kissing among dozens doing the same, Dionysos' reasons blew away like peels of birch bark in the wind.

He was too old for her? Perhaps. But Hermes was older than him—Dionysos wasn't sure how much older, but certainly by at least a decade—and Hekate evidently didn't mind. Dionysos hadn't minded Aphrodite's considerably older age, for that matter.

Hekate would only want to touch someone she deeply loved? Again, she likely didn't feel that way about Hermes, and she was indulging anyway.

He shouldn't debauch the daughter of the Underworld? Well, what were Hades and Persephone going to do if they found out? Have Dionysos killed? It didn't seem likely. Besides, now Hermes would have to take a share of punishment for the same crime. Hermes was a good friend of Hades and Persephone's, and if *he* didn't scruple to touch her like that…

The theatrical heartbreak performances went on and on. Dionysos felt ready to throw the winning wreath at the next person just to end things. Meanwhile, Hekate had turned her head and was accepting Hermes' kisses upon her mouth, and kissing him down his neck, and murmuring and smiling. They both turned to look at Dionysos. Hekate tilted her head to invite him over, and Hermes added encouragement with a nod.

Dionysos swallowed. He began to understand what Hermes was up to, and another reason to give in piled onto his others: how impolite it would be to turn down such a gift, so painstakingly acquired by a friend.

Dionysos answered with a subtle nod of his own, and flicked his gaze at the performers to indicate he had to finish up here first.

His friends smiled in understanding.

Finally the performances ended. The crowd helped him declare a winner, a young man upon whose head he crammed the wreath.

Dionysos let him choose a "bride" from the crowd. Thankfully the performer didn't choose Hekate, but some local girl instead. Everyone cheered, and Dionysos bounded over to Hermes and Hekate and drew them back to the cushioned corner where they had sat during the feast.

"A long evening," he said, his voice breathless in his own ears. "Shall we rest?"

Hekate drew him down to recline against her. "I'm cold," she said, and pulled his cloak around herself. The warm bare skin of their arms touched, and through the fabric of her tunic he felt the soft contours of her body.

Hermes wriggled up against her back, dragging a blanket with him. "You feel warm to me, love."

For some other woman Dionysos might also have made an overused remark about warming her up. But he was too fascinated by her mouth and its shapeliness. He'd never kissed it before, only her cheek and her hand. To make sure he'd remember this, he paid close attention as he leaned down to brush his lips against hers. The kiss was light and lingering. Then she raked her hand into his hair and kissed him harder, and tilted her face and hooked a leg around his knee.

The immortal strength flowing off her in waves ravished him. Aphrodite had been the only immortal woman he'd ever lain with. Though there'd been plenty of mortals since, he always took care with them, though he wasn't likely to hurt them unless he meant to. The heightened strength only blazed forth if an immortal wanted or needed it to. But with Hekate he didn't need to temper his touch. He could roll her around, clutch her tight, push and feel her push back.

Ah, how he'd missed it, the feel of an immortal woman's body, softness and grace sheathing deadly power, and a sexual appetite that outperformed even his own. And this time he held a woman utterly different from Aphrodite, which made it more exciting still.

As he kissed her and their hands explored one another, he marveled at the change in Hekate, from aloof, clever sorcerer bringing lights alive in his wreath, to wanton fleshly woman upon her back in his furs.

Someone with so much magic at her command, the moon and Earth and Underworld at her feet, and she wanted him? "Flattered" didn't cover his reaction. "Moved" was more like it. Enchanted.

He paused a moment to remember the friend who had brought him this gift, and lifted his gaze across Hekate's shoulder, which Hermes was mouthing in leisurely fashion. "Thank you," Dionysos said.

Hermes winked. He climbed onto the pair of them, hugging them both in one horizontal embrace. They squawked and laughed in protest. Then he rose and smoothed down his rumpled clothing. "If I were you, I'd take this fetching woman to the other realm for some privacy."

"But we'll see you later?" Hekate said. Sweet gratitude softened her voice.

"Oh yes, I plan to sleep as close to you as possible. Or to Agria. It's bloody cold out tonight. Bring blankets."

Hekate and Dionysos nodded, and grabbed as many furs and cloaks as they could hold. Then, still lying on the ground, they slid into the spirit realm. Cold air swept across them. A looming hush fell. His ears rang after the noise of the festival. Soon his eyes adjusted to the dark, showing him her coy smile in the starlight.

Without a word, she pulled him on top of her, and wriggled both their tunics out of the way below the waist.

"Are you sure?" he whispered.

She grasped him and tilted her hips to bring him inside her, drawing a sharp breath from him. "Don't I feel sure?"

He tried not to start moving right away, much as he wanted to. "Listen, I've got cloudhair seeds in case you didn't bring any—"

"No need. I've got magic."

He laughed. "Of course. Of course you do. You are a marvel."

And as he moved with her, and their mouths became occupied with kisses instead of words, he thought, *I'll get to know you. It's the middle of the night and we're frenzied and soon we'll be sleepy, but tomorrow, and every day after, I'll learn about you, I'll talk to you, I'll give you the attention you deserve. Oh, you're enchanting, you're delicious, you're amazing.*

CHAPTER FORTY-SIX

"IT *IS* BLOODY COLD," DIONYSOS MURMURED AS THEY RESTED UNDER the winter stars.

Hekate couldn't disagree, shivering despite her tired efforts at a spell to ward off the wind. But her tiredness was of a complacent sort. This body was now properly that of a woman, she thought. By some people's definition, at least. She kissed the hollow of his throat. "Let's go back. The tent is warmer."

He yawned. "And we told Hermes we would."

They hugged one another and switched over. Hekate landed upon Hermes, or at least his arm and leg as he lay sprawled with a passed-out young man.

"Oof," he grunted. He pushed her off, then smiled sleepily at her. "Hello. And goodnight."

"Goodnight, and thanks," she whispered back.

A SUDDEN, BREATHTAKING stab of pain jolted Hekate awake. She opened her eyes to a living nightmare. A sword's blade protruded from her chest. She yanked it out and lay gasping.

The sky was still dark and fires still burned; she could only have slept a short time. But now people screamed around her, and elbows and feet and fists were flying and bruising her and each other. Between the flailing limbs she discerned the cause: masked attackers had swarmed into the tent, seemingly a hundred of them, bristling with swords and knives, stabbing anyone who fought them. But their might was concentrated upon herself, Dionysos, and Hermes.

Thanatos.

The leopard beast Agria had been stabbed and killed, her teeth bared but useless now, her spots marred with blood. She was only a mortal animal, after all, like all the spirit realm beasts.

Blood soaked everything, Hekate now found as she touched the sticky hot furs and smelled the coppery scent. Hermes and Dionysos were covered with it too. They snarled and threw punches and grabbed at blades, and kept diving in front of her to protect her, but each time the assassins sliced new blades into them or smacked them aside with clubs. Hekate tried to struggle free from the middle of the fight, or switch realms to get clear of it, but found herself immobilized by another sword that stabbed her through the leg. Lying on her side, panting in agony and scrabbling to pull out the blade, she sent a desperate glance around.

Some revelers fought the masked attackers, trying to protect their honored god, but dead or wounded mortals lay everywhere now. And the invaders kept coming. Hermes and Dionysos moved more slowly, wounded and bleeding all over, though they stayed on their feet and kept fighting.

But they were losing, as was Hekate. Every time she yanked a blade out of herself and started to reach the magical balance necessary to switch realms, another knife stabbed her. Her friends were suffering the same problem. Panic flooded her.

Someone caught her by the legs and began dragging her away. She kicked free, pulled another knife out of her side, and stabbed at the hand closest to her. Someone yelled in pain and the hand let go. Dionysos lunged for her, knocking five attackers out of the way, and caught her arm. But swords hacked at their joined hands until Hekate, gritting her teeth in torment, had to let go or else they would have lost fingers.

The masked people hauled her off the ground and picked her up as Dionysos and Hermes watched from behind a wall of war, their faces warped in fury. She flung all her energy toward them, willing them to regain their strength and get clear and safe.

Whether it worked, she didn't see: three, four, five more blades lanced through her body. She vomited blood. Several pairs of hands seized her and shoved her into a wooden box, whose lid slammed down with a bang. Blades still impaled her chest, her belly, her throat. With the darkness of the box came the terrifying realization there she could no longer sense where her friends were. *Oak. The box must be oak.*

It was the last conscious thought she had for quite some time. Blood and pain suffocated her, and her mind fell away.

Strength rushed into Dionysos like a flash flood. The debilitating pain all over him faded, and with a bellow of rage he seized a sword from an attacker and sliced open five of the killers in a single whirling moment. They all fell screaming. At his back, Hermes managed the same—he knocked people down left and right, snatching blades and weapons away to use them against their owners.

Still more fighters surged at them, and neither of them could get past to follow the group that had clapped Hekate into a box and carried her off. As soon as they did it, Dionysos had felt his sense of her vanish, and he realized they must know about the properties of oak. It terrified him, and enraged him into a new bout of murderous defense.

But it took too long to dispatch everyone coming at him, even with the help of Hermes and the worshippers. The moment he finally hacked a clear path to the tent's entrance, he sprinted forward and looked around to find out where her kidnappers had gone. Dawn hadn't broken yet; darkness blanketed the world. Sobbing and shouting surrounded him from the poor innocents sprawled upon the ground. The attackers had cut down anyone who stood in their way, even those unarmed and drunk. They were just like Ares that way.

Dionysos had loathed such people before. Now he trembled with the need to send each of them to Tartaros personally, with this stolen sword and his own two hands.

He ran out through the trees to the main road, their likeliest route for escape, and chose the direction that headed into the hills. But running only a short distance in the cold starlight was all his still-wounded body could take. Besides, he couldn't see much in the dark, and it quickly occurred to him that he could be going the wrong direction. He ran back, thinking to try the other way, into Argos. But he returned to the festival site first to catch his breath and fetch Hermes.

Hermes ran to meet him, similarly gasping and splashed with blood, most notably from a deep cut across his eye and another at his throat. "Where is she?" He coughed.

"They took her. I don't know. I—" Dionysos stopped as a hand tugged at his tunic's hem.

He looked down to find a worshipper on his knees, a young stout man, shaking. His cheekbone was bruised and swollen, his lip bleeding, and his hands joined in supplication. "My lord, they instructed me...I'm supposed to tell you..."

Dionysos seized him by the front of his tunic and held him in the air. "What?"

The young man squeaked in fear, then stammered, "I—I didn't know they were coming! I tried to st-stop them, but they hit me, and then said they'd let me live if I d-delivered this message to you."

"What message?" Hermes' eyes looked like green ice as he stared at the man.

He swallowed, still dangling in the air. "They'll let her go, if you'll trade her for one of the greater immortals. One of her parents. The gods of the dead."

Dionysos' arm weakened, and the pain of his many wounds caught up to him. He let the young man fall with a thud to the ground. He kept staring at him, awaiting the full message.

"Sunset, tomorrow," the young man continued, sitting on his rump and returning the gaze, wide-eyed. "One of the death gods is to come here by sunset tomorrow, or else they'll...they'll destroy her."

"And if Hades or Persephone do come by sunset tomorrow,

Thanatos will destroy them instead, is that the idea?" Dionysos said.

The young man nodded.

"Why?" Hermes demanded. "Why trade for one of them, if they've already caught an immortal?"

"They think Hades and Persephone are more powerful, that they control the fates of mortals, that they send plagues to increase their numbers of dead souls. They say those are the immortals that truly must be stopped." The young man raised his hands again. "Please, my lord, it's only what they think!"

"They're idiots," Hermes snapped. "It isn't true. None of us has those powers. They—" He stopped and sucked in a breath through clenched teeth, glancing about in despair.

Dionysos shoved the worshipper onto his back, his hand around the young man's throat. "Which way did they take her? Tell us everything."

"I don't know! I swear I don't. There was so much fighting—all I saw was them carrying the box, then they were gone into the dark."

Hermes seized a torch and ran toward the road, casting his glance around on the ground. "Damn these dancers!" he shouted. "Footprints are everywhere."

Dionysos squeezed the man's throat harder. "Did they have a wagon? Did you hear horses, donkeys, anything? Tell me!"

"I—I think so. They probably put her on a wagon to escape faster, but I don't know, really I don't! Please, my lord, I worship only you!"

In disgust, Dionysos let him go and ran to Hermes. "We're wasting time."

They plunged through the sea of olives and reached the road. Hermes ran toward the faintly brightening sky in the east. The torch flame rippled in his hand. He was still wounded enough to favor one leg, and limped.

Dionysos chased after him, and they stopped as they looked up and down the road. Wagon tracks and the prints of pack animals covered it in both directions from the countless travelers who used the road every day. There was no way to tell where the latest group had gone.

"They could have gone into Argos," Hermes said, "or out into the hills, or to the coast for a ship, or..." He paused, closing his eyes in despondency. Then he opened them and shoved the torch into Dionysos' hand. "Here. You start looking. I..." His shoulders drooped. "I will go tell Hades and Persephone."

Chapter Forty-Seven

WHEN HERMES RUSHED IN AND WOKE UP PERSEPHONE AND HA-des in their bedchamber, his clothes and body streaked with drying blood, Sophie woke with a start too. She lay in the chilly Airstream in the twenty-first century, in the middle of the night, with Adrian asleep behind her. Wind whispered outside the windows. The white holiday lights glowed in fuzzy spots through the closed blinds.

Afraid to move but equally afraid to sleep again, she lay immobile, sometimes closing her eyes and sometimes opening them to seek solace in those gentle strings of lights.

But there was no escaping now. In her mind she turned to the dark gates guarding those most horrible of memories, and opened them.

HALF-DRESSED, HADES STORMED across the bedchamber and yanked open the chest against the wall before Hermes was done speaking. Hades strapped on every weapon he possessed—knives, spear, even bow and arrows though he was no good at using them.

"We'll kill them," he said. "Anyone who had anything to do with this, anyone we can catch, anyone we have to kill to get her back. I'll do it, I don't care if Tartaros holds me for a century."

Persephone thought she might faint, or start screaming like a madwoman, or indeed, rage out of the Underworld and join Hades in a murder spree. Her daughter, her one child, immobilized by blades and locked unconscious in an oak box somewhere, held by Thanatos scum...

She locked gazes with Hermes, who looked both steely and heartbroken. The blood all over him and the hacked-apart state of his cloak and tunic and boots showed how hard he had fought—to no avail. "But we can't," she said, her voice choked. "If we go out killing and attacking, they might hear of it and just kill her, wherever she's being held. Do we...negotiate somehow?" Persephone swallowed and slid out of bed, shivering. "If it comes to it, they can take me. My life for hers, of course I'd do it—"

"No," Hades snarled.

"Listen to me." Hermes held out a hand to stop her, then swiveled to point the gesture at Hades too. "Do not give in to their demands. There is no reason to think they'll honor anything they've said. They haven't shown a shred of honor or sincerity so far. If you turn yourselves in, they might kill you and then go ahead and kill her anyway."

"Then we kill them first," Hades said.

"We need to find her and rescue her," Hermes stated. "As quickly and quietly as possible. Persephone's right: if we go cutting a swath through the country, they'll hear of it within a day and—and could easily destroy her." His voice broke in the last words.

"But what do we do?" Persephone hugged herself and ran her hands up and down her trembling arms. In her mind she raced through the Underworld's gardens and orchards, all the magic Hekate had ever demonstrated. She came up with nothing, nothing that would locate her daughter and bring her home safe. Even the spell to trace someone when holding one of their possessions—only Hekate herself could do that. Persephone was powerless.

"Two of us should go out and look," Hermes said, "and one should stay here, in case she...returns."

As a soul or as a living person, Persephone thought, and shivered more convulsively.

"I'll stay," she said. "But I want to go out looking later."

"Dionysos is already looking too," Hermes said. "As will others soon."

"Let's go." Hades threw on his cloak.

"For Goddess' sake, at least give me the bow." Hermes shoved aside Hades' cloak and yanked it from him. "I can use it, unlike you." He looked to Persephone, and reached out to squeeze her hand with his blood-encrusted one. "We won't give up. We'll find Demeter and tell her, and I'm sure she'll begin searching too, and will recruit others to do the same."

Persephone nodded, and the thought of Demeter was what did it: her eyes flooded with tears at the thought of how agonized her mother would be to learn what had happened to her darling granddaughter.

"Please don't despair," Hermes added, though he sounded desolate himself.

"I'll try," she whispered.

Hades moved close to take her head in both hands and kiss her on the lips. When she blinked her tears away to focus upon him, his eyes looked dark and deadly. "We won't let them," he said.

She nodded, unable to speak.

Then Hades and Hermes were off. The silence of the Underworld fell around her, alleviated only by its perpetual sound of water trickling behind the walls. Beside her, Kerberos whined. She stroked his head, hoping his presence could somehow summon Hekate home or send strength to her from afar.

But nothing could do that. It was the maddening conclusion she kept circling back to all day as she paced through the fields and orchards with Kerberos, thinking, praying, trying not to break down. She did descend to Tartaros early on, and located several of the murderers. Though she questioned each at length, they couldn't tell her with certainty where Hekate had been taken.

The group had meant to kill Hermes and Dionysos straight off, they all said. She felt a grim satisfaction at being able to inform them they had failed. But capturing Hekate in order to barter for Hades or Persephone had also been part of the plan, and that part had succeeded. Only a certain subset of the group, the people in charge of the capture, knew the final plan for where to take her. This precaution was precisely so that no one could torture the information out of the others. It also meant, Persephone noted in frustration, that even a soul in Tartaros, unable to lie, couldn't tell her anything useful.

The possibilities the souls had overheard varied: some said she might be taken to the caves in the hills, some said to a ship that would take her to another coast or island, some said to a house or building tucked away either in the countryside or in the bustling midst of the city. Too many options. Persephone longed to sprint out into the world and investigate every one.

At mid-day, Hades returned alone. He shook his head wearily as he walked to her. "We ran along all the main roads outside Argos, asked after anyone carrying a large crate or box. Threatened and beat up a few people who recognized us and shouted 'Thanatos' at us." He closed his eyes and rubbed his face. "Which we shouldn't have done, I know, for her safety. But no one knew anything that helped."

"Is my mother out looking too?"

He nodded. "She's gone to fetch Rhea, Artemis, Apollo and anyone else near. But without any of us being able to sense Hekate, and with all the places someone can hide in this blasted world…"

"It's my turn. Let me go look."

He nodded again, dropping to sit against a tree in exhaustion, and laid his hand upon Kerberos' head when the dog placed his chin on Hades' knee. "Here. Take these." Hades pulled the long knife and sword from his belt and handed them over.

Though she usually only carried a small knife—and so far had never used it to attack any human being—she took the weapons at once. In fact, upon closing her hand around the finely wrought bronze of the sword's hilt, she experienced a gleam of ferocious eagerness at the notion of driving the blade into a Thanatos captor right before smashing open the oak box and freeing her daughter. If it were as simple as murder, indeed, she'd do it. Even if it meant years in Tartaros later.

But it wasn't that simple. She entered the living world near Argos, and found immediately how vast and full of a million hiding places the world was—even just one stretch of hilly coastline in Greece. The city of Argos was in a panic, everyone grieving and raging over the massacre at the Dionysia. Some forty local people had been killed, and only a few of the surviving attackers had been captured.

Those attackers had all been stoned to death by the angry citizens before even having a chance at a trial. The trial, she supposed, would only have led to execution anyway. Today she couldn't spare any concern for the outrage and suffering of the citizens. She could do nothing but scour the world for her daughter.

Disguised in a shabby cloak, Persephone rushed about the city, listening to gossip and news, gathering any hints she could and chasing them down.

She heard a few accounts of people carting away a large wood box, but no one seemed sure where they had taken it. Someone else had heard that outsiders just before the Dionysia were asking around for private space to rent in outbuildings or stables. So as grievous wails and shouted speeches echoed in the streets behind her, Persephone scaled walls and peeked into windows and pushed past surprised horses and goats in stables to search corners of buildings. Nothing.

As the sun set, she and Demeter and Hermes gravitated toward one another outside the city gates. Persephone fell into her mother's arms and they held each other, trembling, a long while. Finally they stepped apart and the three looked at each other.

"Nothing in the caves," Hermes said, "but there are still probably at least twenty I haven't explored yet. Why the hell do these mountains have to have so many caves?"

Demeter looked ravaged with grief, her face somehow decades older today. Mud coated her boots and splattered the hem of her cloak. "Nothing in the farms and villages I've talked to, either. They say no one's come by, nothing suspicious…" She raised her hands and let them drop. "But how are we to know if they're lying? Who do we trust, who do we believe?"

313

"Who do we torture?" Hermes' fingers curled around the hilt of his knife until his knuckles whitened.

Dionysos approached too. He wore a rough-spun cloak; he and Hermes had evidently changed out of their alarming bloodstained clothes and washed up a bit. But the dust of the road covered him, and he looked ready to drop in defeat.

He walked to Persephone and wrapped his arms around her, his golden head bowed. She returned the embrace delicately. Hermes had said Hekate was sleeping between the pair of them; he'd said no more, but Persephone had her suspicions. And even if her daughter had been dallying with one or both of these men, that didn't bother her much, but she fervently wished Dionysos had arranged for better and more efficient guards while the immortals slept.

"My friend, forgive me," Dionysos murmured, and let her go.

She nodded stiffly. "You didn't wish this upon her. I know."

"Never. If I had even suspected…" He scowled at the sunset. "Clearly none of us will sleep in the living world anymore."

"No sleeping tonight anyway," Demeter said. "I for one plan to search all night."

"And I," Hermes said.

"So will I," Persephone said. "But I'll check in with Hades first. He'll be tearing his hair out. I'm sure he'll want to take a shift in the nighttime."

Which he did. Halfway through the night, she returned to the Underworld and he went out to take over. Other immortals—Rhea, Prometheus, Aphrodite, Apollo—paid brief visits to embrace Persephone and assure her they were leaving no stone unturned, then they rushed out again and kept looking.

But dawn came, then mid-morning, and still no one found Hekate, nor did she return on her own, alive or dead.

When Hades returned at mid-day to switch places with her, Persephone clung to him, and he rested his head upon her shoulder. A pair of hot tears dripped onto her collarbone, and he caught his breath in a sob. Tears overflowed her eyes. She stroked his long, tangled hair. "We won't let them," she whispered.

They separated, sniffling, and she held out her hand. "Give me the blades."

He handed them over.

She was climbing onto her spirit horse, about to leave, with Hades and Kerberos standing near in the entrance chamber, when Hermes hurtled down through the cave mouth. He leaped from his horse, flung the reins around a stalagmite, and called to them, "Kerberos! Give me Kerberos."

"Why?" she said, bewildered.

"Oh, gods," growled Hades. "Of course. We're such idiots. He can sniff her down, track her. Oak wouldn't matter to him."

"I can't believe we didn't think of it." Hermes sounded disgusted. He clicked his tongue to beckon Kerberos, who came forward. Hermes picked him up, gathering the dog's wriggling legs under him. "I'll fetch Dionysos and we'll take Kerberos back to the festival site and see if he can pick anything up. Meanwhile keep looking, and hurry. Sunset isn't much longer now."

"It's my turn to look," Persephone said. "I was going to check the fishing village north of Argos. They've been hostile to us before. I imagine Thanatos is strong there."

"And it's my turn to stay," Hades said, "but I warn you, if sunset approaches and she isn't back..."

"Don't even think it," Hermes snapped. "We will find her. We will." His voice trembled in strange vulnerability.

"Do you love her too, Hermes?" Persephone asked. Exhaustion and distress made her disregard the concern of whether it was a nosy question.

He swung up onto his horse with Kerberos under his arm, and sent her a swift glance. "More than you'll ever know. Up!" His horse shot up and out.

Persephone didn't have time to mull over that odd revelation. She climbed onto her horse, then paused to look into the eyes of her husband, the soul she loved so profoundly, and right now the only one who fully shared her agony. "If sunset does come, and we've had no word..." She clenched her hands on the reins. "You know what I will do."

"No," he insisted. "I'm older. I've had more of a life. It will be me, not you."

"What good will my life be if you're nothing but a soul I can't touch?"

"What good will mine be, with you that way?"

They stared at each other, breathing in trembles, tears welling in their eyes.

"It's a conversation we'll have to save until sunset," she said.

He conceded, nodding, and stepped back wearily. "Find her."

She nodded in answer, and streaked up into the sky.

CHAPTER FORTY-EIGHT

IONYSOS JOGGED AFTER HERMES AND KERBEROS, HIS LEGS WEAK. His body was ready to drop after two nights of hardly any sleep, two days of running and searching, and the constant grief and fury at his beautiful friend being stolen violently from him— all in the wake of sustaining at least ten wounds that each would have killed him as a mortal. Hermes looked to be staggering a bit too. They both needed rest. But sunset was speeding toward them in the winter afternoon, and if they were to find and save Hekate, now was the time to push ahead.

Kerberos' behavior gave them hope. The dog snuffled along the ground, leading them down the road from the festival site. He passed the city gates without turning in, and they continued winding down the slope, picking one road after another, headed for the sea.

Kerberos led them out onto a small dock of wood planks. The salt-scented waves lapped against the posts. At the end of the dock he stopped and whined, and lifted his nose to sniff the wind.

Dionysos and Hermes peered out across the vast blue water. Here and there, the white and brown shapes of boats dotted the surface, coming and going in the endless commerce and travel of the Mediterranean. They looked at each other.

"We need a boat," Hermes said. "A fast one."

A short time later, for an exorbitant price paid up front in heaps of silver, they had acquired a small ship and six strong men to row it. The ship was perhaps a mere three times the length of

Dionysos' height, and only as wide as his arm-span. It had sails, but the sailors only bothered rigging up one of them, explaining the wind was coming the wrong direction for the others to be of any use.

They stationed Kerberos in the bow where he could sniff the air and point them in the right direction. The rowers launched the boat into the bay.

"Is this even possible?" Dionysos wrapped his fur cloak around him for warmth. "Can a dog track a scent across the sea?"

"Well, he is an immortal dog." Hermes held onto the edge of the pitching ship as they sped forward. "If any dog can do it, he can. And it's our last hope." He turned west to glance grimly at the sinking sun.

PERSEPHONE HAD FAILED. She hadn't found her child. And now the sun was about to touch the treetops on the western hills. If she was to return to the Underworld and have that dreadful conversation with Hades, now was the time. But she knew she wouldn't.

She turned and began walking the road back toward the festival site. Best to offer herself up now, on the early side. If she waited much longer Hades would surely come up to find her, or to offer himself as the sacrifice. For the second time in his life, and this time more permanently.

She wouldn't let him. He and Hekate would live. It was her turn to receive the blades and the fire, though the terror of the thought turned everything in her to ice.

She took her gold and amethyst crown from the bag she carried, placed it on her head, then concealed it with the hood of her cloak. She walked steadily, though her heart sobbed and her eyes welled with tears. She longed to embrace Hades and Hekate one last time, and her mother, and her friends. But she couldn't do so without revealing her intention to give herself up, and if they discovered what she meant to do, they wouldn't allow it. Besides, now there simply wasn't time. She would have to beg their forgiveness and tell them she loved them when they came to see her in the Underworld. She closed her eyes a moment, then wiped the tears off her cheeks and kept trudging forward.

A scowling middle-aged man stood by the path to the festival site, wearing dirty armor and slung with at least five weapons. He blocked her way with a spear. "Special meeting taking place this way," he said.

She drew back the hood of her cloak. The crown, along with her face, sparked a flash of recognition in his eyes. "I'm Persephone," she said. "I give myself up for the life of my daughter."

Another heavily armed man, overhearing her, ran up to join the first. They eyed her suspiciously. "If you've got friends coming to attack," the second man warned, "that's it for your girl's life."

"No one's coming, not that I've heard. Please, take me and let her go."

They exchanged a glance, then seized her, confiscated her sword and knife, and tied her wrists behind her back with a heavy chain. They pulled her on a long and twisting path through the olive trees. She could have broken the chain, but there was no point. She didn't intend to fight.

They stopped in a clearing where a large fire burned in the center of a crowd of nearly a hundred menacing-looking men and women. The crowd rumbled with low laughter and shrill remarks. Shouts spread the news of Persephone's arrival, and they surged forward to surround her, grinning and chuckling. An exciting day for Thanatos indeed, she thought gloomily.

A man pushed forward to stand before her. From how the crowd readily made way for him, she guessed him to be their leader. He was of wiry build, brown-haired with a long mustache and a thin face, and looked to be perhaps thirty years old. He would have been handsome if not for the frightening, insane malice in his blue eyes, and the disgusting teeth that revealed themselves when he spoke.

"This is the queen of the Underworld?" He bowed, satirically. "My name is Straton. The king of Thanatos."

His title was clearly meant as a joke, in parallel to her status, and his companions chuckled malevolently.

"I turn myself over to you." Persephone felt a flicker of pride in noting that her voice didn't shake. "Please send word at once to release my daughter."

"Indeed, we have folk ready to do that." He grinned, with only half his mouth. "But not till we've taken care of you. We know how your type can escape at the last minute."

Persephone felt it then: Hades approaching, and fast. She closed her eyes in despair.

"No!" he shouted from down the path. His footsteps pounded forward. The armed villains rushed to surround him, pointing spears at him from every angle. "Stop!" he said. "I'm Hades. Take me. Let my wife go."

"No." Persephone's voice carried over the crowd.

The attackers brought Hades forward to join her near the fire. His chest bled through his white tunic from a spear jab, and he let two of the men hold his arms behind his back. But mainly all she could see was his grief-consumed, radiant dark eyes.

"What a treat!" Straton said. "Well, then. Which of you shall it be?"

Persephone and Hades faced each other, not quite close enough to touch, their hands imprisoned behind them. She blinked rapidly, trying not to weep. "Please let it be me," she said.

"I can't let it be you," he said. "I'm not strong enough."

"Nor am I."

They stared each other down. A tear ran from each of Hades' eyes. With Persephone's next blink, two tears answered, falling down her cheeks.

"Both of us?" he whispered.

"Together," she said. "She's strong enough to bear it."

Hades cleared his throat, and glared at Straton. "If we allow you to destroy us both, you must give us your word you'll end this war against the immortals. You'll leave every last one alone."

"Done," Straton said, rather too airily for Persephone to believe.

The hands pulled Persephone's arms tighter. The crowd converged closer.

"Assuming," Straton added, "the immortals leave us alone, and meddle no more in human affairs, and bring no more plagues and evils upon us."

"We don't cause those!" Hades shouted. "You understand nothing!"

Straton motioned to his soldiers. Swords and knives slid out of sheaths all around with a ringing whisper of metal.

"Release our daughter," Persephone said to Straton. "Send word at once, if you have any honor, please."

"It shall be done as soon as your sacrifice is completed. We do hope you won't take as long to die as your mother did."

Shock jolted Persephone's body. "What?"

Straton pulled a gold crown from his belt and held it up, smiling. Gold wheat stalks and stones of emerald and amber decorated the slender circlet. Demeter's crown.

Hades stared in horror at it, then at the tall roaring fire.

"No," Persephone said. She couldn't sense Demeter—that could mean she was in the Underworld, as a soul… "No! You stole it! You're lying!"

"Let her see." Straton waved toward the fire.

One of the men reached in with a spear and hauled out a burning object. He flicked it across the ground to Persephone's feet. A charred sandal: one of Demeter's. She recognized it by the colored string of beads. Feeling she was about to faint, she looked into the flames and now made out the shape of a human arm and leg there, among the scattered parts being consumed by the fire.

She sagged to her knees. "*No!*"

"She offered herself shortly before you did." Straton sounded smug. "We accepted the opportunity, of course. But we couldn't send word to release your witch daughter, for those weren't the terms of the offer. Only the capture of you, the death gods, could do that."

Persephone kept her head down, weeping, her ears ringing in unbearable grief. Against her will, her mind conjured images of this butchery. Had Demeter come forth with grace and courage, her head held high in her usual indomitable way? Or had she tried to plead, to reason with them, to no avail? And then what had they done to her? *We do hope you won't take as long to die as your mother did.* Persephone prayed Straton had only said that to torment her, that it wasn't true, that Demeter hadn't suffered long... but she would be able to ask her soon. Cruelly soon.

"You'll still die," Hades growled at Straton. "Sooner or later. And when you do, you'll burn for centuries under the Earth, and the forces that will put you there are far greater than Persephone or me or our daughter or anyone who's ever lived. They'll go on whether or not we're alive. You're fools. Murderous fools."

"So you claim," Straton said, "but we don't really know, do we. Come. Let's finish this."

The hands hauled her up.

"Persephone," Hades implored, suddenly sounding tender.

If Demeter could face this doom for the sake of her granddaughter, then so could Persephone for the sake of her daughter.

She lifted her face as she stood. In a quick burst of strength, she and Hades pulled away from their captors and came together for a tear-flavored kiss. The hands grabbed her again and pulled her back.

"We've had a good run, darling," Hades said.

"I love you."

"I love you too."

She drank in the sight of his warm, living skin, his face and body. "See you in the Underworld."

Then a burst of pain incapacitated her—she'd been stabbed through the back, was being stabbed again and again. A blade shot out from Hades' chest in a spray of blood. He choked out a cry.

Someone bashed her on the side of the head, and she collapsed to the ground, fuzzy stars and a sheet of red spreading over her vision. Pain and pain and pain, and screaming—her own and Hades' and others'—and it went on forever and ever.

Then with a flood of calm, the pain and noise vanished and the world was born again. The twilight sky arched serene above the treetops. She stood alone in the wild forest. She lifted her hand and looked at its translucent glow. Though her heart still sobbed, it was a muted pain now, tempered by love and wisdom. The serenity of the dead.

She felt the Underworld pulling her almost as strongly as the Earth used to pull her living feet downward. But she lingered to wait for Hades.

In a short time, his soul appeared. His tunic and body and face were clean again, handsome and eternally young, though sadness radiated from his eyes.

"So you came here first," he said. "I'm glad. It means you suffered a shorter time."

She took his hand. She could grasp it, and though she couldn't feel its texture the way she used to, it provided a comforting tangible presence within her own. "We'd best go to the Underworld," she said. "They'll be looking for us."

CHAPTER FORTY-NINE

URLED UP HALF-ASLEEP IN THE LONG DECEMBER NIGHT, HER BACK against the still-sleeping Adrian, Sophie closed her eyes in anguish. Persephone may have acquired the serenity of the dead, but living biochemicals still teemed in Sophie's brain and body, and tormented her with grief.

It couldn't end like that! Persephone's and Hades' lives couldn't be cut short that soon, that brutally. But the memory spoke true in its cruel, blunt pictures, and flowed seamlessly into the memory she had already glimpsed several weeks ago.

Persephone walked, or rather drifted, beside Hades in the Underworld's fields, both of them souls. She found she was wearing the red cloak and white gown and wreath of flowers she had been wearing when she eloped with Hades. The fabric and blossoms all looked as bright and fresh as they had looked that day, more than twenty years ago. Her violet-shaped amethyst necklace was back too, though in the living world the necklace must have been stolen by Thanatos by now, along with her gold crown.

Hades also wore his garments from their wedding day, cream-colored tunic and purple cloak edged with jewels, and his gold crown with the narcissus tucked into it. Her handsome bridegroom, restored to her.

They passed the edge of the orchard, and she gazed sadly at the graceful trees she had planted and tended, and now couldn't touch.

"Our deaths served their purpose, as long as she's all right," Hades said.

"If only we knew it worked," she said. "If only we knew what happened to her."

Souls kept approaching and following them, curious and sympathetic to find the royalty of the Underworld newly dead among them.

Persephone turned to the small crowd and asked in the Underworld tongue, "Please, can you find my mother Demeter?" Now that she lacked an immortal body, she couldn't sense souls anymore. She had all the memories the pomegranate had given her. All the souls had those. And she had gained a certain clarity and calm she had lacked before. But her vibrant sense linking her to her immortal family had fallen dormant. As Hekate had once put it, a perfect immortal body was required for that ability. Souls found each other here merely by cooperative asking, and seemingly by an unconscious pull sometimes too.

The souls murmured the request outward among them. Soon Demeter walked into view, all eyes upon her. She wore a slim white tunic with embroidered flowers at the edges, one Persephone remembered from her childhood, a favorite of Demeter's. She was barefoot, and a simple wreath of wheat ears decorated her head—the crown she had always preferred over her gold one.

Persephone let go of Hades' hand and stepped forward to embrace her mother. Demeter's arms encircled her, and again Persephone could only feel a soothing presence, not an actual touch. But it was enough.

"Oh, Mother." She drew back to look at Demeter's ever-youthful face, finding the same quiet sadness reflected in it. "You didn't have to give yourself up. You did so much good in the world. You should have stayed."

"Not if it might have saved my granddaughter." Demeter stroked Persephone's shoulder, then turned to look across the fields. "I suppose we'll know soon enough."

The three of them wandered together, waiting.

THE ROWERS PASSED three slower ships without Kerberos giving any of the boats a second glance. He kept his front paws planted on the leftward side of the bow, sticking his nose out as far as he could. Dionysos waved the rowers that direction. They approached a tiny island off the coast of the gulf. A ship was anchored just off it, its sails furled. Kerberos stared at it. The fur on the back of his neck rose, and he growled.

"That boat." Hermes pointed, and the rowers brought them closer.

As they drew nearer, Dionysos could make out a line of burly men on its deck, watching their approach, spears and bows at the ready.

Hermes cupped his hands around his mouth and shouted across the water, "If you have a captive immortal woman on board, hand her over to us at once, and your lives *might* be spared."

"The drunk god and the lecherous trickster," someone shouted back, and immediately three or four arrows flew their direction. One bounced off the hull; the others fell into the sea.

Hermes lifted his eyebrows at Dionysos. "Found our kidnappers."

Kerberos strained and quivered and leaned his head out of the boat, with occasional anguished yips. Dionysos stroked him between the ears. "She's there. All right. Let's get her." He turned to the rowers, who looked at him in dread—the arrows had shaken them. "Get us close enough to jump on," he said. "Then pull away if you wish. We don't want you killed. We'll stand between you and the arrows as much as we can."

Though the rowers muttered desperate prayers and exchanged uncertain glances, they had received their handsome silver payment, and they were honorable enough to obey. They pulled hard in unison upon their oars, and the ship soared toward the anchored boat.

On the enemy ship, two men hastily hauled up the anchor, and others rushed around readying oars and sails, while three stayed at the side and kept shooting arrows at the immortals. But Hermes had found a few thick planks lying loose in the base of the boat, and now he and Dionysos picked them up and used them as shields, knocking aside the arrows as they came. One got through and lodged with a nasty sting in Dionysos' thigh, but he gritted his teeth and jerked it out.

They reached the other boat. In a chaos of shouts and smacking blades, Dionysos and Hermes jumped across and landed on the opposite deck, swinging their planks and swords. The row of attackers toppled over but kept fighting. Kerberos leaped after them, snarling and snapping.

Men converged upon them as they rolled and fought on the deck. All the assassins were armed and stank of sweat. But the ship could only hold about twelve of them, and their numbers dwindled quickly. Hermes scrambled to his feet and flung one man after another overboard. Dionysos did the same. They each spun to meet a rushing attacker, stole the weapons, and sent their owners into the sea with bloody wounds.

Someone shouted a warning and Dionysos whirled around to find a man racing at him with a long knife. But then an oar crashed onto the attacker's head and he screamed and fell overboard. Dionysos grinned in gratitude at the man who had dealt the blow: their rowers hadn't left after all; they had pulled up the boat alongside and were attacking with their oars and fishing spears.

"You're excellent men and we'll pay you double," Hermes shouted to them.

Dionysos chased after Kerberos, who had planted himself atop a screaming man on a large cloth-covered crate. The dog's teeth were sunk deep in the man's shoulder, and Kerberos twisted and whipped while biting the man, as if trying to kill a rat. Dionysos pulled Kerberos free and clutched the man by the throat. The man scrabbled to grab a knife from beneath him and flailed it at Dionysos, but Dionysos easily seized it and threw it into the water, then flung the man in after it.

Kerberos scrabbled at the crate with his claws, ripping at the cloth over it.

The rest of the enemy crew had been thrown overboard. The immortals' hired rowers prodded and stabbed at them with spears to keep them from climbing back aboard. Ignoring the screams and shouts from those in the water, Hermes and Dionysos tore the cloth off and ripped open the lid of the oak crate.

Dionysos' sense of Hekate burst back upon him, close and immediate and wondrously welcome. But with it came a rush of shock. The sight of her nearly knocked Dionysos to his knees. Hermes choked back a cry of outrage.

She was pale and unconscious, and lay in a pool of blood that covered the bottom of the box and swished about with the motion of the ship. Blades and hilts protruded from her throat, chest, belly, hands, and feet. Dionysos and Hermes stared frozen for a moment, then both dived in and began pulling out the blades, gasping and murmuring prayers. Dionysos blinked against a sting in his eyes that spread down his face, and realized he was crying.

After removing all the blades, they lifted her up, her blood dripping down their arms, and cradled her between them on the ship's deck. One of their rowers raced over with a skin of fresh water he'd found on board. They poured it carefully over each of her wounds, and her sticky, matted hair.

"Please." Hermes held her head and shoulders upon his lap. "Please, love…"

She gasped, the sound loud and startling. Everyone jumped. She rolled onto her side, gagging and spitting out blood.

Dionysos knelt by her with the water skin. "Here. Drink. It's all right."

She let him trickle a bit into her mouth, spat it out, then accepted a bit more and swallowed it. Her eyes finally opened, and she fell back onto Hermes' lap and looked in confusion from him to Dionysos.

"Hello," Hermes said, smiling, his voice broken. "Shall we take you home?"

Dionysos looked at the horizon, and caught his breath in alarm. "Fast," he said. "The sun's setting."

CHAPTER FIFTY

ZOE HATED HERSELF FOR CONSTANTLY CHECKING TAB'S SOCIAL NET-work pages, but she did it anyway. Kinda frequently, to be honest. So by now, as she neared the end of her work shift, she learned Tab was somewhere called the Nectar Club in Seattle, playing host to The Luigis—which Tab *knew* was one of Zoe's current favorite bands.

Zoe could jump on her ghost horse and speed to Seattle. But she wouldn't, not without an invitation. She did have pride. She considered using the excuse of going to keep an eye out for Thanatos, who'd been lurking round Washington state these days. But Freya and Niko were already there, and they hadn't invited her either.

Fine, didn't care. She had her grown-up job to attend to, her family, much more important things to do. But in actuality, her job had been so quiet today that the hours dragged, and Zoe had felt unneeded by the whole of New Zealand. She had spent most of the weekend and today brooding upon the life of Hekate.

A few days ago, she'd reached the horrible kidnapping she already knew about, because Adrian had told her of it years ago. But actually "living" it shook her much harder. She had gone over it in her head a few extra times, not because it was easy—in fact, it dealt a good deal of pain—but because it put other problems in perspective. Such as being ignored by an annoying, hot, American teenager.

She clicked her mouse through work records, but her mind

paid no attention to them. Instead it dwelled upon the day when Adrian, still wheelchair-bound but undergoing his pomegranate explosion of memories, had texted her, *Please come over. I really need to hug you.*

She had obeyed, though didn't quite understand why he was so emotional, even when he explained. After all, this stuff happened like how many thousand years ago?

But now she got it. Fully. And if he didn't come back for a visit soon, she'd hop on her horse and go find him and hug him. Sophie too. Invitation or not.

Lovers were a pain in the arse. Your affection for them, and theirs for you, could be there one day and gone the next. But your parents, your children, they mattered forever.

HEKATE'S VISION SWAYED, from weakness as well as from the waves rocking the ship. Hermes picked her up. Dionysos spoke softly to her, reassuring her all would be right soon. Kerberos yipped and whined and wriggled. Hekate lowered her arm to let the dog lick it, his warm tongue comforting her and reviving her depleted blood.

Hermes carried her across the deck, then stopped and swore. "Wonderful. There's more of them."

Dionysos grimaced. "Must have been watching from that island." He glanced at her and explained, "Another boat, headed here."

Hekate whimpered, which she hoped would convey that she wished she could fight them with magic, but couldn't yet; she needed more time to recover. At the moment she still couldn't even talk.

"We could switch realms," Hermes said, "but then we'd be in the water. Our horses are back at Argos. And there's only so fast either of us can swim."

"We can row you fast," a man said. "But only if you get on board now."

Soon Hekate was being transferred down to a smaller boat,

and laid across Dionysos' lap. Oars creaked and the boat began moving. A sail was hoisted; someone shouted that the wind would help now. It chilled her face and hands, that wind, but felt blessedly fresh after the murky confinement of the box, which she had sensed in a half-aware way while floating in pain.

Dionysos tried to smile down at her, but a cringe crinkled his gray eyes. He stroked her temple. "I'm so sorry," he whispered. "I should have done better."

She smiled back. She felt the dried blood on her face crack and flake with the motion. She cleared her throat with an effort. "You found me."

He shook his head, looking across her. "Hermes did that. He was the clever one, thinking to use Kerberos. I'd have been hopeless on my own. I always am."

"How long has it been? Do my parents know?"

"Almost two days," Hermes said. He leaned into her field of view. "And yes, they do and they're mad with worry."

"I sense them." She frowned. "They're moving away from me. Why?"

"Probably to wait for you at home." But Hermes' reassurance sounded a bit brittle. He looked back at their pursuers, and called, "Faster, men! Dionysos, let's take the oars ourselves. Give these poor fellows a break."

Dionysos laid Hekate carefully on the floor of the boat and stepped over the bench seats to take the place of one of the rowers. Kerberos hopped over to lie beside her, and licked the blood from her. Everywhere his tongue touched, a boost of well-being bloomed in her body.

Soon the boat surged ahead with extra speed as the two immortals began rowing. Watching the ruffling sail, Hekate lifted one hand into the air, feeling the wind. She silently asked it for cooperation. This kind of magic took minimal effort when the elements were amenable, which luckily this wind was. A breeze swept in, a small thing directed only into their sail, and helped speed them along.

"The sun's almost set." Dionysos sounded even more despairing. Hekate wasn't sure why. Was sailing that dangerous in the dark? Weren't they fairly near shore?

"They'll have sensed her if they came out," Hermes said firmly.

"I suppose," Dionysos said.

Who, her parents? Indeed, Hekate imagined, they must be frantic. Goddess only knew what madness they were up to out there.

"Damnation," Hermes said. "Look."

From the floor, Hekate glanced around. Everyone was frowning ahead.

"I don't suppose they're coming to tell us something complimentary," Hermes added.

"Another Thanatos boat?" Hekate asked weakly.

"That's my guess. Armed, belligerent-looking men headed straight for us. I'd rather not stick around to inquire." Hermes handed off his oar and stood up. "We're near enough to shore now. It'll be cold, but...Dionysos? Think we can manage?"

Dionysos crouched near her again. He nodded and gathered her up. "You take Kerberos. I'll take her."

Swung up into Dionysos' arms, Hekate could see across the edges of the boat again. She turned her head and found, in the fading sunset, the new enemy boat plowing through the waves toward them, the men shouting something at them. She supposed it could be a surrender or a plea for negotiation, but indeed, she wasn't keen on getting close enough to find out. Last time they got that close, she was clapped into an oak box.

Hermes clicked his tongue at Kerberos. "Here, boy. Time to switch." The dog came to him, and Hermes picked him up. He turned to the rowers. "My friends, thank you a hundred times. Here's your extra silver." He tossed a bag to their feet. "I hope they give you no trouble, but please, tell whatever lies you must in order to save your lives. Claim we took you hostage, if that helps. Or hand over all the silver. We'll get you more. Time for us to go. Farewell and the Goddess protect you."

He nodded to Dionysos, and with a jolt, the boat disappeared and they fell into the sea.

The chill of the water shocked Hekate. All of them gasped; Kerberos grunted and began paddling madly. Dionysos, treading water, helped Hekate keep her head above the sloshing surface. "Get onto my back," he said.

She spat brine out of her mouth and threw her arms and legs around his back. He and Hermes and Kerberos began to swim for shore. Hekate tilted her face to the darkening blue winter sky. The sea was cold, yes, but the water teemed with magic, nearly as much as the waters of the Underworld. She basked in it and invited it in. Healing tingled all over her. Her strength increased.

And at least this way she and her garments were getting washed.

A dark hump rippled upward from the surface, a few arms' lengths away, then went under.

Dionysos twitched. "Did you see that?" he asked.

"Yes." Hekate squinted at the spot, trying to sense through the water what they might be sharing space with. In the spirit world, possibilities were limitless. Hadn't Poseidon claimed he'd seen sea monsters? But animals avoided the immortals. Usually.

"Keep swimming," Hermes shouted between quick breaths. "It's not much farther."

A current beneath them sent a rush of colder water upward.

Dionysos jolted again. "Something just bumped my foot! Something huge."

"Lovely." Hermes sounded tense. "Keep swimming."

Hekate thought of the blood rinsing off her body and clothing. Surely that would attract sharks or other hungry fish. Best not to suggest that to the men. Shore was near enough now that she could see individual logs on the beach. Still watching the water to the side, she spotted another long ripple, some creature skimming close to the surface.

Just as she began composing a silent message to send out, something to announce they were harmless and the creatures should let them pass, the sea's surface burst open in front of them. A huge hill rose up, water sluicing off it. Five or six immensely long tentacles waved and uncurled, lifting up higher than any sailboat mast Hekate had ever seen.

They all yelled in alarm, and Kerberos barked angrily. The water knocked them around together in the new chaotic waves churned up by the giant creature.

"Dear *Goddess*." Hermes sounded half-panicked, half-impressed.

"Don't suppose it'll leave us alone like the beasts usually do?" Dionysos clutched Hekate's arm with one hand while swishing the other through the water to keep them afloat.

Hekate looked for a face on the creature, but in the fading twilight couldn't tell which of the spots and splotches on its dark green body might be eyes. If she could look into its eyes, or touch it, she might be able to get a better reading on its intentions...

The water foamed up around them. A curl of green tentacle, as thick as Hekate's whole body, surrounded Dionysos and Hekate and coiled around them.

"No no, no no no," Dionysos said. The slimy coils tightened, lifting them out of the water. Even with his great strength, he couldn't push or fight free, nor could Hekate.

Next to them, another coil had picked up Kerberos, who snarled and bit to no effect.

And another had captured Hermes, who was struggling to get at the sword on his belt, but the tentacle blocked it. "Come on, you wicked monster," he shouted, "put us down and go back where you came from!"

"Don't shout," Hekate called. "Let me try." Now that she was touching the animal, she closed her eyes and concentrated on its deep-sea energy, the spirit-world magic flowing in its chilly veins.

She found the beast was curious, mostly. It would eat them if no other idea occurred to it, but mainly it had swam up to them because they were unlike anything it knew and it wanted to investigate them.

She sent out her plea, bending the magic to meet her will, asking for the creature's help.

"Hekate?" Dionysos said, nervously.

The tentacles swung them forward, sweeping them dizzily over the surface of the sea. Above the waves that broke white off shore, the creature released them. They plunged in over their heads. Hekate lost her grip on Dionysos and tumbled feet over ears underwater. She held her breath and kicked upward, and broke through into the air. The next wave washed them onto the sand. Kerberos lunged out of the surf and shook off his fur in a spray. Hermes, Dionysos, and Hekate all rose on hands and knees, coughing and snorting and picking off kelp.

She looked back for another glimpse of the helpful monster, but saw only one lazily whipping tentacle, which soon slipped away under a patch of churning sea.

"Swimming in the spirit realm," Hermes panted. "Not recommended. Keep that in mind."

Shivering, Hekate got to her feet with the help of Dionysos.

"Come on," Dionysos said. "Our horses are this way. Let's get you to the Underworld."

On the walk to the horses, and the flight to the cave, Hekate asked them what exactly Thanatos had done. They told her about the slaughter of the mortals at the festival, and the revenge of the citizens there, but she saw they weren't telling her everything. The uneasy glances they exchanged signaled as much.

"My parents," she repeated. "What have they said? What have they been doing?"

"We split up to look for you," Hermes said. "Naturally they're distraught. Probably they're pacing the cave and tearing their hair out." But he sounded distracted, and gazed ahead, following the increasingly thick river of souls as they neared the Underworld.

Hekate's strength was approaching normal by the time they landed in the entrance cavern. Her parents were here. Sensing them again warmed her through and through with relief. She ran along the tunnel with the others and crossed the river.

Then her steps faltered and stopped in the fields as a crowd of souls parted to make way for her. Before her stood Demeter, Hades, and Persephone, smiling sadly at her. They were souls.

"*No!*" The shriek tore itself out of her, seeming to take her own soul along with it.

She rushed to her parents, dropped to her knees, and flung her arms around their legs, but of course her arms passed through the glowing air without any contact. Her hands and forehead fell to the cool white grass at their feet. "No," she wailed again into the ground. "What happened?"

"You fools," Hermes raged, behind her. "How could you? I *told* you I would find her! I told you not to throw your lives away! You insane, stupid..." He choked on the words then and fell quiet. Hekate raised her pounding head to glance back at him, and found he had his face against his arm on a tree trunk, and was weeping. Near him, Dionysos stood staring at the three souls, pale with shock.

"We're sorry, darling," Persephone said, kneeling before Hekate. "Thanatos offered your life for ours. They were going to kill you if we didn't turn ourselves in by sunset. Parents will gladly make such sacrifices."

"Grandparents, too," Demeter said, gazing fondly at her. "We're so glad you're safe, dear."

A trade, their lives for hers. So that was what Hermes and Dionysos hadn't wanted to tell her. Hekate looked into her mother's sweet, familiar eyes, trying to comprehend, but burst into tears herself. She crumpled, bending over her lap, face in both hands.

Kerberos approached and sat beside her so his warm haunch pressed her leg. He lifted his head and began to howl in lament.

"My brave girl." It was Hades' voice this time, near her, as if he were kneeling too. She still had her face covered and couldn't look. "We'll be here for you. We'll stay a long while. But you won't need us, not really. You know so much, and you can do much more than we ever could."

Hekate only shook her head, sobbing, unable to speak. Of course she needed them, of course she did...

A warm hand slid across her back, an arm sheltering her; someone nestled down beside her. Dionysos. She knew him through touch and sense, though barely heeded his presence. The world was shattering, and even magic for the moment had turned into whirling, dangerous chaos. Never did she imagine she would come home to a horror like this.

"It will get easier," Persephone assured her. "It will be all right again, since you're here."

"It can't ever be all right again," Hekate choked out.

She kept weeping, surrounded by the sense of her loved ones so near, but too many of them now intangible.

Hermes recovered faster. She heard his step behind her, and his sniffle. Then he coolly stated, "I still say the three of you are all colossal idiots."

"Perhaps this time you're right, Hermes." Demeter sounded mild and forgiving.

Hekate couldn't laugh, couldn't even lift her face. Tears had bathed her palms and were dripping down her wrists.

She had caused this. It was her fault.

"Darling," Hades said. "Darling, listen. You can grieve, and we know you must. But you'll have to stand strong again. Everyone needs you. Listen, I need you to remember to feed Kerberos, all right? You know how grumpy he gets if we forget. And you, Kerberos, hush. That's enough."

For Kerberos had been howling and whimpering throughout. At Hades' command, he hushed to a whine.

Hekate forced a stable, shuddering breath into her lungs. She slowly lifted her hot, damp face, looked at her kind father, and nodded.

Dionysos squeezed Hekate closer against his side. Hermes, behind her, stroked her hair—still wet from the ocean. Everything had happened so fast.

"We'll take care of her," Dionysos said.

"She'll take care of you two, more likely," Persephone answered, with the pride of a mother.

Hekate was the central living Underworld goddess now. The only one. She wobbled to her feet. She sniffled and wiped her eyes. Looking at her father, mother, and grandmother, she cleared her throat and said, though her voice cracked, "The world grieves to lose you. Your murderers will not go unpunished."

Her parents had said it to souls who came forward with accounts of being unjustly killed. Now it was her duty.

"Indeed they won't," Hermes said, behind her. "We're going to make the bastards pay."

CHAPTER FIFTY-ONE

ADRIAN AWOKE IN THE PALE MORNING LIGHT TO FIND SOPHIE'S side of the bed empty. He rolled over to look around. She sat at the kitchen table in the Airstream, a blanket around her, her face turned toward the window. Kiri lay curled at her feet.

He got out of bed and approached. "Hey."

She glanced at him and his heart constricted. Tears shone on her cheeks and reddened her eyes and nostrils. "Hey," she said, in a strained squeak. "Look. It snowed."

He swiftly checked out the view: indeed, the outside world had put on a layer of white, beneath quiet gray clouds. "Wow, look at that. Um. You okay?"

She planted her elbows on the table, leaning her eyes against the heels of her hands. "You said it wasn't so bad. You said it could be worse. How could you say that?"

Of course. As he dreaded, she had finally reached those memories. He slid onto the padded bench beside her and hugged her. "Well. It could have been. At least we were together. At least Hekate survived."

"It was terrible! Her finding us...and K-Kerberos..." Her mouth twisted in fighting another bout of crying, and she looked away from him, out the window. She drew in a hitching breath. "And I have to take a *final* today. How am I supposed to do that?"

Adrian leaned his cheek on the blanket over her shoulder, the wool catching against his morning stubble. He inhaled the wafts of warmer air rising from her neck. Below the table he found Kiri's furry side, and wriggled his toes under it. With his gaze upon the snowy ground outside, he spoke softly.

"When I first got to that memory, it was in a dream. I was fully asleep. So it felt more vivid, as real as the memories ever feel. You're right, it was horrible. I dreamed it all the way to Hekate and Kerberos grieving at our feet. Then I woke up. I was still paraplegic at the time, at home with Dad. It was almost dawn. I was on my back in bed, as usual. Could only move the upper half of my body."

Sophie sniffled, holding still, listening with her gaze cast down.

He pulled his foot from under Kiri and stroked the dog's back with it. "I sort of gasped like I was drowning," he went on. "Kiri slept in my room with me, and when she heard me she got up and came over to see what I needed. She always did that if I woke up. I leaned over and hugged her and…just started crying into her fur." Though he felt a bit silly about confessing it, a lump formed in his throat at the memory.

Sophie leaned her head against his. "You're just saying that to make me feel better."

"I'm not. It's true. I was quite pathetic."

"How'd you get through the rest of your day?"

"Did the things I had to do. Tried to remember it was ancient history and we'd been given a second chance now. Still…" He nestled his arms more snugly around her. "I wished I could go see you. I went straight to your blog, hoping you'd put up a new post, and luckily you had."

She lifted her reddened eyes to him, a hint of curiosity in them. "What was it about?"

"Kumquats," he said. "And the season finale of 'Nightshade.'" He had watched that show too. Her face softened with a smile, and he added, "I commented extensively upon both."

She turned so her forehead rested on his cheek. "I remember."

"Also," he said, "I had Zoe come over so I could hug her."

"I want to hug her too."

"She does as well. She just got to those memories the other day. I would've told you, but…"

"But then you'd have had to tell me how it ended."

"Right," he said.

"God," she groaned suddenly. "My chem final. I just cannot."

"Yes you can." He kissed her eyelid. "You'll get out there in that snow and you'll be fab."

"It'll do." Betty Quentin looked around inside the small, se-cluded house. "Hard to get to, hard to find, not a neighbor for a mile or more. Handy having people in the group who own cabins, isn't it."

Landon smiled through his shivers. All three of them were cold, despite their coats and scarves. The old house hadn't been occupied for months, and the baseboard heat was taking a while to warm up. But it truly was ideal: less than an hour from Carna-tion, out in the labyrinth of Forest Service roads that snaked all over the Cascades and foothills. Nothing but huge trees, muddy creeks, and the cries of eagles out here.

Krystal glanced out the window with a smile of triumph. "And that fire pit outside is nice and big. We can build a good hot fire and throw in whatever we need to."

The young woman's bloodthirst spread to Betty with a dark thrill. "If it comes to that, indeed we will." Betty rubbed her chilled hands together, smiling. "Feels good to be setting things in motion. So. This fellow you've found in Seattle, he's ready?"

Landon and Krystal glanced at each other and nodded. "He's an untested commodity," Landon said. "Only Krystal's met him in person, and we suspect he's a little…" He looped his finger by his temple.

"They often are, if they're willing to take on this work," Betty remarked.

"But he's focused," Krystal said. "And he keeps the details straight. So I think we should give him the go-ahead."

"This Tabitha does seem to be doing an awful lot," Landon said. "If her posts are any indication. Money and fame everywhere suddenly. A new car yesterday—an expensive one. She posted pictures. And she's still friends with Sophie. There are comments between them; 'likes' and that kind of thing."

"More and more likely." Betty nodded. "Then tell this fellow not to hold back. We might as well make our intent clear to Sophie and Adrian."

"It'll be pretty clear after we hit the farmhouse." Krystal caressed the gun in her holster.

"Then this will help make it extra clear," Betty said.

Sophie was not fab at her chem final. Tired and achy-eyed, she couldn't remember electron configurations or molecule shapes, forgot everything she knew about ionization energy, and was almost sure she screwed up basic math on calculating percentages and pressures. At the end of the two hours, she turned in the barely-finished stack of torturous questions and her Scantron form, and plodded out of the crowded, quiet lecture hall. She didn't even know anymore which part of life was making her more miserable: finals week or the memories.

Waiting for her outside the building, flinging snowballs at each other, were Adrian and Zoe.

Surprised pleasure washed through Sophie.

"There she is," Zoe greeted.

Sophie hurried through the slush to meet her, and hugged her.

"Goddess, how much did those memories hurt, right?" Zoe asked.

"Right." Sophie sighed. "Thanks for coming."

Adrian tossed a snowball up and down in his bare hand, as if waiting for a good opportunity to pelt Zoe with it. The evidence of their battle stood all around in smashed dots of snow against walls, benches, and tree trunks, not to mention each other's coats. "Way to be inconspicuous, you guys," Sophie said.

"We are," Adrian defended. "This is exactly what everyone's doing out here today."

"We blend in," Zoe agreed.

"So you came to help find our enemies?" Sophie asked as they crossed the campus street.

"Yeah. I was hoping to use magic, but..." Zoe flicked a line of snow off a mailbox—without her fingers actually touching it, Sophie noticed. "We don't have anything belonging to Quentin, as far as we know. And we don't know who's with her. So I can't trace them unless I think of some other way. Still, I can look round, do some research, be a spy, the way Freya and Niko are."

"And you can give us good luck, right?" Sophie asked hopefully. "Like on finals, too?"

Zoe grinned at her and placed a cold fingertip on Sophie's forehead as they walked. "Zap. There. You're smarter."

Strangely, Sophie did feel a boost of mental acuity, like instant-acting coffee. "Dang. Wish I'd done that *before* the test."

"Have any more exams?"

"Yeah, one tomorrow."

"We'll do it before that."

"Thanks." Sophie smiled, but looked down at her hiking boots, which weren't keeping her feet quite warm enough on the slushy sidewalk. She felt deeply inadequate, accepting magical protection time and again from these awesome immortals, while she had nothing to give them in return. Unless love counted.

"Your job is to rock your exams," Zoe said. "You do that, and let us worry about the nasties."

CHAPTER FIFTY-TWO

Zoe's confident words to Sophie were a false show. Everything worried or irritated her lately. She had managed to get a week off work, and her parents were covering for her, saying she was visiting friends in Auckland, while in truth she hopped over the Pacific Ocean to help the immortals protect each other and the Darrow family.

Said immortal friends placed a lot of trust and reliance upon Zoe and her magical talents. Way too much, she kept reminding them, though she didn't wish to alarm them. But the truth was, her protection spells weren't bulletproof (as Sophie had put it) and couldn't protect everyone all the time. She hadn't yet figured out a way to divine where the creeps were lurking or who exactly they were, other than Quentin, nor when they'd strike. Realistically, she was down to the same skills as her friends: strength, speed, vigilance, and computer snooping. And in the event of an attack, she could use magic—assuming she was present or at least aware of the attack. Which she couldn't assume she would be.

So Zoe worried. And in addition to that, Zoe fumed. Tabitha had got to the dreadful memory of the kidnapping and the deaths of Hades, Persephone, and Demeter. Zoe asked her if she'd got there in a text this morning, unable to curb her impatience, and the little twit had answered simply, *Yeah. Dude, that sucked.*

That was it? End of evaluation? Tabitha owed the situation rather more analysis than that. And, if Zoe was being honest, she felt Tab also owed *her* a bit more explanation. Zoe didn't know if she and Tab were dating or ever had been, in Tab's view. She was guessing not. But why did Tab offer no comment upon it whatsoever?

She was going to find that blonde Yank, and they were going to have it out.

And if Freya was hanging about, so much the better, because Zoe had a choice word or two for her as well.

I'M NOT GOING to freaking cry about something that happened three thousand years ago, Tabitha reminded herself over her second giant mug of coffee in a 24-hour Chinese restaurant and diner near the college. I'm not, I'm not, I'm not.

She had successfully avoided doing so for the last few days and nights, distracting herself with a nicely full schedule. The Luigis were still in town, doing a couple more gigs, and she'd gotten to hang out with them again last night. Today she turned in a take-home final and showed up to do a final performance in voice, but she knew she'd been half-assed—even quarter-assed, honestly—about all of that. Hell, with everything going on in her life, she patted herself on the back for still remaining in college and showing up at all.

Now she was officially off for winter break, but didn't want to go back to Carnation. Her mom was sure to depress her, drinking herself to sleep at night, stumbling around to get to work on time every morning, berating Tabitha for not helping around the house more. Hanging out with her dad and the over-perfumed Jamie was out of the question too. No, Tab chose to stay in sparkly Seattle, thanks. This year she was old enough to make that choice, and had the money. So much money. It was kind of ridiculous.

She treated herself to a suite on the nineteenth floor of the Miraldo, one of the city's swankiest hotels. Way better than hanging out in the ugly old dorms over Christmas. With the suite plus all her new clothes and her new Jaguar, she ought to be bursting with happiness.

Instead she was moping by herself in a dim, windowless restaurant, surrounded by lurid red wallpaper and tasseled lanterns.

The feel of Zoe approaching startled her. She lifted her head. Sure enough, in a few seconds Zoe's tall, slim, shaggy-haired figure stalked into the restaurant foyer and veered into the dining room.

"Hey." Zoe wriggled out of her parka, threw it over the back of the leather chair opposite Tabitha, and seated herself. "How's the coffee here? I could use a warm drink." She plucked a menu from between the soy sauce and salt shaker.

Tabitha stared at her, trying not to be overly charmed by her fresh skin, her cheeks and lips rosy from the cold air. "Hey. Didn't know you were coming."

"Nice to see you, too." Zoe still perused the menu, and smiled at the waiter who approached. "Hi. Coffee and the Greek omelet, please." As the waiter nodded and retreated, Zoe remarked to Tab, "I mean, how could I not choose the Greek one, right?"

Tab studied her. She felt pretty damn sure Zoe was messing with her, and furthermore, that Zoe had every right to mess with her since Tab hadn't been a very good friend lately. And the guilt made her more annoyed still. She lifted her eyebrows and looked away. "Guess you came to help protect Sophie and everyone?"

"Yeah. And for moral support. She just got to those same horrible memories you and I did. She told you, right?"

Tabitha shook her head. "She didn't. Wow. During finals. That sucks." She swished her coffee around, with a new flash of sympathy for Sophie. Plus it thoroughly bugged her that her best friend was apparently confiding in others more than in her lately. Again, not that Tab had deserved the title of "friend" so much in recent weeks. She'd meant to find some other cool treat for Sophie, had loads of ideas in mind, but just hadn't been able to make them happen yet.

Zoe's touch on her hand, on the table, surprised her and lifted her spirits. But only for a moment, because then Zoe withdrew her hand, somewhat clinically, and sat back to regard Tab.

Defensive anger swept over Tab. "You don't get to just touch me and read my emotions whenever you want! Isn't that an invasion of privacy or something?"

"Yes. You're right. Sorry." Zoe accepted the coffee from the waiter. As he walked back to the kitchen, she picked up a packet of raw sugar and tore it open. Her voice went quieter but sharper. "But you aren't talking, nor texting, and we're in the middle of Thanatos murdering us in the past, and trying to in the present, and I don't have time to play bloody head games with you. *Talk* to me."

"About what?"

"Let's start with all that guilt I just read in you. What's that for?"

Tabitha slumped over the table, defeated. "For—for all that stuff you just said. For being a sucky friend. For not helping more. I—I don't know what to do to help, all right? I'm not as smart and responsible as the rest of you."

"What about the memories?" Now Zoe sounded softer.

Tabitha shook her head, staring across the room at a red lantern hanging from the ceiling, while the ancient terror and grief hauled down on her heart. "What am I supposed to say? I sucked even worse then. It was my fault. I can never, ever fix it. Not all of us are awesome heroes, okay? Some of us make humongous mistakes. A lot of them."

"You think it was *your* fault?" Zoe stirred the sugar into her coffee, her gray eyes somber. A tense line appeared between her eyebrows. "Clearly it was mine. My choice, my carelessness. Me as the hostage who got my parents killed. I never forgave myself. I know that much. I still don't forgive myself." She threw a fierce look at Tab. "So there is no *bloody* way I'm letting Thanatos hurt them again this life. Nor do I want them to hurt you. But you could at least lift a finger to help yourself, and not be such a stupidly obvious target. Could you do more for your friends than throw parties—to which they aren't even invited, incidentally?"

"You...have a permanent invitation," Tab spluttered.

Zoe rolled her eyes. "Are you going to help or not?"

"Fine, yes. Just tell me what to do."

Zoe blew on the surface of her coffee. "Sophie's taking her last final now, and going home tomorrow. We want you to take a shift hanging out at her house and keeping an eye out the windows for spies, anyone suspicious."

"I already do come check on Sophie's folks a couple of times a week," Tab defended. "I do that, at least."

"Good. So do this bit too. Carnation's the one place Quentin keeps cropping up. She's threatened Terry directly. That's where we should focus the protection. Everyone knows you're Sophie's friend, so it doesn't look strange if anyone notices you visiting. Her parents know about the Underworld and everything by now, so you don't even have to pretend around them."

"I know. We've chatted about that." Tab sighed. "Tomorrow? Okay, yeah. As long as my shift doesn't go later than nine at night." At Zoe's accusing glance, she added, "The Luigis have their last gig in town tomorrow. I said I'd come. You should come too. Please?"

Zoe bowed her head, her light brown bangs falling over her eyebrows. "Fine. Sounds good. Cheers." She smirked. "Ade will be wanting the night shift anyway, if you know what I mean."

"Bet he won't get much spying done," Tab tried to joke.

But neither of them smiled much. Letting sex distract you into opening the door to an assassin attempt—yeah, they had both lived through a memory like that all too recently.

CHAPTER FIFTY-THREE

This had to be the most surreal winter break of Sophie's life. Obviously it was the first time she had come home from college for the holidays, rather than simply coming back from the high school down the road. She brought luggage, not just her backpack. But in addition to that, she was escorted back to Carnation in a super-fast flying bus by the king of the dead—or her new Kiwi boyfriend, whatever you wanted to call him—where her parents shook his hand and her mom pulled him aside to have a conversation about her past-life memories.

Tabitha soon showed up too, cheerfully announcing she was here to "guard" Sophie. Sophie's dad hugged Tab and thanked her, because of course everyone in the house now except Liam knew about the immortals and Thanatos. Liam was in his room on his computer, immersed in one of his online role-playing games with his headphones on, and wouldn't have noticed if a parade of hippos walked through the house.

Sophie picked up a sugar cookie from the plate in the kitchen and munched it. She wandered on wobbly legs into the living room. Finals had wiped her out. The brain-boost Zoe gave her before her last test did seem to help; she felt she'd done better on that one than on the chemistry. But she still felt none too confident about her fall quarter grades on the whole. All she wanted to do was sleep, then wrap Christmas presents, then sleep some more, and not worry about terrorists ever. Her immortal friends assured she shouldn't worry; thwarting Thanatos was their job—which of course made her feel bad for ruining *their* holidays.

Adding to the strangeness, Adrian and Tabitha now met in person for the first time.

He wandered up to Tab, where she hung out by the front window checking her texts. He offered his hand. "Hey. Finally get to meet."

Tab lifted her head, beamed, and pumped his hand in greeting. "Yes! Finally. How's it going?" She burst into a laugh before he could answer. "Sorry, dumb question."

He glanced out the window, then back at Tab. "So, um, have you hung out with Grange Redway again, besides that first time?"

"Not so far, but he emailed me the other day about a party around New Year's. I might go."

"Ah, sweet as. I'm *such* a Red Merlins fan."

Lingering by the couch, Sophie watched them talk, and smiled. Adrian could have been stern with Tab, the way Zoe confessed she'd been yesterday. He grumbled and scowled about Tab's behavior, and as Hades he had found Adonis-Dionysos a bit flaky, too. But Tabitha had dutifully come to help today, and for the sake of team harmony, Adrian sought common ground.

Sophie gave him an extra long kiss at the side door to thank him before he left.

"I'll be back tonight," he said. "Off to rendezvous with Niko and Zoe and see what use I can be."

Sophie nodded. "Thank you. See you then."

ZOE FELT UNEASY about leaving with Tab that night to party in Seattle with The Luigis. But Adrian was with Sophie now—apparently her parents were letting him stay in the house, though in a separate room—and Zoe felt no particular threatening vibes surrounding the property. Adrian had turned up nothing in all his scouting around Carnation and vicinity all day. Zoe had poured a fresh salt line and woven a new braid of magic around it just in case. Ignoring the mental warning that reminded her brute force could bash through such things, she joined Tab and they flew side by side on their two horses to Seattle.

"All these check-ins, I still haven't seen a thing," Tab said. They descended to the ground on a hill overlooking the dark Elliott Bay. "Just the neighbors I've known my whole life."

"I didn't find anything in the email accounts I managed to get into, either." Zoe slid off her horse and tied him up next to Tab's, around the trunk of a slim fir. "Mind you, I still can't get into Quentin's, which would be the real jackpot."

"I bet they're just trying to freak us out and spoil our good time." Tab hooked her arm through Zoe's. "Let's not let 'em."

Flattered at the touch, and charmed by the youthful excitement she felt through Tab's skin, Zoe went along with the sentiment. They switched realms and the city burst into loud, colorful light and motion around them. They were standing beside a brick building on a slanting sidewalk, cars and buses swishing down the steep street or laboring up it.

"This way." Tab tugged her arm, and they charged up the hill.

The venue was a small theater that had sold out its seats within the first hour, Tab told her. But she steered Zoe to the back door and only had to beam and say "Hi!" at the guy guarding it. He smiled back, said, "Hey, youngster," and let both of them through.

Zoe was so breathless and stoked at her imminent meeting with The Luigis that she didn't sense Freya's presence until they were all together backstage: the laughing Swedish blonde, chatting with, and charming the leather pants off, the band.

Of course.

Zoe held back a few steps while Tabitha sauntered forward and hugged the band members and Freya. Then she swung around and beckoned to Zoe. "Come! Meet everyone."

Freya hugged Zoe first, without invitation, saying, "Hello, darling."

Zoe barely lifted her arms in response. She smiled awkwardly for The Luigis, and shook hands with each of them, and mumbled that she loved their music. Which she did, absolutely.

But now she felt, without question, that she didn't belong in a scene like this. This was Tab's arena; Freya's and Niko's too. Zoe operated best in quiet, dark, solitary places. And that depressed her, because this was the pinnacle of coolness in the world— standing backstage with one of the most happening bands of the year, with the goddess of love and the god(dess) of partying and alcohol.

But it wasn't like she could go back to Sophie and Adrian, who were likely doing their best to find some private time before retiring to their parent-mandated separate rooms. And Niko wasn't in Seattle tonight; he was staying nearer Carnation, snooping around for enemies. So she endured the evening.

Endured it even when enduring meant watching Freya and Tabitha hook their arms around each other's waists or play with each other's hair. Or when wishing she'd brought earplugs because the volume of the (admittedly awesome) music tormented her ears. Or when catching herself scanning the crowd and the other backstage wanderers grimly, searching for assassins, rather than relaxing as she was supposed to be doing.

She seethed with irritability by the time the concert ended near midnight. They all poured out onto the cold street, everyone mingling and shouting at each other over their ringing ears.

"Come see!" Tab was yelling, and pulled Zoe's arm to follow her. The crowd of band members and groupies came too. "I parked it down here earlier today so it'd be close. Who wants a ride?"

Ah, Tab's new Jaguar. A sleek purple-blue thing that looked like it could take off like a rocket, and probably cost ten times more than anyone should spend on a car. Totally absurd. But all the band members were petting it and cooing over it and Tab was making zoom noises to demonstrate what the engine sounded like, and soon Tab unlocked it and the drummer opened the passenger side and climbed in. Zoe sighed and moved out of the way, leaning her hand on the Jaguar's hood.

The warning shot up her arm like an electric shock. She gasped, spreading her palm on the sparkly blue-purple metal to make sure. Then she shouted, "Tab, no!" and sprinted around the hood, into the street, to grab Tab before she could start the engine. "Stop, something's wrong with the car, stop!"

Key touching the ignition, Tab stared in astonishment at Zoe. "What the hell is wrong with you?"

"I could feel it! A bomb or something. Get out, everyone get away."

Tab sat frozen, eyes wide, then she scrambled out. The drummer did too. Everyone muttered, looking at Zoe like she was mad. She didn't care. She cast a frantic look around, trying to pinpoint who in this crowd of strangers might be the threat.

Tab popped the hood and frowned at the engine in the beam of the streetlight above. The drummer looked too. "I don't know, I think it's all okay…"

Zoe touched the car again, feeling the danger throb as strong as ever. She followed it along the exterior, toward the back of the car. She knelt, looking under the tailpipe, though she had no idea what to look for.

The bassist and a roadie crouched with her, the roadie shining a keyring flashlight onto the undercarriage. It lingered on a greasy plate of metal that didn't match the rest of the glossy new car. "Dude," he said. "I'm thinking that should not be there."

Zoe reached out and let her fingertips touch the plate. Evil sang from it; lethal intent had placed it there, no question. She shuddered and jerked her hand away. "Call the police. Don't start the car or mess with it, anyone."

"Jesus." The bassist stepped back, glancing at Tab, who stood pale with fright, watching Zoe.

The roadie whipped out his phone and dialed, and soon began telling someone they'd found a suspected car bomb.

Zoe walked to Tab, who threw her arms around her and stayed in her embrace, shaking. "It's okay," Zoe said. "We found it in time."

This time. But what else would Thanatos try? If they knew about Tab, did they know about Zoe? Were her parents safe?

Above Tab's head, Zoe met Freya's gaze. Freya stood with her arm around the cutest of the roadies, but watched Zoe with grave and perceptive eyes. She gave Zoe a nod that Zoe supposed meant approval and thanks—though who the hell knew? Zoe wondered if they could even trust Freya. But right now they had to get to safety and tell Adrian, Sophie, and Niko what had happened.

"Listen," she said to Tab. "We better—"

But an enraged roar cut her off. People shrieked. Tab and Zoe jolted apart. A heavyset, bearded young man rushed forward, pulling a large gun from under his coat. As he ran he aimed the gun straight at Tab, yelling, "Thanatos!"

Tab leaped across the sidewalk, perhaps intending to shield the innocent fans and band members. Freya tugged free of the roadie and lunged after the man. But Zoe's strike hit first. With a wallop of protective magic, aimed with her outstretched hand rather than just her mind, she knocked the gun out of his hands. He shouted in outrage. The gun clattered across the sidewalk. The groupies and band members skittered away from it, then five or six of them rushed forward to stand around it and block the man from picking it up again—which he was intent on doing, judging from how he wheeled that direction.

But Freya reached him and shoved him with all her strength so that he slammed hard against a parking meter and fell to the ground. He rose again, roared, and rushed at Tab. The crowd, however, wasn't going to take it. Likely they thought he was trying to assassinate one of The Luigis, and they were outraged. Now over their shock, and inspired by Freya's fighting back, two of the stronger and faster young men rushed forward to grab him, and soon another half-dozen fans and band members joined them, clutching at him and trying to haul him to the ground and hold him for the police.

The man fought like an animal, though, and rolled free of their grip, off the curb, then leaped up and ran into the street—without regard for traffic.

A brightly lit city bus, swooshing down the hill, smashed into the man within seconds and threw him tumbling across the pavement. Brakes squealed and the bus slid to a stop while onlookers shouted in panic. The man lay still.

Zoe leaned weakly against a parking meter, her eyes upon his motionless form.

"What did he say?" people were asking each other, behind her. "Xanadu? Canada?"

"I don't know, man. He was just crazy."

She could switch realms and watch to see his soul appear, if she chose. But even from here she sensed the powerful emanation, the life pulling away from his body and departing this realm.

She closed her eyes, trying not to slide to the ground, and searched for mercy in her heart as she pictured his soul flying across the world and down, down, down into Tartaros.

CHAPTER FIFTY-FOUR

SOPHIE VISITED ADRIAN IN THE MAKESHIFT GUEST ROOM, THE STUDY on the first floor with a sofa where he was going to sleep. Kiri and Rosie and Pumpkin all dozed on the floor. It was after midnight and the rest of the house had gone to bed. But rather than engaging in steamy undressed activities with an ear cocked for the footstep of her parents, they were arguing. Quietly and sympathetically, but still an argument.

Adrian was trying to convince her it might be best if he didn't stay inside the house. "If they find out I'm in here, they could just blow the whole place up to get me—taking the lot of you out too."

"How would they do that with all the magic and spying you guys are doing?" she said.

"I'm telling you, our magic and spying are not that awesome. They could sneak straight past all of it if they chose their moment right. We can't protect everyone, always."

"Well, I feel safer if you're here," she insisted.

"And I'm saying maybe you shouldn't."

They went over and over those same pieces of ground. It was, in a grim way, a relief when Zoe's text interrupted them.

It came to them both, cc'ing Nikolaos, and they stopped arguing to check their phones.

Attack on Tab. We're all ok for now. Need to regroup and plan.

Sophie's stomach clenched in queasiness. She gazed at Adrian. After a few seconds, he advanced and kissed her on the forehead. "I'll keep watch round here. You call Zoe and get the details."

She nodded, though her tongue had turned so dry she doubted she'd be able to speak. Adrian and Kiri departed to the front room, where, in the dark, he moved from one window to another and peered out.

She called Zoe. Zoe gave her the story, and said they'd be finding a different place to sleep tonight, other than either the dorm or the hotel room in Seattle. "You two might think about doing the same," she said.

"But my parents and brother are here. They're asleep. I don't want to wake everyone up and move them, but I also don't want to leave them…"

"Listen, I'll come over," Zoe said. "I'll feel round, same way I did with Tab's car. If there's anything like that bomb planted near, I ought to be able to sense it. Then maybe you can stay for now, but think about a new place to go tomorrow, yeah?"

"Okay. Thanks."

Sophie went out to the living room and caught Adrian up on the conversation, though he'd been hearing details from Freya, who had called him.

He peeked past the curtain to squint out into the night. "We don't know if they'll even target this house anytime soon," he whispered. "They might be concentrating this attack on Tab. We need to figure out if they know she's immortal for sure, or if they were just trying to do damage to your friends. I'd bet on the former, if they went as far as a car bomb, and a high-powered rifle as backup."

Sophie leaned against the wall, shaking. "So what else do they know?"

"That's what we have to find out."

Zoe arrived soon. After giving each of them a reassuring hug, she walked the perimeter of the house and the property, trailing her fingertips on the concrete foundation, the cars, the fence, the planter boxes, every potential hiding place for explosives she could think of.

"Nothing," she reported when she came back in. "Which isn't

to say they won't try some other way, sometime. But nothing for now, tonight, as far as I can sense."

"I wonder if Quentin even knows her assassin failed yet." Adrian's jaw clenched as he scowled out at the empty road. "If I knew where she was, I'd bring her his body myself and dump it at her feet. Then I'd drag her into the spirit realm and leave her for the animals like I told her I would."

Sophie sank onto the sofa, wishing she could find some realm free of all this viciousness. Did any such place exist, besides the fields of the Underworld? Maybe she should just move there. With her whole family. Her father might like it, growing magical produce, but Liam would surely get bored and go above ground and get himself eaten by one of those spirit-world beasts...

Her dazed thoughts tumbled with her into her dreams as she fell asleep on the sofa, with Zoe and Adrian keeping watch in the house.

THE IMMORTALS STOOD or sat about in the fields, some gazing across the glowing expanses in distress, some studying the souls of their fallen companions with stormy expressions, some clustered around Hekate.

Persephone, Hades, Demeter, Zeus, Hera, Epimetheus, Euterpe, Benna. The fallen had all converged to meet their grieving friends and family. Hermes had spread the word, dispatching others to fetch everyone, until all the immortals had come down here to judge what should be done.

Ares had come with the rest, though he looked as uneasy as ever. "Why have you not attacked?" he asked the others. "How can you let a savage insult like this stand?"

For once, no one talked him down, Persephone noted with concern. She tried to do so herself. "Ares, once you reach the state we're in, you'll see it doesn't help, answering violence with violence..."

He rounded on her. "I never want to be in the state you're in!

I don't want it to happen to any of us! We need to wipe out these ungrateful swine, and we need to do it now."

"I agree." Artemis' voice trembled, and her eyes glistened as she took in the row of her translucent companions. "They have gone too far."

Dionysos had found Agria's soul—the only leopard-like animal in the fields—and was kneeling beside her, watching her circle curiously around the soul of a house cat. "They *have* gone too far," he said softly. "We need to take a stand."

"I agree." It was Hekate's voice. Everyone turned to her in surprise. She kept her eyes lowered, staring at the pale grass. "I'm willing to incur black marks against my soul if it means destroying these murderers. The Fates long to get their hands upon them. I can feel it."

"My dear," Rhea said gently, "isn't it possible it's you who long to get your hands on them?"

"Either way," Hekate said, without even a blink. "Who's with me?"

"Truly, I don't think we should initiate bloodshed," Hephaestus said, with some timidity.

Hekate turned a passive glance upon him. "We didn't initiate it. And what if it wasn't us who shed the blood? What if it was nature?"

Dionysos looked from Agria's soul to Hekate, and rose with a nod. "I stand with you."

Hermes waited at Hekate's back, as if guarding her. He squeezed her shoulder. "And I."

"And I," Ares muttered.

"And I," Artemis said.

Apollo joined. Poseidon joined. Aphrodite joined. Rhea joined. Two of the Muses joined.

And in the end, those who declined to join agreed not to stand in the way of the rest.

SOPHIE AWOKE TO the clink of breakfast plates and the white

light of morning. She entered the kitchen to find everything was still surreal: her parents were having breakfast with Adrian and Zoe, and her dad looked up at her and said, "Hey. I'm thinking we have Christmas in some other house this year. Like one in Baja maybe."

Sophie glanced at Adrian, who capitulated in a half shrug. "Works for me," she said. "Kind of like the Witness Protection Program. As long as you don't tell people where you're going."

"We'll work out the details today," her mom said. "Find a good place, get organized, and go this afternoon or tonight. So none of us has to worry so much. Sound good?"

Sophie nodded, the kinks in her neck relaxing in sweet relief. "Very good." She glanced up the stairs. "Liam still asleep?"

"Yeah," her mom said. "We'll tell him when he gets up."

"Tell him everything?" Sophie looked to Zoe and Adrian, who both clearly wore doubt on their faces.

Her dad spread jam on his toast. "I'm thinking at first we'll just tell him it's meant to be a big secret and we can't tell anyone. Course, when he sees how we're getting there, he's going to need more of an explanation."

"He's going to love that bus," her mom said.

Terry shook his head. "Tell you what, your grandma is *not* going to be pleased with us for bailing on her Christmas visit."

"I'll bring her to see you if you like," Zoe said, smiling at him. Hekate smiling at her grandmother Demeter, Sophie thought. Not that her dad knew he was Demeter yet.

She blinked her bleary eyes and turned toward the bathroom to get ready for the day.

KRYSTAL'S DISAPPOINTED SIGH cut through the quiet of the cabin. "Here it is." She glared at her phone's screen, reading aloud. "'A man was accidentally killed by a bus on Capitol Hill last night when he pulled a gun on a crowd after a Luigis concert, and was chased into the street by onlookers. Police also found a car bomb beneath one of the audience members' vehicles parked on the street, and suspect the two incidents are linked.' God damn it. Idiot. We shouldn't have trusted him."

"It's hard to get people to do that kind of work," Landon sympathized, leaning over her chair to look at the phone.

Betty prodded the embers in the fireplace. "So we still aren't sure Tabitha's one of them?"

"No," Landon said. "But then, we wouldn't have been sure if we'd killed her, either."

"I say she's one of them." Krystal thumped her phone down on her lap. "Ugh. Incompetents."

"Sounds like it was mostly bad luck," Betty said. "No plan is perfect. We'll try her again before long. Adrian is still the known enemy, and we still go after him today. You ready?"

Krystal's frown lifted to a calculating smile. She twirled the end of her red ponytail in her fingers. "Ready." She beamed across the room at the case containing her newest purchase, which Betty had helped finance: a grenade launcher to attach to a rifle Krystal already owned, and a few high-explosive rounds. They had all been purchased under the table to avoid legal registration, and had set Betty back a couple of thousand dollars. But that was a small price to pay for stopping a threat to the safety of the human race.

Law enforcement would thank Betty Quentin someday, if they ever found out the whole story.

CHAPTER FIFTY-FIVE

$\mathcal{T}$HE HOURS TUMBLED BY. THE DARROW FAMILY PACKED CLOTHES and Christmas presents, and researched places to stay. Adrian and Zoe, who stuck around to guard them, conferred with them about their options and agreed it was probably safe to stay in a remote cabana in Baja California, and certainly more comfortable than camping in the spirit realm. Adrian would come along to keep watch, just in case. Sophie even dared to let herself become a tiny bit pleased, looking forward to swimming in the warm sea with him in the tropical night.

But organizing it and getting ready was taking all day. Soon it was 4:00, and the sun was setting in the dim December sky.

Sophie checked in with Tab, who was still deeply shaken about the attack, and uncertain about even setting foot in the living world. Zoe agreed to spend the evening near her, though Freya was already there—maybe *because* Freya was already there, Sophie thought. It tired her to sort out the romantic complications among those three. Meanwhile, Niko remained in living-world Seattle, searching for any other would-be killers, though he reported no success so far.

Liam was done packing, and was bouncing off the walls in excitement about the sudden secret trip to Mexico. Sophie smiled dryly as she pictured how much more excited he'd be when he realized they were taking a supersonic spirit horse bus instead of a passenger jet.

Liam wanted to dash down the road before leaving and pick

up a present from his buddy. Since the others were still getting ready, his parents let him.

Sophie watched him bop away in the fading light, and immediately worried about his safety. She decided to send Adrian after him if he didn't come back within half an hour.

Adrian had prowled from window to window most of the day, taking breaks to look at computer screens and messages, and to eat when Sophie reminded him to.

At the moment, her parents were still up in their room, packing and squaring away details by phone or email.

She found Adrian in the study. "Come on, have some leftovers. We should eat them up before we go."

"Suppose so." He went to the window facing the field behind the house, and looked out into the twilight gloom. He frowned. "Do you see someone out there?"

Sophie looked too. "No, but it's getting dark. Wait." Her stomach dipped in alarm. "Yeah, by the fence—I did see—"

The flash of fire sliced across her words. Adrian flung himself at her and seized her. The sounds of glass shattering and a roaring explosion vanished to silence within a second, and instead of hitting the floor they fell a foot or two through space to the wet, cold ground. The landing bruised her hips and elbows and made her grunt in pain.

Sophie flailed free of him in the muddy dead leaves and scrambled up, staring around the spirit realm in panic. "What happened? Oh my God, what happened?"

"This way." Adrian leaped up too, and grabbed her hand, pulling her along. "I switched realms to get us out of the way."

"I know that, but what is happening in the other realm right now?" she shrieked.

His body and voice trembled as he rushed her between trees, counting off paces. "Something not good."

"Is the house burning? Adrian! My parents!"

Rather than answer—and surely he had no answer, any more than she did—he wrapped his arms around her and switched realms again.

Flames bloomed up into the sky, filling her vision as she turned. She and Adrian stood in the field beside the house, far enough away to be out of danger, but even from there the heat licked at her face. The whole house was burning, collapsing, almost unrecognizable already as the humble wood frame gave itself up to the fire.

She screamed, the sound raw and tearing into her lungs. She lunged forward, but Adrian confined her against his chest, holding her as she struggled.

"No!" he said. "You can't go in, don't you dare, don't even try."

"My parents!" She fought with all her strength. "We have to get them out!"

"Sophie, I'll try, but a fire like that…" His voice sounded shredded and broken.

Somewhere in her distraught mind she remembered Kiri had been around the house, not to mention Pumpkin and Rosie. At least Liam was out, but the dogs, her parents…this couldn't be happening.

People were shouting and calling. A car or two had stopped on the road, and Phil Shenk, the retired man who lived in the next farmhouse over, was running toward them.

Adrian looked at him. "Are you safe with him? Do you know him?" he asked rapidly.

Sophie nodded, returning her horrified gaze to the fire.

"Sophie! My God!" Phil said, gasping for breath as he reached her.

Adrian handed her over to him. "Stay here," he told her firmly. Then he jumped the wooden fence, sprinted to the house, and slammed through the side door. He disappeared into the flames. Sophie crammed her hands over her mouth to keep from screaming again. How could she have sent him in there? But how could she *not* send him in there to save her parents?

"What happened?" Phil asked in hushed horror.

Sophie only shook her head to indicate she had no idea. Though of course she did. Thanatos. Grenades. They did things exactly like this. And right at the moment when they must have spotted Adrian in the window…

An animal's silhouette wriggled into view between her and the flames. Kiri! She was pulling someone: a dark body on the ground. Sophie and Phil climbed over the fence and rushed forward.

After one look, a look that stretched forever though it only lasted a few seconds, Sophie spun away and threw up into the bushes by the fence.

Her mother. Burned like a fireplace log. Dead.

Sophie staggered back and dropped to the muddy ground on her knees, her whirling head bent over her lap. Soft dog fur settled against her side. Kiri whined softly. She reeked of burning hair, and Sophie fought the need to scream or vomit again.

New shouts made her look up in dread. Someone had leaped out a second floor window and went tumbling across the garden: Adrian, clothing aflame, holding another body in his arms.

Phil and a woman from one of the cars ran forward to them. Adrian had let go of Terry, and rolled across the ground until the flames were extinguished. But Sophie's father lay still. She didn't wish to go any closer, not when she saw how the other people cringed and covered their mouths and said, "Oh, my God."

Sirens howled. Red lights flashed against the treetops, competing with the flickering fire. An ambulance and a fire truck pulled into the driveway.

Adrian tottered to Sophie and collapsed to his knees before her. Kiri whined, scooting over to place her chin in his lap. He bent over the dog and hugged her, and buried his face in her singed fur. "I'm sorry, Sophie." Smoke or tears, or both, had roughened his voice into unfamiliarity. He lifted his head, and in his face she saw the bleak answer to her hope.

"No. They can't both be dead, they can't be." She couldn't breathe; she squeaked out the words past paralyzed lungs.

He turned his head suddenly, glaring into the fields past her. Soot grimed him all over. "Whoever did this isn't far." He leaped to his feet. "I'll find them and I'll throw them into that fire."

"Don't," she begged. "They were trying to get you. Don't go straight to them."

"I'm stronger and faster than them, and they need to die." He dashed for the fence, startlingly quick, and in seconds he was over it and out into the dark of the fields. Kiri barked and ran after him, leaping the fence and vanishing.

BETTY QUENTIN WATCHED the fiery orange glow light up the sky from across the field while she waited in the nondescript van they had purchased yesterday. Excitement and hope beat in her chest. She exchanged a glance with Landon, behind the wheel, who once again sat ready as the getaway driver. They were parked on the quiet rural road half a mile behind the farmhouse, on the other side of the field. At dusk, Krystal, dressed in full camouflage, had snuck through the tall grass with her grenade launcher. After several silent, tense minutes, the twilight had bloomed loud and bright with the explosion.

That meant Krystal had seen Adrian: identified him positively, and fired. It meant that, as Betty and her companions expected, Terry and Isabel had allowed Adrian into their household and were harboring him.

Betty drew in a long breath, and sighed. "Pity about the family. I did try to warn them."

Landon echoed her sigh in answer, sounding uneasy.

Betty's cell phone rang. She glanced at it to find Krystal's code name, and answered. "Hello?"

"He didn't die!" Krystal kept her voice carefully quiet, but still conveyed intense annoyance.

"He didn't die?"

"Neither did Sophie. I just saw them both. He tried to save her parents, but he survived. I think *they're* dead, whatever good that does us."

"Where is he? Can you still get a shot at him?"

"Too many people around now. I'd get caught." She seethed out an infuriated breath. "Great, and now he just disappeared into the field on the other side. Probably looking for me. Wish he'd come this way."

"Don't wish that," Betty said. "Without the element of surprise on your side, he can too easily win. Just go to plan B. Are you ready?"

"Yes." Krystal cleared her throat. "Yeah, with him out of the way, that should be pretty easy, in fact."

"We'll bring the van around front."

CHAPTER FIFTY-SIX

ZOE STALKED BEHIND TABITHA AND FREYA THROUGH A DODGY neighborhood in downtown Seattle, scowling at how Freya was laughing and trying to decorate Tab's hair with a piece of tinsel she'd pulled from a cafe table earlier this afternoon. Probably the playfulness was only meant to lift Tab out of her worries, but it was working rather too well. Tab giggled right back and swatted at Freya. And annoyed the living hell out of Zoe.

"Ugh!" Zoe stopped on the sidewalk and used a smack of magic to send a plastic soda bottle clattering into the street.

Her companions stopped too, turning in surprise to stare at her.

"What *is* this with you two?" Zoe demanded, more bluntly than she'd meant to. "Freya, are you even gay? Or bi? Or what?"

An embarrassed glance shot between Freya and Tab, then Tab sulked and looked down, while Freya put on a placating smile. "We're all allies, dear," she said. "Just trying to keep each other happy."

"You're messing with her head. Same as you always did. Can't you see that?"

"No, she isn't," Tab insisted. "It's my fault. I'm still working things out. I mean, look, Dionysos had years to get over her and figure out his life, but I've only been doing this for, what, a month?"

"As have I," Zoe returned.

"You have a purpose!" Tab said. "You have magic. It's there for you. You know what to do. I *don't* know—I don't know what to do or what to be. What am I supposed to learn from all the ancient shit? I'm good at parties? None of you seem to appreciate that very much nowadays."

Freya moved between them, holding up a hand on each side as if separating combatants. "All right. It's complicated. Lots of memories, lots of lives—and to answer your question, I do try to be open to anyone, but in this life, this body, I generally am straight."

Generally. Didn't that leave things nice and open. Zoe tore the warm hat off her head and swooped her fingers through her hair. "We're supposed to be on guard here, and every time, you two are—oh, forget it. Why don't we split up, and I'll stalk pointlessly round one part of the city while you two do what you bloody like in another—"

Her mobile rang, interrupting her tirade.

She yanked it out to glower at it, finding "David" as the caller. Adrian. "Yeah?" she answered.

"Come now." He sounded like he was panting. She heard sirens behind him. "All hell's broke loose. Sophie's house, they hit it, it's burning, her parents are dead. She's all right, physically, but—come now, all of you."

The wind knocked itself out of Zoe's chest. "Dear Goddess. What about Liam?"

"He wasn't in the house, I'm not sure where he is. I'm combing the area looking for the bastards and I swear this time I will kill them."

"Ade, be careful. Wait for us, all right? Keep Sophie safe."

"If this is my way of keeping her safe," he said, his voice breaking, "then what good am I to her at all?"

"Be careful," Zoe begged again. "Be safe. We need you. We'll be right there. I'll get Niko. I love you, Ade."

"Cheers." He sniffled, and hung up.

Her two companions gazed stricken at her. Zoe stared back at them, thinking of Terry and Isabel, that nice couple who'd wel-

comed her in—Terry, the soul of her beloved grandparent Demeter, who had sacrificed herself for Hekate…

No, Zoe's irritation with these two women didn't matter, not
at all.

She caught her breath on an inhaled sob. "We have to go," she
squeaked. "Now."

Sophie staggered to the driveway, trailed by her neighbor
Phil. She had to find Liam, stop him from seeing the bodies. She
didn't know yet what had become of Rosie and Pumpkin, but they
had probably died too. She had to be the one to tell Liam, not
some neighbor or paramedic.

Police and paramedics did stop her on the way, asking urgent
questions, looking her over for injuries. She answered automatically, shook her head, refused medical treatment, said she didn't
need any, repeated she had to go find her brother right away.
They reluctantly let her pass, after urging her to come back and
talk to them as soon as she found him.

Phil stayed behind to tell one of the officers what he had seen.
Sophie kept stumbling forward.

At the highway, in the throng of vehicles and concerned
onlookers, a skinny young woman with red hair in a ponytail
stepped forward. A yellow badge on her dark blue uniform proclaimed her Oregon State Police. She stopped Sophie and held her
by the arm. "Sophie, we need your help right away. It's critical, if
we're going to stop these people."

Sophie shook her head, repeating her mantra through numb
lips. "I need to find my brother."

"This is about your brother." The young woman tugged her
forward. "This is the only way to save him."

Fresh, sickening fear pooled into Sophie's stomach. "Why?
What happened?"

The red-haired woman glanced at the fiery chaos, and pulled
Sophie farther. "Let's go where we can talk. Sit in here."

She led her inside a white van that sat ahead of a police car and an ambulance.

Sophie's sense of danger, already overloaded, didn't register until a few seconds late. She followed the woman into the van and sat on the worn sideways-facing bench seat. The door slid shut and locked, shutting out the street and the glow of the fire. Strange paneling surrounded her, wood of some kind. It blocked all the windows and the view of the front seat.

Oregon State Police. This was Washington. And this could not be official police business at all.

In the faint gleam of the dome light, Sophie looked at the wood-paneled wall in dread.

"Oak," the red-haired woman said. She now aimed a handgun at Sophie. "You know about oak, don't you?"

Sophie tried to swallow against her raw, dry throat. Yes, she knew. She shut her eyes. "Kill me, then," she whispered. "Just do it fast." She'd be with her parents. This would be over. The serenity of the dead sounded far better than the agony of the present.

"I'd like to, traitor." Scorn twisted the woman's words. "But unfortunately you're much more useful as a hostage."

A jolt of electricity seared through Sophie. All her muscles seized up, tingling in torture. Gasping and convulsing, she slammed to the van's floor. Probably a stun gun like her own, she thought. Just before losing consciousness, she felt the van begin moving.

ADRIAN STOPPED IN the middle of combing through the dark field. With Sophie present in his mind throughout his homicidal search, it came as a startling silence when her presence disappeared like a radio being switched off. He was aware of a couple of oak trees around, but in glancing toward them, he reckoned she shouldn't be on the opposite side of them. She ought to be near the house, safe with the neighbors.

The sudden realization of what Thanatos must have done slammed into him, strangling him with new fear and fury. He sprinted for the driveway, Kiri at his heels. He burst into the glare of the fire and the numerous vehicle lights, not caring if someone identified him and shot a new rocket at him. He grabbed arms and turned people, looking into one startled face after another until he found the neighbor he had left Sophie with. The man was talking to a police officer, but stopped mid-sentence, eyes going wide, when Adrian seized his shoulder.

"Where is she?" Adrian shouted. "Where'd she go?"

The man, already shaken and pale, looked terrified. "She—she was here a minute ago. She went to find her brother. She was talking to a police woman right over there."

Adrian glanced where the man pointed, in the direction of the street. No Sophie, no sense of her. He ran over and looked up and down the highway in desperation. Several emergency vehicles had pulled over, along with cars belonging to people from town. Other cars and trucks passed on the road, slowing as the drivers gaped at the fire. Total chaos, and he didn't even know what the attackers looked like this time.

He ran along the line of vehicles. He peered into each one, shouted her name, and asked people if they knew where she was. No one did. He stooped over beside the road, hands on his thighs, head hanging down as despair swept over him. Without being able to track her, he couldn't help her. He was at their mercy.

He thought suddenly of Liam and lifted his head. But he could still sense Liam—he was near. He looked over to see the tall, thin, black-haired boy, face contorted in a wail, held back at the driveway by a neighbor and a cop. Heart sinking even further, Adrian tottered to him and shouldered between people to thud his hand onto Liam's back.

Liam turned to stare in near-incomprehension at him, breathing jaggedly through his mouth, his young eyebrows twisted up in agony.

"I'll find your sister," Adrian told him, his voice cracked and unsteady.

Liam gave a sort of nod, an upward twitch of his head, then returned to staring in distress at the smoking ruins of his house.

Adrian couldn't start weeping now. That would do no one any good. He merely staggered down the sidewalk and waited.

It didn't take long. His mobile rang soon, showing Sophie's number. Not that it would be her.

He answered with a subdued, "Hello."

"You'll come to where Sophie is if you want her to live." Hearing Quentin's voice twisted his stomach until he felt like retching. "You see now we're quite serious," she added.

He pulled in a breath. "Where?"

"You can sense her when we take her away from the oak, I presume?"

His head drooped in defeat. "Yes. I can't sense her now."

"Then when you can, come find her. It should be in twenty minutes or so. You come alone. You don't fight. If we see anyone else at all—your dog, your friends, the police, some unlucky person who happens to be hiking at night onto the property—we kill her."

And if I come as you ask, you kill me. He was shaking too much to say it, and in any case it didn't need to be said. It was understood. "Is she all right?" he managed to ask.

"She's unconscious."

Adrian winced, imagining the bastards bashing her on the head with a heavy flashlight. Tears stung his eyes.

"Just come, Adrian." Quentin sounded almost soothing. "This can all be over."

"But it won't really be, will it. You'll always keep looking for us." He knew how wretched he sounded, but hardly cared anymore.

"For those like you, yes. But for you, it can finally be over."

Shows how little you know about reincarnation. But the thought was bleak and didn't console him in the slightest. "Don't hurt her anymore," he said. "I'll come."

"Good." Quentin hung up.

He paced, looking around half-hopelessly, half-murderously for any other attackers, but none approached. The firefighters blasted their hoses, reducing the house to embers and smoldering black ruins. Some neighbor and a friend about Liam's age crouched on the ground, holding Liam while he huddled sobbing. One of the dogs was found, Rosie, miraculously alive though injured with burns. They brought her to Liam and he lunged to seize her and cradle her against him. Adrian's vision blurred with tears again, and he turned away.

He sensed his friends arriving: Zoe, Freya, and Tabitha. Niko approached too, though farther off. The three women switched over into the living realm, and ran to him from the field.

Zoe threw her arms around him. He barely responded, and in a second she drew back and looked at him in alarm. "Where is she?" she asked.

He shook his head to indicate he didn't know.

"This was a diversion?" Zoe turned to stare in horror at the collapsed, smoking house. "*This*?"

"It was an attempt, I think." Forming words felt foreign to his tongue. "Since it failed to get me, they're using their backup plan. Is my guess."

"They have her?" Zoe's eyes widened in rage. "They *took her*?"

Adrian nodded, miserable. "See to Liam. Please."

"We have to do something about Sophie!"

"Yes," Adrian said faintly. "I will."

Tab had come up behind Zoe, and turned her pale face to Adrian after taking in the destruction of the Darrow family house. "Sophie's gone?"

"I'll get her back. I promised Liam I would. Help him, please, all of you."

Tab rushed to Liam and knelt to throw her arms around him. Freya went with her, and soon collected Rosie off his lap, and held and petted her while a paramedic treated the dog's burns and injured limbs.

Zoe stayed put in front of Adrian, eyes narrowing at him. "What are you planning to do, Ade?"

He swallowed against his sand-dry tongue, and guided Kiri forward by the scruff of her neck until she stood closer to Zoe. "Keep Kiri with you, please. Don't follow me. None of you."

"What. Are you planning. To do."

"Soon I'll have to go," he explained in misery. "It's the only way they won't kill her."

"Are you saying they'll kill you instead? And that you're going to let them?" Zoe looked dangerous: cold and furious, gray eyes nearly giving off sparks.

"Don't follow me," he repeated, an edge in his voice this time.

"Fuck that, Ade! You think I'm going to let you do this?"

"Don't follow me!" he shouted. "None of you. Do you understand? Do not! Just let it be this way. Look what they've done." He swept his arm toward the house. "Look what I've done to her, to all her family, by getting close to her. Keep fighting them if you want. I'm sorry you were dragged into it, I really am. But them hurting her, it needs to stop. She's better off without me."

Zoe's hands curled into fists, and a tangible gust of power from her knocked him back a step. "Stop that right now! Have you learned nothing from history? You do not give yourself to them! It doesn't work!"

"There's no other way. If I fight, they kill her. If they see anyone but me, they kill her. Is that what you want?"

Zoe rose higher with an inhaled breath. Her gaze sliced through the crowd. "There has to be a way. We'll think a moment, we'll come up with something—"

But at that second they both jumped, because their sense of Sophie returned. She was farther now to the east, out among those dark mountains. Zoe stepped that direction, but Adrian stopped her.

"Only I go," he said.

"This is incredibly stupid. You know I could pull something off if we got a look at things—"

"But if we messed up at all," he said, "they'd kill her. You know this time they'd do it. They'd *enjoy* doing it, to hurt me."

Their gazes locked. Misery and frustration glimmered in Zoe's eyes.

"You can't let them," she echoed, but the words were weak.

Adrian glanced at the mourning Liam, at Tab and Freya speaking softly to him and to each other. "Tell them I'm sorry. Niko too. I know I'll see everyone…in the Underworld. But…" Giving up on words, he knelt and hugged Kiri tight, stroking her thick, soft fur. She whimpered, gazing at him with her large brown eyes. After kissing the sleek spot on top of her head, he rose and hugged Zoe.

Zoe clutched him with enough strength to crack bones. "This is not goodbye," she hissed. "I will figure something out. You aren't giving yourself to them. Do you understand? I'm letting you go so you can scope out the situation and tell us how to help you. But you aren't surrendering. Got that?"

Adrian didn't believe a word of it. But to keep her from following, he nodded as if agreeing. He kissed her on the cheek, turned, and plunged into the spirit world.

CHAPTER FIFTY-SEVEN

Someone picked Sophie up. Her clothes felt sweaty and damp, and everything in her body tingled and stung. Opening her eyes sent stabs of pain into her skull. From the arms of whoever carried her—it wasn't Adrian or anyone she knew; she guessed that much—she saw the leaping flames of a fire. Not the fire that had killed her parents and razed her house. A smaller one, in an outdoor fire pit, though still large for a bonfire. Beyond the fire was nothing but blackness. Her vision wouldn't focus, and it hurt to keep her eyes open, so she shut them and listened, though the dizzy pounding in her head gave the voices a dreamlike aspect.

"He'll come soon." The voice rattled Sophie's nerves, her body reacting even before her mind caught up and recognized the voice as Quentin's. "Let's keep it simple. Quick and done."

"A grenade would've been fun," another female voice grumped. Probably the red-haired woman.

"You got to fire your rocket," Quentin said. "Don't sulk. You going to be ready for this?" The question seemed directed at someone else.

"Yes," said the person holding Sophie—a man with a tentative voice.

"She's still out?" Quentin asked.

"I think so," the man said.

"With any luck she'll be waking up just in time to see her boyfriend burn," the younger woman said.

Sophie twitched and writhed, panic making it impossible to keep still.

"Whoa." The man clutched her to keep her from falling.

"Hold her," the young woman barked. "I got her."

A few quick steps approached, then another horrible jolt of electricity rocketed through Sophie. She would have screamed, but her vocal cords felt paralyzed. The pain closed around her head and she blacked out again.

Zoe paced the sidewalk like a caged lion, her senses grasping wildly for any hint of what the Fates wanted her to do. But her own agitation warped her judgment, and she doubted every idea that came to her.

When Niko arrived a few minutes after Adrian left, Zoe threw herself at him and clutched his arms. "Adrian's gone to them! But we can't follow or they'll kill her! What do I do? How do I fix it?"

Niko stared at her, then at the smoking house and the fire trucks, then at Liam huddled on the ground with Tabitha and Freya. He looked at Zoe again with sharp green eyes. "Tell me. Quickly."

She explained what happened.

He gave a short, impatient sigh, and squinted a moment down the highway, where cars still slowed as they passed the destruction.

"Right," he said. "I'm the sneakiest. I'll do this." He started past Zoe, back toward the field.

"Where are you going?" she called.

He turned to answer as he walked backward away from her. "To see Thanatos where they can't see me, and figure out a way to save our idiot friends."

"But if they do see you—"

"They won't."

"But Adrian said not to follow!"

"As if he gives me orders. Oh, and if you can send any good

luck spells our way, we'd all appreciate it, love." He leaped the fence into the dark.

She bit her lower lip hard. Anxiety now wracked her for Niko's sake as well as Sophie's and Adrian's. But a good luck spell, protection even—which would be better—that was a useful idea.

Who to direct it to, though? Spreading it to all three of her friends meant a weaker spell, diluted among them like that. Choosing one would be best. Adrian might be muddled with grief and self-sacrifice; she could help clear his mind. Or Niko could use her help in being extra-speedy and hard to spot.

But no. Sophie needed her most. Sophie had no immortal strength, and was being held hostage, probably already injured. Quentin and her thugs didn't expect any special strength or fighting ability from her; they expected despair and surrender…

Zoe rushed toward Tab and Freya. Kiri chased after her with a worried yelp.

Throwing herself onto the damp, cold ground on her knees in front of them, Zoe announced, "Ladies. I need you."

ADRIAN LOWERED THE bus to a stop between the tall evergreens on the mountainside. Darkness as thick as the Underworld's surrounded him, his horses' glow illuminating only a small patch of the forest. He climbed down, tied them up, and murmured, "Thank you" to each horse. With cold, shaking fingers he touched the metal side of the bus one last time, then turned around.

Sophie wasn't far off, a hundred meters perhaps. He switched realms.

The bonfire glared into being, piercing his eyes even at that distance and from between trees. He raised a hand to shield his eyes a moment, then examined the scene when his vision adjusted. The fire burned in a pit outside a ramshackle wood house. The house sat alone in a meadow at the end of a thin gravel road, nothing but black, steep mountains and trees surrounding it.

Three people were stationed around the fire, their backs to it, each watching a section of the meadow: Quentin, a young woman with a ponytail, and a young man. The young man rested on his knees rather than standing like the other two. He held Sophie unconscious across his lap. And he held a gun to her head.

Adrian entertained the briefest fantasy: he'd dive in there, snatch her away before anyone knew what was happening, maybe break the man's arms the way he'd done to Wilkes not long ago...

But Sophie wasn't conscious this time. She couldn't cooperate with a rescue. One false step on Adrian's part, and they'd kill her as mercilessly as they'd killed Isabel and Terry.

And more to the point, wasn't Quentin right? Wouldn't it be best to end all this? Look what Adrian had done to Sophie, to her life. If he loved her—which he did; it was the defining aspect of his eternal soul—then he would give her back what was left of her life by removing himself from it. The choice and the attempt at balance were tearing her apart. He had given himself as a sacrifice before. He could do it again.

Maybe next life they'd have more luck. He could hope for that.

He walked forward and emerged from between the trees, hands raised in surrender.

The young man spotted him first, and shouted, "There!"

At that moment Adrian noticed a soul-signal that his distressed mind had ignored till now. He knew one of these souls. It was a soul he rarely bothered thinking about, and had assumed to be far away, but here he was. Ares. The young woman was Ares.

It seemed it should matter. But after a moment of consideration, Adrian realized it didn't, in fact. This woman hadn't eaten the pomegranate; didn't know she'd been an immortal herself once. Adrian could tell her so, but the woman wouldn't believe it. No, for tonight, it wouldn't change a thing. It served only as a mirthless bit of irony, or fate. And it was also a tidbit of hope, for in future, in the Underworld, he'd tell his friends to track Ares in order to find a member of Thanatos. They'd gain a valuable lead in their fight.

But for this battle, the identity of this soul was irrelevant. And Adrian hated even to think of the ongoing fight. Why couldn't it end?

At least for him it was about to.

The young woman in her police uniform ran toward him with her handgun. He stood still in the cold meadow, hands raised, and gazed in defeat at the uniform, reckoning it was likely one of the same ones someone had worn while springing Quentin from prison in October.

Without so much as a triumphant remark, the woman aimed the gun at him in both hands, holding it point-blank against his forehead. She fired. The bang and the explosion was the last thing he knew.

TABITHA WIPED THE tears off her cheeks and stood, as ordered by Zoe, to go find a trustworthy neighbor or friend to leave Liam with.

She jogged across the crowded driveway on trembling legs, heading for Dr. Marcy Baskin, the town veterinarian. They had all brought their pets to her for as long as Tab could remember. The woman was in her fifties now. Wearing a plaid wool hat and a pink coat, she stood speaking with other neighbors. Distress etched lines in all their faces. Dr. Baskin had seen Tab and Sophie and practically everyone in Carnation through the grief of putting cats and dogs to sleep. She could be trusted now with Liam, even in a far worse grief.

Could it be that a couple of days ago, Tab had cared for nothing as much as her connections to celebrities and sexy goddesses? That crap didn't matter. It was fun, but it was not the center of a person's life. She had begun to grasp that last night after the failed car bomb. All day, all she'd been imagining, even while Freya teased her into smiles, was what would've happened if Zoe hadn't caught that bomb in time. Tab a soul in the Underworld, her parents agonized, innocent bystanders also killed, like The Luigis' drummer who was getting into the car next to her... She had been calming down these past hours by reminding herself those tragedies *hadn't* happened, and she *didn't* need to deal with them, and thank the gods for all that.

But now Sophie and Liam did have to.

A home, like this one now in smoking ruins; and loved ones, like these in tears for their loss—those were the center of your life. Not fame, not parties, not showing the world how cool you were.

Tabitha was going to lift up Sophie and Liam from this tragedy if it killed her. This family needed a dying-and-rising god to show them there *would* be life after death.

Babbling and pulling on Dr. Baskin's arm, Tab got the message across that she needed the vet to stay with Liam and Rosie for a while, just half an hour or so, while they fetched his sister.

"Of course, yes," Dr. Baskin assured. She followed Tab over and knelt to pet the trembling Rosie, now back in Liam's lap. Pumpkin, Tab had heard, was killed in the fire. Someone had found his little body. She couldn't think of it now; she'd only fall apart crying and that wouldn't help anyone.

Liam sat with one hand on Rosie, his head dipped low. Curled in upon himself, he rocked slowly forward and back. Someone had draped a blanket around him. Lately he had been looking tall and defiant and adolescent, but now he seemed to have reverted to the little boy Tabitha had watched grow up.

She wanted to crumple next to him and hug him for at least the next week. But Zoe was pulling on her arm, and telling the vet not to leave Liam's side or let anyone else take him anywhere, no matter who; he had to stay right here until they brought Sophie back or at least brought news of her.

Dr. Baskin understood and promised.

Zoe, running, led Tabitha and Freya and Kiri out into the dark field. She had them all sit in a circle, though the ground was sopping wet and muddy. Chilly water soaked through the seat and legs of Tab's jeans, making her shiver. The brown grass reached over their heads. Its marshy smell closed around them.

"Grab hands," Zoe said. They linked hands. Kiri lay in the center, her back nestled against Zoe.

"What is it you're going to do?" Freya asked.

"Send Sophie our strength. I could do it alone, but it wouldn't be as strong. The three of us together—three immortals, sending her everything we've got—that might give her a fighting chance. A chance to survive whatever they're doing to her." Zoe closed her eyes, gripping Tab's hand harder. "And a chance to stop Adrian from sacrificing himself."

Freya gasped, and Tab's heart kicked against her chest.

"Is that what he's doing?" Freya asked.

Zoe nodded. "So we aren't letting him, yeah? Quiet. Close your eyes and concentrate. Focus on Sophie."

Tabitha obeyed. Sophie. Her awesome best friend, the only one who had stood by her steadfastly when the rest of the world was heartless jerks...Sophie, whose life had just been torn apart and who might be on the verge of having her boyfriend turned into an intangible soul as well...

The blaze of power felt like a blast of heat from the hottest of summer days. Tab opened her mouth in a breath of wonder, but managed to keep her eyes closed, sensing it was important to do so. Heat and love and strength flowed through Zoe and Tab and Freya—and Kiri too, she guessed—swirling in a circle, faster and faster. Tab held on, wanting to sob in humility or laugh in joy.

Then the flow converged into one column, and shot upward and away from them like a meteor.

Tab went limp, as did the other two. Her hands fell out of their grasp. She toppled over backward and opened her eyes, and blinked at the cloudy night sky, barely conscious. But still she focused on Sophie, to the degree she could focus at all.

CHAPTER FIFTY-EIGHT

BETTY QUENTIN HOPED HER OLD HEART WOULD SURVIVE THE SUpreme thrill of tonight. At last, she watched as a bullet shot through Adrian Watts' skull and dropped him to the ground in a spray of blood. The fire awaited, leaping high in the fire pit. At last this fiend would be removed from the world, like that Rhea woman before him.

Krystal holstered her gun and grabbed Adrian by the legs. She grunted as she began to drag him the fifty feet or so to the fire pit. "Little help here?" she called.

"Here, Grandma," Landon said. "You cover Sophie. I'll help carry him."

Betty limped to where Landon sat. He put the unconscious Sophie on the ground, handed his gun to Betty, and jogged over to Krystal. Betty glanced down at Sophie, and nudged the girl's leg with one foot, but she stayed out cold. Oh, well. Betty did feel it was kinder not to make Sophie watch as Adrian's body was burned, whatever harsher ideas Krystal might have. Sophie would have a rough enough life after this already. Even when they let her go, they'd keep watching and warning her. She had her parents' loss to contend with now, and her friend Tabitha was likely to be removed next. Sophie was a smart girl; she would learn to turn against the immortals. What would teach her if these tragedies didn't?

After checking that the gun was ready to fire, Betty held it pointed downward at Sophie, just in case. But she gazed primarily upon the pivotal moment unfolding in front of her: Landon picked up Adrian by the arms, and Krystal by the legs, and they carried him toward the fire. Landon's face was pale and gleamed with sweat. The poor boy had a sensitive nature. He didn't love the task the way Krystal did. It spoke well for him, Betty felt. A nuanced mind was best for directing Thanatos. Brute force was handy for these jobs, but it couldn't run the whole operation.

Sudden movement writhed below her. She looked down, and in that second, Sophie grabbed the gun and ripped it away from her. Betty gaped. Anger blazed in Sophie's wide-awake eyes, and the girl was already climbing to her feet, pointing the gun at Betty.

"What—" Betty said.

Krystal dropped Adrian's body, leaving Landon to fall to his knees, struggling with his half of the burden. Krystal pointed her gun at Sophie. "Drop it!"

Sophie looked at them, and her fury only intensified. Sophie's arm whipped around Betty and yanked her up close, unbelievably tight. The gun's cold barrel dug into Betty's temple. How could anyone be so strong after being repeatedly electrocuted? Was Sophie one of the immortals after all?

"I'll shoot you from here," Krystal shouted. "I am an excellent shot."

"No!" Landon begged, as his panicked gaze took in the hostage situation. "Wait."

"For what?" Krystal kept her aim upon Sophie. "Throw him in the fire! Now!"

Sophie flung Betty away from her, sending her ten or twenty feet through the air before she crashed in the grass. The ground was squishy, thankfully, but the landing still bruised her bones and knocked the wind out of her.

Sophie paced forward toward Adrian.

A bang assaulted Betty's ears: Krystal had fired. But either Sophie somehow dodged, or Krystal missed, for Sophie kept stalking straight at them. Then she raised the gun she'd stolen from Betty and fired at Krystal.

Krystal went down with an enraged scream. Betty struggled

up to her elbow to look, and saw Krystal clutching at her hip, pain contorting her face.

Krystal aimed at Sophie again, though her arm shook. But before she could fire, someone dived in from the darkness and knocked Krystal back to the ground. Soon something went flying—probably Krystal's gun. With a strangled grunt, Krystal curled up on the ground, gasping and still.

The stranger rose: a tall, slender young man with a merry smile. "Hello, dear," he said to Sophie. "You take Adrian while I chat with our friends?" He glanced at Adrian's body. "Don't worry, he's still in there."

Sophie nodded, strangely straight and poised. She swung to point the gun at Landon, who, unarmed himself, immediately let go of Adrian and scrambled backward on his knees with his hands raised.

"Hmm," the stranger said. He gazed at Krystal and then at Landon. "Now that's interesting."

"Please," Landon begged. It seemed to be all he could say.

Betty, struggling to regain her breath, hauled herself painfully upright in the grass.

"Know what?" the stranger told Landon. "You can go. For now. I think it'll be fun to leave you wondering when we'll find you again. Which we will, I assure you."

Landon got to his feet, hands still in the air. He glanced at Betty.

"No, you can't take *her*," the stranger said. "I've got business with her. But the redhead, fine. Shoo now." He fluttered his fingers at Landon.

Landon hurried to Krystal's side and picked her up while she gasped in pain. He rushed to the van with her. "Grandma!" he called desperately across the field.

"Go, Landon," Betty called back. "Drive fast. Don't wait for me."

Sophie had sunk to her knees beside Adrian, and laid her hand upon his chest. Betty couldn't observe more, because now the smiling stranger strolled to her, grabbed her by both arms, and picked her up like she was a rag doll.

Goodbye, Landon, she thought with tenderness. No one but he had loved her in such a long time. He would likely grieve.

The world darkened as the fire disappeared. Across the meadow stood a glowing horse. The stranger threw her over his shoulder and walked toward it. "Know where we are?" he asked.

"The dead world," she said. "Where you'll leave me for the animals."

"The spirit realm," he corrected, "and that's what Adrian said he'd do. But I'm not as patient." He vaulted onto the horse with Betty, jostling her further, and commanded, "Up!"

The ground dropped dizzyingly away. A weightlessness both terrifying and delightful swooped through Betty's stomach. From her awkward position upside-down against his back, she watched the dark ground spread wider. The mountains dwindled, changing from peaks towering over them to an undulation of land below them. Looking sideways, she found a few stars floating between the clouds.

"It's an even nicer view in daylight," the man remarked. "No moon tonight. Bad luck. Oh well, you'll see more of the realm when you fly."

"Fly?"

He hauled her forward so she slid back down his shoulder in front of him.

Instinctively she clutched at him, not wanting to fall—though she began to understand that was exactly her fate.

"It's rare a person can say this literally," he said, still sounding pleasant and conversational. "But in your case I can." He tore her away from him, holding her at arm's length out in the air. Her kicking legs swept through the glowing horse without making contact. "See you in hell," the stranger said, and flung her out into space.

Betty fixed her terrified eyes on the stars as she fell and fell. Then there was a lightning-fast pummeling—branches, rocks, ground—then total blackness.

She rose, pain-free, and beheld her own body in the spirit realm. Her soul illuminated it. But she couldn't stand long in contemplation, for invisible forces were pulling her away, fast and inexorable like rapids going over a waterfall. She succumbed, and flew.

THE BURNING, NUMBING, glorious power in Sophie's body began to ebb. She remained immobile on her knees, her hand on Adrian's chest. He had begun to breathe again, faintly, and twitched once in a while as the gunshot wounds in his head, front and back, started to heal. Niko had vanished with Quentin, probably to abandon her in the other realm. The two younger Thanatos killers had driven away a few minutes ago in a rapid crunch of gravel. It was just Sophie and Adrian, the silent and wounded, in the field. She dropped Quentin's gun beside her with a shudder, hating the slick metal feel of it.

She hardly knew what had happened during the last several minutes. She'd been taken over by what she could only describe, in this dizzy aftermath, as the righteous fury of angels—or, like-lier, gods.

When she had opened her eyes in an unclouded moment of strength to see the stooped Betty Quentin standing over her, not even watching her, not even properly keeping hold of the gun she held, Sophie had let all her howling grief and rage surge forth. It had even felt a bit like someone else's grief and rage. Perhaps Zoe had thrown magic her way.

And immortal strength too. No way could Sophie have flung Quentin across the field like that otherwise. And fear ordinarily would have made her shake as she faced down a Thanatos assassin with a gun. Instead she had walked straight at the redheaded woman, didn't even flinch when the bullet grazed her shoulder, and fired back. She had shot someone.

Now she did more than flinch. The tendon curving from her right shoulder into her neck stung and throbbed. She touched it and winced, finding blood soaking her T-shirt and sweater. The gouge hadn't hurt much before, as if her temporary strength had shielded her from pain too, but now the pain increased with each breath. She'd need medical help. But she had to see Liam first.

And with the thought of Liam, the rest of the evening crashed down upon her mind. She wilted until her forehead almost touched her knees, and let the tears drip down her nose and into her filthy jeans.

Footsteps whispered through the grass. She looked up. It was Nikolaos, his face paler and less merry than when he had arrived. He knelt and hugged her, saying nothing.

She stayed in his arms a long spell, letting her silent tears soak his clothes instead of hers.

Then he sucked in a breath and murmured, "Gods, girl, you're wounded. Why didn't you say?"

"I'll live." It came out sounding mournful. She sniffled and asked, "What'd you do with Quentin?"

He cleared his throat. When he answered, his voice retained its usual flippant quality, but with a strained undertone. "Took her high up on my horse to give her a nice view in the starlight. Very high indeed. Not a height a person would want to fall from." The flippancy dropped away, and he added softly, "At least it was fast."

Sophie closed her eyes and shuddered again. But she stayed huddled against Niko, and whispered, "Good."

"Is it?" He still spoke softly. "Won't the Fates chain me up even longer now, Persephone?"

Wincing at the pain in her shoulder, she glanced up at his anxious eyes. "I don't know," she said truthfully. "But if it were up to me, I'd pin a freaking medal on you."

He smirked and glanced away.

"Did I kill the girl?" Sophie asked.

"Doubt it. Only hit her in the hip. Should give her a good world of hurt, though. Maybe a limp forever, if we're lucky." His gaze slid to Adrian. "Well, come on. Let's get the pair of you back."

Niko transferred them to the spirit realm, carried Adrian to the bus, and attached his own horse to the team before driving them back to Carnation. On the quick ride, Sophie held Adrian across her lap. But he felt and smelled alien, with all the blood, and the pain in her shoulder in combination with the horror at losing her parents had flared into a nauseating headache that marred any possibility of love or comfort.

She did love Adrian. She didn't want him to die. And she refused to let Thanatos win. But she couldn't stand the pain anymore, the fighting. She wasn't strong enough. Life had become a nightmare.

What if she could turn the clock back to the night three months ago when Adrian had texted, *Are you interested in being kidnapped again, then?* What would she answer, knowing what she knew now?

No, she thought, closing her eyes in nausea and agony. *No, please, leave me in peace.*

CHAPTER FIFTY-NINE

AWN WAS FILTERING INTO THE CLOUDY SKY BEFORE ADRIAN could hold onto a thought without it spiraling away into nonsense. He still couldn't talk. His tongue wouldn't obey when he tried. He lay in the back of the bus, piled under blankets. Freya and Niko sat with him. His hair felt clean and damp, and his clothes were changed, so they must have been washing him and taking care of him. They teased him with fake cheer, suggesting maybe the bullet had given him the partial lobotomy he'd always needed, which would surely improve his personality.

He tried to force words out, which resulted only in an angry growl.

Niko looked away, and Freya relented. "Sophie's fine, dear. I mean, not *fine*, of course. She's with Liam, and they're...coping. Together. Tab and Zoe are with them."

He swallowed, begging her with his gaze for more information.

She took his half-numb hand between hers and looked at his fingers. "We haven't been able to take her to the Underworld yet to see her parents. A bullet injured her shoulder, and she needed to spend the night in the hospital. It's giving her some pain, but it isn't serious. Those idiots will need more guns before they can do that to anyone else. Niko stole all their weapons he could find, from their van before he confronted them, and from the cabin too. That should set them back at least a little. Oh, and Quentin's dead. Niko killed her."

Adrian widened his eyes in surprise, and shot a glance at Niko, who only met his gaze for a moment and then looked away as if distracted. The relief Adrian felt at the news soon diminished. Killing Quentin wouldn't matter much. Thanatos would never quit. They would just assign a new leader and keep at it.

Adrian flexed his tongue and managed a word this time. "Ares."

"Oh yes," Freya said. "We know now. Ares' soul is the redhead." Freya gave a scornful laugh. "Ares. Such a douche. He always was. At least we can trace him. We have that against them now."

Soon Adrian could speak again, and not long after that he could sit up and eat. Niko said he had picked Quentin's pocket before flinging her off his horse, and thereby got Sophie's phone back and returned it to her. So Adrian texted her: *I'm awake. I love you. I'm so sorry. When can I see you?*

She didn't answer.

"Don't fret," Niko said. "Zoe and Tab won't let anything happen to her. She's probably asleep."

Thank you, thank you, thank you, Adrian texted Zoe next. *Also, I hate life.*

No problem, you idiot, she responded. *Me too but it'll get better. Sophie's resting. We'll summon you soon.*

When he had recovered his strength and his ability to move normally, Adrian sent Niko and Freya off to spy on the redheaded woman and her accomplice, and to scout around for any other immediate danger. They all knew the errand was unnecessary, merely a measure to let him be alone for a bit.

They were already in the spirit-world region of Carnation, the usual spot he parked the bus when taking Sophie home. When he switched realms now, no farmhouse rose behind the line of trees. Instead there stood a blackened pile of rubble, the stench of smoke stinging his nose even from fifty meters away. Yellow police tape surrounded the lot, and people in uniforms picked through the ruins and spoke to neighbors. Adrian wandered closer, feeling sick.

A family. A home. A business. A dog. Countless possessions and Christmas gifts and dreams of the future. All destroyed because of him, because he loved a girl and stubbornly insisted on having her with him.

His phone buzzed, and he yanked it out, hoping Sophie was texting him with a message of forgiveness.

But it was Zoe. *They're ready to go. Come with the bus and fetch us?*

Be there soon, he responded.

He switched realms again, got into the bus, and automatically followed his sense of Sophie to her location at the hospital.

Probably it was wrong to wish Thanatos had killed him last night. Even that wish was selfish, because if he had died, Sophie might have more pity for him and less reason to hate him. And he shouldn't think such things; he shouldn't think anything except how to help her, how to stop Thanatos and other murderers, and how to take every gram of punishment the universe wanted to heap upon him. He deserved it.

Angrily he smeared away the tears under his eyes, and brought the bus down near the hospital. No, he was not even allowed to cry. He'd be stealing grief that was rightfully hers.

He tied up the horses and switched over, finding himself in a half-full parking lot. He moved to the sidewalk and followed it to the hospital.

Zoe and Niko sat on a bench outside, Kiri and Rosie at their feet. The dogs wagged and whined as Adrian approached, though Kiri of course much more frenetically. He dropped to his knees on the concrete and hugged her, letting her lick his face over and over.

He pulled out a bandanna and wiped his face off, then turned to collapse on the bench next to Zoe and hugged her too.

She held him a long moment, then punched him on the arm.

"Ow!"

"Goddess above, you twerp. Do not sacrifice yourself ever again. I told you."

Adrian only offered a penitent smile in answer. He couldn't promise not to do it again.

He glanced past her to nod a greeting at Niko. Niko barely returned it, then went back to gazing in abstraction at the shrubs. In this life, murder had probably never been among his crimes until now. Even killing someone who deserved it, like the head of Thanatos, would shake up a person.

Zoe nodded to the glass doors. "Here they are."

Adrian leaped to his feet as the small crowd emerged from the hospital: Tabitha, Sophie, Liam, and a pair of older people whom Adrian assumed were relatives or family friends.

His gaze latched with despair onto Sophie. She looked far worse than he had been led to expect. Thick white bandages covered the side of her neck and bulked up her right shoulder. Her face was so pale as to be almost yellow, with purplish circles of weariness surrounding her eyes. Her lips drooped as if she had never laughed in her life. And when her gaze met his, it did so only for a second, then slipped back to the ground.

He stepped up and hugged her as gently as he could. But she flinched and murmured, "Don't touch me."

Possibly she only said so because of the pain of her stitches, and the nausea that the whole experience would leave upon a person. But the words still lodged like thorns in his flesh. He swallowed, pulling back his arms. "Sorry. Um. Shall we take you there? You and Liam."

She nodded.

"You're sure you'll be safe?" the older woman asked, laying her hand on Sophie's uninjured arm. Sophie didn't flinch at that, Adrian noticed. "You have a place to stay? Everything's set up?"

"We've got them covered," Tabitha said. "They can stay with me at first, and we'll make other arrangements later. We'll make sure they keep in touch so no one worries. But right now they have to talk to some people." She had her arm around Liam, who hadn't said a word. He was gazing down at Rosie, who had wandered up to lean against his legs.

"Maybe we should come," the man said.

"Not for this one," Tab assured. "We've got it. But I'm sure they'll need you soon."

The man and woman hugged Liam and Sophie and gave their grieved, anxious goodbyes, promising to check in soon.

Watching them walk across the parking lot, Adrian asked Tab, "Who are they?"

"Their grandma and their uncle," she said.

His soul deflated further. More actual people whose hearts he had helped break. There would be so many, the more he looked around...

"Where do we have to go now?" Liam's voice shook with dread.

"Okay, buddy, this might actually be fun," Tab said brightly. "Like Sophie told you, we have a *lot* to show you and explain to you. And some of it's wicked cool. Are you ready?"

Liam glanced at her in doubt, but a flicker of tired amusement did cross his face. Gratitude for Tabitha bloomed in Adrian's mind. He and Zoe and Niko all stood shaken and damaged and of little use to the Darrow children. But Tabitha, whom he had thought likeliest to crumple under pressure, had stepped up and become their cheerful strength. In this life she had loved Sophie longer than he had, after all.

They moved out to a spot between parked cars. Zoe picked up Rosie. Tabitha circled her arms around Liam. Adrian, to avoid being rebuffed by Sophie again, picked up Kiri, leaving Niko to draw Sophie into his arms. She seemed lost in contemplation, as if barely noticing who held her.

Together they all switched realms. Liam's gasp mingled with the wind in the empty meadow.

"What'd I tell you?" Tab said. "Wicked cool."

Adrian led the group to the bus, which Liam paused to stare at in fascination.

Sophie came to life a little more, turning to her brother and starting to explain in a soft voice. "This is why I told you not to be too upset. I couldn't tell you till now; it wouldn't have made sense. This is the spirit realm. We're going to be able to see Mom and Dad and talk to them, but we won't be able to touch them, okay? And we can't tell Grammy and everyone else, not yet. It'll be hard. Still, it's going to help a lot, seeing them."

"But where are they?" he said. "What do you mean? What is all this?"

"Let's talk while we ride," Tabitha suggested. "It's a long flight."

While everyone got settled in the bus, Adrian tried one last time. Sophie had chosen the seat behind his, so she could sit beside Liam. Standing at the driver's seat, Adrian reached out to run his finger, light as a snowflake, down her cheek.

She twitched away. "I said don't touch me."

She spoke the words gently enough, but he retracted his arm as if bitten.

Her hazel eyes darted to him unhappily. "I'm sorry. But for now, I can't."

He forced a sympathetic smile. "Of course. Understood." He turned and sat down, pretending in his haze of heartache to inspect the willow-and-ivy reins.

Tab leaned forward from Liam's other side, and her hand fell on Adrian's shoulder. While Sophie and Liam spoke, Tab murmured, "Don't worry, bro. She'll come around."

He threw a halfhearted smile back across his shoulder, and gave her hand a pat before she withdrew it. It was tempting to believe Tab, to think Sophie only didn't want his touch today, and would want it again someday. But when he thought of the smoking ruins of her house, of her parents lying dead, he easily believed that a person could never want to be touched again by the fiend who had caused all of that.

His heart frosted over. Setting his expression into impartial stone, he checked that everyone was ready, then snapped the whip and launched the horses off toward the Underworld.

CHAPTER SIXTY

STRATON AND HIS FOLLOWERS HAD OF COURSE LEFT THE SITE OUT-
side Argos immediately after killing Persephone, Hades, and
Demeter. But Hermes and Artemis tracked them down, stealthily
following reports of a band of brigands camping in the woods.
Three nights after the murder, they brought the news back to Hekate that they had caught up with them. They'd found the group,
or at least the better part of them, carousing around a campfire in
the hills.

The immortals choosing to partake in vengeance assembled
there in the spirit realm. Hekate arranged them in a circle, corresponding to Hermes' and Artemis' reports of the boundary of
the enemy campsite. Hekate, Hermes, and Dionysos had collected
the most frightening masks from the Dionysia: those with animal
fangs, or metal blades as teeth, red slits or skull-like holes as eyes,
and horns or beaks or tusks warping their wearers into monsters.
Hekate handed the masks around and each immortal put one on.
The circle of lurid visions stood ready. The moonlight sparkled on
the frost. The wind rippled their wool cloaks.

Wild beasts in the spirit realm as well as the living one usually
avoided the immortals' particular scent. But Hekate could call
them to her if she wished.

Now she lifted her face to the cold wind and closed her eyes,
and reached out through the hills. In the thousands of life threads
crisscrossing the land, she focused on those belonging to large

animals who ate flesh, and who were particularly ravenous to-night, in the desolate winter. She called them to the circle.

After an interlude of windy silence, they began to arrive. Paws and claws rustled the dead leaves on the ground. Growls and predatory panting breaths filled the air. Hekate opened her eyes.

Lions, leopards, crocodiles, wolves, and bears, or creatures like them, drew closer out of the darkness. All the beasts were twice as large as the ones in the living world. Having called them, Hekate now also did her best to send them the message that the immortals were too dangerous to eat, but that the animals would soon have their feast if they waited.

"One apiece," Hekate instructed her companions. "Go."

In a whirl of motion, the immortals turned to the beasts, and each captured one and held it tight. Hekate held a giant black wolf, its dog-like smell pungent as it squirmed and snarled in her hold. Dionysos had snared a striped wildcat as large as Agria. Aphrodite grappled with an all-white lion. Hermes held down a huge crocodile, its armored tail whipping. Goddesses and gods all around stood ready with their living weapons.

Hekate called above the snarls of the animals, "Three, two, one. Switch!"

Everyone switched realms. The torches gave way to the campfire, and a sprawl of travelers appeared across the ground, stinking of wine and sweat. Screams arose as the criminals spotted the giant beasts and their masked keepers, and spun to realize they were surrounded.

"For your part in the destruction of the sacred immortals," Hekate shouted, "the goddesses and gods decree that your blood shall feed the beasts of the spirit realm. Release!"

The immortals let go of the animals.

The carnage was immediate and shocking. Shrieks tore upward and then were choked off as the hungry animals bit into necks. Any victim who managed to dodge and run for the darkness was caught by the circle of immortals and thrown back into the arena. Hekate forced herself to watch, though with each dark spatter of blood and each wrench of jaws that tore a bone from a socket, she wanted to close her eyes. But this was her doing. She should own it and look upon it.

All her companions, warriors and non-warriors alike, kept their terrible masked faces turned upon the slaughter. They might have been closing their eyes behind the masks, but she guessed they were not, though surely most wanted to.

Before long, every one of the Thanatos band was dead, and the animals were settling in to eat. When each beast had consumed its fill, an immortal approached and caught it, and whisked it back to the spirit realm and released it. That was the worst, Hekate found: having to wrap your arms around a wild animal who was now dripping with the warm blood of the people you had thrown to them. All the immortals were bloodstained by the time they released the last beast, pulled off their masks, and dispersed in shocked silence.

Dionysos and Hermes followed her to the Underworld, as they had been doing ever since rescuing her.

They all washed in the cave's rivers and changed their clothing. Hekate trudged to the glowing fields, and lay down shivering upon the pale grass at her parents' feet. Kerberos trotted up, lay beside her, and licked her ear. She hadn't let him come along. She didn't want him taking part in the massacre.

"Forgive me," she murmured.

"Of course we do," Hades said.

"Forever," Persephone said. "But forgiveness isn't only up to us."

She knew who, or what, would have to forgive her. She spread her hands on the grassy ground, but felt the same bland emptiness she had felt in the water, the air, the rocks, all the way back from the slaughter. The magic was gone, withdrawn from her reach. The Fates did not forgive her.

She would have wept, but some part of her had already guessed this would happen. This or a worse rebound of power, back upon herself and her allies. She told herself to be grateful it hadn't resulted in that instead.

Hermes threw himself down under a tree, his back against the trunk. He scowled into the distance while breaking up a stick and flinging bits of it away.

Dionysos approached and sat behind Hekate, his fur-edged cloak settling warm against her. "Whatever your crime, I share it. I will not let you be alone. I serve you."

To think, not long ago she would have floated into the air in happiness to hear him say such a thing. Life was so much more complicated now. Friends and lovers could help you a great deal, but the world held so many dangers, so many greater problems, such insurmountable tragedies.

She rolled onto her back to let her body lean against his legs.

She was still immortal, still as powerful as her friends, even without her magic. And their enemies were far from defeated.

"We have much to do yet," she murmured, and gazed upward into the fathomless black ceiling of the fields.

TO BE CONTINUED...

Afterword

Mythology fans may note that while *Persephone's Orchard* could perhaps be called a retelling of a myth, this volume diverges far enough from the myths that it ventures more into "Greek god fan fiction" territory.

For example, it's basically suggested nowhere in mythology that Hekate (often spelled Hecate) is the child of Persephone and Hades. In fact, she's usually spoken of as a much older deity, one of the earliest and most mysterious and powerful. In the Homeric Hymn to Demeter, she's around at the time Hades kidnaps Persephone, and assists Demeter in the search, and later becomes a friend and/or handmaiden of Persephone's. But I wanted Hades and Persephone to have a child, and I wanted the child to be one of the other Underworld deities, and Hekate was the one who interested me the most. Her position in mythology as the goddess of witchcraft and sorcery made for a lot of tantalizing plot ideas. So I twisted the relations to serve my story.

It's also suggested basically nowhere in mythology that Adonis and Dionysos are the same person. However, some scholars have noticed the two figures do share a lot of interesting similarities. Both are dying-and-rising gods, both are mostly non-warlike compared to the majority of male gods, and both are especially beloved of and worshipped by women. So in wishing to continue Adonis' storyline, and in also wishing to find a place for the intriguing Dionysos, I fused their identities into one. I apologize for any headaches and confusion this gives people who are trying to straighten out the myths.

Hekate loving Dionysos or Adonis is also unattributed in mythology. But Hekate does have association with Hermes here and there in myths. Both of them are fond of rambling about at night on mysterious errands, both cross the living world/Underworld boundary at will, and both are associated with crossroads. There are even one or two tantalizing lines in various ancient stories that suggest they had sex or even had a child together—but then, Hermes was almost as busy a philanderer as Zeus, so for his part that isn't unusual.

The rivalry between Ares and Adonis over Aphrodite is also well established in mythology. Adonis is usually said to be killed by a boar, but some versions say the boar is actually Ares in disguise, jealously murdering his rival.

You'll also note that in some places the immortals adopted existing myths and turned them into a piece of reality, such as adopting the names Dionysos and the River Styx. Given how much people have always loved to invent stories, I reckoned it was just as likely that legends would become truth as that truth would become legends. Whichever way it happens, what matters in the end is whether it's a good story. Which is all I'm trying to write, too.

- M.J.R.

Acknowledgments

I've received so many encouraging remarks from so many people who have helped me keep this series going that I couldn't possibly cover all their names—I'd still be forgetting someone. But the following definitely get special thanks.

First of all, my beta readers:

Dean Mayes, novelist, and one of the nicest you'll ever meet when it comes to supporting his fellow authors—thank you for all the encouragement and the glowing reviews and retweets that help me and so many other writers find more readers.

Jennifer Pennington, for years and years of friendly, helpful, fun writing discussions: your instincts were so very right on this draft and you excelled at asking the important questions and making the insights click for me. Thank you!

Ray Warner, with whom I've enjoyed, again, so many years of smart and geektastic fandom conversations—thank you for turning your wisdom to the task of fixing up this book. I've said it before, but really, you're brilliant.

Beth Willis, musical artist and one of the longest card-carrying fans of this crazy story of mine, for all the exuberant comments that made me laugh out loud (in coffeeshops, even). And thank you also for seeing all the character relationships for what they were and should be, and helping me straighten them out!

I must also thank various friends who helped along the way:

Øystein Bech Gadmar—very belatedly; forgive me!—for the best spelling and etymology of "chrysomelia." Kevin M. Lewis for good-naturedly answering my questions on weapons, and of course for Scotch whisky recommendations. (The latter weren't for the story, but still.) The Mulvey family (Rich and Katy and kids) for daily affirmation in the form of good humor and the occasional tech support. Melanie Carey and family for being lovely friends and keeping me company at book-related events. The incredibly supportive online folks, including but not limited to

Fred LeBaron, Tracy Erickson, Cara Chapel, Erin Eileen Davis, Kim and Kevon Wilt, Kirsten Fleur Boxall, Michelle Murphy, Stephanie Staples Babbitt, and a whole slew of awesome book bloggers…honestly I want to list all of you who have ever left a comment or sent an email or a tweet, and I'd probably still forget someone. Know that you are appreciated!

Though I've never corresponded with Aaron Atsma, I now officially send him my thanks for his compiling of the magnificent Theoi.com, which regularly supplies me with so many valuable Greek mythology details. And similarly, to Walter Burkert (and translator John Raffan) for his incomparably thorough tome *Greek Religion*, which I often thumbed through for inspiration, even though I'm not learned enough to properly understand most of it.

Without Michelle Halket, indefatigable editor extraordinaire, this series wouldn't be what it is or where it is. Thank you for your enthusiasm about it right from its first mention, and for understanding my introvert writer ways and helping me get these books out to the world in spite of them!

Last but never least, uncountable thanks to my family: my children, husband, parents, siblings, cousins, aunts, uncles, in-laws, everybody!—you are all about the smartest and most loving family a person could hope for. Thank you for making me laugh when I need to take myself less seriously, and for being steady when I need it. The world would be a better place if everyone had a family like mine.